To Julie,
Welco

Garage sale world,

GARAGE SALE

Riddle

Garage Sale Mystery Series

SUZI WEINERT

Suzi Weinert

Text and Illustrations copyright © 2016 Suzi Weinert
All rights reserved.

International Standard Book Number 13: 978-1-60452-124-5
International Standard Book Number 10: 1-60452-124-4
Library of Congress Control Number: 2016955242

BluewaterPress LLC
52 Tuscan Way Ste 202-309
Saint Augustine, Florida 32092

http://www.bluewaterpress.com
This book may be purchased online at

http://www.bluewaterpress.com/GSR

Editing by Carole Greene

To Denise Weinert
for opening the portal to
Katy Garretson, Jonathan Axelrod
and Hallmark's Television
Garage Sale Mystery Series

LETTER TO MY READERS

Historical fiction uses imaginative reconstruction of historical events and personages. Like my earlier mystery thrillers, this book and its characters are fictional.

Upon hearing two conflicting accounts of an auto accident, you may begin to wonder about history. Each person brings his own subjective prejudice to whatever he "sees." Civil War eyewitness testimonials often hinged on observations of terrified men rather than dispassionate objective reports. Thus, history we accept as "true" may reflect combinations of verifiable facts and eyewitness "truths" plus the myths and legends growing around such information in generations of slanted retelling.

Confederate Captain John Singleton Mosby, Union General Edwin Stoughton and General Jubal Early were real people and the raid on the village of Fairfax Courthouse, a real event. However, Mosby's "treasure" reflects legend and myth and my accounts of all these people and events are historical fiction.

While Birdsong's a real, fine old name dating back to the 1600s in Virginia, my John and Raiford Birdsong characters are fictional, as are William Early, Ellwood, Hanby and all the others.

Because I'm personally drawn to the relevance and impact of current issues, I like to weave them into my mystery thrillers. As with child abuse in *Garage Sale Stalker* and terrorism, human trafficking and spousal abuse in *Garage Sale Diamonds*, this novel explores another compelling national topic: the challenges facing our country's burgeoning senior population. This group, plus baby boomers (born 1946-1964), have created unprecedented economic, social and practical issues for older individuals, their families and their federal, state and local governments.

While more options exist for seniors than ever before in American history, not all have prepared for this stage of life, financially or otherwise. Nor do they realize criminals target them for exploitation, scams and other crimes that could wipe out their life savings.

To face this, states and counties scramble to create senior support systems, including prevention efforts to increase crime awareness for elders and their communities. I felt it was high time for my Garage Sale novel series to address this topic.

If you'd like to comment on my story, please e-mail me at: Suzi@ GarageSaleStalker.com.

Thank you for choosing my novel.

Suzi Weinert

www.SuziWeinert.com

CHAPTER 1

Glinting fangs ringed the elongated, gaping jaws. Reptilian scales armored the sinewy body. The partially unfolded wings readied for flight as the talons flexed with anticipation. One claw clutched a sphere. The glittering eyes shimmered with intensity. Did this penetrating stare reflect deep knowledge of universal wisdom? Or did the stare reflect a predator's focus riveted on prey?

Lightning-fast, the dragon fired a telepathic barb directly into Jennifer Shannon's brain. The hook pulled tight as she gazed, hypnotized, at the creature in her hands.

A human voice intruded upon her concentration. "Do you want it...the item you're holding?"

"What...?" Jennifer asked, startled.

"Do you want to buy it—the statue?"

"Do I want...yes, yes I do."

"Thirty dollars, please."

Jennifer jerked herself back to garage sale reality.

"I...how about fifteen?"

"Twenty."

"Sold." Jennifer clutched the statue in one hand and produced money with the other. Then she pointed to the statue. "What... what do you know about this piece?"

"It belonged to my parents," the garage sale Seller said. "They told me they got it before I was born, back when they lived in the Philippines. Lots of Asian imports/exports pass through that country, so impossible to guess its origin. The statue means nothing to me except I remember my mother valued it and now I'll never know why. Just another question I didn't ask my folks back when I thought they'd live forever."

Jennifer nodded as her own mother's cherished face crossed her mind. "Point taken," she said.

Back in her van, she studied the dragon from different angles. However she positioned it, the eyes watched her. Even with its face pointed away from her, the rear of each shiny, bulging eye held her in peripheral vision. Reluctant for it to leave her hand, she finally laid it carefully in the wide, shallow box she kept on the passenger seat to prevent items from tumbling around as she drove. The dragon watched her start the car.

This wasn't the first time a garage sale object "called her name." Skilled craftsmanship creating this compelling piece of art was reason enough to buy it, but she had a second motive. Maybe this would make a suitable gift for husband Jason's birthday in a few months. Might it amuse him if she compared life's challenges to fighting dragons, and he the family's protective dragon slayer?

But two other messages came with this impulse purchase: the reminder to tell her five children the stories about some of her own belongings while she still could, and also to learn more about possessions her mother had collected over the years.

Though smug about this unexpected find, what she really shopped for today and had hunted for over a year was a picture frame for a painting she'd bought two years ago at another garage sale. And not just any frame of the right size, but something unusual with a primitive look. Besides estate and garage sales, she'd searched stores and the internet. Maybe what she coveted didn't exist, but she'd know it if she saw it. She didn't give up easily.

She pulled the car to the safety of a curb, shifted into park and studied her notebook. Garage and estate sale listings from her newspaper's classified section were taped in a neat column down the page's left side. At the bottom, she'd written additional addresses from Craigslist.

She'd started at 7:30 this Saturday morning, and would add a few more sales before heading home by noon to prepare lunch. Her fingers moved down her notebook list, hovered and entered the chosen address into her car's GPS.

Fifteen minutes later, she pulled up in front of a property near the border of McLean and Great Falls. A phalanx of parked cars snaked along one side of the road outside a stone fence. She maneuvered skillfully into an empty space and walked up the driveway of the graceful plantation-style house. Huge old trees cast welcome shade across the lawn.

Merchandise filled the veranda and large front yard. Her pulse quickened as she did a quick "overview" for any stunning item inviting immediate claim. Spotting none, she wandered from table to table, past linens, luggage, floor lamps and furniture. Pausing at a table with antebellum era merchandise, she examined old quilts and embroidered linens, a worn but serviceable churn, wooden rolling pins, well-used cutting boards, crocks, tole-painted tin ware, enameled bowls and ladles.

Beside old kitchenware stood weathered leather boots, insignia, canteens and military buttons. Not likely valuable if still here. Antique dealers typically took early first-looks. She could buy them all in hopes of selling them later to a dealer, but realized she didn't know enough about Civil War relics to distinguish rare from common.

Several teenagers wearing "Helper" T-shirts roamed the yard among shoppers. Signaling one, she asked, "This collection of old things, do you know where they came from?"

"From the attic. You might learn more from my aunt. She's in charge."

"Would you point her out so I can talk to her when she isn't busy?"

"Over there at the checkout table."

"Thanks. Say, some of these things look like they date way back," she pointed at some insignia, "maybe to the Civil War. Is that possible?"

The teen smiled. "Gee, no idea. They remodeled the house a few times from that really old stone farmhouse. This seedy stuff lived in the attic. Now my aunt's emptying everything to sell the place. Hauling all that stuff down the three flights of stairs to the yard nearly wasted my friends and me. It better sell so we don't have to lug it back again."

Jennifer flashed a commiserating smile. "I appreciate the info."

"Let me know if you need help carrying something to your car."

"Double thanks."

Moving through the sale, she collected an armful of intriguing small items. About to pay for them, she arrived at the last table before checkout, where the sight of something unexpected stopped her short. Her eyebrows rose and her mouth formed an O.

CHAPTER 2

Jennifer stared at an odd frame with a weird picture mounted inside. The frame's crafter had twisted thin branches and fastened them onto a rectangle of wood, leaving protruding errant twigs. Unlike conventional plain or baroque frames, this primitive folk art seemed alive, as if leaves might sprout any minute. The crafter's clever use of simple materials created a one-of-a-kind original.

But if the frame wasn't arresting enough, the haunting picture inside revealed a circle of trees through which one glimpsed a large flat-topped boulder with other big rocks atop it. Thrilled to find the frame she'd sought so long, she felt equally drawn by the amateur painting's mystique—the way the light filtered through the trees and played upon the glen's stones. Together, the frame and picture formed a stunning combination. Suddenly oblivious to all else, she stared at this item much as her dragon had stared at her. She edged her way through the elbow-to-elbow browsers pressed around this display table to reach for her quarry.

When a stranger's hands closer to the frame lifted it up, Jennifer felt a pang of acute distress. To search this long, at last find a frame she wasn't even sure existed and then have it plucked away so near her fingertips...

She swallowed hard, remembering the unwritten rules: at estate sales like this one, whoever picks up something has "walking rights" until he puts it down again, and whoever pays for something first owns it. She watched the other set of hands rotate the frame front and back before lifting it away from the table.

Panicking, Jennifer followed, willing this person to discard the painting. But it didn't happen. She followed the buyer to the checkout line, desperately shaping a strategy. After the purchase, she'd make this new owner an offer. She'd double or triple the purchase price, anything to own it herself. But if the buyer refused to sell, then what? Karate?

Buyer stacked her purchases for Seller to total and fished money from her wallet, her purse and her pockets before discovering she hadn't enough to pay for all she'd chosen. Seller might let Buyer take it all for the money produced. Jennifer held her breath.

"If you leave out this framed picture, you'll have just enough," Seller suggested instead.

"Or I could take the picture and leave the other things," Buyer thought aloud. "Or would you hold the picture for me until I return with the rest of the money?"

How would Seller respond? Jennifer bit her lip.

Seller pondered Buyer's request and appeared to make a decision. Jennifer feared the worst.

"I don't think so," Seller apologized. "But it'll probably still be here when you come back with the money."

Jennifer felt a wave of relief. Buyer fussed over what to buy or leave until Seller mentioned the long line of other customers. Buyer appeared to decide, picking up the frame. Jennifer blanched. Then in a sudden, last-minute move, Buyer put down the frame and took the other items.

Next in line, Jennifer grabbed the framed picture so fast the Seller looked surprised. "I'll take it, thank you. I've looked for this for a very long time and was inches away from losing it."

"That's $30 for the picture and..." she totaled the other purchases, announcing the sum.

As Jennifer paid Seller, she realized this woman was the only link to this picture's history. Once away from this sale, she'd sever that link forever.

She smiled at Seller. "You're busy now, but when you have a moment, may I ask some questions about the painting?"

"Actually, I'm about to take a break." She called to another woman. "Your turn, Sis."

Folding Jennifer's money into a pocket, Seller stood, untied her money apron and handed it to her sister. "Over here," she motioned to Jennifer.

"Do you know anything about this frame or the picture?"

"We found it in my mother's attic."

"Could I ask your mother where she got it?"

Seller grimaced. "Not any more. She died last month. That's what triggered this sale."

"Any idea how she happened to have it?"

Seller glanced around, making sure the sale ran smoothly before turning back to Jennifer. "My family's been in Virginia since the 1700s and my mother was proud of that heritage. She belonged to the DAR and the UDC."

"DAR? UDC?"

"Daughters of the American Revolution and United Daughters of the Confederacy. To join, you must prove your ancestors participated in those wars. You're accepted or rejected based on those credentials. My mother loved it and was a shoo-in, but it doesn't interest me at all. Those old wars are long over. The South lost and for me, that closed the Civil War book. But not so for Mama."

"So you found this in the attic with other items of similar age?"

"Everything in her attic looked and smelled old. This picture was with those old things. Because I'm forward-looking, I don't dwell on the past, but I imagine the attic stuff was mostly antiques. Whether my mother inherited them or bought them or they're from her family or my father's, I don't know. Still, I loved her and wish now we'd looked through the attic while she was still alive so I could learn more about that side of her—what she remembered and why she cherished these old things."

Seller glanced away. Her eyes moistened. She blinked back tears. "After all, I'm named for her and her mother and her mother's mother, so there's a link after all."

"Oh? What name?"

"Selby."

"Unusual..."

Selby nodded. "Rare, in fact. It's from the Old Norse branch of Old English in the Germanic language family. Selby means 'from the willow farm' or 'from the willow manor farm.'"

Jennifer got a better hold on the items she carried. "You seem to know about the past, after all."

Selby laughed. "Only because my mother told me this many times, having the same name. In grade school, kids teased me about it, so my mother told me what to say back to them. She'd faced the same thing when she was little. But it didn't help me."

"Why?"

"Then they called me Old Norse or Willow Farm."

"Kids!" Jennifer looked down at her new frame. "Where in Virginia did your mother grow up?"

"Right here in Fairfax County. Our ancestors owned a thousand-acre farm once. Back then I guess McLean and Great Falls were mostly farm land." Seller paused, remembering. "I do know one Civil War story Grannie drilled into us when we were young. She said a band of Union soldiers gunned down my great-great-grandfather on his farm during the Civil War. Without him the family couldn't make a go of it, and in time they sold off all but twenty-five acres. About sixty years ago, they sold more, reducing it to five acres surrounding the original homestead here. My mother redid the house beautifully, adding wings, patios and a five-car garage. But times have changed and my sister and I just can't afford to keep it. Heartbreaking. Really. We all grew up here. It's the end of an era for our family."

"I'm sorry to hear that." Jennifer pulled paper and pencil from her pocket. "If you think of anything else about the picture, would you please phone me? There's something about it." How could she explain? "Feels like it has a story to tell." She handed Selby her contact info.

"Sure," Selby said. "Oh, wait a minute. I do remember something. Let me look at the picture again. Yes, before this went to the attic, it hung near my grandmother's back door when I was little. I remember her saying this place in the picture really exists — somewhere in this area, I think. But if she told me where, I don't remember."

"You have my number in case you do. Thanks for my purchases and thanks for talking with me. Good luck with your sale."

Jennifer hefted her newest treasures into her car. She'd intended to visit more sales this morning, but excited about finding the frame at last, she smiled triumphantly and pointed her car toward home.

She glanced at the dragon watching her from the passenger seat box. Was it her imagination or did he give her a knowing smile?

CHAPTER 3

A s her car approached her house in a quiet McLean cul-de-sac, Jennifer pressed visor buttons to open the driveway gate and lift the garage door. Her watch read 9:02am. With her husband playing golf and her just-graduated-college-daughter sleeping late, she expected no interruptions as she examined the startling framed painting she'd just bought. Her other garage sale "finds" could wait in the car until later — except for the dragon. She put him in her large purse, as one might tuck a small dog into a carrier.

On the way into the house, she probed a garage shelf for the painting she'd saved for this frame and tucked it under her arm. Inside, she lay her own painting atop the framed one. Yes, the right size, but not the effect she'd envisioned. Disappointed the frame didn't compliment her own painting as well as did the one mounted there, she'd erase any doubt by substituting hers.

She put the dragon on the table before studying her other purchase again. Besides the unusual frame, something about the painting's haunting scene again gripped her attention. She might end up hanging it as-is.

Turning the frame upside down on the kitchen counter, she pried aside the small rusty nails fastening the backing to the wood. She eased away the cardboard backing, but instead of the rear of the painting, she found cloth padding. She pulled it aside, discovering a second cloth underneath. Was that writing on the fabric?

She spread the cloths open, written side up, for a better view. On one appeared a jumble of words; the other looked like a crude map with a pirate-style "X." What in the world? Folded for so long, the wrinkles wouldn't flatten enough for a clear look at the scratchy pencil marks.

She hustled the cloths to the laundry room and laid them upside-down on the ironing board. With a warm iron, she gently pressed both fabrics on the non-writing side. Turning the cloths over, she saw this flattening improved legibility.

Were these two different pieces of cloth accidentally padding the same frame? She moved the pieces of fabric around on the ironing board, noting torn and even edges. As she brought them together, the torn sides matched exactly. Two pieces from one cloth. So these weren't separate fabrics randomly stuffed in the same place; they were related. Moreover, the same scratchy pencil had marked both pieces.

Back at the table, she grabbed paper and pen to copy recognizable words, line by line. Finished, she wasn't sure what to do next. Glancing up, she found the dragon staring directly at her. Didn't archeologists identify readable words on scrolls or reliefs and then *infer* missing or illegible words? After a couple of tries, she made substitutions for the handful of garbled words which seemed to fit the shapes of partial alphabet-letters, the size of the space to be filled, the logic of each sentence and the rhyming nature of what appeared a poem. Then she shot the dragon a conspiratorial look and read aloud:

"April 30, 1863
A RIDDLE: WHAT IS 'X?'
A Union general stole X for the Blue
from Virginia families whose anger grew.
But the Gray found X in the general's lair
and rescued it back with daring flair.
Then danger loomed for Grays who carried X.
To avoid recapture, they quickly buried X.
When Gray Ghost sent his men to get it,
only one could but he'd regret it.
Pursued by Blues, he couldn't carry X.
His only choice: he must rebury X.
If X you find, your task is clear,
for pride of cause and honor dear.
You'll know it's X by JSM's knife.
Make haste then if you value your life.
Get X to General Robert E. Lee
for return to owners in our Confederacy."

Jennifer leaned back in her chair. Didn't General Lee command the Confederate Army in the Civil War, and wasn't April 1863 a date during that conflict?

Grabbing another paper, she scribbled key words: Union General, Blue, Gray, Gray Ghost, JSM, General Robert E. Lee and Confederacy. She hustled this list to her computer and Googled "Dates of the American Civil War." Wikipedia confirmed 1861-1865. Next, she typed "Civil War Gray Ghost." Up popped links to John Singleton Mosby. This fit the riddle's initials, "JSM." A thrill rushed through her. Had she accidentally stumbled upon something historic? But what was X? Stolen by a Union general and found in his lair, which angered Virginia families.

How did JSM link to a Union general? She Googled "Mosby and the Union general." This provided numerous links to a Union General Edwin H. Stoughton. But nothing about X.

Googling "Gen. Stoughton's documents" yielded nothing. Next, she tried "Gen. Stoughton's valuables." This brought up a "Civil War Treasures" link, describing an alleged cache of gold and silver looted from wealthy southern families by Stoughton's invading army and later captured by Mosby during his raid on the general's headquarters at Fairfax Courthouse.

If Jennifer substituted "treasure" for "X," the riddle made sense. She flashed the dragon a victory smile. Was her imagination overactive or did he return the smile? What a silly thought.

She turned next to the crude map on the other cloth. Nobody could miss Potomac River, lettered on the far right along two parallel lines which ran north/south and then curved west. Might that curve on a standard map help narrow the location? Another line clearly showed a railroad. The printed names, Gentry and Parker, might mean individuals or farms she could trace.

But this looked like two maps in one and drawn to different scales: the larger showing the Potomac, railroad and farms and then a smaller insert detailing a stream, a stone wall, a winding path and a square structure with sharp right angles. Near the bottom was an odd sketch depicting a shape like a box with rounded corners and something she couldn't identify on top—an odd primitive hut?

Except for the river, railroad and proper names, the map's landmarks remained mysteries, but the spot marked by X, wherever that might be, stood clear.

She need not be a curator to realize the fragile cloth and faded writing would suffer from handling and folding, so she made copies of them at her printer. Then she copied her interpretation pages, showing the key words and her inferred substitutions. Gently folding the cloth originals, she slid them into a large envelope for safekeeping and hid it on a laundry room shelf behind some vases.

"Now, why did I think it smart to do that?" she asked the dragon, who said nothing.

Back at the computer, she wiggled excitedly in her chair. If correct, she'd answered the riddle's question: *what* is X?

"But," she said aloud to the empty room, "the riddle's real message targets something different: *where* is X." If the map held the answer, could she follow it herself to discover the location?

If not, who could she trust to help her discreet search for artifacts that might affect history? Who had the important knowledge she needed without the greed treasure hunting often generated?

Now the dragon's wise stare made her uneasy, as if he read her mind. Did he know the secret of "X?"

CHAPTER 4

As she pondered the riddle, the map and the dragon, the phone rang.

"Hi, Jen. Its Mary Ann. Guess what. I think I've met a very special man." It was Jennifer's friendly neighbor who lived three houses away and whose husband had died two years earlier.

"Good morning, Mary Ann. So, tell me."

"Well, you know it took me a year to land on my feet after Dan died. Although you and other friends rallied around me, I began to miss male companionship and signed up for that dating service where I met the losers. But a few weeks ago, I found this ad on Craigslist and he sounded nice and about my age, so we met in a public place, just like you're supposed to. And, Jen, he's quite good-looking—handsome, even. And has an out-going personality. He's English and I love his accent. His name is Charlie and he has nice manners. We've been seeing each other regularly for three weeks, and I think I'm smitten."

Grateful that Mary Ann paused this monologue to take a breath, Jennifer said, "You certainly sound excited. Have you met any of his friends?"

"Not yet and he hasn't met mine. We wanted to see if the two of us clicked before we widened the circle."

"Where does he live?"

"He rents an apartment near Tysons Corner. I've been there and it's beautiful. He said he had a decorator furnish it for him and it looks like it. He let slip a few times that money was no object and he takes me to great restaurants like L'Auberge Chez Francois and Ruth's Chris and The Palm. We're having wonderful times together."

"What does he do?"

"Some sort of import/export business involving antiques."

"Has he been to your house?"

"Yes, several times. I cooked for him one night, and last night on the patio, he grilled delicious steaks. It felt a lot like old times when Dan was alive. Of course, I realize Dan's gone forever and I have to move forward. Charlie may be the one to move forward with."

"Will Jason and I meet him soon?"

"Great idea, like a double date. Also, I'd appreciate Jason's impression of him."

"I understand. Shall I get my calendar?"

"No, I'm driving right now. May I call you tomorrow to set up a time?"

"Absolutely. Okay, bye for now." Jennifer ended the call. Did her friend remember their earlier discussion about potential pitfalls in these blind date situations? Or had infatuation swept caution away? Did this man answer Mary Ann's prayers or embody her worst nightmare? She wished Mary Ann a second chance at happiness. She knew numerous friends who lost a spouse and later found a loving companion to share their golden years.

The dragon stared at Jennifer, as if aware of those answers.

She reached again for the map, but the phone interrupted again. She picked it up. "Hello."

"Help me. Help me...please," a frail old voice begged.

Jennifer immediately recognized this caller's voice but not the fragile, beseeching tone. Her grip tightened on the phone. "What is it? What's wrong?"

"I...it's happened so quickly I can hardly think straight right now."

Alarmed, Jennifer eased into the nearest chair, gripping the phone. Masking her worry, she forced herself to use a calm voice. "Take a deep breath and start at the beginning."

"I...I guess it began at the gas station. When I couldn't start the pump, a friendly young man at the next pump offered help. He said his name was John and we chatted while he filled my tank."

"Go on..."

"He asked if I garden. I told him I used to but now I paid a service to take care of my landscaping until they stopped coming because…well, because I forgot to pay their bill. He said he did yard work and would charge less than the service that deserted me. But he'd have to see my property to give an estimate. He asked how I liked my Mercedes and if I did a lot of driving. I explained I didn't drive much anymore, just for necessities, because…"

"Because…" Jennifer prompted.

"Because…well, I didn't want to tell you this, but I failed my last driving test, so I guess I've been driving illegally for a few months. Instead of chastising me like you're probably about to, he laughed. He'd chauffeured in a past job and suggested the 'Driving Miss Daisy' thing. So John came back to my house, looked around, gave a really low estimate for the yard and said he's also a handyman. I showed him a few chores and he spotted several more. He changed my burned-out light bulbs, opened a window stuck shut for years and suggested a little paint would brighten up the woodwork. I agreed. So he gave me his prices, did the chores and I paid him."

"Yes…" Jennifer encouraged, wondering how this related to the call for help.

"The next day, he drove me to the grocery in my car, which made me feel rather queenly. On the way home, he mentioned his wife does domestic work and is also a great cook; would I like to give her a try? I agreed, thinking what good luck to meet him. She's also pleasant enough. She cleaned the house and cooked a fine lunch and dinner. And then…"

Jennifer shifted the phone to her other hand because she'd gripped it so tightly her fingers tingled. "And then…" she urged.

"Then when they returned the next day he looked sad for the first time. He said they had to move from their rented house because the owner decided to sell it and they had to be out today. They found a nice furnished place but couldn't move in for two days. He said money was tight and they were trying to figure out a place to stay for two nights. Well, I looked around my big, empty house and thought I could be gracious to this nice, hard-working young couple, so I offered to let them stay here. They moved in and…" the voice trailed away.

"And?"

"And it should be wonderful because Jane cooks, cleans house and goes with me every time I leave the house so I have a companion. But…"

"But?"

"But they still haven't left and it's been over a week."

"Did you tell them to go?"

"I don't like confrontations or acting impolite, but I hinted. Weren't they only staying two nights? Yes, but their new place had a roof leak and the owner needed another week for repairs. They always have believable answers for my questions, ones that involve staying here longer."

"Are you all right otherwise? Have they harmed you?"

"Well, yes and no. I feel like a prisoner in my own house. John drives me where I want to go, so he has my car keys and they've hidden the phones so I can't make calls. I wonder if they put something in my food, because I sleep a lot more than I used to."

"Without a phone, how are you calling me now?"

"You know, Chelsea's done my hair at the same beauty shop for thirty years. That's where I am now. Chelsea let me borrow her cellphone, and I'm hiding in the ladies room because Jane stays to watch and listen whenever I leave the house. I wonder now if it's to make sure I don't contact anyone. She listens to every word I say. She's sitting in the shop right now waiting for me to come out so John can drive us home."

"Can you get help from a neighbor?"

"No. Those two watch me every minute I'm awake. They seem like they're just being nice, but they don't leave. They seemed so interested in me and learning all about my family and friends. Since I live alone, I enjoyed someone to talk with. Looking back now, I realize they asked me a lot of questions and I told them much more than I should have. But in the beginning they seemed so... wholesome and likeable that I wasn't at all suspicious."

"What if *I* told them to get out?"

The voiced sobered. "I don't feel comfortable about that. What if it makes them angry? How could I defend myself?"

"I think I should call the police right now. They will..."

"No. Please, Jennifer, just come here yourself to help me. Couldn't you get to Florida tomorrow on a plane...or maybe even tonight? I hate to bother you, dear, but I...I'm scared."

"You are never a bother to me. Look, I'll check flights and get to Naples today if possible, latest tomorrow. Can you manage until then?"

"I...I hope so. Thank you, Jen. I'm so confused, I don't know what to do."

"Try to relax now and don't worry. I'll be with you in less than twenty-four hours. Just hang on and know I'm coming to rescue you." A sudden thought struck her and she added quickly, "Remember, this is our secret. Don't tell John and Jane I'm coming."

"All right, our secret. Thank you, Jennifer. I love you, dear."

"Love you, too, Mom."

Jennifer's mind raced. Would her mother stay safe until she arrived?

CHAPTER 5

Jennifer ended the call, sighed and cradled her face in her hands. She'd balanced small signs of her mother's forgetfulness against her equally strong wish to live independently in the same Florida neighborhood familiar to her for thirty years. This worked if her mother could drive, handle daily living and decision-making on her own. Finding caretakers to deal with a senior's creeping dependence offered solutions but also risks. Paid help could neglect or otherwise take advantage of an elder without a trusted advocate nearby to check.

But now Jennifer recognized having nobody on site left her mother at even greater risk, as today's revelation proved. Should she have insisted on local oversight to prevent her mother's gradual aging issues escalating into this crisis?

Jennifer inhaled deeply, acknowledging this wasn't her first sudden race to Florida. Besides the "want to" trips, when she and Jason visited her mother to exchange Naples' warm winter sunshine for McLean's blustery winters, were the anxious "have to" trips. Her mother's ambulance ride to the ER triggered Jennifer's first dash to Naples. Fortunately, the resulting A-fib diagnosis could be treated with prescriptions—assuming her mother remembered to take the meds.

When her mother's beloved Jaguar developed expensive mechanical troubles, Jason flew down to help select a new car. The Mercedes they chose—he for the dependable machinery, she for the aristocratic lines and plush interior — served her well until today's revelation about no driver's license.

And the lost purse episode, when Jennifer rushed to Naples to resolve the missing checkbook and credit cards and to get her mother a new driver's license at DMV. Because the purse also held her keys, they changed locks on her house. And, of course, replaced the missing cellphone.

Still another time, Jennifer persuaded her mother to simplify life with a Naples home-care group sending someone daily to cook and help with shopping and light housework. After the first week, her mother locked them out, certain they were stealing her sterling silver, one piece at a time.

Forays to Florida to stomp out these brushfires weren't convenient for a daughter living this far away. After today's experience, she knew her mother shouldn't live alone any longer. Should she search out senior housing for her in Naples or coax her here to McLean, where they could keep an eye on her? Getting her to agree to such a move promised a battle.

She glanced at her watch. Ten in the morning. Back at her computer, she pushed aside copies of the riddle, her translation attempt, and the map in order to type in her travel options. She booked a flight, leaned back in her chair, stared at the ceiling and closed her eyes. So much to do to get ready in so little time.

She scribbled a hasty to-do list, wrote down meal suggestions for food already in the refrigerator and packed a suitcase. On impulse, she threw in her copies of information from the cloths. Then she cancelled appointments for two weeks and knocked on her daughter's bedroom door.

"What is it?" a sleepy voice asked.

"Grammy needs me, Becca. My flight's at 1:00. Any chance you could dash me to Dulles in half an hour? I could drive and park myself but I don't know how long I'll be away and don't want to leave my car in the airport garage for weeks."

After a pause to comprehend, again the sleepy voice managed, "Okay, Mom. I...I'll be ready soon."

"Thanks, hon." she said to the closed door. Next, she phoned Jason. "Jay, sorry to bother you on the golf course, but..." and she explained her impromptu trip of unknown length.

"Do you think this is the beginning of what we talked about for your Mom...moving her out of her Florida house and close to us?"

"Maybe, but she won't cooperate. It means stress between us instead of the good memories I'd like in my final years with her. Wish you were there with me, because she'd listen to you. She thinks you're wise and wonderful."

He chuckled, "Well, she got that right."

"Indeed, she did." Jennifer smiled. "I'll make a list for you of things happening while I'm gone, like Celeste cleaning house on Tuesday. I've left a few meals, but you'll soon be on your own."

"Don't worry, just new reasons to appreciate you. Becca and I'll bachelor it for a week. After all, I survived in the military."

"Yes, but the mess hall fed you or you had those meals-ready-to-eat."

He groaned. "Just thinking of MRE's kills my appetite. I'll be fine, Jen. It's you I'm worried about. Go by the police station first and get a cop to go with you before you square off with this John and Jane duo. They think they're on to a good thing and may not give up easily. Your Mom might not realize it, but they could even be armed."

"Jay, I hadn't thought of that, but you're right. Okay, I won't go alone." She looked from her to-do list to her watch. "Becca's taking me. My flight's at 1:00 and I must arrive an hour before, so I'll leave for Dulles by 11:00. Love you, hon. I'll miss you and thanks for being understanding about Mom."

"At least I got lucky in the mother-in-law department."

"You think so now, but who knows what's ahead if she…"

"Don't worry, I'll wear my FH and DSIL hero cape and goggles for the task."

She wrinkled her nose, trying to puzzle this out. "FH and DSIL?"

"Fearless Husband and Devoted Son-in-Law."

* * * * *

Traffic slowed as they drove toward Dulles airport. "Probably an accident," Becca guessed, eyeing the crawling line of cars snaking ahead. "Not even a steady creep, just stop-and-go."

"I can't miss my plane. Your Grammy needs me…"

"Worst case, Mom, you can catch the next flight. Why not reserve a seat right now so you have one if you need it?"

Whipping out her cellphone, Jennifer did.

"Look, Mom, not everybody makes it to the airport an hour before flight time. Your boarding pass and carry-on give you an edge. Once through security and the shuttle train, maybe you can run for it."

Jennifer nodded but then admitted, "Anything preventing getting to Grammy fast is a worry, but you're right, the later plane is Plan B."

They inched along for ten miles as XM radio music played. Jennifer tried not to fidget.

"Look, Mom. Traffic just opened up. No accident or logical explanation for the slow-down. Go figure."

Jennifer's watch read 12:20. "I might still make it if the security line's short and the shuttle train out to the planes is quick."

"...and if your departure gate is near the shuttle gate. Last time I flew they said their new policy is closing the plane door ten minutes before departure."

Jennifer gathered her purse, double-checked her boarding pass and when they reached the ticketing curb, she jumped out. "Love you, Becca. Thanks for getting me here...physically and mentally." She grabbed her suitcase, blew her daughter a kiss and dashed into the terminal.

Inside, she located her gate on the electronic board displaying flight information. The security line moved fast. Once through, she hurried for the shuttle train. At the departure terminal she rushed toward her plane's gate. Empty waiting-area seats told her the plane had already boarded as she dashed up to hand the agent her ticket.

"Sorry, economy seats are full. When you didn't arrive on time, we gave your seat to someone else. We're just closing the door."

Jennifer fought tears. "*Please,* I just learned this morning that my mother's in critical trouble. Her life's in danger. She's desperate for me to help her. I left home with plenty of time but traffic stalled on the highway. Please. *Please* let me on this plane? I must get to my mother."

The ticket agent frowned and shook her head as the boarding agent came up the ramp.

"Ready to close," he said.

With the next flight hours away and her mother at risk, every minute counted toward her rescue. Jennifer choked back a sob, anguish clear on her face.

CHAPTER 6

T he impatient airline gate attendant looked up, studied Jennifer and shifted uneasily. The agent recognized how this passenger's obvious distress mirrored her own only last week when she'd rushed to Chicago to help her ailing father. Sudden empathy softened her standard corporate response, and the agent made a snap decision. She studied the boarding pass in her hand. "Just this last passenger, Jennifer Shannon. Put her in the empty in first."

As the boarding agent motioned Jennifer down the ramp to the plane, she touched the gate agent's arm. "Thank you for this kindness." Then she hurried down the jet way.

Inside the plane, the flight attendant guided her to the last empty first-class seat and hefted her carry-on into the overhead rack. She eased into her seat, buckled up and speed-dialed her phone as the plane pushed back. "Becca, please tell Daddy I made the flight. Yes…a miracle and I *am* breathless. Can't talk now — time to turn phone to airplane mode. Call you tonight. Please cancel that later plane for me." She gave her the flight number, ended the call and leaned back.

The flight attendant approached, "Would you like something to drink?"

"Yes, merlot, please." She chuckled at the wild contrast from her near hysteria a few minutes ago to being aboard and en route to her mother. She'd toast this good luck with the wine.

Grateful to board the flight at all, never mind in first class, she closed her eyes, listening to familiar taxi and take-off sounds. Her pounding heart began to slow. She opened her eyes to find the plane airborne. Glancing initially at fellow passengers enjoying the comfortable first class seats and attentive service, she turned toward her seatmate.

He gazed out the window at the view, a closed book in his lap. The title read, "Civil War Relics." He was clean shaven, dressed in expensive casual clothes. His carefully groomed white hair contrasted with a sun-tanned face. His prominent nose and thin lips combined into a hard profile. The manicured hand resting on the book had avoided hard labor. Something "creepy" about him, although Jennifer questioned superficial first impressions. On his tray sat two small empty airline bottles of Jack Daniels beside an empty glass.

"Hello," she said companionably. "Do you fly often?"

"Yes and I loathe commercial flights. But my own plane's hangared for repairs."

"Do you live here in the DC area or Florida?"

He turned toward her. "Both."

Their drinks came. He filled his glass and she tried again. "How is that?"

"How is what?"

"That you live in both places?"

"I have interests in Naples, business in Great Falls and homes in both."

"Is one of those interests connected with the Civil War?"

A sharp, suspicious look crossed his face, as if uneasy at a stranger's insider knowledge.

She gestured. "…the title of the book in your lap,"

"Oh… yes."

"Do you think many Virginians still feel reverence about the Civil War, even though the fighting ended over 150 years ago?" she asked.

"In history's terms, that's like minutes ago," he admonished.

Jennifer plumbed her cursory Civil War knowledge. She recognized battles like Gettysburg, had read *Andersonville* in college, saw *Gone with the Wind* twice, *Cold Mountain* once and watched some of Ken Burns' Civil War Series on public TV. Plus her latest Google searches relating to the newly found map and riddle. Admittedly, she knew little.

"Why does the Civil War draw *your* attention?" she asked.

He looked pensive before giving her a sudden sidelong look. "Are you really interested or making conversation?"

Surprised, Jennifer still didn't hesitate, "Unless we talk about the Civil War, it's just another ordinary flight. But here's my chance to learn something new. Of course I'm interested."

He held the book, its spine in his right hand, and lightly riffled the pages with his left thumb, as if releasing the volume's mysteries into the air. Abruptly, he shut the book.

"If you're American, our Civil War's results impact your way of life today in a general way. If you had relatives who fought in that war, it impacts your life in a personal way. If you live on the very land where the battles raged, it impacts you in an emotional, even a metaphysical way."

Jennifer sipped her wine, not wanting to interrupt his train of thought. At that moment, the flight attendant offered them refills. Jennifer shook her head, but her seatmate again held up two fingers. Obligingly, the attendant brought him two more bottles, scooping away his two empties.

"So how has it affected you?" she prompted.

"Though bloody, this war's gore doesn't differ significantly from that in other wars. Its leaders' distinct personalities, like Robert E. Lee or Abraham Lincoln, seemed larger than life, but other wars had legendary leaders like MacArthur, Genghis Khan or Alexander the Great. Here, each side fought with passion for the cause they believed in, but that's also common in other wars, except when mercenaries are employed."

"...who fight for anybody who pays them against any enemy their employer chooses," she volunteered. "So those similarities aside, what was different?"

"History's other wars were in other times, on other turf and for other reasons. For Americans, this was 'our' war with causes wrenching enough to pit fathers against sons and brothers against cousins and each other. This war changed our country's course while ravaging the land and the people it touched. Relics from those deadly battles turn up daily in Virginia's fields, woods and urban excavations."

"Relics like the ones in your book?"

He inhaled one of his drinks. "Exactly."

"So what's your role in this play?"

He managed a deprecating smile, as if he were a celebrity she stupidly failed to recognize. "I guess you could say I'm a collector… and very particular about what I choose."

"A personal collection or a public collection, like a museum?"

"A personal collection, though when I find duplicates, I sometimes offer them to museums."

"Then your collection must outshine most other collections?"

Despite his patronizing expression, he chuckled at his own secret joke. "You might say that."

"So what happens if you and another collector vie for the same artifact?"

He turned toward her, eyes beady. A feral grin creased his face. "That's when the real fun begins. Money smooths most deals, and money isn't a problem for me. It's amusing to guess what cash offer proves irresistible for a 'priceless' artifact. Breaking the seller is part of the game. In the end, whether with money or otherwise," his eyes narrowed, "I always get what I want—whatever it takes."

His face had turned cruel. His cold voice and ominous words sent a chill prickling across Jennifer's neck and down her shoulders. She stared with surprise at the raised hairs on her forearms.

CHAPTER 7

As the flight attendant approached, Jennifer hugged herself, puzzled at her negative reaction to her seatmate. The attendant smiled. "Another round?" Her seatmate held up two fingers. Jennifer declined.

"So you're used to getting what you want?" she asked the collector.

"Why not?" he gave a drunken sneer. "The last time I didn't get what I want, I was seven years old."

"What happened then?"

His harsh laugh caused her to turn toward him. Unnerving how his normal expression morphed into slitted eyes and mean mouth. He's reliving it right this minute, she thought. Would he reveal his shelved memory or close up?

He drained another airline liquor bottle into his glass and drank deeply. "Now I'm financially comfortable, but my fortune is self-made." Rancor filled his voice. "My middle-class parents wouldn't buy me the red ten-speed Schwinn Flyer bicycle I wanted that Christmas. When Santa brought one to a six-year-old neighbor one street away, you might say I made the boy an offer he couldn't refuse. The bike was mine. The boy told *his* parents the story I provided him: two men came by in a car, grabbed his bicycle and reached to take him also, but he ran away just in time. I told *my* parents a stranger riding in a limousine gave me the bike. The two sets of parents weren't acquainted and never put the two stories together."

Cautious now, Jennifer asked, "And what was the offer the boy couldn't refuse?"

Alcohol made his eyes rheumy, but he poured another drink. "I told him my plan for his dog," he slurred, "then for his little sister and then I'd come for him. I almost lost him when he said he hated his sister, but fortunately, he loved his dog." His laugh showed a cruel edge.

"And he believed you?"

He downed his last drink. "I can be...*persuasive* when I choose."

His smirk made her uneasy. She changed the subject. "How do you find these relics?"

He didn't answer right away, as if reluctant to pull himself away from the childhood memory. "I prowl sources myself and get input from finders — some on the internet, some in pawn shops or stores specializing in Civil War artifacts, and some collectors like me who want to trade. They earn a nice finder's fee if they locate something I want, so they're eager to deal."

"After all this time since that war, does anything new ever turn up?"

"Mainly documents or buried treasure."

The riddle and the map! He had her attention, but she didn't want to reveal too much. "*Treasure?*" She feigned surprise. "Are you kidding?"

"No. Southern plantation owners buried valuables on their property to protect them from plundering Union troops or deserters or carpetbaggers. Besides the small troves are occasional big ones. For example, in April 1865 as the victorious Union Army marched on the South's capital of Richmond, President Jeff Davis took with him the Confederate Treasury — plus gold reserves from Richmond banks to prevent their capture. But he reached his destination without those millions, rumored to be buried somewhere between Richmond and Georgia. Did plantation owners divide the treasure and bury it in many places? Did soldiers steal it? Jury's out. In theory, large parts remain undiscovered."

"There are others?"

"Sure. Rumors persist about treasure buried at Boswell's Tavern, Carter's Grove Plantation, Portsmouth, Abraham Smith's Poor Valley plantation, Beale's treasure in the Blue Ridge Mountains, Mount Rogers where a Confederate major buried loot stolen by his men, Roanoke, McIntosh Farms where a Confederate general and his slaves allegedly buried $4 million and, of course, Mosby's find."

Her mental antenna rose. She stared at him. "Mosby found treasure?"

"Well, that's one of the rumors. Story goes he rescued it from a Union general he captured in a town called Fairfax Courthouse. Then, with a battle threatening, he buried it somewhere along the road between the capture site and Centreville."

She sat up straight in her seat. "Did Mosby go back for the treasure?"

"You mean if it ever existed. Well, if he tried, he failed, because he died nearly penniless."

"Has any Civil War treasure been found?"

"In the 1970s a treasure hunter found silver coins and plates worth $20,000 in a Roanoke park, but with the state and government wanting all or a cut, most treasure hunters have little incentive now to publically reveal a find."

Could this knowledgeable collector help her better understand what she'd found inside the frame? Something creepy about him warned her not to ask. "So...what if I stumble upon a Civil War artifact or treasure when I'm out in the woods?"

He slid a business card from his shirt pocket and handed it to her. "Why, then you call me."

The name written on the card was "William Early." He looked at her expectantly.

"I don't recognize the name."

"Are you illiterate about this war?" he slurred.

"Apparently."

He harrumphed, then gestured with alcohol-fueled importance, "Confederate General Jubal Early is my ancestor in that War of Rebellion, although the Earlys have lived in America since the 1700s, long before that war."

"No wonder you identify."

He linked words into sentences with inebriated care now. "Identify is too...too shallow a word." Then his tone turned reverent. "For me, the Civil War is a...a living, pulsing entity engulfing me. The thousands of poignant individual tales, the collective tragedy of lost causes. Lost lives and broken families. The dynamic outcome... changed the American way of life, as...as well as history." He breathed rapidly, eyes glistening with manic zeal.

Jennifer felt another chill tingle her neck and arms. Something about him frightened her.

Finally, she ventured, "How long have you felt this strongly about it?"

"Since the day I was born."

She shot him a quick look. Was this drunken exaggeration? But he'd leaned back and closed his eyes. Within minutes, he lapsed into a drunken slumber, snoring gently until the plane landed two hours later in Ft. Myers, Florida.

When the plane taxied to a stop and the seatbelt sign blinked off, she stood, fumbling to retrieve her bag from the overhead rack.

"Out of my way, please," he said impatiently. Making no effort to assist her with her luggage, he lurched past her into the aisle and out of the aircraft.

Was he the sociopath he seemed or just a rude, self-centered clod? Either way, she hoped never to see him again.

CHAPTER 8

After deplaning at the Ft. Myers airport and renting a car, Jennifer zoomed down I-75 toward her Naples exit. Her first stop: the local Collier County Sheriff's office, where she explained her mother's situation to the desk sergeant.

"Senior problem, Cliff," the receptionist said into her phone.

Moments later, a middle-aged man appeared. "Deputy Cliff Goodwin. How can I help you?"

He listened attentively as Jennifer described her mother's phone call, the controlling couple who wouldn't leave and the concern about them administering sleeping drugs.

"Usually you file a report and we look into it later. But I'm heading out anyway and I'll just follow you to your mother's house in case that Doe couple causes trouble."

"The Doe couple?"

"John Doe, Jane Doe. Not their real monikers but handy aliases 'til we know who they are."

Jennifer handed him a piece of paper. "Here's her address in case we're separated. I have a key for the front door. Instead of warning them by ringing the doorbell, shall we unlock the front door and catch them by surprise?"

"Fine, miss, except I'll go in first in case they have weapons. Once I determine it's safe, then you come right behind me."

Ten minutes later, they walked up the sidewalk to the house, eyeing the windows for movement. Jennifer tried to hide her apprehension as the detective slid her key into the lock. He surprised her by pulling out his pistol before gently pushing the door open.

"Police. I'm coming inside. Police." No answer. Repeating what he'd said, he moved into the foyer, gun poised in his right hand while his other hand motioned Jennifer to stay behind him.

As they both looked left and right, Jennifer gasped. Empty drawers lay scattered on the floor in her mother's once-tidy living room; chairs and tables knocked over, rugs pushed aside, lamps askew, empty nails and pale paint showed on walls where paintings once hung.

Again, signaling Jennifer to stay back, the detective jerked open the door to the garage and led the way in with his gun muzzle. Jennifer peered past him into the empty space.

"My mother's Mercedes. It's gone," Jennifer whispered. "And see those boxes and newspapers. The Doe couple must have packed up Mom's things right here, where neighbors couldn't see."

"Do you know her car's license number?"

"No."

"Never mind. I'll radio it in. What's her full name?"

"Frances Louise Ryerson." His radio crackled. "We have a crime scene here." He gave the address. "Send backup."

"My *mother!*" Jennifer's voice rose with urgency. "If they've done this to her house, what have they done to *her?*" She started for the stairs but the detective blocked her way.

"You brought me here in case you found this kind of situation. Let me do my job. I'll look for her, but you need to wait in your car until I say it's safe inside."

"I'm not leaving this house until I know she's all right."

He took her elbow firmly. "Yes, you are. I won't take long and I'll tell you exactly what I find as soon as I come out. The faster you leave, the sooner I can look for your mother."

"But…"

"Do you want me to find her or do you want to waste time?"

"But, I…" Jennifer found herself standing outside the front door and heard the lock click behind her, as if he knew she planned to sneak back in when he went upstairs.

At first, she perched unhappily on the front step, but as Florida's summer heat overtook her, she climbed into her car and turned on the air conditioning.

A car marked "Sheriff" pulled to the curb, and another deputy hurried to the house. He entered quickly when Goodwin opened the door for him.

As minutes ticked by, Jennifer shifted impatiently. What could take this long? Were the "Does" inside? If so, did the deputies subdue them or visa-versa? More important, what about her mother? Was she there? Or had the Does taken her away? Had they hurt her? Was she even alive?

Jennifer choked back a sob.

CHAPTER 9

Pistols drawn, Goodwin and his backup checked the downstairs rooms, trashed like the others but with no sign of the suspects or Frances Ryerson. They crept up the stairs. Easing higher, one step at a time, Goodwin felt a growing concern for the mother's welfare.

At the top of the stairs, all doors but one stood ajar as they edged down the hall, hyper-alert for sound or movement. Goodwin eased the first door open wider and inched inside behind his weapon.

Nobody there, although they'd tossed this room like those downstairs. He checked the closet, bathroom and under the bed. "Clear." His companion repeated the same drill in the second and third bedrooms. "Clear," he confirmed. To leave no space unexamined, Goodwin jerked open the two linen closet closed doors and another bathroom facing the hall. He studied the ceiling for attic access.

Only one closed hallway door left. He flung it open, gun pointed, shouldered his way inside and found himself in the master bedroom. The other deputy shadowed his movements.

Last chance—if Ryerson wasn't here, the Does might have kidnapped her...or worse.

They gazed into the wrecked room. Ryerson wasn't in the bed, on the loveseat or at the desk. Goodwin's partner checked the large bathroom. Empty. Anyone still in the house had to be close. Goodwin turned to the walk-in closet's closed louvered double doors, weapon ready as he threw open the right-hand door and paused, unprepared for what he saw.

Lying immobile on the floor lay a bound and gagged frail old woman, eyes closed.

Dropping to one knee, Goodwin touched her neck. Did he feel a faint carotid artery pulse or just wish he did for the sake of her daughter downstairs? "Need ambulance ASAP. Victim alive but unconscious," he radioed.

He stood and snapped a cellphone picture of the old woman for potential future trial evidence. Then he knelt again. "Frances." He shook her slightly. "Frances?" No response. Goodwin turned to his backup. "Her daughter's out in front. Get her and bring her up here."

The second deputy hurried down the stairs to the front door and motioned Jennifer inside. "Upstairs. Master bedroom."

Panic gripped Jennifer as she raced up the stairs to her mother's closet. She looked into the closet and stifled a scream. Falling to her knees beside the prone figure, she cried, "Mom, it's Jen. You're safe now." She turned to the deputies. "Quick, scissors at the desk to cut the tape on her wrists and ankles."

Goodwin brought the shears. Jennifer tried to gently ease duct tape from the wrinkled old skin around her mouth. Then, leaving the detectives beside her mother, she hurried to the bathroom for lotion to smooth on the irritated skin as they inched away the tape's stubborn adhesive covering her mother's lips.

When they finished, Jennifer forced aside her own shock and fear to focus on her mother's urgent situation. She cradled her mother's frail body as tears of relief at finding her alive mingled with apprehension. They all looked up as an approaching siren signaled help on the way. Goodwin's backup hurried downstairs to bring the medics to their patient.

Jennifer heard feet pounding up the stairs before two paramedics swept into the room. "Stand back, please, so we can do our job." Jennifer and the detectives did, watching them monitor vital signs, start an IV and administer oxygen.

"She has a-fib," Jennifer interjected.

"Do you know her medications?" the medic asked. Jennifer told him.

When another medic wheeled in a gurney, Jennifer sobbed, "Is she alive?" They nodded.

"Look," Goodwin said, "You go with them, while I button up this scene. I'll see you both at the hospital in about an hour to..." he wanted to say to get her statement but given the old lady's condition and Jennifer's desperation, he said instead..."to see how she's doing." He pressed his business card into her hand. "I'm sorry you had to see this, but you did the right thing asking me to come along."

Jennifer imagined stumbling into this situation alone. Despite her anguish, she managed a smile and touched Goodwin's arm. "What if you'd brushed me off instead of taking my story seriously? No, Deputy, *you're* the one who made the right decision."

CHAPTER 10

C utting the siren as they neared their destination, the ambulance crew delivered their patient directly to the Naples Community Hospital ER, where aides rushed the gurney carrying the blanketed body directly to a treatment room.

An attractive woman with a stethoscope over her white jacket strode in moments later. "I'm Dr. Kravis," she said. The lead paramedic presented her with the facts: "Eighty-seven-year-old female: possible overdose, found initially unresponsive but now GCS is 3. Unknown drug or time of ingestion, Pulse 115, blood pressure 81 over 52, oxygen Sat 95%, currently being bagged due to respiratory compromise. The patient has known a-fib history and takes Cardizem and Xarelto."

"Her first name?" the doctor asked.

"Frances."

The doctor performed a sternal rub across her patient's cheek. "Frances, can you hear me. Wake up. Frances." She turned to the nurse. "Intentional overdose?"

"No, possibly drugged by someone robbing her house."

"Injection?"

"Cursory inspection but no injection sites noted."

"How long ago?"

"Best guess, two to seven hours."

"Okay, I need an EKG, head CT, urine and blood tox screens, CBC and CMP. Give her Narcan 2mg IV. If she doesn't respond, we will need to intubate."

The nurse quickly administered Narcan, but when this elicited no response, they intubated their patient and placed her on a life support ventilator.

The doctor sighed. "Someone waiting for her outside?"

"Her daughter."

Dr. Kravis snapped off her gloves and lowered her surgical mask. "Okay, I'll talk to her." She walked into the waiting room and looked around. "Jennifer Shannon?"

Jennifer jumped to her feet. "Yes."

The doctor introduced herself. "Your mother was unresponsive and not breathing on her own when she came in. We intubated her and placed her on life support. We'll admit her to ICU to keep a close eye on her. Until the toxicology tests come back, we don't know what she was given so we don't know what's going to happen, but she's stable right now. It's a good thing you got her here when you did. The nurse will tell you when you can sit with her."

Jennifer shook Dr. Kravis's hand. "Thank you."

The doctor sobered. "Don't thank me yet. I did my part. Now she does hers and, if you're looking after her, you'll soon do yours." She studied Jennifer a moment. Early sixties, worry and fatigue on her face—Kravis saw this same acute anxiety for at-risk loved ones every day. Like all the others, this case would go one direction or the other. Either way, she'd done what she could. Now relatives must deal with the results.

"Try to get some sleep tonight..." the doctor began, but a nurse touched her arm, pointing toward another treatment room.

As she walked away, Jennifer stared after her, wondering what trauma awaited this doctor next. Could she save the next person and all the other ER patients tonight? Or would she lose some...maybe even Jennifer's own mother in ICU...? A shiver coursed through her. She swallowed hard and turned toward the nurses' station. "May I stay with my mother tonight? Her name is Frances Ryerson."

The nurse consulted her chart. "Sorry, we don't have sleep chairs in the ICU rooms."

"Could I sit beside her in a regular chair?"

"All night?" the nurse frowned. "You could, but she's in skilled hands there in case you want to rest up for tomorrow. You can go up on the elevator with her as soon as I find an orderly. Maybe twenty minutes. They're busy now."

Jennifer vacillated. Sleep made sense, but what if this was her mother's last night alive and she wasn't there to comfort her or say goodbye? What if decisions caused her to use her health advocate power of attorney?

She knew her mother would get attentive medical care, but until a doctor pronounced her out of danger, Jennifer felt anxious. Rather than stew alone, she phoned Jason to explain the situation.

"Jen, honey, you must feel crazy. Do you want me to fly down?"

"No, Jay. Once they tell me she's okay, I will be too. Then I only need to coax her to leave behind all she holds dear here to move to McLean." She gave a small, semi-hysterical laugh.

Jason chuckled. "Well, you do the impossible better than anybody."

"On the other hand, Jay, if...if she doesn't make it..."

"Then I'll rocket down to Florida and we'll face it together."

Her voice quavered. "Thanks for calming me down. Love you, Jay."

"Love you, too, sweetie. Call me anytime you want to talk tonight, even if you get the GSOB instead."

She giggled. "The GSOB?"

"Grumpy Sleepy Old Bear."

CHAPTER 11

Jennifer clicked off the phone, settled back in her chair and looked around the emergency room waiting area. Everyone wore troubled expressions like hers. What ER traumas gathered this unlikely group here today at—she checked her watch—6:42pm? These complete strangers sharing concern for someone in extremis became default foxhole buddies of a sort.

The old man with the cane (waiting for his wife?), the young couple with two small children (anxious about the fate of another child?), the bearded motorcycle-jacketed guy nervously shifting his helmet from hand to hand (a traffic accident?) and the well-dressed young man holding a briefcase while glued to his cellphone (an ambulance-chasing lawyer?)

Her natural curiosity and active imagination often led her to play this "what's-their-story?" game. Her alertness for visual clues in such social scenes usually amused Jason. His "little sleuth," he called her.

She pulled out her to-do list but stopped short when two patched-together patients emerged from the treatment area: an elderly woman in a wheelchair with a bandage across her forehead and a child on crutches wearing a foot cast. Seeing who they would join in the waiting room provided a piece of the game for her.

The motorcyclist hugged the child. Before leaving, they talked animatedly with much smiling. But who waited for the old woman? The old man? Instead, the young family greeted her warmly before pushing her wheelchair out the door as the children skipped around her.

Jennifer sobered. What if matches for these waiting-room people did *not* emerge from the treatment area? Might some get rushed to surgery, or ICU like her mom or even… to the morgue?

Another walking-wounded patient limped in from treatment. Wait, didn't she recognize him? She did a double-take. Yes, William Early, with a hand in an elastic brace and arm in a sling. Would he meet the lawyer with the briefcase? No, he went to the old man with the cane, and it wasn't a happy greeting. In fact, the old man pushed William's unbraced hand away when he tried to help him up. What was going on? For a fleeting moment, she considered hailing him, but held back.

Just as well, since the nurse signaled her. "Would you like to sit with your mother now?"

"Oh yes, I would. Thanks."

In the ER treatment room, despite IV bags and an unnatural plastic tube snaking from her mouth, her mother's closed eyes and peaceful expression encouraged Jennifer.

Minutes later an orderly wheeled her mother's gurney to an ICU room, where nurses hooked her leads to telemetry machines whose beeps broadcast her vital signs. Jennifer sat in the straight chair beside the bed, staring at her mother's inert form. Five minutes passed while Jennifer talked encouragingly to the sleeping woman. Then the curtain moved and Deputy Cliff Goodwin ambled in.

"How is she?"

"The drugs haven't worn off yet but they say she's stable. They're keeping her a few days in ICU to see what happens."

"Are you up to talking with me?"

Jennifer sighed. "I guess so. I want to help find those monsters who hurt Mom, ruined her house and stole her things. The Does — you've got me calling them that now — they need to pay for what they did and be jerked out of circulation so they can't victimize others."

Goodwin settled himself in the chair next to her. "First, we need to know what they look like. Our sketch artist can draw what your mother remembers about them. She's the only person we know who saw them. Since they stole a lot of her stuff, we can assume they took her credit cards, checkbook and so on. Can you freeze those for her?"

Jennifer remembered the hassle dealing with her mother's lost purse some years ago, but then her mother gave authorizations. "I have financial and health powers of attorney but haven't used them and am uncertain what they cover. Could you go with me to the bank to verify it's a crime situation when I ask them to freeze her bank and checking accounts?"

"Yes, but you can deal with the credit cards by phone. Can you find their numbers in her files?"

"I'll try, but her filing is unconventional. Instead of putting those bills under MasterCard, Visa or American Express, she files them under 'B' for blue card or 'G' for gold card. It's a 'don't-ask.'"

"When does the doctor think she can talk to me?"

"Who knows? She's out cold and they say may stay like this a few days. Without a description, you can't start a manhunt?"

"We found some fingerprints but need to sift them from friendly prints. If you don't mind, I'll take your mother's prints and yours while I'm here." He held up the portable kit. "But sketches are what we really need."

"Did you ask neighbors?"

"Yeah, but no luck. Again, a sketch might help them remember who they saw and when."

They considered the problem. Then Jennifer sat up straight. "Wait, maybe there is someone."

"Who?"

"My mother's hair dresser. Mom's gone to her for many years. Remember, I told you she loaned Mom a mobile phone to call me from the beauty shop restroom. Mom said Jane waited for her in the beauty shop so Chelsea may have noticed her. If we can find Mom's rolodex in the chaos at the house, it has Chelsea's mobile phone number. Maybe we could contact her tonight or meet her tomorrow."

"The sooner we get a drawing, the faster we can use facial recognition software. Do you know the name of the shop in case they're open this evening?"

"Let me think. Tropical…something. Tropical Tresses? Tropical Styles? Tropical Creations—that's it." She clicked Google on her cellphone. "Here it is." She read the address to the detective, pressed dial and then Speaker so he could listen.

After a few beeps a voice said, "Tropical Creations. May I help you?"

"Yes, may I please speak with Chelsea?"

"Ah… I think she just left. Let me check. Maybe I can catch her." Long pause. After a moment a different voice spoke.

"This is Chelsea."

"Chelsea, it's Jennifer Shannon, Fran Ryerson's daughter. I need to meet with you right away. It's important."

"Oh, Jennifer, good to talk to you because I'm worried about your mom. A spooky thing happened the last time she visited the salon. Look, it's seven o'clock and I'm just leaving work. I skipped lunch and am about to grab some food at Joe's Diner on Tamiami Trail, a few blocks north of Vanderbilt Beach Road on the Naples Park side of the road. Would you like to meet me there?"

"Good idea, Chelsea. I know where it is and I'm not far away, on Immokalee. I'd like to bring someone with me: a detective." He nodded vigorous encouragement.

"Uh-oh, I don't like the sound of that." Chelsea's voice reflected concern.

"When?"

"Maybe 20 minutes?" Jennifer lifted her eyes to the detective for his reaction. He nodded. "Okay, Chelsea. See you then."

Goodwin stood. "Look, why don't I take you to the house to pick up your wheels? Remember, your car's in the driveway there. Then we can meet this possible eye-witness."

Jennifer nodded and kissed her mother's cheek. "Love you, Mom. Sleep well. I'll be back soon."

CHAPTER 12

E ntering the diner, Jennifer recognized the beautician right away. Chelsea's bright eyes and brown hair, cut in a youthful style, made her appear younger than fifty-five. During visits over the years, Jennifer often drove her mother to those weekly hair appointments. On those occasions, while Chelsea worked on her mother, another operator had styled Jen's hair.

Jennifer waved, hugged Chelsea and introduced Cliff Goodwin.

"A detective?" Chelsea frowned. "Is this about Frances?"

"I'm afraid so." Jennifer explained why she came to Florida and what she found.

"How terrible!" Chelsea shook her head in disbelief, "but I felt something was very wrong that day. I mean, not only did your mother borrow my phone, which she'd never done before, but that woman eavesdropped on our conversation and watched Frances every minute except when she went into the bathroom."

The waitress came and they placed orders.

"Do you remember the woman well enough to help our police artist make a sketch?" Goodwin asked.

"I tried not to stare at her but I got a good look and think I could help with a drawing."

"Would you describe her?"

"Long black hair in a ponytail, dark eyes, slim, about my height, maybe in her thirties, serious expression, little smiling. The man was her opposite."

"The man?" Goodwin asked in surprise.

"Yes, when the appointment ended, the woman called him on her cellphone. He came into the shop to get them."

Jennifer and the detective grinned at this piece of luck.

"You said 'her opposite'?" he probed.

"Well, although they're about the same age, he was blond, blue-eyed, husky, about six feet tall, all smiles and personality. I could tell your sketch artist exactly what he looked like."

Their food arrived and they talked as they ate.

Remembering her mother's last conversation about forgetting to pay bills and failing her driving test, Jennifer asked. "Have you noticed anything different about her in the last six months?"

"I see changes in all my older regular customers as the years roll by," Chelsea volunteered.

"Like?"

"This goes beyond obvious changes like adding wrinkles and liver spots or walking stooped over or developing gnarled hands. Their new main topics are forgetfulness and medical problems—arthritis, pains in hips, backs, knees, recent surgeries or those coming up, medicines they take, and so on."

Jennifer chuckled. "I hear that from friends my age in their sixties."

"...and their personal care starts to deteriorate—they bathe less because they forget or it's too much trouble. They forget to brush their teeth, so bad breath. Whew! Makeup works two ways: some older women forget it entirely and others apply it brighter and thicker than ever because of failing eyesight."

Jennifer shared one of her mother's problems. "Or bathroom bulbs burn out and they can't climb up to put in new ones. Their makeup looks fine in the pale indoor light but garish in the sunshine."

Chelsea nodded. "And then there's nutrition. They eat less because buying and cooking food is a hassle, or their appetites change or they just forget. Medicines affect the condition of hair and skin and nails. Aging can change hair texture as blood flow to the scalp decreases. Stress or worry can also impact hair's condition..."

Goodwin grinned, "You mean like that old phrase, 'he was so scared his hair turned white overnight.'"

"Believe me, as a beautician I see effects of strain in hair health *and* color."

Jennifer probed further. "What else do you notice?"

"Well, eyesight, if they don't get new glasses. Hearing loss is another biggie. When they can't hear, they're uncomfortable around other people. Even if they use hearing aids, they forget the regular audio check-ups or haven't the energy to go. Deafness means isolation, even in a crowd. I have one old client who avoids group activities because she hears nothing and feels left out. Now she's a hermit except for her Meals-On-Wheels delivery person and her faithful weekly trips to the beauty shop.

Goodwin chuckled. "So who's she prettying up for at your shop?"

Chelsea sighed. "I guess for herself. She's all she has left. Actually, this is a good sign for an older person, meaning she hasn't stopped caring about her appearance."

They ate silently, thinking this over. Jennifer pushed her empty salad bowl aside. "So if you see older clients develop problems needing attention, what do you do?"

"What *can* I do? I don't want to make them or their families angry by interfering. But I make suggestions; maybe tell a near-deaf client about another customer who said her hearing aid check-up opened her up to the world of sound again. Or maybe ask a client in pain if she's heard of a certain doctor who helped another client with a similar complaint. But believe it or not, some older people don't want to go to doctors at all. They don't want bad news or long hours in the waiting room or finding transportation to get there."

The detective gestured with his fork. "If a problem looks serious, could you call an older client's relative?"

"Before your mother left this last time, I asked her for your phone number. As the man and woman hustled her out, she called back over her shoulder that she'd give it to me next time. But there wasn't a next time. And here's something sad I see: some seniors aren't close to their children to begin with. Or if they are, they don't want to bother them because they're busy with fulltime jobs or young kids. Those seniors don't want to be a burden to their children."

Goodwin set down his soda. "Yeah, independent seniors don't like to admit they're floundering. But they do flounder, right into county hands where police or social services reel them in."

"And children like me who live in another state think our weekly phone calls prove our parents are okay. But, as you say, they may sugar-coat what's really happening."

"Exactly." Chelsea stirred her coffee. "My older men regulars come to the shop about once a month, but my older ladies come every week. I see them oftener than their doctors or dentists or their grown children. I see them fifty-two times a year. Some of them feel like family to me. If they reveal they've had car accidents or failed driver tests, I worry about them and everybody on the road with them."

"With Naples' large senior population, this shouldn't surprise us," Jennifer admitted. "But it should make us a lot warier on the road."

Goodwin picked up on this. "Yeah, the sunny climate and beaches lure them to vacation in Florida and when it's time to retire, they sell the place up north, move here and get old. Causes police all kinds of headaches."

"Such as..." Jennifer encouraged.

He nodded toward Chelsea. "Like you said, such as driving with no license or causing accidents. Their vision and hearing aren't so good any more so they're less alert and may not even *see* traffic signs, never mind *obey* them. Delayed reflexes add to the problem, and sometimes the aging process shrinks them so they can hardly see over the wheel."

They all laughed at that familiar sight.

"And that's only their driving. Elder scamming and fraud are another big problem," he added. "A perp's ideal patsy is an older woman alone—a widow; and since women outlive men, there are plenty around. These senior ladies trust what they hear and expect the best in people, not realizing scam artists deliberately target them for easy fleecing. Like your mother..."

Jennifer nodded soberly. "Back in Virginia, Fairfax County has a "50+" program with scam prevention alerts. But seniors live in every state, so this must be a nationwide problem. "

The detective noticed they'd finished dinner. He dropped his napkin beside his plate. "I could tell you plenty of stories about criminal exploitation of older folks."

"Like?"

"Like identity theft, telemarketing fraud, mail fraud, internet fraud, home improvement fraud, mortgage fraud, investment fraud, caregiver fraud." He laughed. "A new one is an IRS phone scam telling victims they owe money for unpaid taxes and are threatened with arrest if payment isn't made right away through a wire transfer. If they don't cooperate, the caller gets nasty and threatens them."

Chelsea frowned. "Are you serious?"

"You bet. The real IRS never demands payment over the phone or asks for credit card numbers, but many seniors are fuzzy about their taxes, and arrest threats alarm anybody. They think sending a payment will make the problem disappear. Taken together, crimes targeting seniors make a serious problem for police."

Jennifer shook her head. "I didn't realize this—until today."

"Yeah, and the newest one is the virtual kidnapping scam."

"The *what?*"

"Virtual kidnapping. The scammer calls saying a family member's been taken hostage and tries to convince a parent or grandparent of the abduction by having a fake victim scream for help in the background. If the scammed person won't pay the ransom, they say the kidnapped victim will be maimed or killed. A variation is saying a family member has been hurt in a car accident with a gang member, who won't allow medical care until he's paid for damage to his vehicle. The scammer says he'll stay on the phone until money is wire transferred using Western Union. They keep you on the line preventing you from calling or locating the supposed kidnapped victim."

Jennifer shook her head. "People fall for that?"

"They do, older folks particularly." Goodwin gestured toward Jennifer. "Then you have all the home improvement scams. Some of the perps we call gypsies, who travel up and down the east coast bilking homeowners out of their money. Others we call woodchucks—they're the homegrown opportunists. You just had a mean taste of a scam with your mother. As these combined older generation problems increase, they become a national issue affecting us all."

Jennifer and Chelsea stared at Goodwin, trying to process this unsettling information.

CHAPTER 13

inally, Jennifer glanced at the diner's wall clock and counted
out some cash. "This should cover mine with tip. Sorry, but I
need to get back to ICU. You two stay and make your sketch-
artist plans. Chelsea, let's trade cellphone numbers." They did.

"Do you have far to go?" Goodwin asked Chelsea.

"No, only a couple of miles." She sighed. "I'm returning to an
empty house now that my daughter and grandchild moved out
for good."

"Be sure to lock your doors at night."

"Thanks, Deputy. Spoken like a good cop."

Goodwin turned to Jennifer, "And I'll see you tomorrow."

"Tomorrow?"

"Yeah, after we finish our crime scene pictures, we need a list
of what's stolen from your mother's house and you'll want to get
your own snapshots of the damage for your insurance company.
Also, I need your mother's statement the minute she's able to talk
at the hospital, so please let me know when she wakes up. Do you
still have my card?"

Jennifer fumbled through her purse. "It's probably here, but..."

He handed her another. "...Just in case."

Jennifer hurried to her car. Twenty minutes later, she pulled
into the hospital parking lot. Upstairs at the ICU desk she spoke
to the nurse. "Is my mother, Frances Ryerson, in the same place?"

Caught mid-phone conversation, the nurse nodded and Jennifer
threaded her way back among the curtained stalls. But as she

approached, she saw activity in the room and heard several voices. What did it mean? She ran the rest of the way and slipped inside to find three nurses working on her mother.

"What...what's going on?" Jennifer demanded.

"She, ah...she had a bout with hypotension, but we think it's under control. She seems okay now. See, she's resting comfortably again," one nurse added after the rest left.

Jennifer moved to her mother's bedside. The lights in surrounding machines blinked rhythmically to the telemetry's steady beep. Despite the tube protruding from her mouth, her mother seemed to sleep peacefully. The array of monitoring gadgetry confirmed this.

Jennifer touched her mother's hand. No reaction. "It's Jen, Mom. I'm right here with you. The doctor says you're going to be fine." This hedged the truth, but positive thoughts couldn't hurt. "Just get a little better every minute until you're soon back in your own familiar home."

But would her home seem familiar? Still a crime scene, the ransacked house wasn't habitable until straightened up. She didn't know who her mother hired to clean house before the arrival of the "Does." In earlier years, her mother knew everyone on the block, who would gladly offer cleaning referrals. But some died, others moved, and instead of a street of residents her mother's age, now middle-aged retirees and some young families comprised the neighborhood.

She could hire a cleaning team from the yellow pages or Angie's List. She made a mental note.

What about the missing-items-list Goodwin needed? To recreate what they'd taken, Jennifer needed her mother's help because she couldn't remember what belonged where. When her mother recovered enough to return home, would this awful experience still shake her too much emotionally or physically to do this task? Would she even remember what happened to her for the statement Goodwin needed to track and prosecute these criminals?

Jennifer sank into the chair. When young and in college, going without sleep for twenty-four hours was easy, but such marathons betrayed her quickly in her sixties. Her watch said 9:00pm. She could dash to her mother's home, catch a few Z's and return at 6:00am. Her mother didn't need her constant vigilance while in safe hands here, asleep or awake. On the other hand, if her recovery deteriorated enough for serious decisions her mother had authorized her to make, then she belonged at her side. What to do?

She shifted uncomfortably in the chair for half an hour and started making a to-do list for tomorrow when the next concern struck her. With the house a crime scene, she couldn't spend the night there. The missing Mercedes keys were linked onto house keys, now in the Does' possession. What if they returned for something left behind during their hasty departure? Flimsy crime-scene tape wouldn't deter them.

She took a card from her purse, called the deputy on her cell and described her concerns.

"Get a hotel tonight. Maybe off-season rates at a resort or something reasonable near the Naples exits on I-75. Tomorrow you can change the locks on your mother's house. Maybe even install a security system. Just keep your cellphone handy in case I need to reach you. Do you need help finding a place to stay tonight?"

"No, I should solve this with my cell. My laptop's in my rental car. Are you still on duty?"

"Yeah, you might say I work a lot of hours now keeping busy…"

"…because," she nudged.

"It's personal. I hope we'll wind this case up soon. Chelsea's meeting the sketch artist now, which helps us ID them and put out a BOLO. With their head start, they could make it to another state by now, especially if they ditched the Mercedes."

Next, she called Jason, described the day's improbable events and asked his advice for her decision.

"Dear Jen, I know you — you want to stay by your mother. But there's a practical side. At the hospital, she's in capable hands, but soon she'll rely on *your* hands. Even if she were in perfect health, you'd have a super-full next few days just dealing with the crime situation. Add to that caring for her and maybe even starting the moving-north discussion…"

"I see what you mean. Tomorrow *I'm* where the buck stops. You're right, Jay. I'll find a hotel."

"Remember, I can fly down there if…"

"You're a sweetheart, hon. If I didn't already love you, I would now."

He laughed. "Now get some sleep. Tomorrow's a busy day. You'll make a lot of decisions. I have complete faith in your judgment. Love you, Jen."

"You, too, Jay."

When she unpacked her pajamas at the hotel, a pair of eyes stared up from the suitcase. She didn't remember packing the dragon, but that whole hasty departure process blurred in her mind.

Well, why not. Wasn't this her mascot?

CHAPTER 14

S tartled awake the next morning by the ringing phone, Jennifer fumbled for the receiver. "Good morning. This is your 6:00am wake-up call," spoke the automated voice. She hung up, stretched and looked around the hotel room. A fringe of daylight illuminated the perimeter of the room-darkening curtains she'd closed last night. What would this day bring?

She dressed quickly, threw her belongings into the suitcase, grabbed the hotel bill shoved under her door and headed for the lobby. On the way out, she grabbed complimentary coffee and breakfast snacks to eat in her rental car.

At the hospital by 7:00am, she hurried to ICU just in time to see three physicians doing morning rounds. The doctor introduced himself and his two accompanying residents.

"Hello. How's my mother today?" Jennifer asked as the three consulted the chart filed at the foot of the bed.

"Diazepam, urine and blood screens. Looks like an overdose," the lead physician said to his residents in tow. "The half-life effect increases with age and she's," he consulted the chart, "eighty-seven, so she got here in the nick of time. Resuscitation, intubation and life support usually from one to three days. Basically, she's in a drug-induced coma with probable recovery, but it's still too soon to tell. Was this a suicide attempt?"

Jennifer blanched. "No. Isn't it on her chart? We found her bound, gagged and drugged by criminals who robbed her house.

They left her doped, not caring if she died. It's a miracle we found her in time."

The doctor scrutinized the chart before adding, a bit sheepishly, "Sorry about that. Yes, it's here. So she's a mighty lucky woman."

"Is this 'diazepam' a common drug?"

"That's generic for valium."

"Before you go, Doctor, I appreciate your hospital's quick ER diagnosis and your ICU care. Did you just say her coma may last several days?"

"Depends on various factors, but that's typical absent unexpected complications." The three made ready to leave. "Nice meeting you," the doctor said as they left to visit the next room.

Unexpected complications? So her mother wasn't safe yet. Jennifer kissed her forehead. Oh Mom, she thought, please pull through this. Please.

Sitting down in the chair beside the bed, she opened her purse, removed her cellphone and made a 10:00am locksmith appointment. She'd call the bank about freezing accounts. Next, she arranged for the insurance agent to assess damage to the house at 11:00am. She hired a cleaning team to arrive at 3:00pm and in between, she'd try to figure what the Doe couple had stolen. Last, she phoned the detective to explain her plans.

"How's your mother?" Goodwin asked.

"No change. Any progress?"

"We're matching Chelsea's sketches with face recognition. Nothing yet. We should have fingerprint analysis this morning. Police found the Mercedes up in Atlanta. The perp probably traded it for another ride, maybe also stolen. But I have some good news: although they trashed your mother's house, for some reason they respected her car. We'll get it back in Florida in a few days and after evidence-check, your mother gets her car back, ready to drive."

Given the expired license issue, Jennifer swallowed hard. "Thanks, Deputy. What should I do about the crime scene tape? I'd like to spend the day pulling the house back together.... You'll meet me there? Okay. Twenty minutes. See you then."

She ended the call and bent over the sleeping figure on the bed. "Mom, I'm going now to tidy up the house for your return. I hope it will look much the way you remember. Meantime, concentrate on getting better. By the way, I saw Chelsea last night. She sends her love and expects to see you in her salon chair next Saturday, right on schedule. I'll return later today. Love you, dear Mom."

Her mother didn't move, but Jennifer hoped this comatose figure in the bed absorbed her daughter's familiar voice and comforting chatter.

After reminding the nursing station how to locate her, Jennifer drove to her mother's house. She picked up the newspaper in the driveway.

Cliff Goodwin waited in his car at the curb when she arrived. "Good morning." He joined her on the sidewalk, carrying a sack. As they approached the front door, he handed the bag to her while he balled up the crime scene tape. "I'll go in first," he said.

Inside, the trashing looked worse than Jennifer remembered. Shock at what she first saw, coupled with fear for her mother's safety must have numbed the original impact. Now every detail showed the Does' disregard for her mother's belongings in their frenzy to uncover valuables.

Goodwin waited while she pulled herself together. He righted a fallen chair. "When does the insurance agent get here?"

"Eleven."

"Okay, that gives you three hours to go room-to-room and snap pictures of the mess. The agent will take pics, too, but you probably want your own set. And you can start a list of missing items for your mother's verification when she returns. I need a copy and insurance will want one, too. Here," he indicated the sack Jen still clutched, "I brought coffee and donuts."

Jennifer couldn't help smiling. Goodwin's gruff act covered a softer side. "Thanks, they smell tempting. In the two hours before the locksmith comes, I understand what needs to happen. When the insurance agent finishes, I'll try to straighten this place for Mom's return."

"Yeah, and if your mother's like everybody else, her jewelry's in her bedroom or the refrigerator, where you can check to see if anything's left." Jennifer frowned at this just as his phone rang.

"Yeah.... Yeah.... Good. Keep the pressure on." Hanging up, he turned to Jennifer. "Hey, I got some good news. We got a fingerprint match on the guy. Frances isn't the first senior he burglarized and doped. He has an M.O."

"M.O.?"

"Modus operandi. Didn't know I speak Latin, did ya? It means the way he does things. Perps like to repeat what worked last time. It forms a pattern."

"What...what's his real name?"

"Max Roderick. Nothing on the girl yet. Maybe she's new—someone he picked up on the way. We have a nationwide alert out for them. But if Roderick's flush with cash, he's harder to find. Did your mother keep cash in the house?"

"I ...I really don't know."

How much else didn't she know about her mother?

CHAPTER 15

Jennifer parked at the hospital and headed for the ICU. Her day had gone well. She undid chaos at the house enough that the cleaning team found furniture upright, drawers returned to bureaus and desks, cushions on chairs, some paintings rehung and kitchen cupboards refilled and closed.

Roderick had emptied the freezer, looking for hidden valuables, but she made the wet, food-flecked kitchen floor look normal again. She began a list of suspected stolen goods for her mother to complete. Most important, the house felt safe with new locks and security system. Had all this madness really happened in only twenty-four hours since she'd arrived in Florida?

She entered her mother's ICU curtained cubicle. "Hi, Mom," she said to the sleeping figure. "It's Jennifer. I'm back. What a day." She described accomplishments, doubting her mother understood but hoping her soothing voice comforted. She stroked her mother's hand, the one without the IV, and listened to the beeping machines.

"Jason sends his love. He's ready to fly down here if we need him. He thinks you're the best mother-in-law a guy ever had, so you've really won him over." Some people, after regaining consciousness, reported they'd understood nearby conversations while "out." But what to say? "Guess I'll update you on your five grandchildren who are, of course, by default, my children."

"Dylan's the oldest, as you know, and his kiddies are Asa, Christopher, Ethan and Gabe. Then daughter, Kaela, and her husband, Owain, have three little cuties: Christine, Alicia and Milo.

We baby-sat them a few months ago during the diamond scare, which got way too dangerous but somehow ended okay. Those little ones, your great-grandchildren, thought they'd had a great adventure with us, though their parents understandably didn't." She looked for response from the sleeping figure but saw none.

"Son Mike and wife, Bethany, have three children—all girls. Funny how Dylan has all sons and Mike, all daughters. But the cousins are close since their parents live within a couple hours of us, so we get together often for family events and holidays. You attended a lot of those on your many visits with us in McLean."

Jennifer tickled her mother's toes through the blanket but felt no response. "Daughter Hannah and Adam still act like newlyweds, though they've been married a year. After he subdivides extra acres on property he inherited, they'll start building the new house they've designed. He broke his leg during a fire at their old house, but he's fine now. Becca, our twenty-year-old 'baby,' just graduated from college and is looking for the 'right' job. She has a real zest for life. Her current boyfriend is Nathan Sommer, a firefighter and medic who comes from a big family like ours. We hope Becca likes him as much as we do, but she's still playing the field."

She touched her mother's arm, then patted her cheek. The coma wore on.

"You may not hear any of this, Mom, but I hope you sense someone who loves you sits right beside you."

Jennifer eased back in the chair and closed her own eyes after an exhausting but successful day. She'd sleep at the house tonight with the new locks and security system. She'd stock the fridge with several days' meals and some nice wines. With luck, her mother might shake the coma to join her there tomorrow, finding the house much as it looked before this Max Roderick invaded. Would her mother feel paranoia from her traumatic attack? Shouldn't she be allowed to return to "normal" after the drugging and hospital experiences before Jennifer introduced the life-changing move-to-McLean discussion?

She stood to leave, smoothing her mother's hair back from her forehead. "Love you, dear Mom. Hope you hear me and know just as you gave me loving care for so many years while I grew up, I'm returning that trust. Good night. See you again early tomorrow."

She gathered up her purse and started to leave, but wait. Did she hear a new sound among the machine beeps? A moan? She whirled around to see her mother's eyes flutter open. "Mom?"

The tube prevented speaking, but her mother moaned again. Jennifer hurried to her side. "Mom? Feel like waking up?" Her mother's eyes opened, stared and closed again.

Rushing to the nurse's station, Jennifer reported this.

"We'll send someone in a few minutes. Would you stay with her until we get there?"

Back at her mother's bedside, Jen chatted on, hoping conversation stimulated impending wakefulness. She talked of familiar restaurants they liked, places they shopped and friends her mother cherished.

Her mother's eyes opened again, this time trying to focus and understand her surroundings. Jen said, "You're in a hospital, Mom, because you...you felt sleepy. But now you're waking up. Wonderful! We have lots to talk about."

A doctor came in, carrying a chart. He introduced himself. "She came out of it sooner than we guessed. That's a good sign. We'll assess her alertness for a few hours before removing the tube from her throat. When we do, the irritation may cause raspy voice for a few days. Then, we'll move her from ICU to a regular medical ward for observation before discharge."

"Observation for how long?"

"A day or two. Depends on her progress. A doctor will decide when she's ready to go. Once she's up, she'll feel weak from no exercise, so start her walking as much as feels comfortable. Take her to her regular doctor two days after discharge to confirm her progress."

"Thank you."

"She's pretty feisty to shake the drug coma so fast at age eighty-seven," he commented.

"Cross your fingers for more of the same."

"Good luck to you both."

We'll need some, big time, Jennifer thought. But she managed a smile for the doctor.

CHAPTER 16

Despite the doctor's warning, Jennifer felt disheartened at her mother's struggle to talk after intubation removal. But the older woman sat up, propped against pillows, and displayed increasing alertness. She understood conversations, smiled, frowned and responded to questions by nodding or shaking her head. Where sign language failed, she soon wrote messages on a clipboard. Jennifer felt elated: her mother was "back."

Jennifer updated her about her flight down, reaching the house with the deputy, what they found and the ambulance ride to the ER. She described the hospital care the past few days and anticipated discharge soon. She explained recovery of the stolen Mercedes and BOLO for "John" and "Jane." She explained how she'd straightened up the trashed belongings, house-cleaned and dealt with insurance. "Although only your sharp eyes can identify everything missing, Mom."

So far so good, but too early to burden her with decisions for the future.

"We've talked a long time. It's a lot of information to absorb. Want to rest awhile?"

Her mother's eyes closed as she considered the question, but then opened. She shook her head.

"Do you feel confused or pretty normal?"

Normal, her mother wrote on the clipboard and turned it toward Jen.

"Anything you'd like to talk about?"

Her mother wrote, *Yes. Feel like a fool letting those criminals in my house.*

Jennifer patted her mother's wrinkled hand. "You're not the only one. Sheriff's Deputy Goodwin—you'll meet him soon—says many criminals target seniors for scams like this and worse."

To her mother's questioning look, Jennifer explained. "It's a long, scary list. He says skillful con artists can target any age, but find seniors generally come from a time when a man's word and handshake equaled a contract. This kind of trust makes them vulnerable."

Her mother wrote, *How do they choose a victim?*

"They look for a senior living in a big house with nice belongings, like you. A criminal smells money there. He knows many older folks were raised to use good manners and avoid confrontations or hurting feelings, especially women. They're often kind-hearted and generous, making them easy to dupe into giving money to bogus causes. They're usually likelier to believe a sales pitch."

Why? appeared on the pad.

"Because details confuse them or they think it's rude to question someone's statements. They often forget to ask for a workman's license or bond, the very standards for skill and dependability that protect homeowners. And not just with home repair or phone scams but also investments on Wall Street. Older seniors have less energy to disagree when they're being conned. Some are too embarrassed to admit they've been swindled so they don't even call police. You see the pattern?"

Her mother wrote, *Yes. I lived it.*

They fell silent, thinking about what she'd survived. Jennifer paused to remember her dual purpose of this Naples trip: rescuing her mother and guiding her toward safer living. Jennifer did the homework, researching options like hired home care if her mother insisted on staying in her house, or senior living in Naples with a variety of options. The most convenient solution for Jennifer was moving her to McLean, but her mother had been through a lot physically and she knew body and mind shared trauma. Was this the time to bring it up?

"Mom, while I'm down here in Naples, might we talk about your future?" Encouraged by her mother's nod, she asked cautiously, "Do you think living alone here is a good idea now?"

To Jennifer's complete surprise, her mother shook her head. This unexpected breakthrough invited the second pivotal question. "What do you think is the best way to solve that?"

Her mother wrote. *Move near you in Virginia.*

Jennifer tried to hide her astonishment. No knockdown struggle. She couldn't believe it.

"Where do you think you'd like to live there?" This was the big test. Would she want to live with the Shannons? Would she opt to buy a smaller house or condo?

Her mother wrote, *upscale senior housing.*

Jennifer gripped her chair arms for support. Scarcely able to believe her ears, she grinned. "Mom, what wonderful news. I'm thrilled you'll be close by to spend time with your Grands and Great-grands. We can do things, Girls Together, just like we used to do. Remember GT?"

Her mother smiled and nodded. Jennifer didn't want to rock this new boat, but such a complete transformation in her mother's thinking baffled her. She chose her words carefully.

"Have you…have you been thinking about these big decisions for quite a while?

Her mother shook her head and wrote, *"No. This taught me like nothing else could. I was a fool but I'm not an idiot."*

CHAPTER 17

L ater, when her mother fell asleep, Jennifer stepped into the hall to phone Cliff Goodwin.

"Hello, Deputy. She's out of the coma and raspy from the throat tube, but she can write answers for you. She's napping now but you asked me to let you know right away when she woke up.... Yes, she seems lucid, remembers what happened and should be discharged tomorrow or the next day.... Yes, we'll return to her house.... Well, turns out she wants to move to Virginia, so I need to arrange emptying the house and selling it.... Yes, a busy time ahead.... Okay. If I'm not here when you talk with her, will you please let me know afterward how it goes? You have my number? Good. Talk with you later."

Stunned at her mother's willingness to move north, she knew they must next decide when. Frances had survived trauma, unnerving at any age and particularly at eighty-seven, but Jennifer hoped to act before her mother changed her mind. Already away from her own family a couple of days, Jennifer calculated she'd need weeks to make this move happen and get her mother's belongings to their new destination. But where?

Suddenly Jennifer had a wild thought. She dialed her husband and brought him up to date. "Jay," she continued, "I have a far-out idea for a temporary fix."

Jason laughed with a nervous edge, "I wouldn't expect less than a far-out idea from you."

She chuckled. "Well, now, I'm not sure how to weigh that comment."

"Don't ask. You don't want to know."

"What about the empty house across the street? After Tony and Kirsten Donnegan passed away, their children wanted to sell the house, but the market's down right now. Maybe we could rent it for, say three to six months? We'd move Mom in—she'd need only the first floor—and she'd be right across the street where we could keep an eye on her while we ferret out the best senior housing choice. Would you mind contacting the Donnegan kids for their reaction? Absent that, could you check on other short-term rentals in our neighborhood? Hate to say it, but I'm afraid it's a hurry-up assignment."

"I'll get right on it." His voice sobered. "How are *you* doing, Jen?"

"Fine. My job's simplified by Mom's recovery and unexpected cooperation. Now it's logistics to vacate and sell her house. But before I do, have we any interest in keeping it as a place to winter? We'd have the taxes, maintenance and mortgage, if there is one. The place would sit idle nine months of the year but we'd hire a house-checker to visit bi-monthly, just like all the other snowbirds do. On the other hand, without that sale money, Mom may not have enough to rent or buy or pay the entry fee for the kind of senior housing she wants in McLean. We've never discussed her financial situation."

"Let me think that over, Jen. You have your hands full down there."

Always the cook when at home, Jennifer asked, "How are you solving meals?"

"No problem. I grocery shop for breakfast, get lunch near work. Becca and I collaborate on the evening meal. Mike's family brought dinner one night and Becca and I like eating out. So it's win-win."

"So sorry about this problem with my Mom, Jay, but if I can solve it while I'm down here, this is the final trip. And this way, we'll know she's safer near us. But worst case, it could take several weeks, even a month or more to make all this happen."

"She's a special lady and you're doing exactly what you should. She's lucky you're there. Stick with it, and remember, I can fly down if you need me."

"Love you, Jay."

"Love you, too, my Jen."

CHAPTER 18

Aside from the internet, Jennifer needed advice from a long time Naples resident about quality firms she needed in a hurry. No old friends left on her mother's block in the neighborhood, but then she thought of Chelsea, whose salon clients lived all around Naples.

"Chelsea," Jennifer spoke into the phone. "Is this a good time to talk...? Okay, I'll be quick. I think Mom's leaving the hospital tomorrow, so she'll keep her regular appointment with you this Saturday... You'd like to change her regular day to Thursdays, same time? Sure, I understand Saturday's are high demand at beauty shops. No problem, Chelsea. Could you find another beautician to do my hair at the same time? Great. By the way, looks like Mom may move north with me soon. Can you or your clients recommend any Realtors, moving companies or estate sale people...? Okay, you have my number...? Thanks."

Next, she opened her laptop to research companies and check their ratings. She tentatively picked three possibilities in each category. The choice depended on their short-notice availability, as well as ratings and costs. Later, she'd compare her results with Chelsea's suggestions.

After tiptoeing into her mother's room to find her napping, Jennifer decided to use a table in the hospital lobby to work her laptop and make those cellphone calls.

An hour later she glanced up to see Cliff Goodwin lumbering across the lobby. She hailed him and closed her computer as he walked over, asking, "How ya doing?"

"Fine now that my mom's okay. Are you here to see her?" He nodded. "Mind if I come along?"

"Great idea. Are you staying in Naples awhile longer?"

"Just long enough to organize her move to Virginia."

He gave a thin laugh. "A hard sell, exchanging Florida sunshine for mean winters up north."

"True. I'm amazed, but she came up with this on her own."

"You don't know how lucky she is. I see the downside of some seniors here who 'age in place'—that's what they call it now. Without the right support, they can get isolated. To police that means vulnerable. Some get abused, neglected, exploited and even abandoned. More so, if they have disabilities needing major care. Some families opt out when the going gets tough."

"Really?" Jennifer's brow wrinkled.

"Well, your own mother's an example of exploitation, and her perp used his scam on other seniors needing help at home. We see cases all the time of family members or caregivers neglecting or abusing seniors. If the senior uses glasses, dentures, a cane, a walker or special meds, they hide them and won't return them unless the senior signs papers or does whatever they want. One son put bars on windows and locked his old mother inside the house while he went to work. If a senior is assaulted physically, you can be sure he's abused verbally. Senior sex abuse is about power, a grim extension of physical abuse. Some go after the senior's money by making him more dependent. The more isolated and needy the senior gets, the more power the abuser has. If an old person doesn't drive, his phone is taken away and he's physically impaired, how can he get help?"

"Awful..."

"Look, in law enforcement we don't see the happy, kind, good families where everybody loves each other. We see the other kind. But consider this," he pulled a sheet of paper from his pocket and started reading, "the number of Americans sixty-five and older is supposed to double by 2030 when those seventy-four million baby boomers born between 1946 and '64 kick in. And the number of people eighty-five-plus increases even faster. And guess what— about ninety percent of elder abusers are their own family members, and forty-seven percent of those are their own adult children."

Jennifer shook her head in disbelief as they stepped off the elevator.

"And," the deputy tucked the paper back in his pocket, "twenty percent of elder abusers are their own spouses or partners. You see why police look first at the family in those situations?"

She nodded, trying to absorb this disturbing information as they approached her mother's ward. "Here we are. Deputy, I...I'm worried." Jennifer's brow furrowed. Would this brusque detective understand? "She's already physically and emotionally frail, after what she's been through. If your questions upset her, would you, could you delay the interview?" He sighed but nodded.

They opened the door and looked in. "Hi, Mom. Would you like some company? I brought a visitor." She introduced Goodwin.

"Hey, glad you're feeling better. I'm the deputy investigating what happened. I want to compliment you for calling your daughter to help you. That was a smart, brave choice. Now, we want to catch the couple who took advantage of you. I'd like to wait until it's easier for you to talk, but the sooner we get your story, the faster we can move forward." He took out a notebook. "Can you answer some questions about what you remember and look at some photos to help identify the people who harmed you? I see you're nodding. How did you meet these people?"

Picking up the notebook, she wrote, *Vanderbilt Beach Road. I couldn't work the pump. He offered to help. He admired my Mercedes. We discussed gardening. I needed a yardman. He'd give me an estimate if he saw my yard.*

Goodwin read this. "And you asked him to take a look?" She nodded. He handed her the notebook. "And then what happened?"

She wrote, *Had I handyman work to estimate? I did. He did some repairs. I paid him. He'd been a chauffeur and offered Driving-Miss-Daisy for a reasonable price when I revealed I had no driver's license. I agreed.*

Goodwin read this. "How did the woman get involved?"

She wrote, *He said his wife cleaned, cooked and shopped, all for $30 a day. Couldn't believe it. Said I'd try her. She was a bargain. Or so I thought.* She passed Goodwin the notebook.

"So everything seemed okay at first? When did that change?" he asked.

They hid my phones. He drove me everywhere, but once there, she came in, watched who I met, heard my conversations. Since I usually shopped alone, a companion was nice. Then he said they needed a place to stay a few nights. I offered a bedroom. Stupid. Later I felt sleepy daytimes.

Took naps like never before unless sick. Felt like prisoner. They always explained away missing phones and not leaving."

Goodwin read this and asked, "When did you contact Jennifer?"

Borrowed Chelsea's phone at weekly hair appointment. Called from ladies room. Only place away from Jane. Maybe she saw me return Chelsea's phone or heard her ask me for my daughter's number. Back home from the beauty shop, they weren't nice any more. He said they should move fast. When I asked for water, the drink tasted funny. I put it down, but they made me finish. Walked me to the bedroom. That's all I remember until waking here.

"Anything else?" Goodwin prodded. She shook her head.

He pulled a picture array from his briefcase. "Recognize anyone?"

She pointed. "That's him."

At the photo array of women, she shook her head.

"When you're back home, Jennifer will help you list everything missing so we can search for your stolen property. If you have old pictures of the missing items, it's even better. Here's my card. If you think of something more, call me day or night."

Frances reached out a gnarled hand, touched his sleeve and rasped in a gravelly voice. "Thank you, Detective."

Goodwin smiled and shuffled out.

"Good job, Mom. Well done."

Her mother smiled and croaked. "Not well done for me, Jen. Well done for you, dearest—you saved my life."

CHAPTER 19

A t discharge the next day, the nurse went over the home after-care list while they wheeled Frances to the entrance. "Your voice sounds better today."

Her mother smiled, "Yes, but I preserve it when I can."

As they rode, Jennifer began cautiously, "Mom, you might want to prepare yourself before we get home. After they drugged you, they burglarized your house. Deputy Goodwin says some stolen pieces may turn up, but if not, insurance kicks in. Not the same as having all the things you care about, but at least something. They ransacked the place and I straightened it back the best I could, but it isn't exactly as you remember." Jennifer glanced over to see how her mother took this.

A long pause and then her mother said in a small voice, "For instance?"

"For instance, they took some paintings off the walls. You'll see faded spots where they hung."

Her mother sighed. "I understand."

Jennifer made small talk the rest of the way until they pulled into the driveway. She hadn't the heart to mention they had also stolen the Mercedes, luckily recovered in good condition. "We'll have to use the front door because your garage opener...isn't available."

She helped her mother in the front door. This first look at her home brought a spontaneous moan. And she sank into the nearest chair, absorbing the scene.

Jennifer hoped to balance the jarring scene with something comforting. "Would you like some tea?" Her mother nodded. "Want to come with me to the kitchen?" She did, looking around quizzically as she passed through rooms on the way.

When the kettle whistled, they sipped tea together at the kitchen table. Was moving to Virginia just a hospital "foxhole decision" to be recanted now that her mother had returned home? "Are you feeling okay, Mom?"

"Yes, but it's a shock. As I see what's changed here, I know my bad decisions caused this, so I can accept what happened. Your best teacher is your last mistake."

"Shall we take a little tour when you finish your tea?" Her mother nodded.

After visiting all the rooms, main floor and upstairs, Jennifer asked, "Wouldn't life be easier without climbing stairs every day if your new place was all on one floor?"

Her mother gave her a sharp look. Uh-oh, Jennifer thought, here it comes.

"Climbing stairs every day is good exercise."

"Speaking of exercise, the hospital list suggested taking short walks. We could do that together if you want."

"This is Florida, dear. In summer, we walk outside in early morning or late evening. Otherwise, we glisten."

Jennifer chuckled. "You're right. I forgot. So this evening then, if you feel up to it?"

"Yes. How long can you stay here with me, dear?"

Jennifer groped for the right words. If her mother rejected the moving-north plan, she'd have to persuade her to accept a senior housing solution in Naples. "Well, I guess that depends on how you feel and what we need to accomplish together."

Seeing her mother consider this, Jennifer added, "My family in McLean is also your family. Jason and the children love you just as I do. Jason's managing on his own at home now, insisting he's self-sufficient. He'll fly down if we need him." After a long pause, she added, "So what do we need to accomplish together?"

"A good question...."

Sensing her mother had changed her mind about moving north, Jennifer hesitated. At age sixty-one, she knew one day she could find herself in this very situation as her children helped her through similar decisions. How would she want them to treat her? They could gather information and make recommendations, but she'd want to make the final decisions. She owed her mother the same respect. "Have you thought about a good answer?"

"It's complicated, Jen. Change requires energy and I haven't much. Staying here avoids decisions that take energy I don't have. Change means adjustments, while staying here is comfortable and effortless. Also, Florida weather means I never have to face another bleak, cold winter. You understand?"

Jennifer's heart sank. She'd prepared herself to plan her mother's future in Naples, which included her own default commitment to fly here whenever necessary, to deal with future traumas. Moving her mother to a dependable senior housing campus where their staff solved immediate problems, reported her health status and shielded her from exploitation would reduce, but not eliminate, Jennifer's trips. Her mother loved and cared for her when she was little and now she'd return that selfless kindness. She loved this sweet woman, so similar genetically in looks and intelligence, yet a generation apart in age and experience.

"I think I understand, Mom." Jennifer stared at her hands folded in her lap. "We'll make it work, whatever you decide."

"But two other things affect my decision. First, fate gave me a cruel lesson with a wakeup call. Second, unlike some of my friends, I'm fortunate enough to have a daughter I love and trust. While I hate the mechanics of going, my decision is still to move to McLean."

CHAPTER 20

This decision set them both making lists. Her mother concentrated on identifying items stolen. From Jennifer's online search, plus suggestions from her mother and Chelsea, she narrowed names of movers, real estate agents and estate sale specialists to three in each category. "I'll arrange interviews to select the finalists."

Her mother agreed.

"Estate sale options include emptying everything unsold after the sale, leaving the house broom-clean and Realtor-ready."

Her mother sipped tea. "Good to know, if needed."

Jennifer blinked into the phone at the first moving company's logical question, "You say from Naples, Florida, to what address in McLean, Virginia?" Jennifer realized she didn't know yet. "You can use storage on the other end," added the moving company rep, "but it adds cost."

By dinnertime, they'd both put in a busy day. "I only bought breakfast and lunch food. Shall I grocery shop for tonight or shall we eat out or order pizza?" Jennifer asked.

"How about pizza? I know a good place that delivers. They have salads, too."

"Let's have our own little celebration party." Jennifer looked at the menu her mother handed her, punched in the number and ordered.

"Then we should open some wine—unless Jane and John took it all. I haven't checked yet."

"Don't worry, I bought some for us."

"Where's my dripped candle in the raffia Italian bottle?" Her mother checked kitchen cupboards. "Found it. Here's our centerpiece." She used colorful Italian dishes bought many years ago in Tuscany, tulip-shaped wine goblets and a checkered tablecloth and napkins. "We'd better sample a glass of this Montepulciano before the doorbell rings."

Thirty minutes later, they munched pizza with gusto. "A toast." Jennifer lifted a salutary glass and her mother joined in. "To the pressure we two Ryerson gals can face, because pressure turns coal into diamonds."

Grinning, her mother countered with, "To wisdom—may we always learn from our mistakes." They clinked glasses and drank.

After dinner, dishes cleared and kitchen cleaned, they relaxed in the den to call Jason. "Hi, hon. You're on speaker phone with Mom and me. We have lots of exciting news. She's out of the hospital and surprisingly feisty for what she's been through." They heard multiple cheers on the other end. "Who's with you?"

"Hello, Mom and Grammy. It's us, Hannah and Adam. We brought Dad dinner tonight and we're sharing it with him."

"Hello to all," Grammy said. "Jen's taking wonderful care of me and we're having fun tonight."

Hannah giggled. "Lucky you. I'm jealous."

Jennifer grinned. "You won't be jealous for long, Hannah, because—hold on to your hat–Grammy's moving to McLean. Ta-da!"

"Oh, Grammy, what wonderful news. Woo-hoo."

"Jay, any success finding a temporary rental nearby?" Jennifer asked.

"My turn with big news. The Donnegan kids agreed, for three months. They're working out a price. Immediate availability and right across the street from our house, Grammy. Their main floor has a bedroom, so no stairs to climb."

"Good," said her mother, winking at Jen.

"We're going to bed early tonight," Jennifer announced. "Tomorrow's another busy one for us."

"Okay, love from us all," Jason said. More good-byes echoed behind him as they ended the call.

"Mom," Jennifer hugged her mother. "This is terrific news. For three months you'll live right across the street while we figure out where you'll be happiest." They hugged. "Shall we take that little walk the doctor ordered, now that luck has smiled on us?"

As they moved along the sidewalk, Grammy thought about luck during her many years of life. Finally the old woman spoke. "When the winds of change blow, some build walls and others build windmills."

"Mom, where did that come from? I like it."

"My grandmother said it often, when I was a little girl. I haven't thought of it for eighty years until right now. I don't know how, but I'm going to make this work."

CHAPTER 21

As they strolled along the sidewalk, Jennifer talked about her research into northern Virginia's senior housing options.

"Studio apartments have kitchen, living room and bedroom all in one space. Then one-bedroom or two-bedroom units have a small kitchen, living room, sometimes a dining room or den, usually with washer and dryer. They're about 900-1500 square feet.

"Whatever you choose is a serious change from your big 5,000 sq. ft. house to something much smaller. Knowing this will help you decide what to take and what to leave. Even if you choose a two-bedroom, an apartment's rooms are smaller than yours here. The trick is taking only what you need because moving's expensive and storing, a costly nuisance. If you ultimately choose a one-bedroom instead of a two, you could sell that extra bedroom furniture you took once you're up north."

"Will you help me select?"

"Of course, Mom. But comparing square footage alone, you have about four times more here than you'll need there–a big downsize. But we can do it together. Once you're settled across the street in McLean, we'll visit different types of senior housing to see what you like best. Using their floor plans, we can pre-fit your furniture. But don't worry about that yet. We have enough to accomplish here in a short time."

"I couldn't do this without you, Jen."

She smiled. "And here's the good news, Mom—once we select from each room what to take north, the rest automatically goes into the estate sale. We solve two problems at the same time."

"Let's start back home now. I'm tired of walking." As they turned around, Grammy added. "You make it sound easy, Jen."

"Not easy, but lots of seniors have done this and you can, too. How are you coming with that list of stolen items for the deputy?"

"I finished with the upstairs. John Doe, as you call him, found the safe but couldn't get it open."

"You have a safe?"

"Fortunately, most of my good jewelry was inside along with... well, I forget exactly what's there. Which reminds me, put emptying my bank safety deposit box on your to-do list. Should I close my accounts at the same time?"

"Maybe not. We don't know yet where in McLean you'll settle, and you'll probably choose the closest bank for convenience. Some senior facilities have a bank branch right there. Meantime, bring your checkbook and I'll cash checks for you at my bank until you transfer to one of your own."

"So the bank, the post office. What about doctors and dentists?"

"In McLean, why not use mine until you choose one of your own, maybe near your new apartment? We could pick up your files now or by phone from up north. We made an appointment with your GP in two days, as the hospital instructed, so we can ask about those files then."

"Speaking of files, I have four filing cabinets full upstairs. What about those?"

"Glance through them, but if you haven't time or energy now, move them north, where you'll have plenty of time."

"Makes sense."

"What if we give ourselves, say, a week to get ready for the move? In every room, let's tag each item 'take,' 'leave,' 'donate' or 'toss.' That solves the move *and* the estate sale."

"All right. But now, all of a sudden, I feel tired."

Jennifer laughed as they walked up the steps of the house. "I'm not surprised. You're just out of the hospital and busy instead of relaxing. Let's both get a good night's rest and pedal forward again tomorrow."

"It's a plan, Jen. A good plan."

An hour later, they both slept soundly.

On the dresser, the dragon's eyes remained wide open.

CHAPTER 22

D eputy Goodwin dropped by the next morning. "Good morning, ladies. Ya got a list for me?"

"Half a list," Frances said, "the 'upstairs list' with photos from my husband's photographic inventory. Jennifer made copies for you on the printer. Meantime, Deputy, have you any news for us?"

"Would you like some tea?" Jennifer offered.

"Maybe coffee? Instant's fine. Cream and two sugars."

They moved to the kitchen table, where Jennifer brought cups.

"You can pick up your Mercedes later this morning," Goodwin began but at Frances' surprised expression, he turned to Jennifer. "You didn't get around to telling her?" She shook her head. "Max Roderick stole your car, but we located it out-of-state and brought it back." He told Jennifer where to get it. "And here's the big news. Our BOLO netted Max in Michigan and we're extraditing him to Florida. In their preliminary interrogation, he didn't tell Michigan cops the girl's name, but we may have better luck. We're gonna prosecute him and, unless he pleads, we may need you for the trial."

"I'll be there if you do," Frances promised.

"I'll flash your pictures of stuff he stole when we talk to him here. Meantime, we need your 'downstairs list' ASAP. Any chance late this afternoon?"

"We'll work on it together," Jennifer promised.

"You feeling okay?" he asked Jennifer's mother.

"Much better, thank you. And Deputy, I'm grateful you found me and called medical help so quickly."

He shuffled awkwardly. "Just doin' my job, Ma'am. You both staying around awhile?"

The two women exchanged looks and Jennifer detailed the intended move.

"Another couple weeks then? We ought to have things wrapped up by then. Thanks for the coffee. See you late this afternoon." He drained the cup, put it on the coffee table, picked up Grammy's lists and ambled out the door.

"Mom, I'll take a taxi to get your Mercedes. When I bring it back, shall I get rid of my rental and drive your car instead?" Her mother nodded. "Instead of returning the rental all the way to the airport, I'll just turn it in locally. A Hertz lot is only five minutes from here. If you follow me in your Mercedes, we'll be all set."

"Even... without a license?"

"Even without. I think you can do it one last time."

Mercedes back home and rental returned, they finished the deputy's downstairs stolen item list and by late afternoon added relevant inventory photos.

"Dad organized this photo inventory well," Jennifer remarked. "So sensible. I'm going to ask Jason to do one for us."

"Don't forget, your dad had plenty of retired years to do this before he passed."

"Still, I'll phone Jay about it tonight. Meantime, you've wrapped up this list right on time."

"Jen, I couldn't have managed all this without you. Your energy and focus keep me on track. Some of my friends whose children live elsewhere don't get the kind of steady support you've given me. Just want you to know I don't take what you're doing for me for granted."

They hugged. Across time and cultures, Jen mused, women faced problems common to their sisterhood, drawing them close across generations. She and her mother felt this timeless bond now.

"Maybe I'm not just giving back, Mom. Maybe I'm also paying forward. When my kiddos see me caring for you, maybe they'll rally for me some day, if needed."

Goodwin returned at 4:00pm to collect their info and pics. "Great," he said. "Oh, by the way, after they return Max to Florida and before you go north, will you come to positively identify him at the station? Our one-way mirror lets you see him but not visa-versa."

Frances stood up straight. "Yes, I will—for myself and those other seniors you said he duped."

"And the new ones he won't get to scam since he's behind bars. Sorry it cost your difficult experience to find him, but it worked. Thank you, Mrs. Ryerson."

When Goodwin left, Jennifer said, "Don't you think we've earned going out to dinner tonight?"

"Yes, how about Tommy Bahama's? A fun, relaxed place with island music."

Later, Jennifer phoned Jason with the day's report.

He listened before saying, "The Donnegan kids are flexible about when we start renting across the street. They'll wait until you bring Mom back to McLean to sign a month-to-month lease."

"Perfect."

"And Jen, here's a list of people who've called you, including your friend Mary Ann." He read her the names.

"Thanks for playing secretary, Jay."

"Actually, I can play a few more games to show how much I miss you." He heard her giggle. "But what you're doing in Florida is important. I love you, Jen."

Jennifer cradled the phone against her cheek. "Love you too, sweetheart. Goodnight."

CHAPTER 23

The next morning Jennifer turned a notebook page as she and her mother started the take/leave/donate/toss list for the downstairs. "You made terrific progress upstairs, Mom. Just the main floor and we're finished. You suggested starting in the study." They strolled into the room.

Her mother ran a finger across book spines on the nearest shelf. "Books are like old friends." She chuckled. "We even inherited some from *our* parents, "but most we collected during our sixty years together."

Jennifer continued carefully. "Books are heavy to ship and McLean has a great library. Keep those you really want, but maybe now someone else can enjoy them just as you did. Shall we go through one-by-one and divide them into the four piles?"

"When your father died, I kept all his memorabilia on the wall just as he left it. The other rooms reflect us both, but this was *his* room. Not a day passed without his spending time here until… well, the end when he was too sick. Part of him still lingers here. His memory comforts me. Sometimes I come in here to be near him. If I…if I take down his certificates and dismantle this room, it's like saying goodbye to him for the last time. I don't know if I can bring myself to…"

Jennifer crossed the room to hug her mother. "I've been thinking about the plaques and certificates, Mom. If your new apartment had enough wall space, you could take them as-is. But what if we take high-resolution pictures of each one instead and make a book of the photos? Then, you save all the information for family history and you can feel near Dad any time you open the album. You'd still keep the originals—out of the frames since flat paper stores more easily—and then you could add these empty frames to the estate sale."

"I…it's a good idea, Jen, but not the same powerful feeling the room gives me."

Sadness showed on her wrinkled face. Jennifer needed to give this some positive spin. "Wait, you've just given me another idea. Let's make a second album, one with pictures of all the rooms inside, just as they are now, pre-move. Then more photos outside the house and yard. If you feel homesick for this wonderful place, just open your album for a visit."

Picking up on this, her mother smiled relief. "Oh, Jen. What a creative idea. My recall's no longer crystal clear, and I didn't want to lose the memory of living here for so many years once I could no longer see it clearly in my mind. But you've solved that. Oh, I feel *so* much better about the move." She started to cry.

Was this the prelude to a breakdown? Had her mother faced more than she could absorb?

Pulling out a linen handkerchief, her mother wiped at her tears, but the crying continued. "Just so much happening…so fast. Embarrassment at my bad decisions about John—or Max, I guess he is—and then the hospital and now moving from the place I know and love to somewhere new and strange. My logical mind knows it's right, but my heart says it's wrong—my own internal war," she looked up, forcing a trembling smile, "which you're helping me win."

"Next year, with all this behind you, you'll be settled in a beautiful community with lots of new friends and your family nearby to visit and take you on jaunts. Think of it this way: just like the books in this room, your life has chapters. In the first chapter, you're a baby; in the next, you're in elementary school, then high school and college. Chapters about your suitors and meeting Dad and your courtship. More about marrying him and having your own child. More still for your Florida retirement years and now this chapter about the move to comfort and convenience in upscale senior housing." She tilted up her mother's chin. "It's the Book of You."

The tears stopped. They drank tea. They made small talk. Her mother bridged the emotional crevice.

An hour later, back on target, they started through the books again, discussing the background of some. "What's this collection of Civil War books?" Jennifer leaned forward. A surge of excitement swept over her: unexpected new knowledge about her dead father that might also link with the map and riddle hidden back in McLean.

Her mother smiled. "Your dad developed this interest soon after retirement. He joined a Civil War study group here, mostly fellow retirees who moved to Florida from states involved in that war. This evolved into a social group as well, often including wives."

"Did you enjoy this group?"

"Yes. Interesting, knowledgeable folks. One couple participated annually in Pennsylvania re-enactments, acting out famous battles with historical accuracy in mind. She wore long skirts and cooked in iron pots over fires, and he wore replicas of the original wool uniforms over the underwear of the period, growing the beard and hairstyle popular then."

"Re-enactments are big in Virginia, and you're right, players take their roles very seriously."

"Yes. I was amazed. They even used tools, weapons and sanitation of that time. And, of course, their horses wore authentic Civil War saddles or true replicas."

"We've seen some Virginia re-enactments at Kelly's Ford and Brandy Station. So what was Dad's take on this war?"

"Let's see if I can remember. He said the North kept a small regular Army but the South didn't, so they were ill-prepared for war. Both still depended on enlistments—more patriotic enthusiasm than skill. Dad pointed out some generals on both sides were in their twenties, a few brand new West Point graduates. He said some officers even received rank as political-payback or friendship by Presidents Lincoln and Davis. No surprise, those were poor leaders."

"Did Dad favor either side?" Jennifer leaned forward, amazed this unknown side of her father dovetailed with her own new interest.

"He said he 'had no dog in this fight,' but Dad was a gentleman and I think he leaned toward the Confederacy. Probably because they were military underdogs, because he wasn't at all sympathetic about slavery. He thought both sides had good points and bad."

"Had he a favorite person?"

"Maybe one. He would say, 'Col. John Singleton Mosby, now there was a creative man.' You know, 'creative' was a high compliment from your father. He often said *you* are creative."

Jennifer grinned. "He did?"

"Yes, and I agree."

She'd learned new things about her father today, five years since his death. Like her mother, she felt his presence in the room with them—as if his hand brushed her arm.

She ran her fingers along his Civil War books. "Mind if I put these aside to go through myself tonight?"

"Of course, Jen. Then, if I can find the club member list, we might ask if they want the books. If not, put them on the estate sale pile."

By evening, they finished the main floor triage lists, changed clothes and drove to Swan River for dinner. After ordering, her mother said, "In season, you'd see a long line of tourists for this table, but it's also a favorite of locals like me." She lifted her wine glass. "Let's celebrate. Thanks to you, Jen, we accomplished downsizing miracles at the house today. A toast to you, my dear."

"And to you, Mom. If you'd dragged your feet, we'd have little progress." They clinked goblets and sipped. "Love you," they said together, laughing at their like-mindedness.

But then a serious expression crossed her mother's face. "Jennifer, today I faced a harsh reality. I'd be gone now if my phone call hadn't reached you or if you hadn't been able to leave on the first available flight. My being alive tonight hinges on those two coincidences."

Jennifer remembered how she'd nearly missed that flight. "Add a third coincidence. The plane had already boarded when I arrived late, so they turned me away. Only the gate attendant's impulsive decision put me in the one empty seat left on the plane—first class on my economy ticket—got me to you in time. It's pretty miraculous."

"Three coincidences then. Are they unrelated accidents or do things happen for a reason?"

"Mom, I wish I knew. These events we don't control can lead to positive outcomes or the opposite. And if it's all predestined, where does free will fit?"

Her mother looked thoughtful. "Perhaps free will is what you decide to do with what coincidence brings—you can ignore it or embrace it."

Jennifer lifted her wine glass, "However it happened, I love the way it's worked out. Whether good luck or random accident or a miracle, yours is a happy ending, dear Mom."

Grammy's eyes twinkled. "My mother used to say, 'Coincidence is God's way of remaining anonymous.'"

Jennifer lifted her glass. "To coincidence: which keeps us guessing."

Their goblets touched.

CHAPTER 24

At nine o'clock that night, Jennifer picked three of her father's Civil War books about Mosby. Weary from the day's emotional and physical efforts, she climbed into bed and opened the first book.

She read how Mosby's childhood schoolmates relentlessly bullied his frailty, but instead of knuckling under, he crafted dozens of ways to outwit them. Later, like other similar-minded southerners who sympathized with the North about abolishing slavery's injustice, he took no action until the North invaded the South. To fight these Union "bullies," he joined the Confederate Army as a private in 1861 at the age of twenty-eight.

The hit-and-run tactics, ambushes, sabotage, raids and mobility he'd used as a boy worked well then. But as war tactics, they defied current European-style battle form, where opponents traded rifle volleys as they marched forward in long lines directly facing each other. After grim casualties, those left standing in the battlefield faced hand-to-hand combat with bayonets.

Thus, the military frowned upon other methods until General J.E.B. Stuart noticed Mosby. Impressed with his flair for scouting and coolness in crisis, Stuart listened when Mosby explained with these tactics his men could harass the Union at night, cut communication lines, interrupt supply wagons and railroad trains, capture horses and take prisoners. "The Union may rule the day, but we Confederates will rule the night," Mosby promised.

Given the near impossible task of winning every skirmish and thus the war, General Stuart immediately recognized the practical side of Mosby's novel plan to form an army partisan unit using guerilla warfare. He made Private Mosby a lieutenant.

Despite negative votes from other ranking officers, Stuart supported Mosby's vision until Lee finally gave permission to form the 43rd Battalion, Virginia Cavalry—a partisan unit informally known as "Mosby's Rangers."

Jennifer read that the man beneath the plumed hat wasn't imposing, at 5'8" tall and 130 pounds, but Mosby's quick mind, intuitive daring and miraculous success earned him the respect of his admirers and fear of his foes. As Mosby's notoriety grew, stories about his successes appeared in both southern and northern newspapers. His battalion came to be known as "Mosby's Raiders."

Jennifer could see why her mother described Mosby as her father's Civil War favorite. She read further.

In one remarkable daredevil foray on the night of March 8, 1863, Mosby approached the village of Fairfax Courthouse and, in the wee hours of March 9th, captured a sleeping Union general. But she found no mention of his finding valuables Stoughton looted from Virginia families.

Jennifer put down the first book to read versions of this incident in the other two books. Because of her riddle and map, the tale gnawed at her. Her clock read midnight. So completely had Mosby captured her imagination, she'd unexpectedly read for hours.

Closing the last book, she noticed the dragon staring at her from the dresser. Why did she feel as if energy radiated from this inanimate figure? The artist's ineffable craftsmanship?

This new information about Mosby swirled in her mind as she yawned, saluted the dragon, turned out the light and lay in the dark, staring at the ceiling. Then began a vision, plunging her into another time and place.

Hoofbeats thundered through darkness as thirty Confederate cavalry galloped across the snowy Virginia countryside. Riding at point, Mosby signaled a halt and pulled his poncho tighter. His twenty-nine rangers reined up around him, their horses stomping and snorting against the cold temperature and steady drizzle. With the men's gray uniforms covered by black rain ponchos, they hoped to pass in the dark as either Rebel or Union troops, a threat to neither side.

"We must work fast," Mosby warned in his pre-assault briefing. *"Capture every horse and soldier you can find, especially officers, plus food and arms to supply our troops. Share whatever spoils you find in the prisoners' belongings or tents, but remember, we must be away from these Union lines before dawn."*

A sergeant caught up to Mosby. *"Sir, we cut the telegraph lines a mile back so the Feds can't wire their battalion for reinforcements,"* he spoke into the chill, damp night air. *"You really think an unprotected Union headquarters lies ahead?"*

"Sgt. Ames says so. He defected to us from this very unit, and I trust him. He will guide us in through the picket line. This village fits Union headquarter needs — a hotel, stables and large houses to requisition." He thought also of Antonia Ford, the clever lady spy who confirmed *"Big Yank"* Ames' information. *"Big Yank says this headquarters is over a mile away from the brigade it commands, and the very troops who might defend it. This plays right into our hands, and if that dog Wyndham is there, as reported, I'll deal with him personally."*

The sergeant chuckled. *"That Brit general who called you a common horse thief?"*

"The very one." Mosby smiled.

The sergeant added, *"Of course, he didn't mention that all the horses you stole had riders aboard and the riders had sabers, carbines and pistols."*

They shared another laugh.

"I hope to earn a little more respect from him tonight." Mosby grinned.

He signaled his men to fan left and right–to find, disarm and capture sentries before their alarm roused sleeping Union soldiers. Mosby preferred taking prisoners, but if necessary his men would knife resistant guards to ensure the needed secrecy.

Field experienced, the raiders knew what to do. Capitalizing on surprise, in thirty minutes they easily captured all patrolling sentries, their horses and equipment. Then, at 2:00am, Mosby's men crept into the sleeping town to find deserted streets and no light or sound from the houses.

"Each horse is a prize," Mosby often reminded his men. When they reached the provost marshal's stables, they took every serviceable mount, herding them in front of the village hotel.

One raider captured a soldier, who said he stood guard for the headquarters of Brig. Gen. Edwin H. Stoughton, giving Mosby a new idea. *"Instead of capturing Gen. Wyndham myself,"* he turned to Sgt. James Ames, *"you bring him to me, Big Yank."* As Ames left, Mosby grabbed the frightened captive guard by the lapel and demanded, *"Tell me where to find Gen. Stoughton."*

Trembling, the guard pointed. "He requisitioned that one, Dr. Gunnel's house, for himself and his staff."

Mosby chose six raiders close by, led them to the house and knocked loudly on the door with his pistol butt. In a few minutes, an upper window opened and a weary voice asked, "Who's there?"

Thinking fast, Mosby invented, "Fifth New York Cavalry with a dispatch for Gen. Stoughton."

The window closed, followed by footsteps on the inside stairs.

The door opened. "I'm Lt. Prentiss of Stoughton's staff. You can give..."

But Mosby clutched him by the throat, rammed a pistol against his cheek and growled, "Lead me to the general's room. Now!"

The bug-eyed, panicked lieutenant led the way upstairs to a bedroom, followed by Mosby and three of his men, guns drawn. With trembling hand, the lieutenant opened the door and pointed to a figure beneath heavy covers.

Noting empty champagne bottles on the dresser, Mosby whispered to his captive, "A big party last night?" The lieutenant nodded miserably.

Mosby strode to the bed, whipped back the blankets and smacked the curled-up snoring man's backside. The general grumbled awake.

"General, did you ever hear of Mosby?" asked the person leaning over him.

"Yes. Have you caught him?"

"He has caught you."

Confused, the general sat up. "Who is this man? What's the meaning of this, Lieutenant?" he blustered.

Before the subordinate could answer, Mosby interrupted, "It means, General, that Stuart's cavalry has taken over Fairfax and General Jackson is at Centreville." Would this invented story fool the general into thinking his position hopeless against such forces? It worked.

As Stoughton and Prentiss dressed, Mosby told his men to get them downstairs while he and a corporal searched the room for battle plans."

Mosby loaded documents and maps into a large pouch as the corporal said, "Sir, this looks like a chest of pirate treasure. It's crammed with jewelry, coins, gold and silver candlesticks, bowls and tableware." He pulled aside more of the wrapping cloths. "See."

"What the...where did they get this?" Mosby examined a plate. "Solid gold and worth a small fortune."

Picking up a familiar-looking goblet, he recognized it from Belcore, a gracious plantation whose hospitality he knew well. Mosby glared. "That devil stole these precious heirlooms from fine Virginia families. Well, now they'll take a new journey to Robert E. Lee, for return to those rightful owners. Here, Corporal, grab those two canvas bags and load in the treasure. Make sure each one stays wrapped for protection. Then put the bags in one of the confiscated carriages or wagons and guard them with your life. Tell no one about this until I say so."

Back in the yard, Big Yank approached his leader. "Sir." The sergeant saluted Mosby. "Two Rangers captured seven headquarters couriers from tents in the yard plus their bridled, saddled horses. More captured prisoners and horses wait at the square. And Sir, I'm sorry to say, Gen. Wyndham went to Washington yesterday by train, but we raided his quarters, captured his deputy captain. We also confiscated his horse and all the general's uniforms."

Mosby chuckled. "Good job, Ames, but don't worry. We captured us a Union general tonight anyway, just not the one we expected."

The raiders worked the village so efficiently, prisoners thought the entire Confederate cavalry had broken through Union lines. Taking Gen. Stoughton's cue, none offered resistance. One look at the hat with the plume and they knew they faced the legendary terror: Mosby.

He rode among the horses, men, prisoners, carriages and wagons to get the column rolling. They must pass Centreville before daylight to reach safety in Culpeper behind Confederate lines.

Mosby turned to Sgt. Ames, "While we ride, Big Yank, question Lt. Prentiss and several other prisoners about the source of this treasure."

An hour later, Ames reported back. "Sir, the six I questioned cooperated fully and told the same basic story. The general ordered them to loot every large home in their path. He chose the items himself, taking the most valuable things he saw. He said this demoralized owners and enriched the Union, but they suspect he intended keeping them for himself."

"Thank you, Ames. What's the count of captured prisoners and horses?"

"Forty-two men, three of them officers, with arms and equipment and fifty-eight horses, most saddled and equipped. Also three carriages, five wagons, several casks of wine and a cask of bourbon. And Sir..."

"Yes?"

"All without firing a single shot or losing a single man."

CHAPTER 25

W hen her eyes opened the next morning, Jennifer awoke exhilarated.
　　　She had much to delight her: her mother's recovery from the near-lethal drug and the surprise of her willingness to move to McLean. Also producing the deputy's needed stolen-items list on time and easing her mother through touch-and-go separation anxiety she faced yesterday in the den.

But this new excitement stemmed from her remarkable dreamy vision — that imaginary journey to a different time and place that felt so real...and related to the map and riddle mystery high on her mind!

She sat up in bed. For the first time she understood how the past could draw someone inexorably to immersion in a different dimension — like Egyptologists consumed by a centuries-old world of pharaohs, or paleontologists spending their lives hunting dinosaur bones, or archeologists searching out ancient structures and the cultures that flourished there. All wanted to confirm known facts about the objects of their focus, but were also animated by the fever to discover something new about their quarry.

Until this dream fantasy, Jennifer had lived in the here and now. Documentaries about past history educated or entertained, but she never felt immersed. Now, she understood her father's attraction to Civil War history and her airplane seatmate's hunger for its artifacts.

Alone downstairs, she started the coffee pot and booted her laptop. Wasn't her seatmate's last name Early? And his ancestor… did he say Jubal Early? She typed in the name. Up popped dozens of links. She clicked one after another, learning this general's personal history, battle accomplishments and other attributes, while making notes on a pad.

Ten minutes later, she poured a cup of coffee and, sipping it, studied her jottings: 1816-1894, family in Virginia since 1700s, West Point graduate, lawyer, Civil War Confederate general, irascible, white supremacist, blind to own mistakes, a critical fault-finder, not liked by subordinates or generals, short tempered, fiercely resentful of criticism about himself, cantankerous, blunt, relieved of command by Lee in March 1865, never married but had four children with Julia McNealey between 1850-1864 and gave them his surname.

Not exactly a glowing relative, but neither was his great-great-grandson seated next to her aboard the flight four days ago. William Early's personality gave Jennifer chills. Coincidence or genetic? Who knew?

"Do I smell fresh coffee?" Her mother strolled into the kitchen. "Good morning, dear. Did you sleep well?" As she poured coffee, Jennifer told her about the vivid story that played on the screen in her mind the night before.

"I'm not surprised. That active imagination of yours blossomed when you were little, and it's been fertile ever since. Why, I remember reading the Uncle Wiggly books to you then. Know what you said?" Jennifer shook her head. "You said if this rabbit gentleman went out each day looking for an adventure, so could you. And then the Oz series. In those pre-television days, the Oz books were like today's "Star Wars" or Hobbits. Their world fascinated you. You loved thinking out-of-the-box."

Jennifer smiled, remembering the books but not their impact on her thinking.

"And I think your grandmother encouraged this. Drawing from her Irish side, she told you she couldn't prove leprechauns or gnomes or fairies exist, but nobody proved they didn't. So you had one foot in the real world and the other in an imaginary world."

Jen laughed along with her mom. "Your mother was quite a gal, wasn't she?"

"Yes, dear, she was. Oh," she waved a piece of paper, "by the way, I found it last night."

"Found what?"

"The names of local Civil War Club members who might want Dad's books." She passed the list to her daughter.

"Great, Mom." And, Jennifer thought, not just for the practical purpose of fielding the books but also the memory function it proved her mom still had. Understanding her mother's capabilities played into the care level of senior housing they needed to choose in McLean.

"So what's doing today?"

"How about getting a duplicate list of stolen goods, along with photos from your inventory, to the insurance rep today? I made a copy for them, one for Deputy Goodwin and one for you." Her mother nodded. "Then, we can finish up the downstairs move-or-sell, donate-or-toss list and maybe interview estate sale companies or real estate agents. Oh, and today we see your doctor."

"A busy time then. Good, Jen. Let's eat breakfast, get dressed and start."

Though buoyed by her mother's morning energy, Jennifer mustn't discount her age, her drug overdose or the anxiety endured with Max and his accomplice — any of which might cause lingering implications for her mother.

"And I have another idea," Jennifer began, but her mother interrupted her.

"Uh-oh."

Jennifer looked up sharply, disarmed at her mother's smile. "That's what Jason says when I mention a new idea. What's going on?"

"Well, dear, your ideas can seem unusual because you think about so many things at once."

Unsure what this meant, Jennifer continued. "My idea is inviting Becca here to photograph Dad's certificates and inside your house. She just graduated from college, hasn't found a job yet, is talented with a camera and if she'll come this weekend to do photography, it frees you and me for other tasks. What do you think?"

"Let's invite her. Always fun to see Becca."

Jennifer dialed her daughter's cell number to explain the plan.

Becca responded enthusiastically. "Mom, I'd love to help. But isn't Florida full of snakes? You know I freak out around snakes."

"Not to worry, hon. Grammy's neighborhood isn't the Everglades. You'll be fine. So glad you can come. Remember, use the Ft. Myers airport. Just let me know when to pick you up."

Next, she dialed the phone number of the first name on the Civil War study group list.

"Hello, is this Mr. Birdsong...? Okay. Do you remember Bill and Fran Ryerson from your Civil War group...? Good. Well, I'm their daughter. I've come to Florida to help my mother downsize to move to Virginia near me.... Yes, a big job is right. I'm calling because she thought you, or others in your club, might have interest in Dad's Civil War book collection.... You do? Great. Would you like to come to see them...? Yes, this morning's fine. You live in the area...? Fifteen minutes...? Good. Need the address...? All right. See you shortly."

"Would you like to keep some of the Mosby books, Jen?" Her mother pointed at several volumes.

"Yes. Because they were Dad's and because that part of the Civil War interests me."

"This brings up something we haven't discussed. Would others in our family want some of my things before we sell them?"

"How did I overlook such an important idea? My apology, Mom. You're absolutely right. Shall we e-mail Becca's pictures to the family?"

"Let's do it. Then I'll get to see some of my things in their houses when I visit. Why don't we start with you? Please pick from anything I won't take for my apartment."

Jennifer strolled through several rooms, wondering what she might use. Then the doorbell rang.

CHAPTER 26

"Hello again, Frances." He hugged her before turning to shake Jennifer's hand. "I'm John Birdsong."

"Welcome. So glad you could come over."

"Thanks for inviting me. I comb estate sales for books like these, which I'll share with the other Civil War Study Club members. Thanks for offering Bill's books to us, Frances."

Jennifer showed him into the living room. "May we offer you some coffee while you look through them and maybe also ask you some Civil War questions?"

"Well, yes to both. I'm not an expert but for sure a hooked amateur."

"I remember the group fondly," Frances reminisced. "Is it still the same size?"

"No, we've nearly doubled our membership, but not everybody gets to meetings. We average ten to fifteen and now we meet at restaurants for lunch where it's a combination CWSG and ROMEO." At their puzzled expressions, he amplified, "Civil War Study Group and Retired Old Men Eating Out."

They laughed. Then Jennifer asked, "First question: what's your impression of Jubal Early?"

Birdsong stalled. "Remember, we're amateurs, not experts, and our own backgrounds influence our reactions to famous Civil War names and events. We each have personal opinions and don't always agree, but the consensus among us labels Jubal Early an odd duck, a wild card and not in a good way. Many of us had military experience and agree we wouldn't enjoy serving with him, certainly not as a subordinate. And Lee actually fired him for incompetence in 1865. His dismissal is worded in flowery terms, but basically Lee sacked him for cause."

"Has your group any favorites?"

"Another tough question and again, personal opinions." He chuckled. "But I think we all consider General Robert E. Lee a qualified military leader for the South and also a thoughtful tactician. He was a leader who respected and cared about his troops, and a gentleman by temperament and training. We'd have thought it an honor to serve under Lee, even though he lost the war."

"Anyone else?"

"Well, it's hard not to like Mosby. He epitomizes every boy's dream — daring, imaginative, intelligent, clever, incredibly successful and also mysterious. His men emerged as if by magic from the countryside, where folks hid them, and they melted away invisibly after raids. His unit's plumed hats branded their uniqueness. And Mosby's men loved him — not only from pride at their stunning military successes but because this leader had enlisted as a private. They felt he understood them better than other officers did. Like Jubal Early, you might call Mosby a wild card, but this time in a good way."

"What about Mosby's treasure?"

Birdsong smiled. "One of the legends. *If* it existed, and that's the big 'if,' Mosby had the means, motive and opportunity to capture it from Stoughton. But he mentioned no treasure in his personal Civil War memoirs, and he later died virtually penniless. You could argue if he had it and buried it, maybe he tried to find it again but couldn't. Valuables still turn up occasionally where they were buried in yards by frightened Civil War families in fear of marauding troops or looting carpetbaggers. With rezoning and subsequent building on old farms and plantations, today excavation machinery sometimes unearths just such family treasures."

"Like General Stoughton's stolen 'heirlooms'?"

"Yes. But do you know something else Mosby achieved with Stoughton's capture?" They shook their heads and John grinned. "When President Lincoln heard about the Fairfax Courthouse raid and Stoughton had become a Rebel prisoner, he reportedly said, "I don't mind the loss of a general as much as the horses. I can make a new general in five minutes, but I can't make horses and they cost $125 a piece."

"Another salute to Mosby's genius?" Frances asked. Birdsong nodded.

Jennifer touched their visitor's arm. "How did *you* get hooked on the Civil War?"

"Well, a couple of ways. My family lived in Virginia since the 1600s, and my ancestors fought in the Revolution and the Mexican Wars—as patriots, not as a military-minded family. My great-great grandfather fought only briefly in the Civil War because he ran a farm and had a big family. But his bachelor brother, Raiford Birdsong, rode with Mosby's Raiders. Interesting guy: although a tough soldier, they say he wrote poignant poems. In our group's study of 'The War' we learned many war songs started as poems written by soldiers and along the way were given a tune by a harmonica player beside a campfire."

"Do you have any of his poems?"

"No, all apparently lost over the years." He glanced down at the book in his hand. "Let's see. How else did I get hooked? In my youth, prowling the Virginia woods, I found brass uniform buttons, a canteen, spurs, bullets and so on. Just like kids who find arrowheads, I realized the last person who touched this was someone from the past—and in this case, someone who probably didn't fare well or else why would these items lie in a forest? Touching the relics felt like a dead soldier communicated directly with me—a powerful experience. All those vibes from the past combined to grab me."

His passion reminded her of her airplane seatmate, minus the drunken, sinister personality. "Do you miss living in Virginia?" Jen asked.

"Of course. Those were important chapters in my life. But Florida is the latest chapter and also good, though in a different way."

After yesterday's talk about this very thing, Jennifer winked at her mother, who smiled and nodded. Turning to Birdsong, she said, "It's the book of you."

"I hadn't thought of it that way, but you're right. It is."

"Do you have another few minutes? I'd appreciate your comments about something. Excuse me a minute while I get it." Jen hustled upstairs to the bureau where she'd unpacked her suitcase, retrieved her printed copies of the cloth map, riddle and translation and hurried them back to the living room where John and Grammy chatted about mutual friends.

She explained the copies and how she found them. "Can you make any sense of this?"

Birdsong studied the papers. "I'm no expert, but this grabs my attention. They could be fakes, of course. On the other hand,…you may have uncovered something remarkable. The way I read this, it refers to the alleged valuables Mosby discovered when he captured Gen. Stoughton. But this implies for some reason, they were buried, dug up and buried again. A little hard to follow."

Jennifer frowned. "Moving them in wartime meant risk, whereas burying them meant safety."

"True," Birdsong agreed. "The writer, who buried the treasure the second time, wanted southerners to find it and get it to Gen. Lee, but also to confuse northerners."

"Well, it can't go to Gen. Lee anymore, so if it's found, where should it go now?"

"Why, to a museum for protection — even before information of the discovery is released to the public. This would fascinate qualified Civil War scholars, who'd want to research each piece in the treasure for its own unique story. And the find itself would constitute a new piece of American history. May I put out a few feelers without revealing too much? I'll let you know if I learn something. May I have a copy of your copies?"

Jennifer smiled. "I'll make them right now on Mom's printer. And thanks, John."

Hearing about the riddle and map for the first time, Frances looked at her daughter. "Jennifer, Jennifer. You're always full of surprises. You haven't changed since you were small."

Birdsong took the papers from Jennifer. "Thanks for the books, ladies. Good to see you again, Fran. Good luck with your new adventure up north. And Jennifer, I plan to talk with you again soon about this." He waved the copies in the air.

"One last question, please," Jennifer spoke and Birdsong paused in the open doorway. "Can you explain why the South can't let go of the Civil War?"

Birdsong pondered. "That's a hard one. I think after fighting a war with all you've got for a cause you're convinced is right, and then losing, forces you to admit the staggering toll in destruction of property and human life happened for nothing. War's never pleasant, but winning's better than losing. Converting such a devastating loss into something less ghastly makes the awful tragedy more bearable. This defense mechanism recast their role in the war from bitter loss to noble rebellion for a just, albeit ill-fated, cause. This double-think helped them rebound from the crippling catastrophe with some bit of pride, trading humiliation for honor. For many proud southerners who couldn't stomach the truth, this allowed them enough 'face' to stand up, even to stand tall, and to carry on."

Frances took John's hand in her gnarled one. "I understand. Be positive even when it feels like your whole world is falling apart around you?"

Birdsong gave her hand a gentle, encouraging squeeze.

Jennifer blinked back tears.

CHAPTER 27

"R emind me, please, why we're eating lunch at 11:30. What else is on today's agenda? You're so organized, Jen, whereas these days I feel somewhat confused."

"Today we see your regular doctor at one o'clock to be sure your recovery inside is as good as it looks outside." She winked at her mom, "And also to resolve your medical records. Then we'll pass your bank coming home from the doctor, if you want to empty your safe deposit box. For that, you'll need your key. Do you know where it is?"

Her mother looked doubtful.

"If you tell me where to look, I'll run upstairs to get it."

"Maybe in one of my costume jewelry boxes in the closet? Maybe taped under my night table lamp? Maybe in the rose medallion bowl under the jade grapes?"

Uh-oh. Red flag about this weird filing system! "Okay," Jennifer said doubtfully, "back soon." She returned shortly, flourishing the key in the air.

"Where was it?" Grammy looked amazed.

"Taped under the vase of silk greenery." She laid the key on the table.

"You...you said you have a safe. Is that where you'll put whatever's in the bank lock-box?" Frances nodded. "And where is the safe?"

"I'll show you later, when we're upstairs."

"Also, Mom, at 3:00, 4:30 and 6:00 we interview three real estate agents to pick the one you like best. Or I can do it if you don't want to. Then dinner out and early to bed. Sound okay?"

"I could never manage this without you, Jen."

"By the way, I made myself a copy of the Civil War member list, so here's yours. Do you keep it in a special place?"

"In Dad's cuff link box. There's a secret compartment in the bottom."

Second red flag. "Have you or he...ah, filed or hidden things other places? Like maybe in the study?"

"Well, I don't think so, but your Dad might have. He spent a lot of time alone in there..."

Jennifer made a mental note to check that room again. "If you've finished lunch, Mom, I'll tidy up. We have thirty minutes before leaving for your appointment. If you're dressed for the doctor visit, would you mind looking around? Maybe he tucked important papers into some of the books we stacked. I'll join you in a few minutes."

Five minutes later when she walked into the study, Jennifer gasped. Her mother sat in a chair with books in her lap and a circle of paper money on the floor around her.

"Oh, Jen. I had no idea. He must have hidden money in most of these books. We'll have to check every single one." They each took a stack, letting the money flutter to the floor as the riffled pages yielded more. "We were married almost sixty years, thirty of them in this house. I thought I knew him so well, yet he never told me about this."

Twenty minutes later, Jen said. "Time to visit your doctor. Let's leave this as is until we return. Okay? I'll get the lock-box key. Here's a shopping bag for what you take out of it."

* * * * *

"Hello to you, Marilyn. This is my daughter, Jennifer," Frances said to the receptionist as they took seats in the doctor's waiting room.

"Mom, are you sure you want me to come in when you talk to the doctor?"

"Yes. I don't remember much from the hospital, and you're my backup for remembering what he says today."

A nurse recorded her blood pressure, temp and pulse. Then a pleasant looking man about Jennifer's age bustled into the examining room. They exchanged introductions.

He smiled while his alert eyes concentrated on his patient. "How are you today, Frances?"

"Fine now, but I've jumped a few hurdles this past week. I've asked Jen to tell you about it since she witnessed what I mostly slept through."

Jennifer described the call for help, the trip from Virginia, what she found at the house, her mother's hospital stay, apparent recovery and hospital instruction to see her GP. She handed him a copy of the hospital record she'd requested. "Mom, would you like to tell Dr. Grantlan about your moving plan?"

"Well, I've lived independently about sixty-seven years and imagined I always would. Scams can happen to anyone at any age, but this one proved to me I'm not as sharp as I thought. At eighty-seven, I'm slowing down a little, as anyone would, but not passing my driving test dealt a blow. And then the burglary. Moving near family makes sense, and unlike some of my friends, I have a devoted daughter willing to take on her old mother." She smiled at Jennifer. "She asked me to live with her, but I prefer living near her to stay independent as long as I can."

"We've arranged for Mom to live right across the street from our house in Virginia the first three months, while we find senior housing she really likes. She'll have a break after the move before the apartment decision."

"Feeling okay otherwise? No dizziness? No falls?" He checked her ankles. "No swelling. That's good." With his stethoscope, he listened to her heart and consulted her chart. "Looks like your mammograms are current. Also flu and pneumonia shots. Seems you weathered your ER visit surprisingly well. We'll draw some blood for a check, but you look good and sound alert, Fran." He turned to Jennifer. "If you'll step out I'll do a quick EKG to check her a-fib."

While the nurse affixed the EKG leads on Frances, Jennifer followed Grantlan into the hall. "This is the first time I'll be responsible for a senior. Anything I should watch for?"

Dr. Grantlan studied her a moment. "I actually see some elderly patients suffering from neglect, so I'm glad to help a daughter who wants to act responsibly. Knowing when to stop driving is important, but apparently, that's solved for Frances. Many seniors don't ask loved ones for help because they want to feel and act independent or they're experiencing early dementia or they're just plain stubborn."

Jennifer chuckled. She knew about stubborn from her mother's years of resisting a move north.

"Some don't visit their doctor regularly because they forget or it's too complicated to arrange transportation, so they miss flu and pneumonia shots and other prevention that could prolong health. Some are shy about admitting personal problems to health care providers—things like constipation or sexual and urinary difficulties."

Jennifer nodded. "That could be true at other ages, as well."

"Yes, but it can get serious fast for the elderly, as can jaw pain or stomach upsets. We need such information for correct diagnosis and treatment, but older folks don't always volunteer all those puzzle pieces."

"Why?"

"Maybe they're embarrassed to admit they didn't understand or can't remember dosage instructions or timing of medications or other treatments. Or sometimes they understand well enough, but forget to do it. Sometimes they try to fight the appearance of aging like refusing hearing aids, or canes and walkers, or dentures and eyeglasses—all of which could improve their quality of life. So look for signs of new behavior or changing health. Try to find a geriatrician for her if you can."

"A geriatrician?"

"Yes, a medical doctor trained to meet older folk's special health needs. The elderly often have a number of health problems requiring several medications. Diseases and meds affect seniors differently. A geriatrician looks out for the whole person, not just treating one illness or another. They're board certified plus take additional training for geriatric certification."

"Are they easy to find?"

"Unfortunately, there's a shortage of them now at the very time our older population needs even more. A third of seventy-four million Americans who will be over sixty-five in 2030 will have health problems a geriatrician could help best. My nurse can give you some computer links to look for one in your area.

"Thank you, Doctor, for taking extra time to explain this."

The nurse opened the treatment room door. "We're ready for the EKG, Doctor."

Before starting the machine, he said, "Okay, Frances. Your daughter's outside, giving us a few minutes to talk privately. Are you okay with this move?"

"It's a big effort, but I think it's the right choice. Of course, I don't want to fold my tent and take it on the road, but at my age, anything could happen and eventually something will. I should live near Jen then, for her sake as well as mine."

"No coercion? No intimidation?" She shook her head. "Any new physical problems? Anything you want to tell me."

"No, but thanks for watching out for me all these years." She patted his arm.

"Now stay quiet while I do the EKG."

A few minutes later when he finished, she asked, "By the way, can you recommend a new doctor in McLean and should I take my medical records with me today?"

"I've suggested a geriatrician to your daughter and links to find one. Ask your new doctor to request your records from our office to avoid the per page charge you'd have now. Be sure Marilyn knows how to reach you up north."

"Thank you and thanks again for your good care for so long a time."

"My pleasure, Frances. Stay well."

"May I give you a goodbye hug?"

After the embrace, he patted her arm and grinned. "You make the most of this new adventure in Virginia."

In the car, Frances mused. "Such a nice man and a good doctor. After thirty years, he and his staff almost feel like family. And did you notice all the tall, healthy plants in his waiting room?"

Jennifer gave her mother a sharp look. "Ah...because?"

"Because Erma Bombeck says, 'Never go to a doctor whose house plants have died.'"

Jennifer shot her a look and, seeing her mother was serious about this, choked back a laugh until her eyes watered. Though managing to retain her grip on the wheel, she couldn't stifle a strangled-sounding cough.

"Are you all right, dear?"

"Yes, thanks," Jennifer croaked, grateful to stop at a red light while she regained control.

The doctor's plants she'd noticed were artificial.

CHAPTER 28

J ennifer waited at the bank while her mother and a teller entered the vault. Surprised at the bulge in the bag her mother toted when she emerged, Jennifer wondered about the contents. As they reached the car, her cellphone rang.

"Hi, Becca…. Okay, tonight…. Wait I need to copy this. Yes, I'll wait in the cellphone lot. Call me when you're outside the airport front door. Safe trip, sweetie, and thanks for doing this."

Back at home she asked, "Do you want to go through these things now, Mom, or put the bag directly into the safe?"

"Why don't we do it together? Then you'll know about the safe and the combination."

Upstairs at home, Frances pulled out a file drawer. "We didn't file it under "S" for Safe because a thief would look there first. We considered "W" for Wall-safe, but Dad said it's too obvious. So we settled on…wait, what was it? Ah yes, "T" for This-and-That. Nobody would guess that one."

Jennifer winced. "You're right, Mom. Nobody would." But a new worry pushed aside these otherwise amusing eccentricities. Her parents' wacky filing system and weird hiding places complicated preparing belongings for the sale. Now she'd need to check inside and underneath every single item before "clearing" it. Thank goodness Becca would arrive soon.

"Could you please help me move this small bookcase, dear?" Behind it, Frances lifted away the large rectangle of wallboard, revealing the door of an imbedded safe the size of a dorm-size mini-fridge. "This came with the house when we bought it." She pulled a slip of paper close to her eyes, squinted and read the combination's numbers as Jennifer rotated the safe's dial. "Should open now when you turn to the right." The door swung forward. "Please put this card back in the filing cabinet before the combination gets lost."

Stifling a giggle, Jennifer turned to the "T's" and refiled the card. "Do you want to pour the lock-box stuff on the bed and put it in the safe piece-by-piece?"

"Do we have time before the first real estate visit?"

"No, it's 2:45. The first one's due in only fifteen minutes. Why don't we use that time to clean up the money on the study floor?"

"Let's put the bag in the safe first."

Just as they pushed back the bookcase, the doorbell rang. Jennifer ran down the stairs, her mother close behind.

"Hello," Jennifer said, opening the front door.

"Hello," I'm Mona Giuseppe from Ferrero Real Estate. I'm early but I finished with another client sooner than expected."

"Well, I…" Jennifer thought of the money scattered on the study floor. "I guess it's okay. Come in. I'll get my mother."

When they assembled around the kitchen table, Mona opened her notebook. "First I'll get the facts I need. Square footage?"

"5,000 square feet," Grammy supplied, turned off by the agent's ultra-high heels, plunging neckline, garish make-up and powerful perfume.

"How old is your house?"

"Forty years. I've lived here thirty of those years," Frances supplied.

"Number of bedrooms and bathrooms?"

"Four bedrooms, four and a half bathrooms."

"Den?" Grammy nodded. "Enclosed lanai?" Another nod. "Property size?"

"Half acre."

"Type of heat?"

"Electric."

"Garage?"

"Two car plus workshop."

"Window treatments and chandeliers convey?" At Grammy's nod, the agent snapped her notebook shut. "Okay, now give me a quick tour."

Jennifer and her mother exchanged frowns at this agent's appearance and her "it's-all-about-me" attitude.

"You take her around, Jen. I'll wait in the study." She gave her daughter a meaningful look, which Jennifer deduced meant her mother would pick up the scattered money before they got there. She led the way upstairs, where the agent asked brisk questions while looking impatiently at her watch. They toured the downstairs and garage and returned to the kitchen table. The agent withdrew papers from her briefcase.

"Here's our contract. Sign here..." She pointed. Jennifer and her mother stared at the woman.

"What price would you propose to put my house on the market?"

"Well, I'd have to check comparables at the office to give you a figure, but I guess around $500,000. Pricing it low is good for both of us because it sells quickly so you get your money and I get my commission."

Frances tapped the pen on the contract. "Houses on this block are similar in age and size, and one is for sale down the street. Do you know what they're asking?"

Mona shifted impatiently and snapped, "I told you I won't know until I check comparables."

"Where are you from?"

"Jersey."

"How long have you been a real estate agent?"

"A year."

"How many houses have you sold?"

Mona shifted uncomfortably. "What is this, Twenty Questions?"

"I want to know about you and your company to decide who to choose to sell my house."

"Okay, okay. I sold two houses but I only worked part time for six months. So two houses in six months is pretty good, huh? Here's where you sign."

"You know, dear, turns out I may rethink selling the house. Sorry to have taken your time but I'm not ready to sign today."

Mona stood, incensed. "As a matter of fact, you *have* wasted my time and I don't appreciate it. I'll let myself out."

As the front door slammed, silence filled the kitchen. Finally, Jennifer chuckled, "Was that the real estate agent from hell?" They dissolved in laughter.

Through tears of mirth, Frances managed, "I don't have your imagination, but even I can invent a 'what's-their-story?' explanation about her."

"Okay, let's hear it." Jennifer folded her arms across her chest.

"Her Mafia boyfriend from New Jersey started a new operation in Naples and brought her along. But lounging at the pool and shopping bored her so she badgered him to find something for her to do. To quiet her he said if she took the real estate test he'd provide her clients from his Mafia friends who moved here." They both giggled. "She passed the real estate exam on the third try, *but just barely*. Now she's loose in public and we were her first non-Mafia test."

They doubled over with laughter. Jennifer managed, "And the next agent's due in ten minutes. What will happen then? As the Vikings say, 'shields up.'" They giggled again.

CHAPTER 29

W hen the bell chimed, they both went to the door.
"Hello, I'm Joan Langley from Langley Properties," said the professionally dressed woman.
"Here for our 4:30 appointment."
They introduced themselves and invited her in.
Joan smiled and glanced around. "Your home looks lovely, and this familiar neighborhood has many positive memories for me. Growing up, I often visited relatives living down the block. Did you know them? Scott and Wendey Langley?"
"Oh, the Langleys. Yes, we played bridge together in the old days. Small world."
"That means you've lived here awhile. What's changed your mind about staying in Florida?"
"In a few weeks I move north to settle near my daughter and her family."
"A lot of folks do just that. Hard to leave Florida's climate, but nearness to family is the right decision for many seniors. How might I help you accomplish this?"
"For starters, we'd like to know about you, your company and what price you suggest we ask."
"Let's talk about your second question first. I came prepared with a CMA–a comparative market analysis for your neighborhood. A house down the street, similar to yours, is priced at $925,000 and three have sold in the immediate area for $889,000, $909,000 and $913,000." She showed them the printed page of information.

"Notice how little the selling prices differ from the original asking price? You said you'll move in a few weeks. Summer in Naples may be off-season, but many property-hunters come now to buy instead of the winter, to avoid the in-season crowds. You're in a coveted location, right off US 41, so that's a plus. I'll have a better price idea after walking through your house. While other houses nearby are similar age and size, some have upgrades that others don't.

"Now for your question about me. You might say I was born into the business because my last name is the same as my company's name. I've been a licensed, full time agent for fifteen years. My primary area of expertise is Naples and Bonita Springs, although Langley Properties deals in multiple listings in Florida and around the country. If we decide to work together, Langley would advertise your property weekly on Craigslist plus newspapers in Naples, Ft. Myers and Marco Island. Also, real estate periodicals and direct mailings to people who've asked us to tell them about houses available in certain neighborhoods. I've sold thirty houses in the last twelve months and can offer you referral names. Other questions?"

Like Frances, Jennifer sat back, impressed at this jaw-dropping difference from their previous agent interview. Reaching for her list of questions, she found most already answered. At last she said, "What sets you apart from other agents? Why should we choose you?"

"A smart question. I know my job extremely well, work at it fulltime and have a proven track record of success for fifteen years. Having lived here most of my life, I know Naples. Making my clients happy and treating them fairly are my prime focus. Our company has references to title companies, closing attorneys and mortgage brokers for your buyer. We also have outreach to painting, plumbing and electrical contractors, carpenters, roofers, HVAC, movers, estate sale companies and landscape professionals."

"Have you references?"

"The client names I'll offer you I think will confirm I'm honest, capable, a good communicator and negotiator, quick to return calls or e-mails and committed to client satisfaction. If we decide to work together, please study my contract or run it past your lawyer. No need to sign it in haste, but I begin working for you once we have a signed agreement. Then I'd take still pictures of your house, inside and out, as well as recording a videoed on-line tour for prospective buyers."

Jennifer glanced at her to-do list. "I'd appreciate your mover leads and estate sale company list."

Frances added, "Maybe I'll think of some questions while we tour the house. Jen, will you please lead the way?"

They started upstairs, where Joan made positive observations about each room and asked a few questions. When they finished the tour Joan said, "Thanks for your time. I would be happy to sell your home. Let me know if you want to talk further." She gathered her briefcase and turned to leave. "The housing market here recovers fast from national blips because Naples is a go-to destination — and not just for the climate or the Gulf. The medical community promotes Naples' top-notch medical care plus a pleasant place to convalesce. And what attracted all those high-caliber doctors? The climate, the beauty and an endless supply of retirees for their patients. Here's my business card. I hope to hear from you soon."

Grinning, Frances stepped forward. "Joan, I think I'd like you to sell my house."

Jennifer added quickly, "Yes, please leave us your contract and your client referral list."

Frances said, "To speed things along, could you meet with us tomorrow or the next day to work out details?"

"If we give you an empty house in two to three weeks, can you work that fast?" Jennifer asked.

Joan consulted her calendar. "Yes, I can. How about tomorrow at 4:30? Will that give you time enough?"

They nodded in unison.

As they closed the front door, Frances answered the ringing phone. "Hello, this Flora Finney, your six o'clock real estate agent appointment. Someone just ran into my car at an intersection so may I reschedule?"

"Sorry, Flora, but I've just chosen an agent. Thanks anyway for your interest." Hanging up, she turned to Jennifer and added with a pixie expression. "Was that fate at work?"

"Almost, Mom. Fate is what you're given. Destiny is what you do with it."

CHAPTER 30

"**M**om, it's almost 6:00. Becca arrives at 7:30 and the airport's about thirty minutes away. She won't have had dinner. Would you like to come with me to get her or stay here and rest? And shall we all go out to a late dinner or have something here?"

"Have you time to dash over to Publix for one of those cooked whole chickens and their deli mashed potatoes? I think I have a veggie." She searched the freezer. "Yes, right here. Then I can have everything waiting for you both when you get home about 8:30."

"Great plan, Mom. Want to come along to the grocery?" She nodded. "Then, off we go."

* * * * *

On the drive home from the airport, Jennifer updated Becca on recent events. They discussed how Becca could fit in.

"Grammy's a year older than when you saw her last. A year can make a difference at her age. I find her normal and lucid one minute but tired and confused the next."

Becca laughed.

"What's so funny?"

"I'm twenty-one and you could say the same about me."

Jennifer smiled. "Okay, me, too. But maybe this is different. Even when she seems perky, remember she's been through a lot recently — imprisoned in her home, the hospital, then the move. All this effort is a challenge for *me*, never mind her. And in a couple of weeks I'll return to my familiar home while she's entering the unknown."

"Got it, Mom. So besides taking pictures to fire off to the family showing things they might want and making sure estate sale items aren't hiding treasures inside or under, what else can I do?"

"The usual stuff like three meals a day, laundry, grocery shopping. We still must interview estate sale companies and movers and we're working with the sheriff and insurance companies about stolen items. How long can you stay?"

"No job offer yet after graduating, so I'm at your service. I could share driving when you and Grammy head north or you two could fly and I drive the Mercedes back. Or we could all fly home and have a car transport company bring it. I'm here to be useful."

"Thanks again, honey, for dropping everything to come. How's your cute beau, Nathan?"

"He's the same. And yes, he is cute, isn't he?"

"We'll see a lot of Grammy soon in McLean, but while here you'll see her house again for the last time." She turned onto another street. "Beginning to look familiar? We're almost there."

"Mom, what are those lights up ahead?"

Jennifer's heart raced. Her foot pressed the car's accelerator. Because Becca's bag took forever to appear on the carousel, the Ft. Myers airport round-trip had taken almost two hours. Surely nothing more could happen to her mother in such a short time, right? Yet her concern showed on her face.

"Calm down, Mom. What are the chances...?"

They turned onto Grammy's street, startled by emergency lights gyrating across two fire engines and an ambulance parked in front of her house.

"Oh, no!" Jennifer cried, screeching to a halt behind the fire trucks. They leaped from the car and dashed to the front door as two firemen exited. "You the daughter? They'll talk to you inside," one said.

They hurried in. Grammy sat in the kitchen with two uniformed firemen, one taking notes.

"What...what happened?"

"Oh, Jennifer, there you are. I...I must have dozed off while the food cooked. The vegetable pan burned dry and the smoke set off the fire alarm. The shrill noise woke me up, but a neighbor already heard the sound and called the firemen. Then these nice gentlemen came to take a look."

The medic and lead fireman didn't look amused. "I'd like to speak with you privately," the medic told Jennifer as his crew prepared to leave.

"Becca, would you and Grammy visit together in the study for a few minutes? I'll be right in."

When they left the kitchen, Jennifer again noted the medic's somber expression. "This woman's your mother? She's eighty-seven, right?" Jennifer nodded. "Do you realize an incident like this could have been fatal?" Jennifer nodded again. "You can see she needs assistance with cooking — and maybe more. Every day we face preventable fatalities, and prevention saves lives. If you care about her, take action to keep something like this from happening again."

"You're right. I've been here a week making arrangements to take her north to live by us. I was away only long enough to pick up my daughter at the airport. I'm so sorry you had to come tonight, but thank goodness you did. It won't happen again."

The fireman added sternly, "You understand this could have been a conflagration. It could have been fatal. Thanks to her working smoke alarm and quick action from a neighbor, we prevented worse smoke damage. We turned on the exhaust fan over the stove, opened kitchen windows and closed off doors to the rest of the house to contain the smoke odor. What's left of the pan is in the sink. Your mother should not cook unsupervised again."

"She won't, I promise. Believe me, I see the situation here with my own eyes. Thank you for rescuing her, for your sound advice and for caring."

The man sighed and glanced around the kitchen before starting to leave.

"And thank you for the important work you do for all of us."

"Good night, ma'am," he said in a tired voice as she closed the door behind him.

Just as the burglary had clanged a wake-up call for Grammy, this fire scare did a similar favor for Jennifer. Was this accident understandable given the recent stress and exhaustion, or did her mother need full assisted living now?

CHAPTER 31

J ennifer cooked another package of vegetables from the freezer, nuked the mashed potatoes, and soon all three ate dinner at the dining room table, avoiding the smoky kitchen. Becca chattered amiably about her flight and her joy to see her grandmother again in this wonderful old house they all loved.

"It's nearly ten," Jennifer yawned. "Don't know about the rest of you but I'm ready for bed. Becca, would you lock up while I take Grammy upstairs? You know what bedroom you're in?"

"Yes, and I'll be up shortly. I may take a few downstairs pictures to start my project. Any particular wake-up time tomorrow?"

"No, but anyone up early could look through the remaining books in the study."

Jennifer settled her mother before slipping into her own bed and locking eyes with the dragon perched on the bureau. If the know-everything aura he projected was real, what did he see in their future? Would she get her mother safely to McLean? Would she find the map's treasure?

She picked up one of her dad's books from the nightstand. For total escape from today's trying events, she'd read more about Mosby capturing General Stoughton. Despite each book having the same basic take on these and surrounding events, each book had slightly different versions about who said what and when. After all, history hinged not only on facts, but on who assembled those facts and what they included or omitted. The morning meeting when John Birdsong described his Virginia ancestors bubbled through her mind.

The last thing she remembered was glancing at the dragon, who stared right back. Gradually her eyes drooped, the book slid from her fingers and she again fell into a trance, soon pierced by another vision.

In his isolated makeshift camp, Corporal Raiford Birdsong shivered in the cold as he stared up through the dark at the stars twinkling high in the black sky above the trees. He fought to recall the chain of events five weeks earlier, the actions bringing him here this night.

He had stood, he recalled, in the town of Fairfax Courthouse beside another soldier, Private Orwell Hanby, an endless talker.

"You writin' again in your book, Birdsong? What ya write about when ya never say much?"

"About what I think."

"So whatcha thinkin' about there?" Hanby pointed to the journal.

"Mosby."

"Ya know he enlisted in this here war as a private, just like me an' you," Hanby had said. "The men respect him but it ain't outta fear. No, they like him, too. Now he's rose to Cap'n, he expects tight discipline from us in battle, but that there's one of our success secrets. We're glad to do anything he orders outta regard for the Cap'n hisself, and," Hanby cackled, "a' course, splittin' the spoils after one of them successes don't hurt none either."

Birdsong had nodded, but he felt Hanby's description fell short. Birdsong more than respected and admired Mosby, he worshipped the man – as he knew, did many of his fellow raiders.

Hanby spat tobacco on the ground. "An' he got this spooky way o' readin' people. He can see a man's soul, as if he looked inside him and knowed all about him. Take that Sgt. James Ames, ya know, our 'Big Yank.' When he come into our camp, wantin' to leave the Union and join the South, we all saw him for a gull-derned spy. But Mosby heard him out and sized him up and brought him in. Turned out he saw true, because Ames is one of our best."

As Mosby approached them, the two men jumped to attention. He said, "Hanby, go with Gifford to find us more horses. You know how to quiet those animals when they get skittish."

"Yes, sir. My farm upbringin', sir."

Hanby saluted and left.

"Birdsong, come with me. We're going to hunt us a general."

Hardly believing his luck that Mosby chose him to join the few soldiers picked for that special raid, Birdsong replayed the capture of Stoughton over and over in his mind. Moreover, Birdsong knew he himself showed Mosby the Stoughton cache of plunder that looked like a chest of pirate treasure.

After Mosby examined the valuables and directed Birdsong to load them into two nearby empty canvas bags, he'd added, "Now hide these bags in one of those Union carriages or wagons we confiscated and guard them with your life."

"Yes, sir." Birdsong had said, feeling deep honor at his leader's trust to personally protect something this rare and valuable. Mosby's uncanny judgment of human nature showed he trusted Birdsong. This realization increased the corporal's respect for himself and for his leader.

An hour later as the column of horses, prisoners, wagons, carriages and stores captured by Mosby's Raiders moved through the night from the town of Fairfax Courthouse toward Culpeper, Birdsong's legs protectively encircled the canvas bags beneath his cradled rifle as his wagon bumped along the dirt road. They'd traveled ten miles when he looked up, surprised to see Mosby and Big Yank double back to his vehicle.

"Birdsong," Mosby said, "our scouts say a large group of Union cavalry heads straight toward us from the northeast. If we must fight them and still escape with these horses, guns and prisoners, we may need to abandon the carriages and wagons of food. We can't risk them retaking this treasure. Ames and I will bury it off the road in the woods. I want you to come back with him and some others later to find it and get it to General Lee. Go now and choose a horse because this wagon must stay."

"Yes, sir. My horse, Blackie, is tied behind the wagon."

"And a fine-looking animal he is." Mosby turned to the driver. "Pull this wagon off the road, take this cart horse ahead with the others to trade in for one that's saddled, because we're leaving the wagon here."

The driver jerked back the reins, rolled the vehicle to a stop, jumped down and saluted his commander. "Yes, sir."

Astride Blackie, Birdsong had watched Mosby and Ames enter the woods along the side of the road, Mosby brandishing a shovel and Ames lugging the bulging canvas bags. Birdsong searched vainly in the dark for some landmark by which to remember this place so they'd be sure to find it later — any distinguishing feature along the road. And then he spotted one. Not twenty feet from the road was a huge tree hit by lightning, its split trunk and broken limbs tipped at odd angles that formed a crude "w." Memorizing this, he hurried to mount his horse.

Five weeks later in early April, Mosby called for Whitehall, Elwood, Birdsong and four other raiders.

"Men, it's time to move the two bags of Stoughton's treasure. 'Big Yank' and I buried it in a shallow pit between two pine trees on our way from Fairfax Courthouse to Culpeper. I notched X's in those trees with my knife and then shoved the blade to the hilt in the dirt over the bags. General Lee's battle location changes daily, and battlefields are no place for these valuables, but there's a safe house near Great Falls, which Lee knows well. They'll hide the heirlooms until he can return them to their rightful owners. You men get those bags to that safe house." He gave specific directions to their destination.

Honored at this important assignment, these soldiers saluted the man who'd earned their loyalty with his charismatic leadership, never mind the camaraderie borne of their daring teamwork.

That night as the seven rode toward the treasure, Lt. Elwood drew his horse alongside Birdsong's. "You the one the men call 'Poet'?" he asked conversationally.

"Some call me that."

"Can you sample me why they do?"

Birdsong considered his reply. Shy about this side of his nature, he wrote poems privately, not liking to speak of them. Yet with little choice but to answer an officer, at last he spoke,

> "Nobody closer than the father and son,
> till the war began and the closeness was done.
> The father loved home and chose the Gray,
> but the son chose Blue to stop slave-eray.
> Then raged a battle on a wooded hill,
> a beautiful spot never meant for a kill
> Where two soldiers met with pistols drawn,
> not knowing who they'd come upon.
> As shots rang out and both men fell,
> their eyes locked hard in silent hell,
> The father saw he'd shot his son
> and the boy, his dad. The deed was done.
> I love you, Son, and I say farewell."
> "I love you, Dad," and there he fell.
> Their blood drained out to stain the ground
> and mix together where they were found.
> The mother went not to the railroad track,
> no train would bring their bodies back.
> Her tears joined those of women past,

> *with loved ones dead from war's cruel cast.*
> *Where dying for the winners is an awful cost,*
> *but dying for the losers is a total loss."*

Elwood felt a sudden catch in his throat, for he and his own father supported opposite causes in this anguished, wasteful War Between the States. He hid this emotion with a cough. "The...the men call you Poet for good reason. Ever tried putting those words in a tune? You'd have you a strong song."

"No, sir, but I thank you for the mentioning."

Then another sound reached Elwood's ears. He cocked his head. "You hear that?"

Birdsong looked and listened in the dark. "Horses. Galloping hard. Maybe ten of 'em?"

As ranking officer, Elwood took charge, "Ride out two each in different directions." He pointed. "You north, you east, you and me south. Birdsong, you ride west alone since there's seven of us. They can't catch us all. Whoever breaks free, find the treasure and get it to the safe house."

They spurred their horses and peeled away at a gallop, but the Union troops also split directions, following tight on the heels of each pair. In the darkness, only Birdsong eluded his pursuers by hunkering down in a chance clump of thicketed evergreens dense enough to hide him and his horse.

Half an hour later, from the east he watched Union troops leading two raiders back, on their horses, hands tied behind them. Later, from the south, he saw Elwood riding with tied hands, the second raider's body thrown face down across his horse. And from the north came Whitehall and a second Raider, both captives.

Birdsong felt a stab of fear. Only he could complete the task.

Now his memory had brought him full circle, to why he sat in his makeshift bivouac behind shielding evergreens, staring at the twinkling stars above him and shivering in the cold.

Gradually, his anxiety about the difficult task that lay ahead for him changed to resolve.

* * * * *

Birdsong slept as best he could in the thicket of firs during the day, but when darkness fell, he mounted his horse. Should he return to Mosby to report what happened? Should he get more men to share this job or should he recover the treasure himself and attempt taking it to the safe house?

He had food and a canteen for himself and some oats for his horse, but he needed to find a stream and a grassy spot for the animal to graze. Staying alert for these necessities — while riding undetected and ready to blend invisibly into roadside cover at any sign of human presence — made the nighttime journey exceedingly tense. He did not make good time.

This normal one-night trip at a gallop would take him several nights, but not at his current pace and then, only if he could water Blackie. In the original plan, the seven men would divide the treasure's weight seven ways. Could he carry the two heavy, bulky bags alone through potentially hostile Union territory? Battle lines changed daily, dictating which side controlled an area at any given time.

If he took two nights to cover the distance to the treasure, how many would it take to Great Falls? He might need to walk his horse with the extra weight aboard. Three? Four? More? Assuming he even found the treasure's burying place, could he transport it that distance traveling at night without allowing it to fall into hated Union hands?

At the edge of a farmer's field, he found a rusty trough with enough rainwater to temporarily slake Blackie's thirst and his own. Much later, he came upon a creek, where he watered his horse properly and filled his canteen. By dawn's light, he thought the terrain looked familiar and calculated his bearings. He might find the treasure tonight.

Once again, he slept by day and rose at dark. He began looking for the landmark split tree, grateful for a clear night and light from the moon. At about 3:00am, he thought he saw it, dismounted and walked into the woods to confirm. A lightning- struck tree, all right, but split differently than the "w" etched in his mind. Guessing the place he sought near at hand because both trees were probably struck during the same storm, he brushed Blackie's flank with his boot heel and peered into the woods as his well-trained horse moved forward.

Birdsong's head jerked forward at a sound ahead. Reining in his horse, he leaned forward in the saddle, intent upon the dark road before him. Yes, hoofbeats, but hard to tell how many. He edged his horse into the woods.

The galloping grew louder as five horsemen rocketed past his hiding place. In the dark at their speed, he couldn't count them friend or foe. When their noise receded, he ventured again onto the road. He hadn't gone fifty feet when he saw his landmark lightning-damaged tree.

Dismounting, he led his horse into the wooded glen. When dawn broke, he searched vainly for two slashed pine trees. They had to be close. He returned to the road to reconfirm the landmark before trudging back into the woods to search again.

Though tree trunks and some deciduous tree branches stood bare, a pale green aura fringed the tips as April's leaves budded into springtime and native dogwoods and redbuds blossomed fully. The poet inside him contrasted the timeless natural beauty of this scene with the bloody war men waged nearby. He gazed at sunlight-dappled fall leaves on the ground, their earth-hued layers compressed against the soil by recent winter snows, when his eye distinguished a different shape on the ground. He hurried over and fell to his knees. Mosby's knife. He looked up. Two pines notched with X's.

CHAPTER 32

T he first one awake the next morning, Jennifer dressed quickly, hustled downstairs and prepared coffee. Again, she felt enlivened and eager for the day, energized by the vision pulling her into the intriguing world of the past.

She collected the newspaper from the driveway and perused it while savoring her steaming coffee. Next, she opened her daybook. Surprised to note it was Thursday, she realized she'd arrived in Naples almost a week ago...though it seemed longer.

Starting the day's to-do list, she jotted: 10:00am beauty shop, evaluate real estate contract, call Langley's customer referrals, 4:30 Joan Langley appointment, firm up movers and estate sale company appointments the following day. Scour the pantry, refrigerator and freezer to produce three meals for three people...and possibly a grocery run.

She phoned their first moving company choice. They had her target date available, so she recorded their prices and made a 1:00 appointment to meet their agent.

Also today, Becca would take pictures from which the family could request something of Grammy's before everything sold. This meant furniture *and* contents like china, silver, crystal and linens — anything tucked in any room that must disappear in only two weeks. Would Becca do this well?

At 8:30, Jennifer roused the others, reminding Grammy about the new beauty shop appointment time, and showed them the to-do list. Becca announced she'd start snapping pictures in the house while they beautified at the salon. Jennifer fitted in three client referral calls, all raving about Joan Langley's skill, personality and results.

At ten, they settled in side-by-side chairs at the beauty shop, talking with Chelsea and Jen's stylist, Corky.

"Jennifer, welcome back. And Frances, how *are* you?" When they described what had happened since seeing her last, Chelsea added, "You think my sketches helped the deputy?"

"I know so because they arrested the guy in Michigan. He's on his way back here for prosecution."

Chelsea leaned into the hairstyle she combed for Frances. "Are you willing to face him in court if necessary?"

Grammy hesitated, but then said with resolve. "Yes, because I want him out of action."

"Good for you. Moving north is a big decision for you, Frances. Were any of my suggestions about movers and Realtors useful?"

"Yes, and thank you," Grammy answered. "In fact, we hired the very real estate company you mentioned. Today we select a mover and tomorrow, estate sale companies."

"Bet you didn't know your bad news turned into my good news," Chelsea announced. They turned toward her, curious.

"Well, you know I'm a divorcee for fifteen years and my daughter and her little girl lived with me until just recently. At first, being by myself felt wonderful, like a reprieve, but then it began to feel lonely — really lonely. So now I'm dating and you had a hand in it."

Jennifer saw no connection. "What do you mean?"

"Cliff Goodwin, the deputy we had supper with at Joe's Diner, has dropped by every evening since. Turns out when his wife died a year ago, he threw himself headlong into his work. I'm not calling this a romance, but it's comfortable for now." Chelsea grinned. "But there's even more to my story." Their eyes riveted on her.

"At Cliff's suggestion, I'm taking a self-defense course on my day off. The purpose is keeping yourself safe by improving your mental and physical preparedness."

"Gee, that's a course I'd like to take," commented someone in another chair, overhearing the conversation. "What have you learned so far?"

"We learned the five A's for trouble situations: attitude, awareness, assessment, action and avoidance."

Several customers chimed in, asking when's-and-where's about the course. Chelsea told them.

"What else can you tell us?" someone asked.

Chelsea thought a moment. "Since this course is about your own personal safety, if you see a fight or a crime or other trouble, don't get involved yourself. Call 911 because the professionals have the training plus manpower and firepower. You've done your part by calling them for help."

"What else?"

"Under Awareness in those five A's, they list various kinds of frauds to recognize and avoid."

"For instance?" Jennifer asked.

Chelsea took a folder from her beauty station's drawer, flipped some pages and read. "Identity theft, telemarketing fraud, mail and internet fraud, home improvement fraud, mortgage fraud, investment fraud, caregiving fraud and a prevention checklist."

"What's on the prevention checklist?" queried another voice.

"Use a hidden wallet instead of a purse; don't carry your social security card unless you need it that day; don't talk freely to strangers on the phone, at your door or on the street. Use a crosscut shredder on tossed financial mail and documents... Look, I'll put the list here so any of you can take a look."

The beauticians finished Jennifer and Grammy about the same time. They paid their bills.

"I'll keep my regular appointment for a few more weeks until we leave. Thanks, Chelsea, for your wonderful care over the years *and* for the sketch you gave the deputy to catch my thief."

"Fran, you know I value your friendship. You've been my client longer than any of my other customers. Working with you has been my pleasure." They hugged.

"See you next Thursday," Jennifer said, waving as they left the shop.

As they drove home, Jen's cellphone rang. She answered, pressing the speaker button.

"Hello, this is Hannah with big news. Adam sold the lots to a developer today but kept the one for us to build on as we planned."

"That's exciting." Jennifer grinned. "He's worked hard on this."

"Yes, and he negotiated a great price, so we're thrilled. Next, we start work on our own lot. You know how overgrown the property is? We're going to hire a bush-hogger."

Grammy frowned. "What in the world is that?"

"A man with a machine for clearing brush from overgrown land. In our case, it's light bush-hogging where they spare trees but remove ratty thickets and undergrowth. Then we can see what the property looks like for the first time. It's almost a football field length from the main road, up the driveway to the house, and neglected for so many years nobody knows what's there. Now we'll find out."

"Keep your eyes open for Civil War relics." Surprised she said this, Jennifer wondered at the powerful tentacles with which this new subject had encircled her mind."

CHAPTER 33

Back at the house, Jennifer served lunch and they talked as they ate.

"How's the photography going, Becca?"

"Faster than I expected. I'll finish tomorrow and e-mail the pics to the family then."

"Mom, how are you doing?" Jennifer looked with tenderness toward the frail elder who'd been the vibrant, energetic figure from her memory.

"My stamina's not what it used to be, but I'm trying to keep up."

"You're amazing, Grammy. A major move like this is *huge* at any age," Becca observed.

"She's right, Mom. But now we all need to pool our ideas about some big decisions. On the computer, I made this calendar showing the next few weeks. We want to choose reasonable goals we can reach without going crazy." Becca giggled at this. Jennifer continued, "So let's think about practical ways to move forward."

"First, let's talk about getting to Virginia," Grammy suggested.

"Okay. Shall we fly or drive? If I'm guessing right, we need another three weeks to do what's left at an acceptable pace. Becca, will you still be with us then?"

"If you want me, I'll stay. If you don't need me, I'll go back. If I stay and you don't fly, I could share driving."

Grammy adjusted her glasses. "This is a nice time of year for a drive. We could travel leisurely, maybe even sightsee along the way. And it may be the last car trip of this kind I'll take, so I vote for driving. All in favor?"

Three hands whooshed into the air.

Jennifer picked up a pencil. "If we schedule movers first, then everything left in the house goes to our estate sale. Grammy has four bedrooms, but we'll move furniture from only two, leaving the two bedrooms of furniture useable for us here after the movers leave and before the estate sale starts. A few nights before that sale, we should move to a hotel until we go north. That gives the sale folks time to arrange the house for the event. Afterward, we hire the estate sale people to remove all unsold stuff or we call Salvation Army or one of Naples' upscale thrift shops. Then we turn the empty house over to Miz Langley. We should be able to leave for Virginia right after the house is empty. What do you think?"

"Sounds logical to me," Becca said. "Grammy?" She nodded.

"Then, back to our calendar. If we schedule movers next Thursday, a week from today, that gives the estate sale company a week to prepare for their sale. They like more time, but we'll select a company that can make it happen. Their sale would be on this weekend right here, eight days after the movers." She penciled these events on the calendar and the day they'd move to a hotel.

"Is this okay with everyone? Because once we agree and schedule these people, we must make it work. Now's the time to decide together."

"Looks okay to me," Grammy said. Becca agreed.

"All right, I'll make the calls to set this up."

When the doorbell chimed, they all looked up.

At the door, Deputy Goodwin asked to come in. "Roderick arrived in Naples this morning. Mrs. Ryerson, can you come down to headquarters for a positive ID?"

"When?" Grammy asked, an edge to her voice.

"How about 1:00? We'll put him in a lineup to please the prosecutor. All by the book."

Jennifer knew she must stay for the moving company appointment. "Becca, could you drive Grammy there?"

"You bet. I've wanted a chance at the Mercedes' wheel. Just give me the address."

"Okay," Goodwin handed Becca the information. "See you at one. Oh, and while you're there, Mrs. Ryerson, could you ID some stolen jewelry? What we found looks similar to your pictures. Gotta go."

"Thank you, Deputy."

"Just doing my job, ma'am.

But suddenly, Grammy touched Jennifer's arm. "I...sounded braver than I feel. So much has happened...." She crumpled into a nearby chair. "I don't know if I can...can face that awful man again."

Becca and Jennifer exchanged looks. "Grammy, it's just like 'Law and Order' on TV," Becca explained.

"Yeah," Goodwin added. "You see the suspect through a one-way mirror. He can't see you. Each man holds a number. You tell us the number held by the man who drugged and robbed you. It's easy, and your family can stand right there with you."

But Grammy's frightened expression didn't change, nor did the hand she clutched to her heart.

CHAPTER 34

B ecca led Grammy to the living room. "Maybe if you relax on the couch a bit you'll feel more energetic..." Becca started to add "for-going-to-the-sheriff's-office," but didn't.

Meantime, Jennifer focused on the mover coming in only one week. Could they really make all this work? She sighed and dialed her first estate sale call.

"This is Caring Estate Sales. How can I help you?"

"My mother's moving out of state from the 5,000 square foot, four bedroom house she's lived in for thirty years here in Naples. We need a sale rather quickly." She gave the date. "Could you arrange that sale...? You don't have that date free? Would you please suggest someone else who might?" She wrote the information. "Thank you."

The name they suggested matched the next one on her list. She dialed.

"Golden Estate Sales. How may we help you?"

When Jennifer repeated the same spiel, the phone voice said, "Yes, we have that weekend open. Could you tell me about what you'll sell?

"Mom's taking only enough to furnish a small two-bedroom apartment, so most of the house. Besides furniture, she has silver, china, crystal, linens, Royal Doulton figurines, a Toby mug collection, Dresden and Meissen figures, Lalique figures, linens..."

"I'd be happy to make an appointment when I can answer your questions and take a look. Is one o'clock today okay...? Good. Your address, please?"

She phoned one more estate sale company, making another appointment for 3:00, enough time to finish before Joan Langley arrived at 4:30.

Grammy's apprehension returned as Becca hustled her to the car for the drive to the sheriff's office. Before they closed the door, Jennifer heard Becca say, "We might even stop for Royal Scoop ice cream cones on the way home, Grammy. Would you like that?" She didn't hear her mother's answer.

Preparing for the mover, she freshened up in the bathroom, surprised at the tired face looking back at her from the mirror. If this experience had aged her, what about her mother's life-altering stake in these decisions? In her zeal to hurry the move and return to Jason and her own normal life, had she pushed them both too hard?

The door chime interrupted her confusion. She fluffed her hair and put on a smile to greet the mover.

"Hello, ma'am. You got a mighty nice place here. Is everything headed to Virginia?"

"No, in each room we've marked what stays and what goes. Shall we start upstairs and take it room by room? Good."

She explained about the upcoming estate sale. He took a pen from his clipboard as he followed her up the steps. Showing him each room, she realized they'd readied the upstairs surprisingly well. When she opened the walk-in closet, he said, "Looks like about four wardrobe boxes here. Will you pack any boxes yourselves or do you want us to do it all?"

"You should. If we pack any, there won't be many."

Downstairs was a different situation. Grammy hadn't had time for decisions about all the china, crystal, linens, and so on. Nor had the family yet selected what they might want. Grammy still hadn't made her final book selections and they knew they must check every volume for hidden cash. The kitchen was the easiest room of all: take basics, leave the rest.

"Don't worry, we always bring extra boxes. We won't leave anything you want to take. These paintings need crates." He made more notes. "What about the garage?"

Jennifer glanced around at tools, sand toys and equipment, a bin of inflated beach balls, Christmas decor, hammock and garden equipment. "Nothing out here."

In the laundry room, he asked, "Washer? Dryer? Ironing board? Mops and brooms?" She shook her head.

"Okay, shall we sit down to talk?" They settled in the kitchen. "This should take us almost a full day for pack and load. We can arrive Thursday morning early, say 8:00. By then we must know exactly what goes and stays. On the other end, we'll off-load and put things where you tell us. Will you be at this McLean address to accept delivery?"

"No, but my husband will, so no problem. They'd appreciate a day-ahead notice."

"That simplifies things because we estimate five to seven days until delivery. I'll need his contact information as well as yours. If a client packs everything himself, we call it a no-pack & load. Yours is a full-pack & load. An interstate move is charged by the pound rather than the hour. I estimate yours at about 2700 lbs." He quoted a price. "The company accepts credit card, cash or certified check at the destination. Here's our contract." He explained about standard and optional insurance.

Jennifer had a few questions. He answered them with confidence, adding. "The crew leader is the driver and he'll have three to five men with him. They wear company uniforms, are experienced and professional at their jobs. Tips are optional for the pack and load crew."

"Thanks, sounds like we're in capable hands." She signed the contract and handed it to him.

"You definitely are."

Just then, her cellphone rang. "Sorry, I must take this call."

"No problem. I'll let myself out."

Waving goodbye she answered, "Hello."

"This is Deputy Goodwin. I'm afraid I have some bad news..."

CHAPTER 35

"**B**ad news? Is...is it my mother?"
"The ID process shook her up pretty bad but... Just a minute, I have to take another call. I'll get right back to you."

Jennifer stared incredulously at the phone before pressing end-call. Was her mother back in the hospital? Had her heart given out, weakened by her a-fib? At eighty-seven, could she make it through another medical crisis?

She looked down, surprised to find herself wringing her hands. The suspense was awful. Besides anguish for her mother, if they had to call off the move while she recovered, everything they'd accomplished so far was in vain. Should she call the sheriff's office and ask for Goodwin? The hospital?

She jumped when the phone rang and snatched it up. "Yes."
"Goodwin again. Sorry about the interruption. Where were we?"
"My mother! Is she..."
"Doing the ID was tough on her and we almost called it off, but she made it through. No, I'm calling about what happened afterward."
Jennifer clutched the phone, "What *did* happen afterward?"
"I can hardly believe it myself, but they say it's true."
"*What?*" Jennifer tried not to scream this, but couldn't hide her anxiety.
"The fact is, in the process of returning Max Roderick to his cell, he escaped."

Jennifer stared, flabbergasted. Unwanted though it was, this news paled compared to relief that her mother had survived this ordeal.

"Okay. How did this happen?"

"When we do a line up, we need people who look similar to the suspect. Sometimes we use other perps already in cells; sometimes we use detectives, whoever's handy to solve the situation. They put on similar clothes so the perp looks like the rest. When the lineup ends, we take the same number of men back to the cells, but they weren't the same men. One of them was a substitute janitor. Confused about where to go, he ended up in the cells, and Roderick just walked away."

Jennifer's mind raced. This embarrassed the sheriff's office and, unless they recaptured Max, he wouldn't pay for his crimes against her mother. A disappointment, true, but with no threat for her family. Figuring Goodwin felt miserable enough at this awkward turn in his case, she chose a noncommittal response. "I see."

"Yeah, well, normally this would be just our problem and not yours, but something else changed that."

Uh-oh. "What?" A lump sprang into her throat.

"Roderick's cellmate says he threatened your mother. He blames her for his arrest and says he's 'gonna get her for it.'"

Jennifer faltered. "What does that mean, 'get her for it'?"

"The cellmate says he didn't spell it out, but it doesn't sound good."

Jennifer sank into the nearest chair. "What happens next?"

"Well, you and I should talk about security at the house, how much longer you'll be there and so on. Then we'll figure out a plan."

"Where's my mother now?"

"Your daughter's bringing her home. They don't know about this yet. It happened after they left. I thought you could tell them and keep them at the house until I get there. See you in about twenty minutes?"

"We'll be here," she managed.

Goodwin arrived just as Becca and Grammy strolled in from the garage, taking final licks of their ice cream cones.

Goodwin repeated what he'd told Jennifer. "Here's the deal. He didn't give up the name of his female accomplice. She may still be in Naples. He might even hide at her place, so be alert for either of them. Here at the house, only Mrs. Ryerson knows what they look like, so I brought a mug shot of Roderick and here's a sketch of the woman your friend Chelsea helped us make."

Goodwin gave a slight smile at the mention of Chelsea's name.

Well, well, thought Jennifer.

"Do we just keep the doors and windows locked and the alarm primed?" Becca asked.

"Yeah, and report anything unusual to me, like phone calls where the caller doesn't speak and then hangs up. He could be trying to learn if you're at home."

"If he breaks in, how...how do we protect ourselves?" Grammy wondered aloud.

"Call 911. Meantime, get some cans of wasp spray. Here, keep this one I brought as a sample. It sprays twenty feet and temporarily blinds whoever it hits. Don't panic and accidentally spray it on each other."

"I have my husband's pistol," Grammy announced, to everyone's surprise. "And a permit, so it's legal."

"Potentially deadly and not necessarily for the bad guy. Unless you practice regularly at a shooting range or are an experienced hunter," his frown at Grammy showed he doubted this, "then shooting a gun could take out a family member. Are you weapon proficient?" Grammy shook her head. "If Roderick has his own piece, an encounter could escalate into a gun fight where *you* lose. Even with wasp spray, be sure he's your target before you press the button or one of you could end up in the hospital. Here's my card again to report anything unusual."

"Would we be safer at a hotel?" Becca asked.

"Don't know. Sometimes these guys brag to their cellmates. Act like big shots. Now that Roderick's on the run, avoiding arrest should be his highest priority, not revenge."

"He does know details about the house since he lived here a week," Grammy said, her voice rising an octave.

"Yeah, but you changed the locks and got the security system. You got what...a couple of weeks left here? We'll have the neighborhood patrolman drive by oftener than usual. If you need more protection, we'll figure out something. Just use common sense. Lock your house whether you're at home or out somewhere. Always lock your car when you're not in it..."

"We routinely do that anyway," Grammy offered.

He looked down sheepishly. "Sorry this happened. I am and the department is." He looked up with a wry smile. "You can imagine how tight department security is now, after-the-fact."

As he left, a woman came up the stairs. "Hello. I'm Peggy Perkins, here for our 3:00 estate sale appointment."

They waved goodbye to Goodwin and greeted the newcomer. Once inside, the woman gave a double take as they locked the door behind her. Jennifer didn't want to frighten her or reveal the whole story. She invented a plausible and essentially true explanation as the four of them sat down in the living room. "We had a home invasion, so forgive us for being safety freaks."

CHAPTER 36

"Here's our company brochure." She offered a copy to each of them. "We can help empty the house however the owner benefits best. These lists," she pointed to her copy, "offer problem-solving sources. For example, not every item sells at an estate sale, so we've listed Naples thrift shops that pick up large items they think resalable. You might consign some and donate others for a tax deduction. You might prefer liquidators who make everything left disappear. To ready the empty house for sale, we list handyman services, a construction company and a landscaper. We also list Realtors you might consider when the house is finally ready for sale. Our goal is to assist our customer in achieving what he wants in the time he has."

"What do you charge for your service?" Grammy asked.

"We charge thirty-five percent of the receipts from the sale, and we pay you within five days of the sale's last day. To earn this, we advertise, organize and run your sale, pricing every item individually. We have a staff member or camera in each room to discourage sticky fingers. At the end, we give you receipts showing item and price for each thing we've sold."

"Where do you advertise and who pays for it?" Becca inquired.

"You pay $100 toward all our advertising, which includes the Naples, Marco and Ft. Myers newspapers, Craigslist and our e-blast customer list."

"E-blast?"

"People who want advanced info about our future sales sign up for our weekly e-blasts describing them. Also, we have a website listing our sales, with photos and directions. You might check that website — the internet address is here on our brochure."

"How many days would you run the sale?" Grammy wanted to know.

"Depends upon how much you have. Once we take a tour, I'll have an exact answer."

"Girls, will you please take Peggy upstairs for show-and-tell?" Grammy asked. "I'll rest here while you do."

"The movers come Thursday and your sale would start eight days later, the date we agreed upon on the phone."

Peggy checked her notes and nodded. "After the movers leave, will the estate sale handle everything left in the house?"

"Yes. We'd like to stay in two of the bedrooms a few days after the movers finish and then go to a hotel to make your work easier. When do you suggest we do that?"

"We can arrange all the rest of the house, so two days before the sale starts would work fine."

"Can we stay here during the sale?"

"Yes, if you like. But if you think watching her things disappear will distress your mother, you might want to whisk her off to a movie. Some people feel such strong attachment to their belongings, it's painful to let go. For her sake and ours, if you see a meltdown start, please intervene. It's your call because you want a successful sale as much as we do. Crowding is another consideration. Our staff plus the customers add up to a lot of people moving around. It's a busy time. You know what I mean."

"Actually, I do. I'm a regular customer at these sales in Virginia, where I live."

"Then I don't have to explain."

Peggy jotted notes in every room upstairs, then started the main level in the downstairs study. Twenty minutes later, the three of them joined Grammy in the living room.

Peggy addressed Grammy. "You have many beautiful things here. If you choose our company, we'd suggest a three-day sale: Friday, Saturday and Sunday. This time of year is different from high season in Naples when we're flooded with tourists, but we'll alert local antique dealers north and south of us and some in Miami, Boca and West Palm. I think we'll have good success."

Jennifer smiled. "Your company's thoroughness has my attention."

"May I leave our contract and my card so I can answer any questions you have after I leave? We don't have much time, so please let me know by tomorrow, because I don't think we can organize a sale this size in less time."

Grammy stood. "Good presentation, Peggy, and with what we've learned about your company from other sources, I'm ready to sign now. What do you think, girls?"

"I'm in," said Jennifer.

"Yes," Becca agreed.

"Oh, I almost forgot, our company gives an estate sale this weekend nearby. Here's the information if you'd like to drop by. You'd get a feel for how we do things... to anticipate what's coming in two weeks."

Grammy smiled. "Good. We'll take a look. Peggy, I'm glad we're partners in this venture."

"One more thing," Peggy began. "We must unlock your doors for the sale. You understand that means strangers coming through your house. Are you okay with this?"

Peggy didn't know what to make of their stunned expressions.

Finally, Jennifer answered her. "We'll make it work." To herself she added, we have to.

CHAPTER 37

W hen Peggy left they sat down together in the kitchen.
Jennifer pointed to the calendar. "In thirty minutes
Joan Langley comes," she glanced at the clock, "at 4:30, to
finalize the Realtor phase. She'll put the house on the market here,
in three weeks." She tapped the date with her pencil point.

"Looks like everything's in place," Grammy acknowledged, her
voice tired. "How do we deal with Peggy's question about strangers
coming through?"

Becca looked thoughtful. "If we move to the hotel here,"
she pointed to the calendar date, "and if Max is around..." she
sidestepped knowing he was only after Grammy, "we'll all be
safe there. He doesn't recognize me or you, Mom. So one of us
could oversee the sale and the other stay with Gram. Thanks to the
deputy's mug shot and sketch, we could recognize this Max or his
girlfriend and call Goodwin if we see them."

Grammy stood. "You two work it out, I'm going to curl up
on the couch a few minutes before the Realtor gets here." She left
the kitchen.

Becca whispered, "Mom, maybe this Max has another angle.
We hope Goodwin's right, that he bragged just for an ego trip.
But what if he meant it? If he can't vent his revenge on Grammy
herself, might he still try to hurt her by destroying something
important to her?"

"For instance?"

"For instance damaging something in this house... or even the house itself — like burning it down."

Jennifer registered shock. "Becca, I hadn't considered this, but you're right. Let's ask Goodwin what he thinks." She checked her watch. "We have time to call him before Joan arrives." She dialed, pressing speaker so they both could listen, and explained their concerns. "Locked doors, the alarm system and wasp spray you say work for routine protection, but what about the estate sale... when the public wanders through the house?"

"Interesting twist. I'll think about this and get back to you. Gotta go." Goodwin ended the call.

"Let's not tell Grammy we're concerned," Jennifer sighed. "She'll just worry."

Becca nodded. "While you deal with the Realtor, I'll dash out to buy wasp spray. How many cans?"

"A dozen?"

"Got it."

The doorbell chimed. Instead of opening the door, Jennifer peered through the side glass to see their caller. "It's Joan. Before you go, Becca, please tell Grammy that Joan's here and we're coming to the living room to talk."

After negotiating the fee and explaining how to complete the sales contract closing from McLean, Joan answered their remaining questions, then stood to leave.

"If you like, I can schedule improvements after you leave. Painting the front door and sprucing-up the property outside add curb appeal. Selected touch-up painting and carpet cleaning inside are also smart, and of course, the kitchen needs painting now after the fire. I've already explained staging, but we may not need it. You'd pay for any of these services, but I'd give you cost estimates before hiring workmen. You could veto any you don't want. First impression is important for a buyer, and we want your lovely house to display its best face."

"Thank you, Joan," Grammy said.

When she left, the three sat down.

Jennifer sighed with relief and satisfaction. "Let's celebrate somewhere special tonight. We've hired everybody needed to complete the move. Only three weeks more. McLean, here we come."

"And I have good news," Becca announced. "I finished all the photos and e-mailed them to the family, explaining we need quick decisions. The movers could take north whatever they choose for distribution from Virginia. And Grammy, I found something I'd love to have... with your okay."

"What, dear?"

"Even though I'm at Mom and Dad's house now, once I get a job I'll look for my own apartment. I'd be honored to have a few of your beautiful crystal wine goblets. They're elegant and practical, and they'd remind me of you as they add your touch of class to my simple digs."

Grammy smiled. "It would be my honor. Show me which ones right now."

As they went to the dining room, Jennifer dialed Jason. "Hi, honey. You're driving home...? Have you dinner plans for tonight...? Good. Sounds like fun. Bet you thought you were up to speed about what's happening here because we talk every day. Wrong. There's yet another new wrinkle." She described the new Max threat. "At least we've hired everyone we need for the move and house sale. It's been a marathon, Jay. I can't wait to get home to you.... Yes, you're right, TGITCH. Thank God, It's The Cocktail Hour. Miss you, too, love. Bye for now."

She no sooner ended the call than she heard a crash in the next room. Was Max breaking in through a window?

Heart in her throat, she grabbed the wasp spray can Goodwin left and raced from the kitchen toward the dining room.

CHAPTER 38

G rammy and Becca stared at the shower of glass fragments, some sprinkled beneath the broken pane and others skittered around the dining room floor. Seeing Jennifer rush in with wasp spray at the ready, Becca pointed to the floor at Grammy's feet.

"A baseball?" Jennifer laughed with relief.

But Becca frowned. "Didn't you say they installed a safety system when you changed the locks? If it's turned on, why didn't the security alarm sound?"

"We installed one, all right," Grammy verified.

Jennifer remembered now that their chosen protection package didn't include everything. She winced, realizing Max could break the glass in any window and climb in undetected. She and Becca exchanged meaningful looks but neither wanted to worry Grammy. "System must be off," Jennifer said quickly, "because if it's on, an opened window triggers the alarm. Unless you press the main key pad to show the situation's under control, the security company automatically calls police."

Jen hoped her mother didn't catch the subtle difference between window-opening and window-breaking.

When the doorbell chimed, they hurried to look out a side window before opening it.

"This isn't Max, is it, Grammy?

Grammy looked and shook her head.

Becca continued. "I mean he doesn't look like the photo but if he dyed his hair…"

Jennifer opened the door. "Yes?"

"Hi. I'm George Bixby from that house across the street." He pointed. "This is my boy, Georgie. I was showing him how to bat but accidentally gave him a terrible example by hitting your window. My apologies for this inconvenience. Of course, I'll pay for the repair. Now if this ever should happen to you, Georgie, you'll know just what to do."

The boy, about eight years old, eyed them with interest.

Jennifer winked at the father. "Would you like to see your baseball?" The boy nodded. "Then let's all go to the dining room."

Seeing was believing for the boy. "Anybody can make a mistake, even a Dad," Jennifer continued, "but when you damage somebody else's property it's good manners to get it repaired." The boy nodded and eyed the window and glass shards as she handed him his ball.

Grammy shook George's hand. "Nice to meet a gentleman. There aren't enough around anymore."

George smiled, handing her his business card. "Just send me the repair bill. Rumor on the street is that you may move soon. True?"

"Yes, in about three weeks. Hate to leave my home and this neighborhood… and Florida's beauty and climate. But…time marches on," Grammy said, on the verge of tears.

Seeing this, Jennifer thanked them. "Good to meet you both."

Becca asked if the boy could have some candy. She exposed the end of a Hershey bar in her pocket. When the father nodded, she offered it to Georgie.

"By the way, do you have wasps in the yard?" They looked blank.

"…that can of wasp spray in your hand."

"Oh," Jennifer laughed. "Just…just in case we do."

"Bye, George and Georgie. Nice to meet you both," Grammy said. They closed the door.

"Becca, sorry to ask, but would you look up glass repair shops on your computer and make a few calls? I remember a TV ad for a company with 24-hour service. The sooner solved, the better. Meantime, I'll get the ladder and tape cardboard over the hole to keep bugs out and air conditioning in."

Grammy shook her head. "I've had about all I can take for one afternoon. I'll lie down a few minutes while you two decide where to eat dinner for our celebration tonight. Call me ten minutes before you're ready to go."

She went upstairs while Becca worked her smart phone and Jennifer made a list of likely places to eat. Becca scheduled the glass repair for 9:00 the next morning. Jennifer settled on a favorite restaurant, Bravo at Mercato, and made a reservation.

Becca looked thoughtful. "Mom, in a way we learned something important today."

Jennifer lifted a questioning eyebrow toward her daughter.

"Max can get into the house through a broken window at night. With no alarm, we won't know he's here until he appears in our bedrooms. He knows the house and where they are."

Jennifer nodded. "Glad you thought of that. Max may not know or care where you and I sleep, Becca, but he certainly knows Gram's in the master bedroom."

"...and she's the one he's after."

"We haven't heard back from Goodwin. Could wasp spray possibly offer enough protection?"

Becca frowned. "And how well does it work against a gun?"

CHAPTER 39

T he next morning, Jennifer checked garage and estate sales in the *Naples Daily News*. The classified section showed an area map dividing the sales into Bonita Springs, North Naples, Naples, South Naples and Marco Island.

She liked Golden Estate Sale's catchy ad for the event they'd visit first, but she also wanted info about others in the vicinity. Scrolling Craigslist, she found additional Naples listings.

Becca enjoyed these sales almost as much as Jennifer did, but had Grammy the stamina or motivation to attend any while downsizing her belongings? They couldn't leave her alone at home with Max on the loose. After critiquing Golden's sale with their own upcoming version in mind, Becca and Jen decided they'd stop the minute Grammy tired.

The glass repairman came on time and finished work quickly. Jennifer explained about the bill.

"You pay me," he made clear. "Then work it out with your neighbor however you want."

By ten o'clock, they locked the house and set off for sales. They nodded approvingly at Golden Estate Sales signs at intersections blocks away from the sale, with arrows pointing the correct direction. The large sign in front of the sale was an attention-getter. "I like their advertising," Becca said.

"Are you looking for anything in particular?" Grammy asked.

"Yes, I am," said Jennifer. "Something for Jason's birthday next month. I'll know it if I see it." Her bonding with the dragon she'd thought would make a good birthday gift seemed more like fusion. She didn't want to part with it, even within her same household. So she'd find Jason another gift. They reached the front stairs.

"Ready to go in, Mom?" Grammy nodded.

Inside the house, they saw like-items grouped together. China, silver, linens and crystal in the dining room, all kitchen cupboards open to display contents and the counters covered with bowls and pans. In the garage were tools, ladders, mops and seasonal decorations. Upstairs bedroom closets stood open with clothing and shoe prices listed on the door. Folded bed linens, curtains and pillows were stacked neatly on the beds. In the home office, half-full boxes of new file folders, envelopes, paper clips and other supplies covered the desktop and surrounding shelving.

In one of the bedrooms, Grammy exclaimed, "Oh look. Here's a piece of Blue Danube china I always liked: the biscuit jar. Didn't I give my Blue Danube china to you some years ago, Jen?"

"You did, and I use it every day. It always reminds me of you and happy times around the table when you used it as I grew up. I love it."

Becca picked up the piece Grammy had admired. "A biscuit jar?"

"Yes," Grammy explained. "The English call our cookies 'biscuits,' although theirs are usually smaller. But you could store other things here or even remove the top to use it as a vase."

As they moved among the rooms, Jennifer whispered. "Notice how they've put one of their people in each room to deter shoplifting?"

Grammy scoffed, "Why would anybody steal at a sale where everything's already a bargain?"

"In psychology, we learned some people don't even need what they take," Becca said. "It's the addictive thrill of stealing; outsmarting the system, breaking rules and feeling clever — assuming they get away with it, of course."

Grammy examined a figurine. "I think Golden does a great job. I'm glad we chose them."

They headed for the car, Becca catching up behind them. "Shall we visit some more sales today?"

"Don't think I will," Grammy said, "I shouldn't buy anything and we have so much to do at home preparing for the move."

Jennifer pulled the Mercedes into the garage, lowering the door as they went inside.

Becca hurried to her laptop. "Here are responses to the inventory pictures I e-mailed yesterday. Do you want to decide about these family requests, Grammy?" At her grandmother's nod, Becca added, "I'll print them out. Glad your printer works wirelessly."

"Yes, and I'm glad I remembered the password!" Grammy grinned and turned to her daughter. "Becca chose some of the goblets, Jen. Is there something you'd like?"

"Mom, the beautiful things you've collected over the years are all treasures to me because I remember them from childhood. Even when you moved here, you brought along most paintings and furniture. If I feel an emotional attachment to them, I know yours is even stronger."

"I want to show you something." Grammy pulled a box from a drawer in an end table. "There are the pictures I meant to put in albums. Each one is small freeze-frame of a moment in my life or of the ones I love." They each took a handful to look through, exclaiming over people and places in each scene."

"Mom, why not take all these with you? We haven't time now, but in Virginia, we can group them by year and make books of them. Wouldn't that be fun?"

"Yes, it would, dear. Because these and everything here in my home are proof...."

Becca and Jennifer exchanged questioning looks.

"Proof?" Becca raised her hands, palms up.

"Proof my life wasn't just a dream."

CHAPTER 40

The doorbell chimed. They were careful to peek out the window before opening the door.

"Georgie. How nice of you to visit." Grammy said.

"Could I...could I please look at the broken window again?"

"Of course. Come in." They led him to the dining room and Grammy eased into one of the chairs while the boy studied the floor under the window and the window itself.

"Those broken pieces...how did you connect them together and get them back up there?"

Becca explained, "We swept up the broken pieces and threw them away. Then we called a glass repairman to install a brand new window pane."

The boy processed this chain of events.

"I play third base."

Becca grinned. "And I used to play first base."

The boy smiled acknowledgment of this unexpected kinship. "Do you...have any more of that candy?"

"I do." Becca produced a Hershey bar from her pocket. "Do you like chocolate?"

"My favorite."

"Mine, too — another thing we have in common besides baseball."

Georgie grinned.

Jennifer had a sudden idea. "Georgie, do you play outdoors a lot now that it's summer vacation?" He nodded. "If you ever see a bad man on our street or in our yard, would you please come to tell us right away?"

The boy looked doubtful. "What does a bad man look like?"

She handed him Goodwin's mug shot of Max. "Like this."

The boy appeared confused. "He looks like a regular man. What makes him a bad man?"

"He's a bad man because he was so mean to Grammy she had to go to the hospital. She told the police and they arrested him but getting arrested made him really mad. Then they took him to jail, which made him even madder. *But* he escaped from jail. Now he wants to hurt Grammy again. If he comes near our house, do you understand why we must call police right away to arrest him and take him back to jail?"

"Yes, I get it. Would he...ring your doorbell?"

"We think he'd sneak around the house and find a bad way to get inside. He's a criminal."

"What's a criminal?"

"A bad man who does crimes like stealing, cheating, hurting people and being cruel to nice old ladies like Grammy."

"Oh." The boy headed for the front door. "Thanks for the candy."

Grammy laughed. "Do you think he understood a word you said?"

The phone rang and Grammy put it on speaker. "Deputy Goodwin here. Any sign of Roderick?"

"No," Grammy answered.

Jennifer turned away and lowered her voice, hoping Grammy couldn't hear. "But we learned our security system doesn't respond to broken panes, which is the way he'd likely break into our house. We're not feeling very secure with only wasp spray for protection."

"Yeah, well I can't spare anybody right now to stay there. Does your community do Neighborhood Watch? If so, you could at least alert them."

"I'll look into it."

"Meantime," Goodwin continued, "keep your doors and windows locked and your car parked inside the garage. Call me with any news."

They agreed.

Grammy sat down with a sigh. "Jen, don't we have George Bixby's business card? What if you took the repair bill to his house and asked if he knows about a neighborhood watch? I've become rather isolated now that I'm older, but they're a young family and should know."

"Okay. While I do, Becca, why don't you and Gram organize one of the rooms for movers, making sure go/stay signs are on every item? The packers may work in several rooms at the same time, so we want them to be clear about what to do. Lock the door after me."

Jennifer found the Bixby house. George answered the door. "Nice to see you. Please come in."

Jennifer did, producing the repair bill. "Thank you again for taking responsibility. I have five children and respect the positive lesson you showed your son."

"Glad to do it and, again, sorry about the window."

"Does this community have a neighborhood watch?"

"Not that I know. Some discussion about it once but I think nothing came of it. Why?"

"Have you a few minutes for me to explain?"

"Sure. Have a seat."

Jennifer told a short version of Max's cruelty to her mother, his criminal behavior pattern and the new threat he posed. "Here's his picture."

George considered the situation. "Not the kind of man we'd want around here. Look, why don't I make a flyer with his picture and text like, 'Max Roderick wanted by police. Possibly targeting this neighborhood. Call 911 if you see this man.' My family would willingly knock on doors and hand out the flyers on this street. As a side benefit, if neighbors draw together in a common cause, this might even lead to formation of an official Neighborhood Watch. Good could come from this bad situation."

"Thanks, George, for this great idea. We'll move north in another two weeks, but until then this flyer could be very important."

"Look, I work in computer graphics. If you let me copy this mug shot right now, I can create a flyer for you to proof before I print and distribute it. Is a particular detective working on this case?"

"Deputy Cliff Goodwin. I know his phone number by heart."

George wrote it down.

Jennifer rose to go while George fished out his wallet and removed several bills. "This is for the window repair."

"Thank you. Actually, some good came from that, too. We learned of a security system flaw at the very time we need to know where the house is vulnerable." She explained the window situation.

She left and crossed the street, inadvertently peering around, half expecting Max to leap from behind a bush. This was no way to live.

As she put lunch on the table, the doorbell chimed. Peering out first, she opened the door for George. "How does this look?" Below Max's picture the flyer read:

Max Roderick
WANTED BY COLLIER COUNTY SHERIFF'S OFFICE
Possibly targeting our Pinewood Neighborhood
If you see this man, call Deputy Goodwin
at 239-801-8688 or 911

"Perfect." She showed it to Grammy and Becca, who agreed.

"Please keep this copy."

"Thank you very much, George."

"This is what neighbors are for."

As he left, Goodwin's car pulled in front of the house. The deputy shuffled up the front steps.

Inside, Jennifer showed him the flyer. "Good idea and timely, too."

"Timely...?"

"Yeah," he continued. "New development. In interrogating the cellmate further, we learned your mother's not the only one Roderick's afraid could ID him and his girlfriend. Also on his list is your beautician friend, Chelsea."

Chelsea mentioned these two becoming an item, Jennifer remembered. If so, for Goodwin this was no longer just part of his routine job. Now he took this personally.

CHAPTER 41

From Saturday through Wednesday, Grammy, Jennifer and Becca prepared for the movers, adding items requested by family members to the "take" category. Finalizing choices became crucial.

More important, no sign of Max. Had he changed his mind about "getting" Grammy? Moved with his girlfriend across country to start over? Focused revenge on Chelsea instead of Grammy?

Becca confided, "Mom, as each day passes quietly, I feel less anxious about Max."

"Me too, but the opposite could also be true." At Becca's puzzled expression, she explained, "This isn't to scare you, honey, but to keep us both alert. If Max hopes to lull us into a false sense of safety, we might get careless about security. And if Grammy's still in his sights and he hasn't struck yet, then we should be even warier." When her mother walked in, she changed the subject. "Grammy, you've been a trouper through all this. With Becca's excellent photos, soon you can remember how every room looked by flipping through her pictures."

"Which I'll put in an album so they're easy to see and store in your fancy new apartment," Becca promised.

"Have we overlooked anything before the movers come early tomorrow?" No one spoke. "Then why don't we walk through one last time, room by room?"

They followed Grammy into the kitchen. "What about this ceramic chicken and rooster set?" Becca asked, realizing they'd missed categorizing something obvious.

Grammy sank into a chair. "This is why it's hard to give things up. I'm the steward for these pieces of the past. These were my grandmother's," Grammy said wistfully. "Her farmer husband encouraged her to start her own small chicken business — exciting for a woman back then. After producing chickens and eggs for the family table, he said any remaining profit became her own money. These ceramic figures symbolized her independence, and she treasured them for sixty years, into her eighties. Then they sat in my mother's kitchen another twenty and in mine for thirty. Letting them go feels like betraying a piece of family history placed in my care. See why I cling to things others consider dust catchers?"

"Yes, we do." Jennifer put a loving arm around Grammy's shoulder as they walked toward the lanai. "Now this room should be easy. Virginia apartments might have outdoor balconies, but this is indoor furniture. Let it go?"

Grammy nodded and they moved to the study. "Dad's desk is too big for a small apartment," she decided. "I'll take the file cabinets because I haven't time to sort through them now. I'll need a place to keep my papers. Most books are for the sale, except for this pile.

They studied contents of the remaining rooms, ending up in the master bedroom.

"Have you separated take-and-leave clothes, Mom?" Jennifer called from the walk-in closet.

"Yes, but I haven't pinned signs on them for the packers."

"Also take-and-leave shoes. I'm getting rid of all my hats and most purses. They're old styles now."

"'Vintage,' Grammy, not 'old.'" Becca giggled. "Vintage shops sell the very things you're discarding. Some older fashions are even making a comeback, like platform shoes."

"Did you go through every purse to make sure nothing's inside?" Jennifer asked. "No? Why don't we all do that now?"

They divided the purses and found some empty, one with a grocery list, another a program from the Naples Philharmonic and another with a $20 bill. Grammy unzipped a zippered pouch in the last purse and pulled something out. Unfolding it, they exclaimed over three $100 bills.

"Didn't Peggy Perkins recommend checking clothes pockets, too?" Becca reminded. Together they did so, finding handkerchiefs, miscellanea and more paper money.

Stacking the purged purses, Jennifer looked at the curtains and bedspread. "Do you want these or shall we have some GT fun fixing up your new place?"

Becca laughed. "You did Girls Together? So *that's* how it started."

Grammy smiled at the memory.

Jennifer's gaze traveled around the room. "Guess we're finished in here."

Suddenly Grammy gave a sharp intake of breath. "Good grief, I almost forgot—the safe!"

CHAPTER 42

G rammy's hand flew to her mouth. Of all the important things to take, the safe topped the list.

"Becca, help me pull this bookcase away from the wall while Grammy gets the combination. When the safe's empty, should we leave the combination with Joan Langley for the new owner?"

"Makes sense. Here." Grammy handed Jennifer the paper, "Would you please see she gets it?"

"I'll put it back in the file for now. Nobody should have this combination until we empty the safe. Okay if I e-mail it to her after the move?"

Nervous, Grammy ran the combination twice before the safe's door swung open. Anticipation mounted as Jennifer and Becca waited for revelations within.

First, Grammy lifted out two accordion files of papers. Then a shoebox-size container covered in quilted material. And a wooden chest about the same size. Then a cloth bag with a drawstring top. And papers folded together in a plastic newspaper sleeve. Last, she removed a large box. "Becca, would you please kneel down to make sure the safe's empty?" Becca did.

"Nothing left. Wait...in the back are a bunch of loose...," she drew them out and handed them to Grammy, "...silver dollars?"

"Yes, they are. Frankly, I've forgotten what's here." Grammy looked bewildered.

"How about spreading everything on the bed? Do you prefer to look at these things privately?"

"No, I think we should all look together." She put aside the drawstring bag. "Those are papers from the safety deposit box. Let's do them last."

She opened the quilted box and gently poured the contents on the coverlet. Diamonds flashed and gold twinkled in the light as earrings, bracelets, necklaces and other jewelry tumbled out. "The good jewelry Max didn't get." She moved the pieces around. "So beautiful. Some I haven't worn for thirty years or more. A shame, when keeping the pieces safe seems more important than enjoying them every day."

"Has each one a story?"

"Oh, yes. This locket belonged to my mother." She opened it, revealing two photos, one of Grammy as a toddler and one of her father. "She said we were her two most precious possessions." As they ooh-ed, she continued, "Your father gave me this bracelet for an anniversary — funny, I can't remember which one. And check the engraving on the back of this gold watch, a wedding present to my father from my mother. See the date and their names?" She began putting them back in the box. "When we get to Virginia, we'll have time to look at them all. Maybe you or your girls would like to have some of them. We'll see."

Next, she opened the cloth bag. Out tumbled a worn, stuffed teddy bear with only eye sockets left, the eyes long gone. Beside it lay a tattered bunny, with only stitching where eyes once attached. Next to the animals lay a cluster of lead soldiers and a bronzed toddler shoe made into a bookend. "These were your father's when he was a boy. His mother gave them to him shortly before she died. Your daddy died at eighty-four so adding the five years since then, these are close to ninety years old." She gently returned them to the bag.

She pulled forward a shoebox-size wooden chest secured with a padlock, and studied it. "I don't remember this." She shook it but heard no sound within.

"Have you the key, Gram?" Becca fingered the lock.

At Grammy's bewildered look, Jennifer suggested gently, "Maybe inside a vase or taped under a lamp or in a costume jewelry drawer?"

As Grammy circled the room, investigating possible hiding places, Jennifer watched, intending to check those same places later for clues to more hidden belongings before the estate sale closed the door to that opportunity.

Empty-handed and dismayed, Grammy ventured. "Could we force it open without a key?"

Becca studied the lock. "Yes, but it'll probably ruin the chest. Should I try?" At Grammy's nod, Becca jumped up. "Tools in the garage?" Grammy nodded again. "I'll be right back."

When Becca left, Grammy spoke to Jennifer in a conspiratorial voice. "After your father died, I re-discovered many single women friends who I hadn't spent much time with when I was part of a 'couple.' My widow friends and I, especially those of us who took care of our husbands during their final illness, found we enjoyed the self-indulgence of living alone instead of always considering our husband's tastes and needs. We looked for happiness as singles because we agreed most marriageable men wanted a nurse or a purse for their old age."

Jennifer laughed. "Are you serious? Someone to care for them or support them?"

"Very serious. But I...after a while, I realized I missed a man's companionship. At a party one night, I met someone I liked. We became...friends...then very close friends for several years. He lived in Miami but preferred the Gulf Coast and especially Naples. So he visited here regularly. He explained his job with the FBI involved travel and danger, so if he disappeared one day for good, I must assume he'd died in the line of duty. Somehow, his mystery and secrecy added to the thrill of our friendship. He asked me to keep this box for him in my safe and if ever he failed to return, the contents belonged to me. To please him, I agreed. Two years ago, he disappeared, leaving me heart-broken for the second time. First losing your Dad and then...him." She sniffled into a hankie.

Stunned at this news, Jennifer comforted her mother before asking, "What was his name?"

"Anthony Venuti." Her voice quavered as tears rolled down her cheeks. "Although his friends called him 'Big T.' He...he was a charming gentleman. He had a warm sense of humor and lovely manners. He dressed well, liked the finest food and wine, enjoyed opera, had access to yachts and private planes and always plenty of money. For example, we often flew to the Florida Keys for dinner. But what appealed to me most was his interest in me." Now she wept openly.

Becca returned, brandishing pliers and a screwdriver. But coming upon this scene, she hesitated. "Everything...all right here?"

"Grammy's just sad for a minute," Jennifer explained. "Moving's tough."

Accepting this, Becca busied herself with the tools. "I'll try not to ruin the chest, but you see the problem."

Grammy nodded. After several attempts, Becca pried the hasp from the box and the lock with it. She handed the chest to Grammy, who gave Jennifer a deep look before opening the lid.

They gasped.

CHAPTER 43

Inside the chest, flush with the top, lay five stacks of paper money. The top bills in each stack read $500 and $1,000, each circled with rubber bands. Grammy lifted out the top layer of each stack, revealing more packs of bills beneath and more under those. Finally, she emptied the chest.

They stared at the money piles on the bed, some packs thicker than others. "Wow," Becca marveled. "Wow, again. Should we... count it? I could get post-it notes and pens to put the amount on each stack under the rubber band," Becca offered.

"Yes," Grammy whispered.

"Do you think it's real or maybe counterfeit?"

"Let's ask for change for one of them at a bank tomorrow to see what we learn."

"Would they arrest us if it's fake?" They exchanged uncertain looks.

After counting, an hour later they put the money back into the chest and closed the lid. "It's a fortune, Grammy. How could you not remember it's here?" Becca probed.

"Perhaps my father put it here without telling her," Jennifer invented, to cover the true Big T story. "In any event, let's put it back in the chest and into the safe for now."

Then they considered the remaining items. "What's in this case, Gram?" Becca handed it to her. Grammy opened the clasp and lifted the lid to display a matched pair of old dueling pistols.

Jennifer lifted one, turning it this way and that. "Do these have a story?"

"Not that I remember, but they look old and probably valuable to a collector. Maybe some of those papers explain, but we can read them any time. Let's finish this job."

"Just this quilted box left." Becca pushed it across the bed to Grammy.

"Only your father and I used the safe, so if I didn't put this there, he must have. What do you suppose he's hidden inside...?" She shook the box. Rattling sounds confirmed loose contents.

Grammy poured it out onto the bed: aged coins, a rusty belt buckle, old insignia, a worn bible with a bullet in the center, a knife, a daguerreotype photo, mini-balls, old uniform buttons, some yellowed papers and a wad of modern paper currency.

"Grammy," Becca exclaimed. "This is better than Christmas. I've never seen so much money in one place except a casino."

"These look like Civil War relics." Jennifer touched the items on the coverlet before picking up the bible. Only the cover barely opened because of the bullet wedged inside, but the date on the first page inside read "June 12, 1864." She showed it to the others.

Just then, the doorbell chimed. They exchanged who-could-that-be? looks.

Becca stuffed the Civil War items back into their container. "If you two put this stuff back and lock the safe, I'll answer the door. Hearing her feet pounding down the stairs, they finished this task and hurried downstairs after her.

CHAPTER 44

In the foyer responding to the doorbell, Becca performed the now-standard window check before opening the door.

"Hello, Georgie. How are you today?"

"I'm okay. He's here."

"Who's here?"

"The bad man in your picture."

"You mean," Becca grabbed the mug shot from the foyer credenza, "this man?"

Georgie nodded.

Jennifer knelt down to Georgie's eye level. "Where?"

Georgie pointed. "Up the street that way. He walked along the other side of the street, past my house, but he looked at your house the whole time."

Becca grabbed the photo. "He looked just like this picture, Georgie? You're sure?"

"That's him, except for the hair. It's brown now."

"Good work, Georgie." Becca handed him a Reese Cup from her pocket. "You're a detective. Tell us what he does and where he goes whenever he's nearby. Okay?"

Georgie grinned and nodded.

As Jennifer and Grammy reached the doorway, Becca stopped Georgie from popping the candy into his mouth. "Would you please tell them what you just told me, Georgie?"

He did and then backed out across the porch, his mouth full of peanut butter and chocolate.

Becca closed the door. "Do you think he really saw Max?"

Grammy looked uncomfortable. "How can we be sure? He's just a little tyke with only a picture to go on. The hair color change seems doubtful. Or is that wishful thinking?"

"Let's tell Deputy Goodwin what's happened." Jennifer dialed her phone. "Hello, Deputy?" She described the situation.

"How old is the kid?"

"Maybe seven...eight?"

"Think he's fabricating for chocolate? Kids' imaginations can get pretty wild for a tasty payoff."

Jennifer considered this. "We didn't see the man, so we don't know if it's Max with a dye job, or someone else, or if Georgie invented the story."

"I'll send someone over to look around. Meantime, be sure you've locked your doors and windows and turn on the security system even though you're inside and it's daytime. Do it day and night."

"Movers come tomorrow morning at eight. I don't see how we can secure the house while they wander in and out."

"Narrow their activity to one door and lock everything else. This is only a child's alleged sighting, but no harm in sensible precautions."

The three women gathered their personal items in an upstairs bedroom's empty closet and put a "Not for the Move" sign on the door. "And what better place for the valuables than in the safe while the movers work?" Becca asked.

"Should we park the Mercedes outside on the street in case they need to get bigger items to the moving van through the garage?" Grammy wondered.

"Good idea. We'll do that first thing tomorrow morning. And shouldn't we offer the movers donuts and coffee?"

Becca grinned. "I'll get donuts. Maybe they have chocolate ones."

"You and your chocolate," Grammy clucked. "Where do those calories go? You stay so slim."

Jennifer tapped her calendar. "Tomorrow's your regular beauty shop day, Mom. You've prepared for the movers, so Becca and I can handle the situation for that hour you're away. I could drop you off and..."

Grammy looked concerned. "You'll stay with me, won't you, Jen? With Max on the loose I...I feel uncomfortable outside the house. After what he's already done to me, I'm *scared*."

"Well...sure, Mom, if Becca will supervise the movers. Do you mind, Becca?"

"No problem."

"And could you pick up a quickie dinner for us tonight while you're getting donuts at the grocery? Their deli has some good ready-made choices."

Jennifer trudged upstairs feeling worn out. She felt the final responsibility for every decision resting on her shoulders. Had she forgotten anything? Orchestrating her mother's move was enough of a challenge without the added threat of Max–*if* Max was a threat. Not knowing what to expect next created its own nerve-wracking tension for her.

And then she heard the scream...

CHAPTER 45

Grabbing wasp spray, she careened down the stairs toward the shriek, unsure whether the terrified cry came from Grammy or Becca.

"Where are you?" she shouted, reaching the bottom step.

"In the garage. Hurry!" Grammy called.

Uncapping the wasp spray, Jennifer ran in that direction. "What is it?" she huffed from exertion.

"There," Grammy said in tremulous voice, pointing to Becca, who shrank in horror against the far wall, cornered by a four-foot-long snake, its upper body coiled in strike position.

"Don't move, Becca," Jennifer cried. "He's attracted to motion."

Jennifer quickly pressed the garage door-open button. The snake's head moved at the mechanical sound the rising door made. When she shook the aerosol can in her hand, the snake's head snapped its gaze again toward her.

"Grammy," Jennifer directed, "lift that beach ball near you and roll it toward the snake. Hurry!"

Reacting to the rolling ball moving toward it, the snake struck, plunging its fangs into the plastic sphere. The deflating ball hissed as its air escaped. Apparently satisfied at dispatching this threat, the snake slithered under the car and out the open garage door. When it reached the driveway, Jennifer quickly pressed the door close-button.

Becca's eyes, wide with panic, squinted shut as she whimpered, "I can't go to the grocery now." She ran into the house, sobbing.

Grammy shivered. "How...how do you think that thing got into the garage? The car door was closed, but could someone have left the people door ajar? It opens right into the garden..."

"If snakes can climb into airplane wheel wells," Jen said, "survive the flight and later drop onto the tarmac of another continent when the plane lands, they could curl up in a car's wheel well and later drop onto the garage floor." She hurried to the kitchen, where her daughter still trembled. "There, there...it's gone now, Becca. Where did you get this fear of snakes, honey?"

She spoke through sobs. "Remember the snake Mike had, the one you made him keep outside? One day I found the box inside, so I opened it and the snake jumped out and bit me. He said it was only a garden snake, but it hurt a lot. I wanted to tell you but Mike made me promise not to since he knew he'd get in trouble for having it in the house. He gave me three chocolate bars if I promised to keep it a secret. But I never forgot what happened, and ever since then snakes terrify me."

Jennifer shook her head. "And I thought I knew everything about you children growing up."

Grammy stood. "I have a set of books about Florida in the study. I think one volume covers local snakes. Shall we try to identify it? Maybe it's harmless."

"Harmless ones can still bite," Becca mumbled.

Grammy retrieved the Florida snake book, riffling across the pages as she did. "Was it this one?" She passed the book to her daughter.

Jennifer took the book and immediately saw a picture of their snake. "Eastern diamondback rattlesnake," she read silently and skimmed the remaining text. "Largest venomous snake in North America; bites intensely painful and can be fatal to humans; range North Carolina, Georgia, Alabama, Mississippi, Louisiana and throughout Florida. Excellent swimmers. As construction diminishes their habitat, they can be found in parking lots, golf courses and residential gardens."

"Still looking," she pretended, continuing her silent reading, trying to maintain a neutral expression as she absorbed the frightening facts: most dangerous venomous snake in North America; extremely potent venom delivered in a dose four times the amount needed to kill a person; venom simultaneously attacks prey's nervous system and its blood and tissues; purpose of the venom is to kill and partially digest prey with enzymes. Symptoms:

severe pain at the bite site, intense internal pain, bleeding from the mouth, hypotension, weak pulse, swelling and discoloration.

Jennifer drew a deep breath, glanced toward Becca and snapped the book shut. "Nope, don't see our snake in here," she said, slipping the volume into her purse.

"I don't even want to look at the pictures to find it," Becca moaned.

"Well, you survived that adventure just fine, Becca." Jennifer picked up her purse. "Look, I'll dash to the grocery, get dinner and we'll have a quiet meal here. See you in half an hour."

To distract her daughter from the garage confrontation, she asked Becca as she left, "Would you mind setting the table while I'm gone? Maybe something festive?"

As she drove to Publix, Jennifer shuddered, realizing how close Becca had come to being attacked by the deadly snake.

Her cellphone rang. "Oh, Jen," Mary Ann's voice came through the speaker, "I just had to let you know my good news."

"Hi, neighbor. What's happening?"

Mary Ann squealed. "Charlie asked me to marry him and I said 'yes.'" She squealed again. "It's so exciting and wonderful and improbable. I just had to let you know."

"I hear how happy you sound and I have to agree, this is amazing news. But are you...are you really sure? Not just swept off your feet by a schoolgirl crush? I mean, marriage is a huge step."

"Oh, yes. It's the real thing, all right. Yet only a few months ago I'd never have dreamed it could or would happen to me. And there's another side to it, Jen. Older women outnumber older men, and he's a very eligible, attractive guy. If I don't get him while I can, somebody else will snatch him."

Uneasy at this sense of urgency, Jennifer hesitated. "Do you know much about him?"

"Well, I told you he's from England so I haven't met his friends or family. But he's the one I'm marrying, not them."

"Have you set a date?"

"Not yet, but I hope very soon. At my age, what's the point in waiting around? Every moment of life is valuable now that we're older and have less time left. I don't want to miss a minute of sharing it with him."

"Really good to hear you so happy, Mary Ann. Eager to meet him."

"When do you return from Florida?"

"Not exactly sure. Probably two, maybe three weeks."

"Is everything okay?"

Jennifer grimaced. She could take hours answering that question. Instead she said, "I'm bringing my mother back to McLean. She'll rent the Donnegans' house a few months until we find a senior residence she likes."

"Sounds like a good plan. Let's go out together as soon as you get back. I can't believe you haven't even met him."

Jennifer turned into the grocery store's parking lot. "It's a date, then. Bye, Mary Ann."

"Bye, Jen."

Jennifer wondered why she didn't share Mary Ann's unbridled excitement. She certainly wanted her friend to find and enjoy happiness. Was it because she'd just learned her own mother endured some frightening scenes in her own life caused by a man she hardly knew?

CHAPTER 46

After finishing the dinner Jennifer brought home, Grammy sighed. "Are you two as tired as I am?"

Becca's usual cheery face still looked somber. "I still don't feel good after the snake. I'll just crash here on the couch tonight to get my groove back." Seeing concern on her mother's face, she added defensively. "I'm not a freak, you know. Lots of people have Ophidiophobia. Fear of snakes. We studied phobias in psychology at college. If you have one, for you it's real."

Grammy patted her shoulder. "And a reasonable fear it is, especially after your childhood experience. Most of us don't know bad snakes from good ones, so avoiding them all's a safe solution."

Jennifer changed the subject. "I'm exhausted, too. Let's turn in early." Like Becca, she wanted to push aside the day's urgencies and shelter her mind.

"Night, Becca." They said, going upstairs.

Jennifer climbed into bed, turned out the light, lay in the dark and thought about her father. In her early life and teens when she lived at home, he played an important daily role in her life. But once she left for Virginia Tech and after graduation, launched a life on her own, he and her mother faded to fringe players—people she loved but understood from a child's view rather than as adult friends. A parent's job is arming his child with the tools to live a life independent from them. Wasn't that exactly what she and Jason tried to do with their brood? Wasn't it natural, then, that finding her own parents less primary in her life only meant her folks had done their job correctly?

Still, she wondered about the artifacts her dad had saved in the quilted box. What made them important enough to him to keep and store in the safe? How had each item drawn him strongly enough to salt it away, yet tell no one?

Reaching for another Mosby book by her bed, she held it, feeling closer to her father than she had in years. This Civil War mystique seduced so many. But what had pulled him into its vortex? Too late to ask him now.

She noticed the dragon watching her. "I'll bet you know the answers," she told him as she turned off the light and snuggled beneath the covers. Closing her eyes in the dark, she gradually let go of all worldly connections. Her weary body finally surrendered to sleep, but her mind drifted into another vivid scene...

The two notched pine trees. The landmarks fit Mosby's description. But before unearthing the treasure, Corporal Birdsong wanted assurance he couldn't be seen from the road in daytime. Satisfied, he dug out the two bags and experimented with different ways of roping them onto his horse.

Bulky and heavy, they'd made awkward cargo. Removing the bags from his saddle, he mounded dried leaves over them and set out into the woods to find a glen with grass and a creek for Blackie. His journey's success depended upon his mount's survival.

Despite excitement at completing the first important step in his assignment, he slept as best he could during the day and traveled north two more nights with his burden. But as he reached Old Dominion Road, two Union soldiers came unexpectedly around a bend in the road from the opposite direction, one on a limping mount. Despite the dark night, he hadn't had time to take cover.

His raincoat covered his uniform and the tops of the bags. Who did they think he was? What did they want from him? They hailed him as their horses met on the road. "I'm Lt. Wilson. My sergeant's horse pulled up lame and I need yours." He eyed Blackie, appraising the large, superior animal. The soldiers pulled out their pistols, aiming at Birdsong. "Dismount," the lieutenant ordered.

Birdsong couldn't allow this, but with a gun muzzle already pointed at him he couldn't shoot his way out. Then two things happened instantaneously. Birdsong threw his canteen into the air, both Union soldiers reflexively shot at it while Birdsong dug his spurs into Blackie's flanks. The animal careened away at a gallop, taking the soldiers by such surprise they needed a few moments to process what had happened and begin chase. Needing this head start, Birdsong headed Blackie toward the nearest woods, aware the lieutenant would follow. Because his large horse had longer strides than the lieutenant's, Blackie outran him at the start, but Birdsong knew his cargo's weight would quickly diminish that lead. Thus, he hadn't the speed or mobility to escape on horseback.

Using guerilla tactics, Birdsong dodged and feinted after plunging into the woods. Riding headlong in a forest at night risked trauma from low hanging branches and impediments in the path, but he crouched low in the saddle, head down, trusting Blackie to find a way through the trees, up hills and across streams. He felt himself tiring and knew Blackie's stamina ebbed from racing full-tilt with a heavy load.

In the darkness, he pulled one last trick. He reined in so sharply, Blackie rose on his hind legs. In one swift motion, Birdsong pulled the slipknot releasing both bags, slid from his horse and whacked his mount on the rump.

"Go, Blackie." Hearing the command and relieved of the weight, the energized animal sped away with new zeal, the lieutenant racing after in close pursuit.

When the galloping hoofbeats distanced into silence, normal night sounds returned to the place where Birdsong fell. His heart pounded with exertion, fear of capture and frustration at his unfulfilled task. He fumbled in complete darkness to find and gather the bags then cover them with leaves. He sat beside them.

Lost, with no food or water and without his beloved horse – so critical to this mission's success – he lay miserably on the cold ground, fighting physical and mental exhaustion. He covered himself with leaves, hoping for some warmth in the frosty spring night. Despite his desire to remain alert, he drifted into heavy sleep.

He awoke suddenly in pre-dawn's pale light. Had he dozed despite his resolve to stay awake? Not moving, he listened intently, sifting natural woodland sounds from those of humans or their pursuit. He stared up through tree branches at the wonder of the wakening dawn above him as pastel colors painted the clouds with shades of pink across the sky's blue backdrop. His poet's soul struggled with the jarring coexistence of nature's magnificent wonders vis-a-vis the stupefying horror of war.

Listening intently, he heard no sound suggesting danger. He stretched and peered around. As the morning light increased, he saw for the first time where he'd landed – near the stone foundation wall of an unfinished building.

No sign of Blackie. This created a major problem – not only had he lost his transportation but also his rifle and the saddlebag with his remaining food. His pistols remained holstered to his body, but their short range didn't match a rifle's reach, needed to bring down game if he were to survive in the woods.

He whistled once, not risking a second attempt in case enemy ears caught the sound. If Blackie were within earshot, he'd come. If heard by an enemy soldier, one whistle might invite misinterpretation, but two whistles left no doubt. So he fell silent, surveying his immediate surroundings.

He saw a workbench, presumably where this house builder organized his plans and materials for construction. But no tools. In these uncertain times, hammers and nails became scarce, like every other commodity. What careful workmen would leave behind anything worth stealing? Quietly, he moved away from the foundation walls.

Beside the ashes of an old fire, a pale, limp rag drooped from a six-foot-tall pole firmly stuck in the ground and, beneath it, stood a bucket and two empty wooden vegetable crates. He examined the bucket. Reasonably clean, it would hold water if he found a stream. He studied the pole's cloth – plain weathered cotton. Was this a surrender scene? Had Union troops come upon this workman and captured him, his food and supplies? Did that explain the absence of tools?

Birdsong didn't know which army dominated this area at the moment. The Union soldier chasing him last night forced him into enough evasive maneuvers to disorient him. The sun's direction would offer clues later this morning, and he'd scout the area on foot for more, avoiding enemies while cautiously seeking friends. He'd return quickest to the Confederate cause by eluding capture. Lucky prisoners of war might be exchanged, but the unlucky were hanged or sent to a formidable Union prison.

Not only his own fate but that of his cargo depended upon correct decisions now.

He needed to eat to survive and fight, never mind find another horse to complete his mission. Only then could he get Mosby's treasure bags to their destination. Yet even that seemed problematic, since Union soldiers roaming everywhere had turned even harsher toward Virginians. He recognized the serious risk attempting to ride through more populated areas and towns with the conspicuous bags only partially hidden by his rain poncho. He decided to hide the treasure and go himself to the safe house to get help for this last phase.

Confirming where he'd stashed the bags last night, he wouldn't move them until he devised a better hiding place. He picked up the wooden crates and walked around the foundation, destined to become a cellar for the house built above it. The builder had already tamped dirt tight against the rectangle on three and a half sides. If Birdsong hid the bags against the outer foundation's stones and covered them, he'd complete the foundation's earthen support. With that phase of building completed, no one would undo finished work, thus leaving the treasure safe until he and other trusted Rebs rescued it.

He pulled the cloth from the pole, tore off a fourth of it and spread the piece open on the worktable before stuffing the remaining cloth inside his coat. Removing a rectangular pencil stub from his pocket, he whittled at the point with his knife before scratching an experimental mark on a corner of the cloth.

He could make this work.

Unlike many Confederate soldiers, Birdsong read and wrote well. His mother, a teacher, had educated her children at home since they lived too far from a school.

He licked the end of the pencil and wrote, "These items were looted from Virginia families by Union Gen. Stoughton, but recaptured at Fairfax Courthouse on March 9, 1863. Capt. J. S. Mosby orders you to deliver them to Gen. Robert E. Lee for return to their rightful owners."

He re-read what he'd written, folded the cloth and placed it inside one of the bags holding the golden goblets, silver trays, precious jewelry and other valuables. He put Mosby's knife, initialed JSM, on top of the second bag. Then he maneuvered a bag inside each wooden crate and pushed them flush against the earth-free base outside the uncovered foundation wall.

Scouting the area for a stick to gouge enough surrounding dirt into clods to pack over the treasure, he came upon a weathered man-made pole poking from the ground behind a bush. Wiggling it away from the soil and roots surrounding it took considerable effort but worth it when he discovered a long-buried shovel with rusted blade still attached. He dug it into the earth, grunting satisfaction that it remained a serviceable tool.

Convinced fate smiled on his plan, he shoveled dirt over the bags until the soil reached the top of the foundation, at equal height with the rest of the earth packed against its other sides. He tamped down this new earth, compacting it to prevent erosion and to match the other foundation walls. He stood back, pleased at the uniform look of this construction.

Now he needed landmarks to find the cache again himself or direct others to do so. Grabbing the bucket, he strolled off to find water, clues to his whereabouts and landmarks for a map.

As he strolled, he noticed the wooded area with the house foundation opened quickly into farm fields. He knew farms in this area numbered hundreds, even thousands of acres. Very soon, he found a stream, cupped *his hands and drank greedily. Feeling new energy, he hid the empty bucket behind a bush to explore the creek a mile in both directions, discovering a stone wall paralleling a road. He walked along the road, ready to dart into the growth on either side if he encountered anyone. At last, he returned to the house foundation by a different route and then retraced his path to the nearby stream. He knelt, absorbed in filling the bucket, when the sudden sound of rustling leaves and snapping twigs electrified him into action. He drew his pistol, assumed a defensive crouch from which he could shoot in any direction, and spun toward the sound, aiming as he did.*

CHAPTER 47

Jennifer's eyes snapped open the following morning. She sat up, instantly awake and wary. Her dream vision's elasticity enabled her to *watch* what happened to another person while simultaneously feeling as if she also lived *inside* that person. Incongruous, yet so real was this fantasy that she shared the danger he felt.

Moreover, these visions weren't exactly dreams, which often came in disjointed snatches. No, this felt more like a movie playing across the screen of her mind. She knew she had an active imagination, but she'd never had this experience before. Or was it more than imagination?

It took a minute to reorient herself. These vivid, imaginary sequences might *seem* real, but the movers arriving this morning *were* real.

Her clock read 7:30. She dressed quickly and hurried downstairs to start breakfast. Today began her second week in Naples.

Grammy and Becca drifted downstairs soon after, and by the time they finished eating, they heard the distinctive whine of a large truck motor in front of the house. The doorbell announced the crew chief and his men.

After introductions, Jennifer walked the crew through the house, explaining the desire to load through only one door. "We've had an invasion threat and ask that you and your men let no strangers inside without consulting us. None."

The crew chief's expression showed he thought he'd already heard everything except this. He shrugged. "Okay, ma'am, we got it. We'll start packing now and load later. We should have your household on the way to your new house by evening. We'll start upstairs and stack the packed boxes and wardrobes here in the living room. Then we'll load them all at once."

Grammy finished her coffee. "Becca, dear, would you please move the car? The van's in front of the house, so maybe park it down the street a bit... out of the way?"

Noticing Becca looked hesitant at risking another garage snake experience, Grammy added, "Maybe you could pick up some chocolate donuts for us and for the movers. Your Mom forgot them last night when she went to the grocery."

Becca brightened. "Glad to, Gram. And this way they'll be fresh." She smacked her lips in anticipation and grabbed a broom.

"Why are you taking that with you to the garage?"

Becca gave a mirthless laugh. "In case of any surprises."

Grammy chuckled. "Fine, dear. But don't linger too long. We need to reach the beauty shop by ten this morning."

The packers knew their jobs. At 9:30, Jennifer mobilized Grammy for their appointment. Becca returned with the car, a chocolate crumb on her chin. She smiled sheepishly when Jennifer pointed it out.

"Call my cell with any questions. And thanks, Becca, for overseeing the movers. We'll be back in about an hour."

"Relax, you two. Everything's under control."

Jennifer hoped so.

Thirty minutes later with shampooed hair, they settled into salon chairs as Chelsea chatted amiably. "In the awareness part of my self-defense course they talked about the color of danger."

"The what?" Grammy looked confused.

Chelsea laughed. "Not real colors but a way to measure danger levels. For example, white is safe—like in your house with the doors and windows locked. Yellow is outside your house but not in risky circumstances, like shopping in the daytime in a familiar area. Orange indicates the circumstances are riskier, but without an obvious threat, such as leaving a store at nighttime to get your car in the lot. Red means you see an actual threat, someone suspicious in the vicinity, or people nearby in a fist-fight, or someone robbing another person."

"Oh my, that sounds scary enough." Grammy shifted uncomfortably. "Is there more?"

"Oh yes, the worst danger level is black. That's when the problem is right in your face; you're the target and someone's coming at you with their hands or a weapon. You are in urgent trouble."

Grammy absorbed this.

"And how does this color knowledge help you?"

Chelsea gestured with the curling iron. "The purpose is to learn to protect yourself by making safer choices. Bad choices mean risk. Your decisions affect the likelihood of danger. So if you find yourself in a 'red' situation, you get away from that harm and when safe, call 911 to get help for the others in trouble."

"And in a 'black' situation?"

"You hope someone calls 911 for you. Also, you could carry pepper spray or some other tool for protection."

"Like?"

"Well, they say if you have a flashlight you can shine it in your attacker's eyes to temporarily blind him or whack him with it. Or you could carry a tactical tool like a special pen in a sharp-pointed, extra-tough case, and use it to gouge your attacker."

Jennifer looked doubtful. "Could you get this weapon out fast enough if caught by surprise?"

"That's part of the awareness. If you're in an orange or red situation, you could have pepper spray in your hand when you walk into the dark lot from a store. Only takes a few seconds and gives an edge. Plus you always have one ever-ready tool."

"What's that?" asked an eavesdropping customer a few seats away.

"Your voice. You can shout 'GET AWAY' to the suspect. He likely wants an easy target and you're showing him it's not you. I don't mean a ladylike tone saying, 'Would you please get away,' but shouted like a drill sergeant because your life depends on it. Or you can scream. Someone nearby who overhears may call 911." She giggled. "Since most of us don't shout or scream often, the instructor told us to practice at home."

Finding a moment, Jennifer whispered to Chelsea. "Has Cliff talked with you about Max Roderick?"

"Yes. I live alone now, so I let Cliff move into my guest bedroom to protect me. He presented this idea to me in a funny way. He said if I were a celebrity in this situation, I would hire a bodyguard for protection. And Jennifer, I admit, it's a relief to know he's somewhere in the house with his police skills and a gun he knows how to use. I guess you could say we're dating, but I'm... very cautious about men. They've broken my heart a few times."

Jennifer hugged Chelsea. "Mom has only one more appointment with you and then, if our plans stay on target, she's headed north. We'll miss you. Any chance you might move north?"

"Are you mad? Leave this beautiful climate and magnificent sunsets over the Gulf? No way. And I'll shed a crocodile tear for you when winter rolls around and I'm in my swim suit."

"No cruelty, please. Nobody can fault your choosing to live in paradise. Wish we all could. Cross your fingers for Mom's good adjustment."

Jennifer and her mother returned home to find the movers finishing the upstairs packing.

"You boys move fast," Grammy complimented them.

"Well, we've had a little practice, ma'am," he said. "By the way, those donuts helped us stay focused. Thank you. Also, a little boy's trying to get in. I couldn't find your daughter, so we kept him out until you returned. He's on the front porch."

Jennifer hurried to the porch, where Georgie stood shifting from one foot to the other. "He's here again."

"Where?"

"When I came back from swim club, I saw him down the street."

Becca approached with a chocolate donut. They exchanged conspiratorial smiles as she handed it to him.

"What was he doing?"

"Just walking slow. He's gone now."

"Remember, you're our detective," she said. "Please let us know if you see him again."

"I will. I promise."

When the door closed, Becca asked her mother. "You think Georgie's for real or a clever chocoholic like yours truly?"

"Wish I knew. But I'll phone Goodwin so he knows what we know. When the movers leave for lunch, let's lock up until they return. It's not foolproof protection, but..." Jennifer's voice drifted away, as she realized how vulnerable they were in the face of a determined intruder.

But no point in further alarming Becca and Grammy.

At noon, the movers took the sandwiches and Cokes Becca offered, to eat in their truck. They were all business when they returned forty minutes later.

One of the movers spoke around the side of the box he carried. "The boy wants in again."

Becca sighed. "Thanks, I'll take care of him." She hurried to the door. "Hello, Georgie. How's it going?"

"The man—he's down by your car. He got in and sat there doing stuff. Then he left."

"In the car? Doing stuff?" She knelt down to his same eye level. "What do you mean?"

"I mean he isn't sitting still or looking out the window. He's... doing stuff."

"Is he still there?"

"No, he left a little while ago, but the moving men wouldn't let me in to tell you about it."

"A few minutes ago?"

"No, a little longer than that."

"Thanks, Georgie. I'll take a look."

"Do you have a snack for me?"

Becca hesitated. Was he fantasizing events for treats, after all? "Sure. Wait right here. I'll find something."

Getting the boy's chocolate surprise in the kitchen, she told her mother what Georgie reported.

"We better take a look. Send Georgie home with his reward and let's stroll down there."

They followed Georgie out the front door.

Suddenly a horrific explosion thundered. They turned startled faces toward the sound, to witness Grammy's car engulfed in ballooning red and yellow flames. Beneath a cloud of black billowing smoke, charred debris rained to the ground.

CHAPTER 48

At this horrendous blast, neighbors rushed onto front porches, many dialing cellphones. Almost immediately, distant sirens filled the air. The charred Mercedes skeleton smoldered, with small flames licking the vehicle's interior walls and fluttering at the windows. Jennifer, Becca and Georgie stared open-mouthed.

Georgie recovered first. "Told ya."

Becca stared at the Mercedes' smoky framework as she and Georgie walked toward it. She patted his head. "Yes, you did. Thanks, Georgie. Stay on the job, detective."

Meantime, Jennifer rushed inside for her cellphone. Reaching Goodwin's voicemail, she spoke quickly. "That little boy across the street who's seen Max's picture said he saw Max on our street 'doing stuff' in my mother's Mercedes, which just *exploded*. The car's a total loss. Please call me ASAP. Doesn't this prove Max is in Naples and nursing a vendetta against my mother? We're scared. We need protection. Please hurry."

A fire engine arrived, accompanied by an EMS van. Becca stood near the car, watching them in action as the crew satisfied themselves they'd extinguished the fire and the lead member asked to speak to the car's owner. Becca directed him to the house.

As Jennifer described what happened, Grammy struggled to the door, aghast at the sight of her smoldering car's charred outline. They walked down the sidewalk to the scene.

The crew leader asked Grammy routine ownership questions for his report. "Any idea about what happened to your car?"

Jennifer explained Deputy Goodwin's involvement and Max's probable sabotage.

"Then this is a crime scene until the deputy clears it. Meantime, we'll treat this as arson and look for the cause. Stay clear of the crime scene tape and tell your insurance agent to check with me for the report." He handed her his card.

Ever gregarious, Becca chatted with a handsome fireman about her age. "I'm impressed with your crew's speed and skill. My boyfriend's a fire fighter and lead medic... back home in Virginia."

The firefighter said, "Well, then, on behalf of the brotherhood, we'd like to invite you to join us after shift at a watering hole we favor." He winked. "As a professional courtesy to your boyfriend, of course. I'm Tony. Here's my card. Nice to meet you."

He extended his hand and she shook it, laughing. "Tell me where and when and I'll think about it."

As the men boarded the fire truck, Becca overheard two talking together. "Ever hear of a guy pulling off a daytime car-bombing in a residential neighborhood like this?" said the first.

The second said, "Nah. He must think he's smarter than God or he's a crazy who doesn't care if he gets caught."

Becca mulled this over as the fire engine pulled away. Tony waved at her through the big truck's window as it moved down the street.

Standing beside Grammy on the sidewalk, Jennifer needed to invent some positive spin to downplay the explosion. This added still more to Grammy's stress list of traumas—being doped, waking in a hospital, facing Max for the ID, downsizing and uprooting her life to start again in a new place.

"Look at it this way, Mom. This isn't something you expected, but now that it's happened, you probably wouldn't have driven it much anymore." She didn't mention her having no driver's license. "And now you can use the car's replacement insurance money for decorating your new apartment. Fate worked for you this time. Deputy Goodwin should come soon, and meantime, let's call your insurance company."

But her mother's troubled expression told Jennifer this elderly lady couldn't take much more. Nor did she fail to connect her exploded car with Max's revenge. She was right to feel upset.

Where was Goodwin when they needed him?

CHAPTER 49

As if magically summoned, the deputy's car appeared, maneuvering to park between the moving van and the gutted Mercedes.

"Hey, looks like some excitement here. Mind if I come in?"

As they went toward the living room, the mover crew chief came over. "Shall we continue until we finish?"

Jennifer confirmed quickly. "Yes, of course. The explosion was down the street. Everything's under control." She wanted to believe this.

"Good. I thought I'd seen everything during a move, ma'am, but I have to admit, yours is a first." He gave an uneasy laugh and returned to his tasks.

Hands on her hips, Jennifer faced Goodwin. "So, *is* everything under control?"

He barked a mirthless laugh. "Well, not entirely or you wouldn't have a burned-up Mercedes outside. Although a shock for you, we assume this incident is Max's work, meaning he's in town, a fact that we weren't sure of before. I got a guy interviewing the boy across the street and I'd like to send a deputy to reinforce your security in the house tonight."

The three women relaxed a little. "Thank you, Deputy," Grammy said.

"Sorry your get-away to your new life in Virginia hasn't been smoother, but my personal goal's to get you safely out of Naples and on your way. I'm a phone call away. I'll stay until my man arrives. Meantime, I suggest you stick close to home for a while."

"But we were going out for dinner," Becca reminded.

"Well, I don't feel too adventurous after what's happened but," Grammy turned to Jennifer, "do we have enough food here for dinner?"

"I think so, Mom."

"I want to feel safe right now," Grammy continued. "When will your man arrive?"

Goodwin glanced at his watch. "Any time now."

Jennifer stood. "One small problem. We need a car. Maybe Georgie's father would give me a lift to the car rental place."

"Why not ask?" Becca encouraged. "Do you still have his business card? And shouldn't I go along to the rental office to qualify as an authorized driver?"

"Good point. Wait here while I walk over." She gathered up her purse and turned to Goodwin. "Will you stay with Grammy until we return or your deputy arrives to take over?"

"Absolutely."

"Good. By the way, Mom, have you an extra garage door opener?"

Grammy produced one and Jennifer hurried across the street. When she knocked on Georgie's front door, he rushed to open it with his father at his heels. In the boy's earshot, she praised his detective skills to his parents before asking for a ride to the nearby car rental company.

George picked up his keys. "Of course, I'll take you. Want to come along, Georgie?" The boy frisked to life and skipped ahead of them to his dad's car. They paused for Becca to climb in.

Returning forty-five minutes later, they noticed Goodwin's car gone and a police car parked in front of their house. They parked their rental car safely in the garage. Entering the house, they were met by a man in a sheriff's department uniform.

"Hello, ladies. I'm Deputy Ryan. Cliff Goodwin sent me."

"Come right in. Glad you're here."

Grammy's relief showed. "He's already been through the house and made sure all windows and exterior doors are locked." She even hummed a little tune as she set the table for dinner.

"Don't set a place for me," Becca announced. "I, ah...one of the firefighters invited me to join him tonight at a pub where they meet. Mind if I take the car, Mom?"

This caught Jennifer by surprise, but why not? Becca was a young, attractive, unattached woman spending a couple of weeks in romantic Naples, Florida. Why shouldn't she have a good time? She handed her daughter the car keys. "With this Max situation on-going, honey, would you mind phoning to tell me where you are, and would you come home early so we don't worry?"

"No problem, Mom." She hooked the keys on a finger, grabbed her purse, and checked her makeup in the powder room. She again took the broom with her into the garage. "Don't worry, I'll bring it inside when I come back."

"Watch out for snakes," Grammy called impishly. When the door closed behind Becca, she harrumphed to Jennifer, "That'll get her thinking about caution this evening."

"*Mother*," Jennifer admonished. "You naughty girl."

The mover's crew chief interrupted them with a clipboard of papers. "We're finished, ma'am. The numbers in this column match numbered stickers on each box we packed and on each piece of furniture. If you'll sign here, we'll be on our way."

Jennifer tipped each man. "Thanks for doing a good job for us."

When their truck pulled away, she turned to Deputy Ryan. "Would you like to have dinner with us?"

"No thank you, ma'am. That's not necessary. I brought something to eat."

She showed him how the security system worked and headed for the kitchen to prepare dinner. "The estate sale people may come tomorrow to start organizing. Mom, can you move to the guest room tonight since the movers took your bed today? Becca and I will move into the twin bedroom. After we talk with Peggy, we can decide when to go to the hotel, where we might as well stay until we go north."

After a quiet dinner, Jennifer said, "Let's walk through the house to make sure the movers took everything slated for McLean." They started with the downstairs rooms, then prepared to go up.

"Good night, Deputy Ryan. Would you like a pillow and blanket for the night?" Grammy offered.

"No thanks, ma'am. I'm on duty the whole time. You may hear me moving around the house during the night. Don't worry. That's my job."

After checking the movers' thoroughness in the upstairs rooms, they moved their personal belongings to their new bedrooms.

"Good night." Jennifer patted her mother's shoulder. "This is like olden days when you were the mom and I the little girl. We couldn't imagine then someday I'd have five children of my own."

"True enough," Grammy agreed. "Want a melatonin to help you sleep? I'm going to take one."

"No, thanks. I'm tired enough. With the movers finished today, we're another step closer to our goal."

The phone rang. "Just checking in, Mom." Becca explained where she was. "I'm having a great time. Home in about an hour."

"Good, I've moved your things into the twin room. Your bed's the one nearer the door. Talk to you tomorrow. Love you, hon."

"Love you, too, Mom."

"Ah, to be young again," Jennifer sighed wistfully. She hugged her mother and they headed to their bedrooms.

Her hand on her bedroom doorknob, Grammy turned, her smile melting into concern. "Oh, Jen, I just had a thought. How will we get the contents of the safe north? They were going with us in the car, but now…"

They exchanged puzzled looks. They hadn't considered this.

CHAPTER 50

With so much on her mind, Jennifer doubted she'd fall asleep easily. The evening's parting shot about transporting contents of the safe hung heavy on her mind, with no practical solution. She'd face it tomorrow. She wished to escape this chaotic Naples world to rewire her equilibrium, if only for a night. She wished she could transport herself to a faraway Alice-in-Wonderland place—a place where the buck no longer stopped with her.

She eased into bed, amazed at the relief of stretching her limbs against the cool, smooth sheets. Too exhausted to read, she looked over at the dragon on the bureau. "I bet you already know how this will all turn out," she said to him. He stared back with his knowing look. "Will you make a spell to help me fall asleep?" she asked him as she turned out the light.

She lay in the dark, trying to turn off her conscious mind, which bristled with deadlines and decisions to get her mother north. Finally, her eyes closed. Her breathing slowed and deepened. Gradually, her thoughts drifted upward into clouds where she floated without purpose or destination. Then an unexpected scene below pulled her toward it…

Staring at the steel muzzle leveled at him in the hands of a menacing stranger, a young boy froze in fear.

Warily, Birdsong glanced about and, satisfied the boy came alone, he holstered his weapon.

The boy barked a nervous laugh. "Thought you was goin' to drill me right here."

Studying the boy, about seven years old, Birdsong looked down. "Sorry, son."

"You ain't from around here. You...you lost, mister?"

"Naw, just gettin' a drink and some cookin' water."

"Whatcha cookin'?"

"Well, I don't know cause I ain't caught it yet."

The boy laughed and so did Birdsong. He hadn't laughed for a long time and it felt good.

"You want an apple?" the boy offered. "I got two."

"Well, sure enough I do."

The boy fished his hand into his overalls, produced the fruit and extended it toward the man.

"Why thank you, sir." Birdsong said, biting through the peel.

The boy giggled. Nobody ever called him "sir" before and it made him feel important. He took out the second apple and they ate together.

"This is mighty tasty. You grow these?"

"Yeah, in our orchard. Them trees got spring flowers now but when the apples come, my maw stores 'em in baskets in the cellar for the winter."

"You know your way around these parts?" Birdsong asked amiably.

"Sure do. Lived here my whole life."

"You know where the Potomac River is?"

The boy pointed.

"You ever been there?"

"Lots of times. My paw and me and our handymen fish there sometimes."

"So...is your paw a fisherman?"

"He fishes pretty good for a farmer."

Birdsong laughed and the boy joined in.

"Have you seen any soldiers around here lately?" asked Birdsong, doing some fishing of his own.

"Time to time." The boy hesitated, eyeing Birdsong with caution. "What...what side you on, Mister?"

"Born and raised in Virginny, just like you."

"So...so you a Reb then?

"Love my homeland enough to fight for it. But peace is what I really long for. Do you know what a poet is?"

The boy thought. "Selby says it's someone who writes down thoughts about what he sees to help other people understand life clearer. If you's a poet, can you do a poem about me?"

Birdsong smiled. "All right. How about this? 'A boy's excited about every day, he frisks and funs along the way, he learns from chores and what others say, and his family's love's the best kind of pay.'"

The boy grinned at him. "Guess you remember being a boy, huh?"

"Yes, son, I do. Now what does your paw say about these soldiers who come around?"

"He hopes them damn Yankees leave us be. We won't bother them if they don't bother us." He covered his mouth with his hands and grinned. "I'm not supposed to say 'damn' even though my paw does."

"And do they bother your paw?"

"All the time. They crawficate our crops and animals."

Birdsong smiled. "You mean 'confiscate'?"

"Yep, that's what they do. Makes my paw angry something fierce. He says 'thank God for Mosby, even if his men can't be everywhere.' But we ain't seen 'em for some time now."

"You've seen Mosby's Raiders?"

"Well, not up close, but my paw says they're the likeliest protection we got these days."

"I know Mosby."

The boy jumped to his feet, face animated. "You do? Oh mah gawd." He covered his mouth guiltily at saying this. "My maw told me not to say them words."

Birdsong chuckled. "I won't tell. Who's this Selby who told you about poets?"

"She's my big sister. Real smart. Reads books when her chores is done."

"You live close by?"

"Coupl'a miles."

"Happen to see a stray horse around last night or this morning?"

The boy stared at the ground, fudging his answer. "What's it look like?"

"Black mare wearin' a brown saddle with a rifle in the hitch."

The boy kicked at a stone, knowing that this same thirsty, hungry animal had wandered into their barn lot at dawn, a windfall his paw aimed to use or sell.

"Maybe..."

Birdsong read this as a yes. "Any chance I could say hello to your paw?"

"Sure 'nuf. He's in the north field today. Want me to take you there?"

"Why, that'd be good, son. Thank you. By the way, is someone building a house up the hill over there?" Birdsong pointed toward the foundation.

"Yeah, that's ol' man Parker. He started building but then them Yankees killed his oldest son and right after that, his wife died. My maw says her heart broke when her boy died. My paw says Parker turned old *real fast, and bitter, too. Paw thinks the son that's left will finish the new house for the ol' man one day, but up 'til then, the two of 'em still live at their old place."*

"What's your name?"

"Wilbur. Wilbur Gentry. What's yours?"

"Raiford... Raiford Birdsong. Real glad to see you today, Wilbur. Didn't think I'd be lucky enough to meet up with someone like you."

"Them's funny names, specially Birdsong."

"Yes, they are. But we can't help what our parents name us, can we? Now would you point me toward your paw?"

"You jes' foller me." *The boy skipped ahead.*

Birdsong fell in step behind the boy, thinking as he walked he'd make a map on the piece of cloth tucked inside his coat, a map he'd give to the safe house or Mosby or Lee, since taking the treasure to either of them himself was far too dangerous now. But how could he make a map clear for the intended recipients to find the burlap bags, yet cryptic enough so nobody else would?

How indeed?

CHAPTER 51

Jennifer awoke next morning, refreshed by her nighttime escape into the past. The fantasy scenes had pulled her again into a seductive world a century and a half old. Their actions back then impacted lives a century and a half later just as her actions today would influence lives a hundred and fifty years hence. This thought energized her to face decisions she'd make today here in Naples. She thought of Jason and how much she missed him—his comforting voice, his thoughtful counsel and his loving touch.

Although two self-sufficient adults, they'd been together forty-one years and, during that time, blended into a synergistic whole. Though she yearned for him and for home, responsibility would keep her in Naples another ten days to finish the tasks to shepherd her mother north. Thank goodness, Becca had come to help.

To her surprise, Grammy's physical and emotional outlook seemed upbeat. Enduring moving's disruption and disorientation was challenging at any age, but especially when a senior yearned for familiarity and simplicity rather than newness and complexity.

Grammy sailed through the movers' actions yesterday with ease, knowing she'd see these belongings again in McLean. But the estate sale in one week foretold the exact opposite—abrupt loss forever of long-valued treasures.

At least the remaining logistics of the move seemed well in place. All on target...except for Max. After deciding Grammy ruined his life, albeit a life of crime, what kind of revenge did he want? According to Goodwin, Max's previous M.O. included only opportunistic *scamming* of older folks—crimes, yes, but not *killing* anyone.

Yet he'd shown disregard for life by drugging and binding her mother. Had he intended her to die or starve to death in that closet, calculating a dead witness couldn't testify against him? Or did his clumsy timing show no forethought for unintended consequences? Or had he anticipated help reaching her quickly because of her phone call, which apparently triggered his hasty departure? Did blowing up her mother's car satisfy his anger at last or warn of worse to come? Had his hunger for vengeance grown insatiable? Had his original M.O. escalated to new deadly potential?

And why couldn't Goodwin find him?

She looked at the dragon on the dresser. Its knowing eyes followed her around the room. "Do you know what will happen next, you wily rascal?"

She patted the dragon, dressed, went downstairs and started breakfast. Sipping coffee, she perused the morning paper and started the day's to-do list. Writing "Contents of Safe "at the top, she realized they'd have to study every item there to determine the safest way to ship it north.

Next she wrote, "Estate Sale Prep." Peggy said they'd like a week for "arranging" and with the sale a week away, this meant they'd start today. Then "make airline reservations."

Pausing with her list, she flipped instead to the *Naples Daily News* weekend classified section's Garage Sale heading. Quite a few listed, some in pricey neighborhoods, suggesting higher quality merchandise.

Jennifer's draw to these sales included not only what she might buy, but what she might see—a glimpse into another person's life as reflected in the belongings he'd gathered. She glanced around Grammy's main floor—just as her own mother's house told exactly such a tale.

Each sale's story captivated her, for it sprang from some special reason, as did her mother's. Attending the sales relaxed her, like getting on the course relaxed a golfer—a familiar, positive experience garnished with a splash of the unknown. This stimulation, plus her curiosity about people and situations, made each sale an adventure for her.

Any shopper understood browsing for the unexpected, but her quest for that particular frame had fueled her with special purpose for two years. That quest exploded into unanticipated excitement when the frame at the McLean sale also revealed an intoxicating mystery. Her mind wandered, following the lead of the riddle and map until a sudden voice startled her to the present.

"Good morning, ma'am." Deputy Ryan strolled into the kitchen. "My replacement should arrive any minute. Glad to report an uneventful night. The new deputy will introduce herself when she arrives."

"When *she* arrives?"

"The Collier County Sheriff's Office is an equal opportunity employer open to anyone with qualifying skills. I think you'll find her *very* qualified."

"Good. Thanks for your help last night, Deputy."

"I'll just wait in the living room until my replacement gets here."

As he left the room, Grammy appeared at the kitchen door, smiling. "Do I smell bacon?"

"You do. Did you sleep well?"

"Oh, yes. Living to tell about the movers gives me new confidence for what comes next."

Uh-oh, Jennifer thought. Movers were the easy part.

Grammy answered her ringing phone.

"Hello... Peggy? Yes, this morning at 9:00 is fine. How many...? Four? Okay. See you then." She turned to Jennifer. "They want to start preparing the estate sale today. Will 9:00 work?

Becca's sleepy voice came from the door. "It will now." She sniffed the air. "Only bacon can save me until then."

Studying her list, Jennifer said, "Each day we need to shrink our presence here so Peggy and her crew can get every room ready for the sale. We should move out soon, tonight or tomorrow." On her list, she wrote "select and reserve hotel."

Before the others could comment, the doorbell broke the silence. Jennifer hustled to do the window peek, saw Goodwin and unlocked the front door.

"Morning, ladies." Goodwin's nostrils flared at the aroma permeating the main floor. "Bacon?"

"Not just any bacon but Nueske's bacon."

"What?" Goodwin asked.

"Applewood smoked with an unforgettable flavor. Most devotees order it from Nueske's Wisconsin catalog, but here in Naples it's for sale in Fresh Market's deli."

"Want some?" Becca waved her slice toward him before gobbling it down.

He sidled to the serving platter. "May I?" he asked Grammy.

"Only if you have good news for us."

"Does good advice count?"

Jennifer pushed her list aside. "Depends upon what it is."

"You still plan to move to a hotel in the next couple days?"

They nodded as Goodwin munched on a bacon slice. "Whoa, this bacon is amazing."

"The advice?" Jennifer prompted.

"Don't tell anybody where you're going and check in under an alias. Give friends your cell number, not the hotel phone."

The women exchanged confused looks before Grammy spoke for them all. "Why?"

CHAPTER 52

"Let's call it a 'precautionary measure.' With Max free," Goodwin sidestepped the recent car-arson, "why create a possible way for...," he glanced at Grammy's worried expression, "...for him to...cause any mischief?"

The doorbell rang again. Through the window, they saw and welcomed in a uniformed woman. She handed Jennifer a card as Deputy Ryan joined them from the living room. He nodded to her as she took over and he went off-duty.

"I'm Deputy Julie Martin, your security detail," she introduced herself, then closed and locked the front door. "Would one of you like to show me through the house or shall I just take a look myself?

"Here, I'll show you. Let's start upstairs," Becca volunteered.

As they started up the steps, the doorbell stopped them. Deputy Martin paused, hand on her holstered weapon. Jennifer peeked through the side window. "It's Peggy and her team. They're here to organize for the estate sale." Jennifer opened the door for them."

"Where would you like us to start?" Peggy asked.

"How about downstairs?" Becca suggested.

An awkward silence ensued. Deputy Martin understood why Peggy's team was here, but they didn't know why a uniformed policewoman stood on the stairs. Jennifer thought fast. She didn't want to alarm the estate sale team by identifying Martin as a sheriff's deputy guarding the house. She explained, "Miss Martin's here helping my Grammy." This seemed to satisfy everyone.

Back in the kitchen, Grammy apologized to Goodwin. "Sorry about my robe. Time for me to get dressed."

As she left, Goodwin rose from his chair. "Time for me to go, too."

Jennifer touched his sleeve. "Before you do, is my mother in real danger from Max?"

"We don't know, but safe choices are smart choices. Don't you agree?"

"Yes, but does this mean you have no new information?"

"Afraid not."

"Have you heard the name Antonio Venuti?"

"Now that's a segue." He scratched his chin. "Geez, that name sounds familiar but I...wait, it's coming to me. Yeah, I think... isn't he that Miami Mafia guy with the Saluti family? Didn't they rub him out a couple years ago? Seems like he stole some of their money. I can look it up to be sure." He eyed Jennifer curiously. "Why you asking about him?"

Jennifer invented, "When a friend knew I'd be in Florida, she mentioned the name. Guess splashy news draws attention. Up north many don't know Florida's Atlantic coast from the Gulf coast." She changed the subject. "Thanks for providing protection for us until you catch Max."

He stood. "Don't know if it'll last that long, but maybe a couple days. You head north in what, a week?"

"Eight, nine days. Right after the estate sale. Ah, Deputy. Another quick question?"

"Sure."

"If we drive north with some valuables from the safe—jewelry and such—what's the safest way to transport them?"

Goodwin's hand turned the doorknob then halted. "You mean short of an armored car?" He barked a laugh. "Put them in one of those carry-on bags with wheels. Pull it wherever you go, into your hotel room at night, by your chair in a restaurant, into the ladies room. Burglars might notice parked cars packed high or empty hotel rooms with guests out for meals. Keep the carry-on always close, but act like it's not important." He stepped out the front door.

"Thanks." Jennifer closed and locked the door behind him as Becca and the deputy started to tour the downstairs.

Deputy Martin came over. "So your mother's planning an estate sale soon?"

"Next weekend."

"Is the dragon statue up in the twin bedroom part of that sale? If so, would it offend her to ask if I might buy it?"

"The gold dragon statue holding the pearl?"

Deputy Martin nodded. "These creatures fascinate me, and I have a collection."

"Sorry to say, that one's actually my dragon and I'm very attached to it—almost seems like a wise friend. So, I'm afraid it isn't for sale. But you collect dragons?"

She nodded. "You might think it odd since police work is real-world fact-oriented and dragons are imaginary-world legend-oriented. But the contrast sharpens me for both."

Jennifer grinned. "Tell me more."

"Well, I'm no dragonologist, just an amateur," Deputy Martin explained, "but versions of these creatures appear in most cultures around the world. My detective mind says this isn't coincidence, so I look for explanations. One clue comes from trying to think like a primitive person to figure out how he reasoned—which is similar to trying to think like a criminal reasons in planning a crime. If ancients invented a believable explanation for what they feared, they might hope to protect themselves. Without explanations, they lived in constant terror from unpredictable danger."

"Danger such as…?"

"Storms with horrendous thunder and lightning. Volcanoes rumbling before belching fire, smoke and lava, then raining ash and debris. Earthquakes where the ground shakes, the earth opens and solid things break or crash. Floods where life-giving rivers go mad, destroying all around them. Hurricanes or tornadoes when wind goes crazy."

"So you're saying they reasoned angry dragons did these things."

"That's part of it," the deputy said. "The ancients also feared certain animals. Large birds that could grab animals or children. Bats sucking blood. Predators with fangs and claws like lions and alligators. Animals with sharp horns and antlers to gore and maim. Scaly reptiles, many poisonous, living in trees, water and on land."

"I get it." Jennifer looked at the figurine in her hand. "They mixed the dangerous animals they feared with the natural events they didn't understand. Dragons fit both."

"And they found evidence."

Jennifer looked skeptical. "Evidence? But…"

"Yes. Fossilized dinosaur footprints and bones existed then as now. Finding them seemed to *prove* dragon existence for ancients, and the word spread as cultures grew and trade developed."

"This is fascinating."

Deputy Martin nodded and smiled. "Yes. Maybe we can talk more about it later, but now I need to start my rounds to keep the house secure."

CHAPTER 53

Grammy stretched comfortably on the lanai chaise. "Is it dinner time already?"

Becca stood. "If you don't mind my borrowing the car, my friend Tony invited me to dinner and a movie tonight. Or are you dining out?"

Jennifer checked her watch. "Almost seven o'clock. What do you think, Mom?"

"I'm tired. Let's order pizza and salad again. We can make it a party like last time. Julie, would you like to join us?" She turned to Deputy Martin, who had just appeared on the porch.

"My shift here lasts another two hours. Yes, if it's not too much trouble, I'd enjoy it."

They locked the door when Becca left, studied the pizza menu and ordered.

Jennifer put her dragon figurine on the kitchen table and explained to Grammy their earlier conversation about it.

Julie picked it up. "I saw it right away upstairs because once you're 'into' dragons, you notice first thing if one's around."

"What can you tell us about this dragon, Julie?" Grammy asked.

Deputy Martin lifted the statue, examining all sides.

"Beautifully carved wood, so well-crafted the figure almost seems alive. I'm no expert, but this looks like an Asian or Eastern dragon. But they normally have no wings, yet this one does. Any maker's mark on the bottom?"

"No, but I haven't used a magnifying glass." Jennifer got one from the kitchen desk and studied the figure's underside. "Nothing here. Want to take a look?" she passed them.

Deputy Martin squinted through the glass. "I don't see any mark. So this is a puzzle. Most all dragons have scaly, serpentine bodies, but Asian dragons typically have no wings because they started as water snakes. As centuries passed, some 'evolved' a dragon head, a spiked spine and reptilian legs, which enabled it to prowl on land *and* water, increasing its range and scope of power. Water dragons have power over storms, rains, drought or floods. That's especially true for Japanese dragons, which rule rivers, lakes and oceans, as well as controlling rain."

Grammy raised an eyebrow. "But aren't they all imaginary?"

"If imaginary, why do they continue to fascinate us? Why did Alice in Wonderland face the Jabberwocky or the Hobbit confront Smaug or Harry Potter endure a terrifying dragon contest? And have you seen the recent movie series, *How to Train your Dragon*?"

"But," Grammy interrupted, "we expect fantasy creatures in fantasy stories."

Deputy Martin tried another approach. "As I said, early people didn't understand what caused horrific natural disasters like tidal waves, earthquakes, avalanches or volcanoes. A fire-breathing dragon provided as good an explanation as any. Asians thought by admitting his existence and power, they could show respect and honor, which might keep the dragon from getting angry and causing trouble. Instead of facing a hopelessly random and dangerous world, this gave the illusion of some control over otherwise chaotic natural events."

Jennifer picked up the figurine. "Are you saying Asians didn't consider their dragons evil? Because in Europe…"

"You're right on target." Martin leaned forward in her chair. "Asian dragons had enormous power, which careful humans might influence. Europe's dragons were all vicious and hungry for human blood. Western dragons have wings, and not bird wings but bat wings or pterodactyl wings. At first, they too represented natural powers beyond human control, but under the church's powerful European influence, dragons began to symbolize evil that humans should destroy or slay. Here's one example of the East/West difference: Eastern dragon blood's positive power to heal is the opposite of Western dragon blood's lethal power to poison."

"Did Indians on our own continent conjure up dragons?" Grammy looked doubtful.

"Yes. Statues of feathered Quetzalcoatl dragons are common in South America, and our Cherokee Indians worshiped a snake dragon that carried a magic stone on its head. Similar creatures are found in Hopi, Huron and Zuni religions. Many are more like huge, frightening birds, like the legendary thunderbirds."

When the doorbell sounded, hand on holster, Deputy Martin accompanied Jennifer to open it. A man held a large quilted pizza warming bag. Grammy indicated the foyer table, where he pulled the pizza boxes out of the bag and handed them to Jennifer as Grammy tipped him. The deputy twisted the door lock.

"I'll take a quick look upstairs before I join you," she said. "Please start while the pizza is hot."

By the time they set the table, arranged the salad and pizza and lighted the candle, the deputy returned. They ate with gusto. Jennifer offered key lime pie for dessert.

As they finished the meal, Grammy asked, "What other cultures told dragon stories?"

"As I mentioned earlier, just about every culture has dragon tales. That's part of the intrigue for me, because it's a mystery and I'm a detective. Sorry, I can't help more with your own dragon. Maybe ask at an Asian antique store. Whatever the verdict, this dragon looks unusual and is exquisitely crafted."

She looked at her watch. "My replacement should be here any minute. Don't know if I'll be sent back again, so I'll say good-bye as if I won't be coming back. Good to meet your family. Stay safe here and on your trip home."

The doorbell rang as if on cue. Peeking outside, Jennifer announced, "Deputy Ryan's back." They welcomed him in and said farewell to Deputy Martin. Ryan immediately started his rounds of the house while Jennifer and her mother tidied the kitchen.

Jennifer yawned, "I'm a tired cookie again tonight, Mom. How about you?"

"Add twenty-six years to your age and you'll know just how weary I feel tonight. I think it's more than what happens each day, but the accumulation of non-stop challenges day after day."

"Amen." Jennifer found the list she'd started that morning and yawned again. "Estate Sale Prep Day 1," she read aloud and crossed it off. "Transporting contents of Safe," she read before describing Goodwin's roll-along suitcase suggestion for valuables. "Mom, you said earlier this trip north might be the last one for a while. Do you still prefer driving to flying?" Grammy nodded. "Then why don't we rent a big, comfortable luxury car?"

Grammy smiled. "I'd love it, Jen, and it simplifies taking what's in the safe. At an airport they'd X-ray the carry-on suitcases."

"Okay, I'll cross off 'Airline Reservations Home' and substitute 'Rent Touring Car.' Last item is 'Select and Reserve Hotel.' This afternoon I called several nice places for good rates and picked a two-bedroom suite at a Naples hotel on the beach, subject to your approval. One room has a king bed and the other has two twin beds for Becca and me. It overlooks the Gulf and we could move there tomorrow to give the estate sale planners the run of the house."

"Superb choice, dear. Staying there will be a posthumous gift from my dear Antonio because of the cash he left for me in the wooden chest."

Jennifer hugged her mother. "I love you lots."

"I love you, too, dear."

They both yawned on the way upstairs.

After Jennifer's head touched her pillow, she lay quietly. Pushing the day's events aside, she glanced at the dragon's outline, barely visible in the night light's glow. "I learned a lot about your kind today, but you remain a mystery." Her mind segued to mysteries, which brought her to her riddle and map. She thought about Wilbur and Raiford meeting by the creek and suddenly she felt super relaxed. Then came the visions...

CHAPTER 54

*I*n the north field's extensive acreage, three horses pulled three plows guided by three strong men. Working side-by-side, with each plow a horse-length behind the next, they plowed three parallel rows at a time and turned in unison at the row's end to continue the same process aside the previous rows. The boy led Birdsong to the end of a row where he knew the men paused to water their horses and themselves.

"This here's my paw," Wilbur said. "This here's Mr. Raiford Birdsong, Paw."

The sweaty farmer wiped his brow with a soiled sleeve before extending his callused hand to the newcomer. He noted the six-shooters strapped around the stranger's waist. "Frank Gentry. This here's Gentry Farm."

"Your son tells me Yanks been hassling you."

The farmer eyed his boy sternly. The lad knew not to tell strangers who they backed in the war.

"May I speak with you privately for a moment, sir?" Birdsong asked.

Gentry looked around cautiously, but with his field workers and son nearby, he saw no risk and walked with Birdsong out of earshot of the others.

"Sir, I respectfully ask for your help. I'm Corporal Raiford Birdsong, who rides with Capt. Mosby's 43rd Cavalry. I'm in these parts on a special mission with something important for Gen. Robert E. Lee. Last night Union soldiers took me by surprise and chased me through the woods. In the dark, I lost my way and my horse, a saddled black mare. If I can find my horse or borrow one of yours and if you can give me directions toward Great Falls, I'll be on my way."

The farmer studied the stranger before him with new interest and made a decision. "Wilbur'll take you on back to the house, where you'll find your horse. It wandered in this morning. When we come in from the fields for lunch, we'll give you a bite to eat and some provisions for your ride."

"I thank you, sir, for your help and for your good will."

Birdsong followed the boy home, waiting outside while the child fetched his mother.

"Missus Gentry," Birdsong said to the harried farm wife, her forearms covered in flour as she eyed him from behind the screen door. "I met your husband in the field. He told me to wait here for him until he comes in for lunch."

She pushed the screen door ajar with an elbow, her floured hands held limp in front of her chest. "You do that then." She gave him a polite smile, though still focused on kitchen distractions. He wondered how many hungry farm workers she fed three times a day.

Wilbur took him to the barn where his horse stood in a stall. "Well, hello again, my Blackie." He patted the mare's neck. The horse gave a low nicker of recognition. He turned to Wilbur.

"Any chores I can help you with while I wait for your paw?"

"One of my jobs is mucking out them stalls. Here's a pitchfork. You can help if you want to. Watch out for the milk cow. She kicks at anybody edging up behind her."

While they worked, Birdsong asked: "You got a surface here in the barn where I could do some writin'?"

"Sure do. I'll show you when we finish. And, mister, thanks for helping me out with my job."

"We men got to stick together. You fed my horse and then you found me. It's fair I do for you in return."

Swelling with importance, the boy smiled as they finished the job together.

"You got any writin' paper?" Birdsong asked, waving his pencil stub.

"No, but I can get you a flour sack."

"That'll do," and when the boy brought the sack, Birdsong spread it out on the barn's work table while the boy perched on a nearby hay bale. "I want to make a map of that house foundation where I spent the night. You know this area purty well? Think you can help me with landmarks?"

"Landmarks?"

"Landmarks are things that don't change much even if hundreds of years pass by. Things like big rocks, trees that live a long time, bridges, lakes, stone fences, mills, farms, plantations..."

"Roads and railroads?" Wilbur volunteered.

"Yep, and towns and villages and important buildings like stores or taverns. Also streams and rivers. For instance, one important landmark in this area is the Potomac River."

"Well, my paw done told you the name of our farm and the one you're talking about over there is the Parker farm. It's only about three hundred some acres but our farm is a thousand. I'm only seven but I know my numbers and I can cipher, too. Selby done taught me."

They heard a loud bell clanging. "That's just three rings. It's the coming-in bell. Maw'll ring the dinner bell next."

"So we got us a river and two farms. What else?"

"Well, Colvin Run Mill's in Great Falls. And over there is the AL&H Railroad. Sometimes we hear a train whistle if the wind's blowing right. My paw says it connects Alexandria with Falls Church and Vienna and all the way to Leesburg. I ain't never been to Leesburg, have you?"

"Matter of fact, I have. Nice place. Those railroad letters you said, would that be the Alexandria, Loudoun & Hampshire?" Wilbur nodded. "Hey, boy, you're real good at these landmarks."

"Down the hill from that foundation isn't really a dirt road, more like a wide path, but folks around here use it all the time for horses and small wagons."

"Does it have a name?"

"They just call it the "windin' path," cause of the way it twists around. But I got something even better." A knowing smile brightened the boy's face. "On that Parker property between their foundation and the trail below is a rock so big my paw calls it a boulder – only it's flat on top. And it has a second flat rock set on top of it and more on top of that. And all that sits inside a circle of trees. My paw says in olden times it was a holy place for the Indians. He says he ain't never seen nothing quite like it. One of our hired hands who draws real good, he drew a picture of that place on a piece of wood. My maw nailed it on a wall inside the house. I'll show you when we eat lunch."

Birdsong rolled up his flour-sack list, intending to pace off exact distances before he drew his map. When he left this farm, he'd return to the foundation to get his map right.

Just then, they heard the farm bell ring six times. "That's dinner," cried Wilbur. "Come on. We gotta wash up first. I'll race ya to the pump."

Since the farmer and his hired hands already circled the pump, they got in line to share the same chunk of strong soap and drink from the same tin cup when their turn came.

"You gotta take off your gun belt. My maw don't allow no guns past the back entry."

Birdsong hesitated, but complied. Still, he chose a seat where he could see his holster and get to it fast if necessary.

Inside, the missus and her helpers waved them to tables with an empty dish at each place before passing serving bowls of stew and a platter of biscuits. The women bustled around the men, grateful their hidden stores of flour and lard had evaded earlier Union raids but concerned about the mostly vegetable chicken stew.

"When the Blues stole our cows and pigs," Wilbur confided, "they only left chickens because they couldn't catch them. I catch chickens all the time for Maw but when they told me to help 'em, I pretended I didn't know how."

Birdsong wondered what the family would do when they used up these birds. He felt guilty adding another mouth to feed on their diminishing stores. He looked at the women and girls.

"When do they eat?" Birdsong asked Wilbur.

The boy mumbled through a full mouth of food, "When the men finish and leave."

Birdsong couldn't help noticing the blond-haired girl. Their eyes locked for an instant of shy but powerful attraction. In another life, he thought, they might meet, court, marry and live long, happy lives together – maybe right on this farm. But not now. Not during this God-forsaken war.

He couldn't keep his eyes off her. Every time when he glanced up, she gazed back at him.

When the meal ended, the farmer told Selby to prepare a food package for Birdsong. His wife frowned but told Selby to hurry it up. Gentry gave Birdsong the requested directions and brought his horse to the hitching rack outside the back door. While Birdsong waited near the kitchen for the food, the blond-haired girl approached him. "My name is Selby. Here's your food. I put in extra biscuits and buttered 'em, too. Wilbur says you want to see the picture."

"Why, yes, Miss Selby, I do."

She led him down the hall and they stared together at the artwork while filling their peripheral vision with each other. An energy passed between them, followed by an awkward moment.

"You…you leavin' today?" she asked.

"Yeah. Got to deliver something important for the military."

She reached out to touch his arm. "Take…very special care of yourself. This war is fearsome for everybody but worst of all you soldiers."

"I thank ya for the kind thoughts, Miss Selby."

"You'll come see us next time you're out this way?"

"Yes, Miss Selby. I'd like that. Thanks for…for showing me the picture and…and for your family's hospitality." With effort, he turned to go, but faltered. "Don't you worry, I will come back."

"I'll be waitin'… to see you." She waved and he raised a hand in acknowledgement, before mounting and turning his horse for the ride back toward the treasure and his task there.

Would it still be where he left it? Or were the Blues lying in wait for his return?

CHAPTER 55

Jennifer woke with a wistful smile at the shy romance budding in last night's strange vision. She remembered the electricity she and Jason felt when they'd first met.

Any war's fear and insecurity triggered a hunger to link safety with stability like marriage. The sooner a lass wed in hostile times, the safer she thought she'd feel with someone strong at her side to protect her. But war's reality dashed this wish, for besides her own life to lose came those of her beloved husband and children. Jennifer contrasted this with the peacetime gifts she took for granted in the very country the turbulent Civil War's victory had created for her.

In a count-your-blessings mood, she descended the stairs, greeted Deputy Ryan, made coffee, brought in the newspaper and started a to-do list on fresh notepaper.

The first entry: "Rent Touring Car." She sipped coffee before adding "Move to Hotel."

Picturing this move underway, she wrote "More Carry-ons?" followed by "Inventory Safe to Assess Carry-on Needs."

Grammy appeared in her robe. "The coffee aroma lured me." She poured a cup and sat down to peruse the *Naples Daily News*.

"Coffee for you, Deputy?" Jennifer offered.

"Why, thank you, ma'am."

"About what time did Becca get in last night?" Jennifer looked up at him.

"Ah, around 2:00?"

"Everything without incident last night?" she asked. He nodded. "Your shift ends in about an hour at 8 o'clock?" He nodded again before leaving to make his rounds in the house.

"Mom, could we look at all your suitcases this morning? Then we'll know if we need to buy more carry-ons. Could you and I do that after breakfast? Becca may sleep in after her late night."

Grammy nodded. "When do we move to the hotel?"

"Three o'clock check-in, so later this afternoon."

"Does Peggy's team come again today?"

"They said yesterday they would."

Deputy Ryan came into the kitchen holding his cellphone. "Looks like they're not sending another deputy to you today, so you're on your own. I've double-checked doors and windows, the yard and garage. You're okay now. Just be extra alert about who comes in, and maybe ask your granddaughter to make rounds periodically."

"Thanks for keeping us safe."

"Just doing my job, ma'am. We think it's only a matter of time until they get Max Roderick. They're looking hard for him."

"Then, keep up the good work. Good-bye...and good luck."

When he left, Jennifer and her mother went upstairs to empty the safe. They stacked boxes in piles the size of a carry-on.

"Two should do it," Grammy calculated, "but let's get three for extra room to add anything important we might discover around the house. With three of us, each of us could pull one carry-on, just as Goodwin advised."

She opened a box they'd skipped before, sighing over what lay within. "Mementos of my years with Anthony. See, ticket stubs from philharmonic concerts, match folders from restaurants we liked, unusual shells we found walking the beach, birthday and Christmas cards and these little cards from flowers he sent me. And," she picked up a folded paper, "here's his last letter to me. I've read it so many times it's almost falling apart."

Unfolding it tenderly, she handed it to Jennifer.

"My darling Frances,
When I look at you, everything I really wanted is right in front of me. The first time I saw you my heart whispered, 'she's the one.' Our love, growing with each new moment we share, brings me the greatest happiness of my life. I told you once I would never leave you voluntarily, so it could happen only if I have no power to prevent it, such as if I'm dead.

Tomorrow I face my last dangerous mission. If (when?) I do come back, will you marry me, my love? If I don't return from this or from any departure from your side on any day, you'll know my last thought in this world will be of you, dearest one.

With a heart overflowing with love for you, I am always your very own, Anthony"

Speechless, Jennifer locked eyes with her mother, seeing for the first time a very different dimension in a woman she had thought she knew so well. Stunned at the letter's power, emotion and suggestion, she managed to refold it, ease it into the envelope and lay it softly on her mother's lap. Then she jumped up to hug her, wordlessly sharing what women the world over understood about the joy and pain of love.

Grammy wiped at a tear. To draw their attention elsewhere, she pointed toward the boxes. "Shall...shall we lock them in the safe until our last day in Naples instead of coping with them at the hotel?" She straightened, tucking the letter gently back into the box. "Let's each copy the combination so it can't get lost."

"Good thought, dearest Mom."

Grammy blew her nose into a delicate linen handkerchief. "Let's inventory the luggage," she said briskly.

* * * * *

Becca appeared for lunch, still in her pajamas. "Such a good time last night. I'd like you to meet my friend. Maybe when he picks me up tonight?"

"Great. By the way, we move to the hotel around 3:00 today. Can he pick you up there?"

"Oh, right. I forgot." She munched a sandwich. "Say, isn't Thursday your new salon day, Grammy?"

Grammy nodded.

"I need a haircut. If you can get me an appointment with someone really good, could I come along with you two?"

"Let's see if I can arrange it." Jennifer reached for the rolodex. "Chelsea's info in here, Mom? Good. What's it listed under?"

"'B' for Beauty Shop. The shop's not open yet — summer hours — so you might try her home number."

"Ah, here it is." Jennifer dialed the home number and pressed speaker. "Hi, Chelsea, this is Jen. I..."

"Glad you called. I have a solution for your problem. You remember the colors we talked about last time in the shop? Well, forget yellow and red. Black is the right hair color for you. So concentrate only on black.

"You need to make an appointment quickly because I have a special on right now. Black's a winner for you. You'll be stunned at the power of this color and what it can do. Do you still have that sketch I made for you, the...the one showing your face with the three different hair colors? Study it and you'll see I'm right. Black's the correct choice. I...I have to hang up now but good talking with y..."

The call cut out, mid-word.

Jennifer frowned at her phone and exchanged puzzled looks with Becca and Grammy as she processed this odd message. Then she remembered Chelsea's self-defense course colors. In a flash of understanding, she dialed Goodwin's number but reached his voice mail.

Frustrated, she phoned the sheriff's office. "This is Jennifer Shannon reporting a life threatening emergency. I must speak to Deputy Goodwin.... Not there? Can you reach him...? Okay, then Deputy Ryan or Deputy Julie Martin? I'm giving you names of your people who know what this is about and can arrange help fast.

"All right, from the beginning. Send armed deputies immediately to rescue Chelsea Amaryllis, who just called me begging for help. An escaped felon named Max Roderick has broken into her house wanting revenge. She's in terrible danger. Get your people there fast or he will kill her. Her address?" She read from Grammy's rolodex card. "Here it is. Hurry. Her life depends on it."

CHAPTER 56

J ennifer ended the sheriff's office call to try Goodwin's number again, this time leaving him the same message.

Becca and Grammy frowned. Had Jennifer gone off the deep end?

Grabbing purse and car keys, Jennifer started for the garage door when she felt a hand tighten on her arm.

"No." Grammy spoke in a firm voice Jennifer hadn't heard since childhood. "You put the rescue in motion, but your job ends there. Deputies have the men, the training and the weapons Chelsea needs now, and they can reach her faster with their sirens."

Jennifer hesitated, then drooped. "You're right. What was I thinking?"

But she knew the answer: her mother and Chelsea weren't safe until Max returned to prison.

She wrapped her arms around her mother just as she'd done as a little girl. Together they eased back into the house.

"It's always something with our family," Becca mumbled. "Just when I think it can't get any crazier..."

Jennifer's phone rang. "Goodwin here. I'm on my way to Chelsea. Tell me what happened."

Jennifer described Chelsea's cryptic phone conversation and how she translated it into danger from Roderick.

"Thanks." His terse response reflected concentration as he sped toward the crime.

To ease the tension they shared, Jennifer turned their attention to something else. "Let's...let's inventory Grammy's suitcases while we wait for the other shoe to drop."

"They're in the under-the-stairs closet," Grammy reminded.

"I'll do it," Becca offered. "I slept the morning away instead of helping, so it's my turn."

She returned in a few minutes to report. "Two very large suitcases, three medium and three carry-ons. All on wheels."

"Good."

Grammy looked at the list over Jennifer's shoulder. "So all that's left to do is just renting a car for the trip and moving to the hotel. That's easy enough."

"And solve the Thursday beauty shop appointments," Becca reminded. They exchanged looks of uncertainty about how this might unfold now.

Jennifer added it to the list. "Why don't we stage everything we'll take to the hotel near the front door, the way the movers did? You two get started while I rent the touring car." They all jumped at the doorbell chime. "Becca, please see who's there, but be careful."

Becca looked out before unlocking the door. "Hello, Peggy. More tagging? Sure, come in? How many of you? Just two. Fine. Finish upstairs and then start down here? Good." She returned to the kitchen and said quietly, "Come on, Grammy, let's gather our stuff."

Jennifer's recent conjuring intruded as she gathered her belongings for the hotel. The riddle's mystery nagged at her, bringing to mind her father's Civil War Study Group. If only he were here to share insights about her riddle and map, but instead, maybe his friend, John Birdsong, could. She searched for the number and dialed.

"Hi, John. It's Jennifer, Fran Ryerson's daughter.... Yes, she's feeling well, thank you for asking, and she's also adjusted well to her decision to move to Virginia.... When do we go? In another week. If you have a minute, may I ask you some Civil War questions...? Okay. First, do you know what happened to your uncle, Raiford Birdsong, the poet who fought in the Civil War?"

"Funny you should ask. We really don't. They listed him 'missing in action' and later 'presumed dead.' He failed to return from the war, which wasn't that uncommon. Many soldiers were buried where they fell. Circumstances didn't always allow those burying casualties to check a deceased's pockets for identification, or even if they did, to get that information to headquarters to filter it back to relatives. I suppose it's possible he survived and lived a long life, but our ancestors back then insisted it was inconceivable he wouldn't tell them he was alive, even if he chose to live elsewhere."

"You said you put out some feelers regarding my map and riddle. Any responses?"

"A lot of curiosity but so far no leads to help you. If your riddle and map are genuine, this could be a remarkable find. Mosby's treasure fits the riddle's first part, but I know of no historical accounts to confirm its existence, never mind anyone burying it, digging it up or reburying it."

"Any other observations?"

"Yours isn't a true map. It's what's called a field map—more a sketch than an accurate map. Supplying field offices with maps was tough for the South throughout the war. They had no established government mapping agencies capable of printing large-scale maps and almost total absence of surveying and drafting equipment. Add to that the lack of printing presses and paper and you see why few real maps existed. Some areas had never been mapped at all. These landmarks—the Potomac River, Arlington, Falls Church and the railroad on your field map— suggest it's what we now call Great Falls, but that covers miles of acreage. My guess is the smaller insert showing a rectangle with the X against one side is in that area. Unfortunately, every bit of it is privately or publicly owned now."

"Hopeless then?"

"Never say never. This area isn't too far from Fairfax Courthouse, where Mosby allegedly rescued the treasure from Stoughton. The treasure legends I read suggest he buried it on the way south to Culpeper. So it's all geographically possible, as the riddle says. But why would he take it north?"

"To Gen. Lee's home or headquarters? Or," she thought of what she'd seen so clearly in her vision, "to a Mosby safe house?"

"Now there's an idea...yeah, maybe so." He laughed. "Are you about to get a metal detector to go relic hunting?"

"Why not?"

His second laugh had an edge. "If you do, proceed very carefully. Relic hunting was simple enough forty or fifty years ago, but now you need an owner's permission or pay a fat fine if you don't and you're caught. And this includes parkland, where the fines are huge. So learn the Virginia rules before you start."

She remembered her reverie. "Have you a way to research owners of old farms in the McLean area, like Gentry or Parker?"

"I'll look into it, but why do you suggest them?"

How could she explain? "Just something I dreamed up." She smiled at that truth. "Thanks for your interest and your help, John. Would you mind sending me the information about your relative, Raiford? Here are my phone number and e-mail address." She rattled them off.

"Got it," he said. "I'll do it when we hang up. Oh, by the way, apparently your dad tucked money into some of the books you gave me. The bills fell out when I looked through the volumes. I collected $37 in all. Shall I mail you a check?"

"Thanks, John. We discovered he hid cash in a lot of books in the study. Appreciate your honesty. Please contribute it in his name to your Civil War Study Group. We leave for Virginia soon. You have my contact info. Nice meeting you and thanks for your efforts on my behalf." She ended the call and hustled to put her hotel items near the front door with the others.

"What about the safe?" Grammy whispered when she returned.

Becca considered this. "We can't protect the contents at the hotel because we can't be with those carry-ons every minute, and there's too much to haul to the hotel safe."

Grammy added, "So let's leave it all securely locked in the safe here at the house. Let's tell Peggy the bookcase hiding the safe is not for sale. Nobody will even know the safe's behind it. Then the morning we leave for McLean, we can come here first to empty the safe into our carry-ons for the trip as planned."

Jennifer smiled. "Good thinking, gals.

At 3:00 when Peggy and her estate sale helpers finished their organizing for the day, Jennifer and Becca loaded the car, helped Grammy in and drove to the hotel.

As a bellman handled their luggage and a valet took the car, Jennifer approached the front desk. "The reservation is in my name but Deputy Goodwin of the Collier County Sheriff's department told us to check-in under another name to protect us from someone trying to harm us."

"We'd need the deputy's signed authorization form to do this," the desk clerk explained.

"Then I'll phone him." Her call reached his voice mail so she left a message. She told the desk clerk, "Look, I can't reach him now but what if I check in with my real name, then when we get his authorization, can you change it to the name he provides?"

"I guess so." They completed registration and the bellman took them to their suite of rooms.

"Oh," Becca cried, looking out the floor-to-ceiling sliders to the balcony, "the view is breath-taking."

Grammy grinned. "I couldn't ask for a lovelier place to say goodbye to my Naples."

After they unpacked, Becca donned bathing suit and cover-up. "I'm headed to the pool. Want to come along to see what else this place offers?"

Grammy sat on the bed. "I'll just lie down a minute. You two go ahead."

On the elevator Jennifer asked, "What time is Tony coming?"

"Six."

"That's in two hours. While you swim, I'll explore the lobby stores and peek into the dining room and lounge. Then I'll come poolside to cheer you on."

An hour later, Jennifer returned to the room and asked her mother, "Any word from Goodwin?"

Grammy shook her head.

"Then I'm going to call him." But she reached his voice mail. Next, she tried Chelsea's number. No answer, voice mail full.

"Why would Goodwin wait this long to tell us what happened when I alerted him about Chelsea's danger? Doesn't he owe us that courtesy?"

She'd barely hung up when the cellphone in her hand played its tune. "Jennifer? Goodwin here. Can't talk now but thanks for your call about Chelsea. Will explain later tonight."

She told Becca about this when she returned from the pool to prepare for her date's arrival.

"We need to know if Max was involved and if he's in jail. I think it's rude Goodwin hasn't told us what happened. Grammy's safety's involved here, too." Becca complained.

Jennifer agreed. "Because if he's captured, we can relax. If not, we should be on guard still. And I want to know if Chelsea's okay."

At six o'clock came a rap on the hotel room door. Becca jumped to her feet. "Normally they'd call about a guest in the lobby, but I told Tony our room number."

She greeted a nice-looking young man with a kiss on the cheek and turned, smiling, to her family in the hotel room.

"Mom, Grammy, this is my friend, Anthony Venuti."

CHAPTER 57

Instead of the friendly welcome Becca anticipated for her friend, she stared in dismay at two faces frozen in shock. Embarrassed at this awkward greeting for Tony, she wanted an explanation. "*What?*" she demanded irritably.

Recovering first from the surprise, Jennifer said to the young man, "Your name sounds familiar…"

Tony laughed. "Yeah, I get that all the time. You must mean my uncle. My parents named me for him."

Grammy found her voice. "You knew him?"

"Sure. We didn't see him much—just family events—but he was my father's favorite older brother, so that explains our same names."

Realizing their ill-mannered reaction to his introduction, Jennifer stepped forward to shake hands. "Glad to meet you, Tony. Here, have a seat. Can you tell us more about him?"

"Well, I guess so. He was like our family's rock star. Lots of personality, snappy dresser. Well-heeled. Whenever I saw him, he slipped me a hundred dollar bill. 'Walking around money,' he called it. A c-note's big money to a kid from a blue-collar family. I worshiped him even…even after I learned the truth."

"The truth?" Grammy asked, her lips drawn into a thin line.

"Yeah, I mean, all my information's second hand through my family, but they talked about him a lot because, like I said, he's the closest thing we had to a celebrity."

"And the truth?" Jennifer invited.

"The truth? The Mafiosi recruited him as a kid. He was a made guy." Tony sensed their shock turning to distaste. "In fairness, Italians get the bad Mafia rap, but remember, they're just one among other organized crime groups like the Irish mob, the Jewish mob, the Russian mob, the Chinese Tongs and a lot more. I majored in psych, where they see a parallel crime structure between today's city street gangs and the Mafia."

An amazed Becca also sank into a chair at this unexpected development. "What do you mean parallels?"

"The Mafia is a kind of gang, but not all gangs are Mafia. Some large gangs are loose collections of small street gangs. The Mafia's traditional rigid hierarchy and specific territories contribute to their success at organized crime for profit."

Jennifer nudged, "Does he still visit you?"

"No, he's dead. At least that's what we're told."

"Really?"

"Couple of years ago. Here's how it went. My ancestors came from Sicily to New York to Jersey. They cozied up with the Bollato family. But some of our ancestors pulled away and went straight. My own father's father was one of those. When he got sick of those cold New England winters, he moved to Florida. Our branch has cousins in law enforcement and fire-fighters, like me. We're the good guys. They're the bad guys, but I admit they're flashy and loaded with cash."

Grammy cleared her throat and managed, "What...what happened to him?"

"The Jersey mob liked to winter in Florida, always on the Atlantic side—Miami, Boca, Palm Beach and up the coast. But even on vacation, old habits die hard. They wet their beaks, getting a corner on their standard stuff like extortion, smuggling, prostitution, money laundering. Drugs were big down here with so much shoreline for deliveries and the source countries so close."

"And..." Grammy's voice sounded frail.

"And the story goes he got greedy, didn't ante up the right percentage to the don. They don't just break your arm for insider stealing from the mob. My dad says they had a sit-down where Uncle Anthony's accusers and defenders told their sides and asked the don for a ruling. If guilty, they'd kill him to send a message to anybody with the same idea. If innocent, he'd walk out free, but they'd never forget the stain. Meantime, he'd already decided he liked the Gulf Coast better. Rumor says he moved here, rented a fancy apartment on the water, fell in love with some local woman and retired from 'the life.' But this alleged stealing incident humiliated his accusers, and in an honor society, they don't take humiliation well."

"So?" This story had hooked Becca.

"So, according to my dad, one day Big T—that's what my Dad called Uncle Anthony—Big T disappeared. Vanished. We assume he took a hit, but like Jimmy Hoffa, they never found the body. My dad thinks they rubbed him out."

"How did you know his name?" Becca asked. "Mom? Gram?"

Grammy's voice faltered as she answered, "I...I think I read about it in the newspaper."

Tony grinned as he stood. "Yeah, the news played big in Naples a few days. On all the TV stations. But without a body, it's only rumor and then cold news. Well, Becca, ready to roll?"

She jumped up to join him. "Another person's fifteen minutes of fame?" She took Tony's arm as they left.

When the door closed, Jennifer and her mother exchanged looks before Jen embraced her. "Are you okay, Mom?"

"We loved each other," the older woman mumbled, wiping tears.

"How about a glass of wine before we go downstairs to dinner? It's the cocktail hour and I brought a bottle of your favorite pinot noir;" she smiled, "coincidentally, my favorite, as well."

Two hours later, after a sumptuous dinner in the hotel's waterfront restaurant, Jennifer and her mother returned to their room.

"It's only 8:30 and I'm grateful to put on my pajamas," Grammy observed. "Each day lately seems more draining than the last. But one benefit of exhaustion is sleeping well."

Jennifer agreed, doubting dreams—or whatever they were— like her own distracted her mother's slumber. "Hey, we can even watch sunset in our PJ's on our private balcony. Getting in synch with the planet should help us sleep peacefully."

They'd no sooner settled into their balcony chairs when Jennifer's cell rang. She answered.

"Goodwin here."

"You're on Speaker so Mom and I can both hear."

"Okay. There's good news and bad news. Good news: thanks to your tip, we nabbed Max at Chelsea's house. He's in jail with no chance of another escape. Bad news: Chelsea's in the hospital for overnight observation. Roderick strangled her nearly to death.

We stopped him just in time. Doctors say prognosis good for complete recovery."

"Would she like visitors?"

"Not yet. I'll let you know. How are you?"

"We've moved to the hotel. They insisted we register with our own names but will reverse that if you sign an authorization. We'll go back and forth to the house during the next few days. The estate sale starts Friday morning and we drive north the following Monday."

"With Max in jail, you should have no worries about your real names at the desk. Relax and enjoy your remaining time in Naples."

"Please let us know about Chelsea's progress."

"Oh, you'll definitely hear from me before you leave because of something else."

"What?" Jennifer held her breath.

"Can't tell you yet... but soon."

CHAPTER 58

An hour later, Jennifer stretched between the silky bed linens in the heavenly soft hotel bed. She plunged swiftly into a reverie. Her mind empty, her gentle breathing wafted into the air... and then, the images rolled in, more powerful than ever before.

Convinced of little success in delivering the bags of valuables to the safe house with Yankees all around, Birdsong spread his piece of cloth on the worktable by the unfinished house foundation. Using his flour-sack notes about landmarks, he composed a map showing the Potomac River, the winding trail, the stone wall, the stream and the massive rock surrounded by a circle of trees and the two farms.

Then he paced the distance from the foundation to the tree-circled flat boulders and from there, down to the winding trail. He marked an X on the exact foundation wall where the treasure lay buried. On the second piece of cloth he wrote what he hoped would instruct Mosby or Lee but confuse anyone else. Satisfied, he stuffed the folded cloths into his shirt.

But he couldn't get that girl out of his mind.

He removed a guarded small scrap of paper from a pocket. Only 3"x4" and much too small for a map, he kept it for an emergency. Unfolding and flattening it on the worktable, he wrote:

> *"Selby with the golden hair,*
> *Eyes of blue and skin so fair,*
> *When peace returns and war is done,*
> *Selby, Selby, you're the one."*

Filled with thoughts of this promising maiden, he allowed hope to push back the horrors of war, if only for a moment. His heart felt lighter than it had in months. The dreamy thoughts of his own future with her and their loving family temporarily assuaged war's grisliness. He folded the paper and pressed it deep into the shirt pocket over his heart. This scrap of future anticipation galvanized him for the dangerous tasks ahead. Who knew what or who he might encounter on the road ahead?

Like all Mosby Raiders, Birdsong knew to keep his holstered six-shooters loaded for action and ready at his fingertips. Raiders preferred pistols over the rifles or sabers used by traditional cavalry units because of their mobility, accuracy and reloading advantages. Nothing beat their effectiveness in close quarter combat. Making sure he'd also loaded his extra, hidden, pistol, he mounted his horse and prepared to start his trip to the safe house.

A sudden flurry of distant shots jerked his attention He turned Blackie abruptly and dashed to the top of the hill for the overview of cleared farm fields stretching below. A column of smoke billowed above the farmer's house. He noted the squad of mounted blue uniforms between the house and barn and bodies on the ground. Union Cavalry had attacked the very family who'd given him help.

Selby!

He spurred Blackie into a full gallop toward the farmhouse. When fifty feet away from the patrol and closing fast, he screamed the blood-curdling Rebel yell and ploughed into the fray, shooting two soldiers right off their horses. Recognizing Mosby's trademark shriek, the small band of Union troops fully anticipated one of his regiment's legendary ambushes underway. Two of the men tried to gallop off but Birdsong shot them dead. The others exchanged fire, and Birdsong brought down two more with his rapid-fire pistols.

Wilbur stood open-mouthed at the kitchen door, unable to process the carnage before him.

Astride his horse, Birdsong recognized the farmer's body sprawled on the ground among those of the hired hands. Such anger surged though him that he rushed upon the remaining four bluecoats.

Kicking his horse into a fierce gallop, he charged in, firing at close range. Three more fell. Only one Yank remained. This last one turned in fear and galloped away as Birdsong dismounted to check the downed farmer and others for life signs.

Dismounting to concentrate on the devastating scene before him, Birdsong failed to notice the escaping Union soldier rein in at a safe distance, turn in the saddle, raise his rifle and fire.

Despite the Bluecoat's distant, poorly aimed shot, in an inscrutable twist of fate, the bullet tore through the air and punctured a small, lethal hole in Birdsong's forehead.

In the last image his mind held, he saw a smiling blond-haired girl wearing a white veil framed against the fresh blue of the spring sky. Then he fell dead beside the farmer, one arm stretched protectively across the man's chest.

Wilbur moved like lightning. He snatched up Birdsong's pistol and ran as fast as he could toward the distant Yankee holding the rifle, shouting. "Mister. Hey, mister. I got somethin' for ya."

Surprised by the sight of a small child, so ludicrous at this gory battle scene, the mounted Union soldier hesitated. He jerked his rein hard right, pulling his agitated horse in a circle as the boy closed the distance.

"Mister, wait up. This is for you." Now only five feet away the boy held up the pistol, handle first, for the soldier to take. But as the man bent down from his horse to grasp it, Wilbur spun the weapon around and fired at him.

The soldier slumped, clutching in disbelief at welling blood staining his jacket. In slow motion, he slid from his horse to the ground. The frightened horse whinnied in fear and fled.

The soldier on the ground moaned. Wilbur walked closer.

"I told ya I had somethin' for ya. It's for stealin' our hogs and our cows and our grain. It's from me and my dad and my friend, Corporal Birdsong. It's from all us Rebs in Virginia."

Wilbur fired the gun at him again.

The Union soldier lay still, staring at the sky through dead eyes.

CHAPTER 59

As Jennifer woke the next morning, the drama's despair lingered. This war's horrors a century and a half earlier once seemed remote–long-ago pictures and descriptions in books, stories unrelated to her. But her miraculous visions these last two weeks had transformed those past echoes into something immediate, compelling and powerful.

These thoughts remained in her mind as she slipped past Becca's sprawled shape in the adjacent bed. Collecting shoes and clothes on the way, she glanced at the dragon, watching her from the bureau. She tiptoed from the room.

In the hotel suite's sitting room, Naples' golden morning sunshine spilled in through the large windows, lighting the tropical scene for whatever might unfold today. The beauty of the day nudged the grief of her fantasy deeper into the hidden recesses of her thoughts.

She dressed slowly, looking out the window at deep blue Gulf of Mexico waters lapping soft sand just beyond swaying palm tree branches. Tucking a room key into her pocket, she left a note describing her destination, found the local paper in the lobby and drank her morning coffee sitting on the dining terrace.

From habit, she turned to the classified and read: *Estate Sale. 50 years of collecting. Final move. One day only, 8am-4pm.* "...and just a few blocks away," she noted with a grin. She could attend before the others woke up. This one had her name on it.

She signed the bill, tiptoed to her room for purse, keys and to revise her whereabouts-note. Fifteen minutes later, she reached the address, expecting to fight for a space in the slew of cars. But no, someone pulled out right in front and she expertly nosed her car into the space. Why did she always feel this pre-sale excitement?

The new owners of this old-style one-story house surely bought it as a teardown because the close proximity to the Gulf made the location highly desirable. They would doubtless substitute a grand multi-story, high-ceiling, Mediterranean-style home on this same lawn. After one enjoyed high ceilings, older homes like this felt claustrophobic, even when main rooms opened onto a swimming pool oasis.

She moved through the foyer, living room and into the den, where she stopped short. A collection of dragon figures covered many shelves; books on another shelf bore dragon-related titles. She hurried to the cashier. "Your sign says you're an estate sale company, but I have questions about the dragons in the study. Are the owners here today?"

"Yes, the two seniors sitting in the kitchen."

Jennifer found them. The old woman typed at a laptop computer while the old man sat beside her, sipping coffee. "Would you please tell me a little about your dragons?"

"You noticed them, did you?" smiled Old Woman.

Old Man nodded to his wife. "Actually they're my collection," he explained. "What would you like to know?"

"How did dragons hook your attention?" Jennifer asked.

He chuckled. "When we first met, my girlfriend asked what I collected. Everyone in her family collected something. She collected miniature pitchers. I had no collection at all, but as we walked along the beach that day, we found a little dragon at the water's edge–no, not a *real* dragon but a plastic toy left by a child or washed up by waves. She suggested this might be a fortuitous sign about what I could collect. That girlfriend later became my wife." He nodded affectionately to Old Woman. "So mine's a sixty-eight year collection."

"Not just dragon figures but books, too?" Jennifer held up one she'd brought from the den.

Old Woman looked up from her keyboard. "Collecting sparks curiosity. Why are some dragons different from others? What have they in common? The books help to find answers."

"And why *are* some dragons different from others?" Jennifer asked.

Old Man smiled. "Depends on the culture where they originated. Some dragons are sea serpents. Some resemble huge birds. The smallest ones look worm-size; the biggest, dinosaur-size. They come in various colors. Eastern dragons typically have no wings but Western dragons do. Eastern dragons may not breathe fire like Western dragons.

"Then, have dragons anything in common?"

Old Man scratched his head. "They're scaly, reptilian-looking and most have legs with claws. The traditional description includes feet like eagles, wings like bats, forelimbs like lions, heads like reptiles, scales like fish and horns like antelopes. All covet shiny objects like jewels, which they collect in their lairs. That's why replicas often hold a pearl and why cultural tales describe them as treasure hoarders."

Old Woman added, "Some legends say their pearls hold wisdom and a power to take them to the 'highest level.' Whatever that is. Water dragons like ocean caverns while land dragons prefer remote caves to hide valuables, which they zealously guard. Dragons always represent enormous, formidable power. They're telepathic so you can't hide your thoughts. They're cunning, proud and sensitive to ridicule, and so often insolent. They are homothermic."

"Homothermic?"

"That means they don't depend on the sun for warmth like other reptiles. They're clean, competitive and antisocial. Some speak and although they have their own language, many are depicted as speaking our languages, if they choose, or communicating with telepathy. They're exceedingly intelligent, which makes their enormous power even more staggering."

"Should you mention riddles, dear?" asked Old Woman.

"Ah, yes. Many like the challenge of riddles. In fact, posing the riddle a dragon can't answer could win your escape from him."

At the riddle connection, Jennifer's eyes sparkled with interest. She pulled up a photo on her cellphone. "Can you tell me anything about this dragon?"

He studied the picture. "Hm… unusual. The golden color of the scales and also — see, here — the number of toes suggest royalty. I think not even the Chinese imperial family, but only the emperor himself, was allowed a five-clawed dragon. So this must be a very special Chinese dragon, but with wings. Strange. If I'm right, and that's a big 'if' because after sixty years I'm still an amateur, maybe your dragon represents a union of some sort between China and Europe—perhaps symbolizing some East-West alliance or agreement."

"Thank you." Jennifer studied the cellphone picture for these new clues.

"How did you happen to photograph this dragon?" asked Old Man.

"I bought him at an estate sale similar to yours. Seemed more like he found me, since dragons didn't interest me at all until this particular one wouldn't let me leave without him. I'm curious about people and things, so now that he's mine, I'd like to better understand him. He almost seemed to have a live quality about him."

"Besides his value to you, he may have tangible value as well. Did the owner know his origin?"

"He belonged to her parents, who got him while they lived in the Philippines."

"Well, this may be your clue."

"What do you mean?"

"Along with their own distinctive culture, the Philippine Islands have had strong Eastern and Western influences for centuries."

Old Woman's keyboard clicked as she searched and reported. "Magellan found those islands in 1521 and the Spanish colonized them from 1565 until their rule ended in 1878 with the Spanish-American War. The Philippines became a U.S. colony and later an independent nation. Of course, before their European discovery, they had their own indigenous population dating back unknown centuries."

"So," Old Man picked up on this, "the Spanish ruled there about 300 years. Then America rescued them from Japanese occupation in WWII in the 1940s. But despite this Western influence, the Philippines' location is clearly Asia. How might this dragon link the Philippines to a Chinese emperor? I have no idea."

Jennifer considered this. "So what other cultures told dragon stories?"

Old Man searched his memory. "Before biblical times, Mesopotamian and Babylonian creation stories involved dragons. Those stories spread west to Greece and across the Mediterranean world to Europe, and East to India, China and all of Asia. More dragon myths appear in the Icelandic sagas, Norway, Denmark,

Ireland, the red dragon of Wales, England, Turkey, Egypt, Ethiopia, Persia and the Middle East. Just about every culture has dragon tales."

Remembering Deputy Martin searching for underlying reasons dragons appeared in so many cultures, she asked, "Do these planet-wide dragon myths reflect common symbolism?"

Old Woman sat back from her computer. "Some philosophers think dragon myths represent basic cosmic dualism."

Seeing Jennifer's puzzled look, Old Man explained: "The most basic dual symbolism is life-versus-death. From that evolved good-versus-evil. You see this easily in Western dragon legends, but Eastern legends also show human survival depends on the power of divine sources that created the world. In this way the dragon myth is also the creation myth."

Old Woman's eyes twinkled. "And here's a recent New Age angle. In Erich von Daniken's book, *Chariot of the Gods*, he suggested ancient aliens visited our planet's early cultures. These primitive people later tried to describe what they'd seen in terms of their simple experience. They couldn't begin to understand fiery space ships, but the arrival of space men was a huge event they wanted to understand and share with the future. Had visitors from the sky traveled here on birds? No, birds didn't leave smoke trails, and smoke, they knew, came from fire. But if they arrived on fire-breathing dragons — this could explain what they saw. Von Daniken and other ancient alien theorists expand this theory convincingly. Since those ancient aliens displayed powers baffling and mysterious to early humans — think of the technology and ideas such visitors would have brought–then didn't the dragon bringing them have those powers, too?"

"Wow," Jennifer marveled. "This is a lot to absorb."

"But stimulating, wouldn't you agree?" Old Man smiled.

"Absolutely. Thank you both for sharing your time and knowledge with me. Which of your dragon books do you recommend I buy today to increase my knowledge?"

"Follow me into the den and I'll select some for you." He pulled several from the shelf. "Please take these with my compliments. Look, here's my card. If you ever solve your own dragon mystery, please tell us what you learn."

"Tom O'Bannon," she read aloud from the card. "Your estate sale ad says you're moving?"

"Yes, to a senior complex right here in Naples. That address appears on this card."

Jennifer flipped open one of the books to a picture of an ancient map showing land on the left, ocean in the middle and a blank space in the right. In this open space she read, "Here be dragons."

"What does this mean?"

"When men thought the world was flat, they couldn't imagine what lay past the outer edge where the land and ocean dropped off into oblivion. They capsulized this scary unknown and unknowable with the ominous saying, 'Here be dragons' or 'There be dragons.' It came to stand for something you knew must be there but you couldn't possibly understand."

Jennifer clapped her hands. "Fascinating. I'm so glad I stopped here today. You're a dynamic duo and your energy is contagious. A pleasure to meet you both." She extended her hand to shake theirs. "The best of luck in your new adventure. Will all your dragons go with you?"

"Many will and are already boxed for the move. Those in the den are some extras. And thank you for the good luck wish." His wife nudged him and whispered something. "Ah, of course. Just a minute, please."

He reached into a kitchen drawer, removed something and handed it to his wife. "Speaking of good luck, Tom and I would like you to have this." He smiled agreement as she held out a jewelry-size box covered with intricate symbolic gold tracings.

"What in the world?" Jennifer lifted the lid, looked inside and smiled. "Oh, my."

CHAPTER 60

Inside the box against a black velvet background lay a silver-dollar-size cloisonné dragon, red with gold trim, on a slender gold-colored chain.

"So unusual," she marveled, lifting the necklace from the case. "May I buy it? After all, this is an estate sale."

They shook their heads. "No, because you'd break the charm. One day you'll give it to someone else, and you mustn't accept payment either or your good luck changes to bad."

"Who gave it to you?"

"An old Chinese shopkeeper insisted I accept it for my wife when I bought a dragon from him many years ago," Tom explained.

Marie smiled. "He told Tom the luck works for its owner whether the dragon's in the box or worn around the neck, but I enjoyed wearing it until last week when I knew it was time to pass it on. Shall I help you put it on?"

"Yes, please." She touched the amulet hanging at her throat. "How can I thank you for this?"

"By exploring the meaning of dragons and sharing your knowledge with others, as we did with you."

Spontaneously, Jennifer hugged them both. They waved as she left.

Excited about this unexpected development, Jennifer drove back to the hotel to find Grammy enjoying a room service breakfast on their suite's balcony overlooking the Gulf. After show-and-tell about her morning excursion, Jennifer sat in a chair to thumb through one of her new dragon books.

"Things happen to you, Jen, that don't to other people. Today's an example."

"Or maybe if you just show up where things happen, you might become part of them."

"Speaking of which, any events on today's to-do list?" Grammy asked.

"No, and with Max caged again, we have a relaxed day to catch our breath. I expect we'll hear from Goodwin about Chelsea. We might even visit her if she's ready for company."

When Becca awoke, they ate lunch together and the day proceeded in leisurely fashion. Becca spent the evening with Tony while Jennifer and Grammy ate at a restaurant. The two of them watched TV until Grammy fell asleep and Jennifer also went to bed.

She riffled through another of her new dragon books, glancing at pictures, but felt too tired to read. Remembering info learned at the O'Bannon's sale this morning, she stared at her own dragon, perched on the bureau. His gaping mouth looked to her tonight more like a grin than a roar. "So, you like solving riddles, do you? You watched me struggle to figure out mine and laughed all the while because you already knew the answer." Did his eyes twinkle or was it a trick of sheer fatigue?

She slid under the covers, smiling into the dark. "If I envision anything tonight," she guessed, "it's bound to include dragons." In a few minutes, she began taking slow, deep breaths.

A vision came all right, but not what she anticipated. No, her subconscious rocketed her again onto a farm in 1863.

When the ear-splitting firearm explosions, shouting and turmoil ended in the farmyard, a deadly silence replaced it. Birdsong, Gentry and the field hands lay motionless on the ground. Suddenly the house door burst open and the women tumbled out.

The missus screamed, "Quick, see if any of 'ems alive. Why didn't he let them Yanks just steal whatever they want? Why did he cross them? Why?"

Searching for signs of life, the women rushed to each downed man, but to no avail. Soon their wails of grief echoed through the air.

"What should we do?" cried one.

The missus sobbed with anguish for her husband's death and for the hopelessness this new calamity brought. She couldn't begin to run this farm without him and the other hands, even in peacetime — never mind during this terrible war while robbed of supplies, animals and crops. What would happen to them all? To their land? How would she feed her children? With Frank gone, they'd all look to her for answers...but she had none.

Then one clear thought blinked into her mind. With every man dead in this improbable skirmish, only the women and children knew what had just happened. If the Union found out, they'd take further revenge. To protect what little she had left, she must erase all evidence of this tragic event and deny what occurred here. Spurring the other women into action would mask her true helplessness with the appearance of purposeful action. Motion, if not progress.

"One of you help me carry Frank and the corporal into the house. One of you hide these extra horses in the barn. The rest of you check for anything valuable on the bodies to use or sell. Then we must bury the bodies — the Yanks in the swale behind the barn and our farm hands in the orchard behind the house. It's hard, but we have no choice."

Selby hurried to Birdsong, her blond-hair trailing across his still-warm cheek as she knelt over him. She smoothed back his hair, above the trickle of blood oozing from the round hole in his forehead. She curled her fingers into his warm hand.

Stricken at the mindless waste of life of this man whom she'd welcomed to play an intimate role in her future, she shed tears upon his still face. "Why? Why him?" she whispered into the wind. She sobbed as despair invaded her soul.

At her mother's frightened shout to "get a move on," Selby jerked from her lost dream to face heartless reality. With a shudder, she removed Birdsong's holster, spurs and boots, placing them neatly beside his guns. Inside his shirt, she found some cloths with drawings and added them to the pile, together with the contents of his jacket pockets. Something caused her to open the small folded paper. As she read the poem he'd written her, a strangled sound rose in her throat and she cried at the sky, "Of all the men in this terrible war, why did you have to take him and Paw?"

Doubled over his body, she wailed her torment at the tragic waste of war's dead. She gently brushed her lips against Raiford's before she straightened and with a final sob, forced herself to move on to the next body.

Hours later, exhausted and in semi-shock, the women and boy slumped in chairs around the kitchen table, the life they'd known altered forever by fate's random intervention.

"The bodies are hidden," the missus managed, "and tomorrow we give all them extra horses to the Rebs, who'll ask no questions. If them Yankees

return, we deny this ever happened. We say our men are away helping other farmers with spring planting." She looked around at the others, emotionally and physically wrung out as she was. *"We accomplished the impossible outside today and I couldn't a done it without you. Besides the big shallow grave for them Union killers, we laid out Frank, the help, and the corporal in plots in the orchard."*

Selby dried her reddened eyes. *"The apple trees are blossoming over them. Looks like a white fairyland they're lying under with the petals starting to fall."*

"Remember," warned the missus, *"their graves must stay unmarked until this awful war ends. The Blues must never learn what happened here."*

Wilbur smiled but said nothing, for he had marked the graves his own way to honor the memory of these men. From his rock collection, he'd placed a special quartz stone atop the graves where each hired hand lay. On his father's grave, he tied his father's handkerchief to the end of a stick and pushed the other end into the ground. On the corporal's grave, he'd placed the bucket the man filled at the stream where they first met.

The missus's short-term plan worked, but within a year circumstances forced her to begin selling off parts of the large farm, which eventually dwindled to a twenty-five acre *"farmette,"* composed of the land surrounding her house, the out buildings and orchard.

When the war ended in 1865, many men of marriageable age lay dead or returned home physically mangled or emotionally traumatized. Sixteen years old when the Union soldiers shot her father, his farm hands and Raiford Birdsong in April 1863, blond-haired Selby had more suitors than most because of her beauty. In 1865, at age eighteen, she married a man with one arm, his other removed during a field amputation when this standard solution for gunshot wounds saved some lives, if not limbs. By 1870, she'd borne her husband two children. In 1901, Selby's daughter married and had four children of her own.

In 1920, Selby's grown granddaughter prowled through the attic of her grandmother's farmhouse. Poking among the trunks and suitcases, she found a box containing two six-shooter pistols, a holster, spurs, and two pieces of cloth with odd pencil scrawls.

She also found a frame of twisted branches and a primitive painting-on-wood of trees surrounding a flat boulder with another rock atop it and more small stones atop that. The frame and painting sizes matched, but the picture's wood had warped slightly. She folded the two cloths to the right shape and smoothed them across the back of the painting as filler. Then she cut cardboard to the correct size and nailed on this backing to give it a finished look. The granddaughter stared at the picture, seeing how the *twig frame brought out something haunting in the way sunlight spilled on that big rock pile in the circle of trees and the odd, short, crescent-shaped stone beside it...*

Later that day, she sat by her grandmother. "Nana, what can you tell me about these things on the table that I brought down from the attic?"

Selby, then seventy-three, walked along the table. She touched again various items, which kindled forgotten memories. When she reached the picture, the holstered pistol, the spurs and boots, she grabbed the edge of the table to steady herself as tears filled her eyes. These had survived, unlike the small piece of paper she'd re-read so many times that the folds frayed until the paper disintegrated. Until today, she'd shelved the memory of that heart-wrenching day in her young life when Union soldiers murdered the men in her life. She wept again for her slain field hands, her father and Corporal Raiford Birdsong, the first man she'd ever loved.

CHAPTER 61

Jennifer awoke slowly the next morning and lay in bed, temporarily immobilized by the power of this mysterious drama haunting her mind. These flashbacks weren't disjointed dreams — they felt more like visions. This entire slice of the Civil War exactly fit facts she knew *could* have happened at that time, but did they?

Unlike her friend, Veronika, Jennifer was no psychic. Yet she felt these events, so clear in her mind, had occurred exactly as they unfolded in her vision.

Was this all a figment of her fertile imagination or a glimpse into the past through a portal, perhaps one opened by the mysterious framed painting? Her logical mind promptly discarded this notion.

But it crept back into her thinking. Hadn't she searched restlessly for two years for a frame she saw only in her mind until it lay on Selby's estate sale table in Great Falls with the haunting painting inside? Was that coincidence? Or had that object begun pulling her toward it three years ago when she bought the first yard sale picture that she intuitively knew needed a special one-of-a-kind frame existing only in her imagination — the frame housing the painting of the Indian sacred place, the riddle and the map?

She looked at her dragon. Did primitive man have trouble separating dreams and visions from reality when both seemed equally vivid? During recent nights, she'd vision-walked in century-old shoes of people she felt she *knew*. What was going on here?

Her fingers touched the dragon necklace, surprised she'd forgotten to remove it last night. She scoffed. Wasn't this necklace just a silly modern version of early man's desire for charms, beads, figures or other talisman magic to gain that vital edge for survival — good luck? How could this stubborn primitive urge for protection still entice, despite scientific knowledge to the contrary? She thought of four-leaf-clovers, a rabbit's foot, of gamblers who always wore their lucky socks to the craps table, or ball players their lucky number, or lucky pennies tucked into loafers. She shook her head in confusion.

Getting dressed, she looked expectantly at her own dragon sitting on the dresser. It seemed he returned an equally expectant stare.

Her mind swirling with questions, Jennifer made a cup of coffee in the suite's kitchenette and took it to the balcony to compile today's to-do list. Gazing over the seemingly endless waves lapping the shore below her, she sat back, closed her eyes and invited cosmic connections to engulf her. She felt at one with these natural rhythms and ancient sounds of the universe.

When her pen dropped noisily from her lap to the balcony tile, her imagination rocketed her back from space to her planet to her balcony chair. She sighed, opened her eyes and started the list. "Let Peggy into Grammy's house at 9AM to tag" and beneath that, "Call Goodwin" and "Visit Chelsea?" She thought a moment and added, "Call Birdsong."

The sale would begin Friday morning, end Sunday at 4:00 and they'd start their drive north Monday morning. So one week left in Florida before Grammy's new life began in northern Virginia. She glanced at her watch: 8 o'clock. She must hustle to dress and drive to Grammy's house to admit Peggy's crew at 9:00. When she tiptoed back into the bedroom to get her clothes, Becca lay comatose in the other bed, doubtless having returned late from her date.

Jennifer dressed in the suite's living room, wrote a note explaining her whereabouts and drove toward Grammy's house, stopping on the way for coffee and a bag of donuts. As she unlocked her mother's front door, her phone rang.

"Goodwin, here," said the voice. "Could I come by for a few minutes? Are you at the hotel?"

"No, at mother's house."

"Good. See you in five."

Peggy's group arrived to continue their tagging and arranging inside, as Goodwin's car pulled up curbside. He approached Jennifer on the porch. "Look, a couple of things. Chelsea's at home, resting. She's going to be fine—just shaken up and nursing some bruises. She'll be back at work Wednesday. I..." he sounded uncomfortable, "I want to thank *you*, especially, for figuring out her odd phone message and calling 911. You...you saved her from Roderick... and we captured him besides." He laughed. "And I thought I was the detective here." She chuckled with him. "Also, that other reason I needed to get back to you, we think we found some more of your mother's stolen jewelry. We need her to identify it, maybe later today?"

Jennifer grinned. "Wonderful news. You name the time and place and we'll get her there."

"And what's your interest again in the Venuti case? You asked me about him."

Jennifer considered her answer. If Goodwin thought her interest casual, he'd give her a casual response. But if he knew her interest was significant, he might tell her more.

"If I speak to you in total confidence, will you keep what I tell you a secret?"

Goodwin looked doubtful. "So long as what you tell me breaks no laws, I will."

Jennifer took a deep breath. "He and my mother had a three-year love affair and planned to marry. He told her he worked for the FBI on dangerous assignments and if he failed to return from one of his trips, it meant he was dead." She shrugged, "It sounds fishy to me, but she believed him. Then one day he didn't come back or message her why. She assumed he died in the line of duty. It broke her heart that they wouldn't be together, but worse, she worried he'd met a horrible end. It's like that when you love somebody."

Goodwin stared at Jennifer a long moment. He wanted to say he knew something about loving somebody, his wife who died last year and now a new spark with Chelsea. But he discarded that impulse as unprofessional, never mind unmanly. "Look," he said instead, "I got a buddy in the FBI. We grew up together and stayed friends over the years. Yesterday we talked about another case when the Venuti matter came up. My buddy said..." Goodwin's phone rang, interrupting his sentence. "Sorry, got to answer this." He spoke into the phone. "Okay. Okay. When...? I'm on my way." He ended the call and turned to Jennifer. "Got to go. I'll let you know a time later today for Frances to ID the jewelry." He hurried to his car.

"But..." Jennifer said to no one because Goodwin pulled away from the curb, seeming to entirely forget their Venuti conversation.

She sighed and went inside. Was volunteering the confidence of her mother's relationship with Venuti an unforgiveable mistake? She had no right to do so. If Goodwin let this slip, might criminals connect her mother to Venuti and come looking for their missing money? Money enough for her to buy into any upscale senior residence she chose? Yet Jennifer couldn't take back what she'd told Goodwin. Words are free, she thought, it's how you use them that can cost you.

Feeling regretful, she wandered into the house and sat in the kitchen. With time to kill before Becca and Grammy asked her to pick them up, she dialed Chelsea. After the phone rang several times, she prepared to disconnect, thinking Chelsea might be asleep, but then she heard, "Hello."

"Chelsea, its Jennifer. How *are* you?"

"Well...okay I guess." Her voice sounded very hoarse. "Had the scare of my life, but thanks to you, Jen, a happy ending. I'm amazed and grateful you translated the hair colors into danger levels. I doubted anybody could understand. It was a pathetic long shot, but my only chance."

"Give yourself credit for paying attention in your course and then explaining it so well to us all at the beauty shop. So the hospital discharged you?"

"Yeah, I'll take it easy a couple of days and start back at the salon on Wednesday. I'll wear a scarf to cover the bruise on my neck. He...he strangled me, Jen. I...I almost died. If the police had arrived a few seconds later, I'd be gone. I couldn't talk for a day and a half. I'll never forget the cold, zombie stare in that man's eyes."

"Oh, Chelsea, I'm so sorry you had to go through this."

"Yeah, well...stuff happens." She changed to a safer subject. "You two coming for your usual Thursday appointments?"

"Yes, and could someone give Becca a haircut?"

"Sure, we'll fit her in. And Jen, thanks again for getting my meaning and calling 911. I owe you."

"Take it easy and we'll see you Thursday. Bye."

When the doorbell rang, Jennifer looked out the glass. She couldn't believe her eyes. William Early! She eased the door open, leaving the chain attached. "Yes?"

"Hello. My name is William Early. May I talk with you a few minutes?"

Obviously, he didn't appear to recognize her from the plane when he'd been so drunk. She closed the door enough to remove the chain but didn't intend letting him inside. She opened the door six inches and braced her foot against it so he couldn't push it further. "What do you want?"

"Are you Jennifer Shannon?" She nodded. "May I come in?"

"I'm sorry, it's not convenient now. What do you want?"

"You don't know me, but I think you may have something to sell that I'd like to buy. A Civil War map and a riddle?"

"Where did you get such information?"

"Many folks know of my Civil War interest and tell me when something interesting surfaces, like your two items. May I please see them?"

"No, sorry." She started to close the door.

"Wait," he called. "I'm prepared to offer you $50,000 each for them. That $100,000 could help fund a college education for one of your grandchildren."

"What makes you think I have grandchildren?"

"I know quite a lot about you because you may have something I want. If so, I'd like to make you the right offer."

"I have nothing to sell, thank you."

"Oh, but you do, and if it's what I want I'll double the amount to $200,000."

"No, thank you." Jennifer again tried to close the door but he'd wedged his foot in so she couldn't.

Just then Peggy appeared behind her and spoke loudly, "Is everything all right here or should I call the police?"

At this, William Early withdrew his foot. Jennifer slammed and locked the door.

"Thank you, Peggy."

"Glad to help."

CHAPTER 62

Jennifer reattached the security chain, leaned her head against the closed door and tried to breathe normally. From the window, she watched Early leave the front porch and get into a car, but the car didn't drive away. Was he sizing up the house to break in?

At least he hadn't identified her from the plane, although that encounter gave her knowledge about him. She knew he had a drinking problem and was prepared to do *anything* to get what he wanted.

While waiting for his car to depart, she dialed John Birdsong to describe what happened. "Have you any idea how he learned about my riddle and map? You're the only person in Florida who knows they exist. Who did you tell?"

"Jennifer, I'm sorry about this. I've never met him myself, but William Early gives all Civil War buffs a bad name. I told you I'd put out a few feelers regarding your riddle and map. Many Civil War enthusiasts talk together on the internet about our theories or ideas or discoveries, and he has a lot of 'spies' — contacts wanting payoffs from him for leads they provide. This internet network extends beyond Florida. Civil War fans anywhere in the U.S.A. or elsewhere might participate.

"But my questions revealed nothing about you and I only asked probability questions, like what they thought the chances were that Stoughton had a treasure that Mosby rescued. Or, if somebody found a map and a riddle that appeared to address this treasure, what were the chances it might be authentic? Could anybody suggest who had the knowledge to authenticate such documents? And so on. I don't know Early personally, but by reputation he's a very aggressive private collector with big bucks and atrocious manners."

"Is he dangerous?"

Birdsong laughed. "That I don't know, but I'd guess more obnoxious than dangerous." A buzzer sounded in the background. "I have to get something from the stove. My wife's visiting her mother for a week so I'm playing bachelor and cooking for myself." The clang of pans sounded in the background. "There, all set now. Sorry to interrupt."

Confused, Jennifer said, "From what you describe, I see how he found you, but how did he find me?"

"I really don't know. Rumor says he's used private detectives to track people down if they have something he wants."

"Well, thanks for wanting to help me, John, but please stop your inquiries as of now."

"Done, Jennifer. Did you get the info I e-mailed you about Raiford and links to research on the treasure?"

"Not yet, but thanks for sending them."

"Shall I contact you with any feedback from inquiries already made?"

"Yes, please."

Jennifer no sooner ended the call than her phone rang again.

"Morning, Mom," Becca chirped much too cheerfully. "Would you mind picking us up at the hotel? We could eat here or go out for lunch or buy groceries for lunch at Grammy's house."

"Let's use up groceries already in the pantry. Could you be in front of the hotel in fifteen minutes...? Good, I'll swing by then."

During lunch, Jennifer told them about William Early. "We want to avoid him and keep him out of the house, because he's after the copies I printed of the cloths from the frame." She explained the Mosby treasure theory.

Grammy clucked, "Well, if Mr. Early thinks these papers are valuable enough to buy for $200,000, let's hide them in the safe."

"Good idea," Jennifer agreed. "Who has the combination?"

"I thought we all did."

"You're right. I put mine back in the This-and-That file but the movers took the file cabinet."

Jennifer stood. "I have a copy in my purse. Let's go upstairs to solve this while Peggy and her people are away for lunch."

As they started up the stairs, Jennifer's cell rang.

"Goodwin here. How about 3:00 for the jewelry ID? I'll meet you and Frances at the Property Evidence Room in Building J at the Sheriff's Headquarters, 3319 Tamiami Trail East. Got it?"

"Got it. Thanks, Deputy. See you at three." At the top of the stairs, she confirmed this plan with her mother.

The doorbell sounded and as Becca raced downstairs, Grammy called, "Must be Peggy's gang returning to work on the estate sale, but look out through the window before you unlock."

Becca looked out, then hustled back to the foot of the stairs. "It's a man I don't recognize," she said in a stage whisper.

Jennifer and Grammy trotted down the stairs to the window.

Looking apprehensive, Jennifer said, "It's William Early again." As they stared, he rang the doorbell again.

"Should we pretend we're not here?" Grammy whispered.

Jennifer whispered back. "Becca, get the wasp spray from the kitchen."

When her daughter brought the can, Jennifer opened the door but left the chain in place. Holding the can out of sight, she looked out at the man on the porch.

"Hello, again, Mrs. Shannon. Look, I'm really sorry we got off on the wrong foot earlier. I apologize for upsetting you. I told you I'm William Early, but I didn't explain I'm a Civil War historian and collector of relics. Many enthusiasts, like me, read extensively on this subject and form study groups to learn more about this momentous period in our American past. Our common interest connects us like a fraternity, and we often talk on the internet about our slant on various battles and events.

"That's how I learned about something you may have found recently, a riddle and map." He shifted his weight and moved his briefcase from his right hand to his left. "Because of my long-standing fascination with this war, you can understand why I'd like to see what you've found. From my extensive knowledge, I might be able to help you decipher codes or otherwise offer academic assistance or clarification. And on the offhand chance it's something to round out my collection, I might offer to buy it from you at a very good price."

Grammy whispered, "He sounds reasonable and looks harmless. Should we let him in?"

Jennifer shook her head before speaking again to Early. "Thanks, but what makes you think I have something that interests you?"

He cleared his throat, shaping his answer. "Among my staff of close associates are some computer experts who have...special skills for finding who has put a piece of information on the internet and then tracing further to learn those he communicated with about it."

Jennifer realized this fit John Birdsong's internet feelers on her behalf. Had they checked his phone records, too? But there must be more. "What made you think I have grandchildren?"

"Most facts about everyone are public record these days. You probably know that."

"But even if you traced my e-mail address to my home, how did you find me in Florida?"

"Maybe my associate checked an internet user's phone records. Or maybe you have chatty neighbors who mentioned your vacation to one of my associates?"

Under other circumstances, Early's Civil War expertise would seem exactly what she needed to better understand the cloths' messages, just as John Birdsong's had. But now her intuition warned danger. She shivered — something creepy about him from the outset but way stronger now that she realized he'd stalked her.

"I'm afraid your detective work's in vain because I haven't anything about the Civil War to show or sell. You've made a mistake." From the corner of her eye, Jennifer saw Peggy's car pull to the curb. "And I would appreciate it if you never bother me with this again. Because if you persist, I *will* call the police to arrest you. Now, please leave these premises and don't ever come back."

Early started to protest, but seeing Peggy's group coming up the sidewalk, he turned to leave.

"Afternoon, ladies," he said, albeit through clenched teeth, as he passed them on the way to his car.

CHAPTER 63

At the Property Evidence Room, Grammy studied the jewelry arrayed before her. "This one's mine and this and this but not that one. She picked out nine of the ten pieces. "May I take them home now?"

"Yes," Goodwin confirmed. "We'll add your photos to the ones we took for backup in case they're needed at trial. Just sign here," he pointed with a pen, "stating the jewelry is yours and today's date when we returned them."

"Where did you find them?" Jennifer asked.

"At a pawn shop in Michigan close to where they apprehended Roderick. The other missing pieces may be at similar shops between here and there. We have bulletins out, trying to track them down. Some shop owners are forthcoming, some aren't."

"Deputy Goodwin, thanks for your good police work." Grammy patted his hand. "Jen, is this a good time to tell Cliff about William Early, in case we need help later?"

They did.

"See, here's the problem," Goodwin shuffled his feet. "He hasn't actually committed a crime yet, and we can't arrest him unless he does. You could consider a restraining order if his threats accelerate. But to deliver that order we have to find him. Sometimes that's easy, sometimes hard, especially if he avoids his home or his office—places we'd typically serve him the restraining order. Anything else?" They shook their heads.

"Then I gotta go."

"Here, I'll lock the door after you," Jennifer offered, following him to the porch. When they were out of earshot of the others, she added, "You started to tell me about Venuti earlier."

He looked uncomfortable. "Yeah, but this isn't the place. How about next time I see you?" His phone rang. "Sorry, I gotta take this.... Yeah. Yeah.... When...? Who...? Birdsong? That's a real name...? Okay, I'm on the way."

"Wait a minute. I know a John Birdsong. He's the link between William Early and me. Has...has something happened to him?"

"You say you know him? And he's connected to this man you're afraid of?"

"Yes."

"Then I'll come right back to see you as soon as I finish with... with this development."

Back at home, they found Becca at her laptop. "Catching up on my job search," she explained. "Peggy's gone for the day. I double checked windows and doors and distributed wasp spray cans around the house so we have one in most rooms here and several for the hotel suite."

"Good work, honey, since it's our default weapon of choice," Jennifer said.

"Any plans for dinner?" Becca wondered.

"How about BhaBha?" Grammy suggested. "Do you like Persian food?"

"Absolutely. What time?"

"Six o'clock sound good?" Jennifer suggested.

"I'll make the reservation for two," Becca offered.

"But we're three, not two," Grammy pointed out.

"You are the two. I'm having dinner with Tony." She grinned. "He'll be here in an hour. But you don't have to wait for him if you want to go to the hotel sooner. Beautiful as your house is, Grammy, the hotel's ocean view is even better."

Grammy eyed her granddaughter. "But should we leave you two here alone?"

"Old fashioned rules, Gram. These are modern times."

"That's what the young always say, but some things never change."

Jennifer picked up her keys. "Come on, Mom. Off to the hotel and dinner."

Becca grinned and called after them, "Blessed are the mischief makers for they shall always wear smiles."

CHAPTER 64

After a dreamless night, Jennifer awoke to a perfect Naples day—pleasant summer temperature, warm gentle breezes skimming the placid Gulf of Mexico as wavelets lapped the hotel's beach shoreline.

Jennifer let Peggy's group into Grammy's house at 9:00, reminding them to admit no one without specific permission. Moreover, the day unfolded peacefully, in sharp contrast to the recent chaotic fare they'd almost come to accept as "normal."

"Let's all go to the beach," Becca suggested. Once ensconced in a cabana's shade, she asked an agreeable passer-by, "Would you please take a picture of three generations having fun together?" Eyeing Becca, the beach-walker willingly agreed.

That night they dined at the hotel, sipped wine while watching the sunset, whooping at the shared sight of a green flash. Later in bed, they slept long and well.

But the next day unfolded very differently.

While Peggy's people prepped on Thursday, the last day before the estate sale's start, the three of them skipped off to Grammy's regular weekly salon appointment with Chelsea, where they beautified and schmoozed.

"Chelsea, do you feel up to telling us what happened with Max Roderick?"

"The nasty story I'm trying to forget?"

"Well," Grammy touched her arm gently, "don't if you're uncomfortable. But remember, we share your involvement with this scary man… and Jennifer played a role…"

"You're right," Chelsea acknowledged. "I still can hardly believe it really happened."

"Could you just walk us through it, step by step?"

Chelsea nodded, protectively crossing her arms across her chest. She spoke in a small voice. "Goodwin told me Roderick slit the screen door, unlocked the handle and broke into my kitchen. I heard nothing until he appeared in the living room, where I sat watching television.

I recognized him immediately. On the inside, I panicked hysterically, but on the outside, I tried to act casual. I go, 'Hi. Can I do something for you?'

"He goes, 'Do you know who I am?'

"I say, 'No, afraid I don't, but beer is in the fridge.' He didn't expect this so he got a beer and sat down in front of the TV.

"I thought maybe I could bluff my way through this, but then he says, 'You got a beauty shop customer named Frances Ryerson?'"

"I go, 'I remember their appointments, not their names.'

"He goes, 'You let her borrow your cellphone last time she was in?' Now he's sitting forward in the chair, but I stayed relaxed.

"Not likely. Way too many customers to do that.'

"Then he goes, 'My girlfriend saw her take your phone to the ladies' room where she made a call that ruined a deal I was running.'

"'Oh,' I said, trying to look surprised, 'I don't remember that. Sure your girlfriend gave you the right story?' That surprised him. I pretended to look at TV but watched him out of the corner of my eye. He was getting agitated and I knew he meant trouble. I couldn't get to my pepper spray in the bedroom. The time would come very soon to run for my life. But then the phone rang and it was you, Jennifer. I tell you my hair color story, which really means I'm in serious danger. Thank God, you understood and called the cops."

She grabbed a tissue, wiped away tears and blew her nose.

"And before the police arrived?" Grammy nudged gently.

"I asked him was he from around here, if he had a favorite watering hole or restaurant. He didn't take the bait. I said I hadn't seen him around but did he live nearby. I steeled myself to try anything to buy time for someone to save my life. I asked him to get me a beer. He did. When he handed it to me, he ran his fingers over my cheek.

"I invited him to sit down by me on the couch to watch TV. I asked what shows he liked. He didn't answer but I knew he looked at me differently now than when he came in, sizing me up now for sex before he killed me. I asked him what kind of music he liked.

"To my surprise that got him talking but when that banter ended, he leaned over and kissed me. Now I'm praying Cliff will storm in and shoot him, but no, his hands went all over me. If I rejected him, I knew he'd kill me. So I...I let him do stuff to buy time.

"But then he kissed me again and this time his hands fastened around my neck and squeezed. Choking for breath, I kicked him you-know-where and when he doubled over, I ran for the door. But he recovered and grabbed me before I got outside. He looped something around my throat and pulled it tight from behind.

"I tried to fight but I couldn't get at him behind me and — they told me later — I passed out. Next thing I knew, I woke up in the hospital."

Quiet permeated the beauty shop because everyone had strained to eavesdrop on this emotional story.

Jennifer jumped up to hug Chelsea, whose tears appeared again.

"It was the scariest thing in my whole life," she cried into Jennifer's shoulder.

"It's over now and you helped capture a really dangerous criminal," Becca reminded her.

Chelsea whispered in Jennifer's ear. "Thanks also, Jen, for introducing me to Cliff Goodwin. He...he promised earlier to look out for me. Because he did and from what I learned in the self-defense class he suggested, I fought back instead of giving up. If I hadn't, I'd be dead instead of here today."

Jennifer whispered back, "My mother suffered too, Chelsea, but you both stood up to him. That's why he's in jail."

When the three women returned home from the beauty shop, Goodwin sat in his cruiser at the curb. Putting down his phone, he asked them, "Got a few minutes?"

They welcomed him inside and went to the lanai to evade Peggy's taggers.

"What can you tell me about John Birdsong?" he asked.

Grammy described her Civil War Study Group connection. Jennifer explained consulting him about the cloths she'd found in Virginia and his offer to put out feelers for more information.

"I don't know him at all, but why are you asking us?" Becca wondered.

"He's dead and I want to find out why," Goodwin responded.

"He's *dead*?" Jennifer gasped.

"Oh, no." Grammy collapsed into a chair, visibly shaken. "His poor wife..."

Jennifer remembered, "John said his wife was visiting her mother for a week, so he was home alone."

"Yeah, we reached the wife. His death looked like a bizarre accident but when you," he nodded to Jennifer, "told me he's connected to this man you're afraid of, I did a re-take."

Tears filled Grammy's eyes. "I can't believe it. John was such a nice person. He and his wife were our friends for years. My husband liked him, and he gave Jennifer information for her research."

Touching her mother's shoulder to comfort her, Jennifer added, "Early said his associates connected me to John by hacking his e-mails and phones. They even talked to my McLean neighbors to find out where I am. He offered to buy the map and riddle for $200,000, but I said I had nothing for sale. He gave me the creeps and I asked him to leave and not return."

"So you didn't tell this William Early guy you owned such items, never mind showing them to him?"

Jennifer licked her lips. "No, but what if Early *thought* John had seen them? Might he want to learn what John knew?"

Becca looked confused. "You called this death a bizarre accident, Deputy. What does that mean?"

"Looked like someone tried persuading him to talk first, though that's not the cause of death."

"What is?" Grammy asked.

"Venomous snake bite."

"What?" Becca jerked her feet off the floor and tucked them protectively underneath her in the chair.

"Yeah, we found an eastern diamondback rattler closed up with him in a small bathroom at his house."

"Murder by snake?" Becca wailed. Her wide-open eyes searched the floor for slithery movements.

"Becca's terrified of snakes," Jennifer explained. "But what did you mean by someone trying to persuade John to talk?"

"Besides four snake bites he had some body bruising and several smashed fingernails—maybe unrelated to his death, maybe not."

Jennifer tried to put it together. "Do you think because I refused to give Early information, he tortured John Birdsong to learn what he knew about my map and riddle?"

Becca huddled back into her chair. "And part of that torture was shutting John in a small space with a...a poisonous snake?" She shivered.

Jennifer calculated. "Closing him in the room with a big snake could frighten him into talking. And when his tormenters finished with him, the scene implied accidental snakebite death instead of murder."

Goodwin sighed. "I gotta consider every explanation for what we find at a crime scene. You've described one scenario."

"Wait a minute," Jennifer said. "A few days ago Becca got a bad scare from an eastern diamondback in our garage." She fumbled in her purse for the "Florida Snakes" book she'd earlier hidden there. "This says diamondbacks are common in Florida, meaning two snake events related to us and people we know could be coincidence. Or could these two encounters mean someone interested in my relics has access to such snakes?"

Becca's face contorted into a grimace of fear. Her voice rose two octaves and she cried out, "That was a *rattlesnake* in the garage with me?" She curled into a ball in her chair, whimpering. Jennifer rushed over to soothe her daughter as Goodwin rose to go.

"I don't believe in coincidence," he called over his shoulder as he left.

CHAPTER 65

Peggy's group arrived at 8:00 to start the weekend estate sale. "We put a box of numbers on the front porch for buyers who'll line up when the sale opens at 9 o'clock," she explained to Jennifer and Becca. "Friday's technically a weekday, but usually very popular because it's the first day. And dealers will come today."

As her associates fanned out into each room to assist customers and deter sticky-fingers, Peggy continued. "I notice Mrs. Ryerson isn't here with you."

"No, she's not psyched up yet to watch her belongings go to strangers. Maybe tomorrow."

"I understand. Will you and Becca stay?"

"Not the whole time, but we'll drop back periodically. You and your team have arranged everything well and tagged every item. That's a big job in a house this full."

"We've had a lot of experience and enjoy what we do."

Jennifer thought about Early and his minions. "You'll use only the front door for traffic?"

"Yes, unless someone needs to load furniture in the driveway. Then we'd open the garage briefly for that purpose."

Foolish for Jennifer to say they didn't want strangers in the house, because everyone shopping the estate sale was a stranger. She sighed.

Peggy opened the door promptly at 9:00 and the first twenty buyers in line streamed inside. Some asked immediately about an item they'd seen in the online photos describing the sale while others roamed, picking up and carrying smaller items they fancied lest someone else get them. For large items, they quickly cornered a sales person to attach "sold" signs before they'd paid at the cashier table. Peggy greeted many by nod or name, including dealers she knew or regulars who followed her company's sales each week.

Sales moved at a brisk pace indoors while cars on the street outside jockeyed for parking spaces.

Jennifer went upstairs to assure herself the low bookcase in the master bedroom remained in front of the wall-safe, clearly marked NFS.

One of Peggy's helpers found Jennifer. "There's a young man at the door who wants to see you."

Jennifer hurried down where the boy waited. "Good morning, Georgie. What do you think of all this excitement?"

"Okay, I guess, but he was here last night."

"Who was here?"

"A man in your yard, walking around to the back of the house."

With Roderick in jail, Jennifer suspected he invented this for a chocolate reward. "Did you recognize him?"

"Yes and no."

"What does that mean exactly, Georgie?"

"Yes, because I also saw him in your yard the day before and no, because he isn't the bad man in the picture."

What could explain this? Jennifer wondered. Maybe one of William Early's so-called "associates," casing the house for a way inside to steal her map and riddle?

"When was this, Georgie?"

"My bedtime's nine o'clock on summer nights. My bedroom window faces your house. Sometimes I don't fall asleep right away, so I look out the window. The last two nights were real dark by ten and the moon was out. There he was, both nights."

"Come with me. Let's see if he left any clues. Please show me exactly where he walked."

"Hi, Georgie," Becca called as he scampered ahead. He gave the come-along gesture as she and Jennifer hurried behind him. "What are we doing, Mom?"

"Georgie says he saw a man he didn't recognize in our yard two nights in a row. Maybe we can figure out why."

At the back door, they saw scratches on the lock as if someone tried opening it with wires or tools. Also, pry marks on several lower windows.

"The security alarm signs in the front probably deterred him from breaking a window to trip the signal." Jennifer gave a dry laugh. "Little did he know that wouldn't have triggered our particular system, which we learned only because of Georgie's dad's mistake."

"We should tell Cliff Goodwin about this." They started to go inside when Georgie cleared his throat meaningfully.

"Ah, thanks for reminding me." Becca pulled a handful of chocolates from her pocket. "You earned these, young man."

He smiled broadly as the candies fell into his hand. "Gee, thanks," he beamed before trotting away.

They sat in the gazebo as Jennifer dialed. "Hello, Deputy. We have some news for you." She described their discovery.

"I'll get there soon, but a lot going on right now. Maybe an hour? Maybe more. Okay?"

"Just call my cell when you're ready, and if we're back at the hotel, we'll meet you at the house. And thanks, Deputy."

"Let's take another walk around the sale and then rescue Grammy at the hotel," Becca suggested and Jennifer agreed.

When Deputy Goodwin arrived at the house three hours later, they welcomed him inside. "Can I buy stuff at your sale, too?" he joked.

"Anything you can't resist," Jennifer laughed.

"First, how about showing me what you found."

They did.

"Yeah, looks like an attempted B&E."

"B&E?" Becca asked.

"Breaking and Entering. Roderick's in the can so maybe somebody wants to shop your estate sale without paying for what he buys?"

"Or maybe William Early's men are trying to find what he wants inside," Jennifer suggested.

"You got something in there he wants?"

The women exchanged looks. "I made copies of the writing on the cloths, of the riddle and map. The copies are upstairs in the safe, but the original cloths are at my home in McLean."

"I guess you got other valuable stuff here too, because you asked me how to travel safe with it. When do you clean out the safe and go north?"

"Monday morning we say goodbye for the last time."

"This is Friday so you have three more days here."

They nodded.

"What kind of safe?"

"Gosh, I don't know the brand. A big one. Want to see it?"

"Yeah."

"By the way," Jennifer opened the door for them to go in, "any news about what happened to our friend, John Birdsong?"

"We got feelers out to local herpetologists."

"Who study reptiles and amphibians," Becca volunteered. "Your college investment wasn't wasted, Mom."

"And..." Jennifer encouraged Goodwin as they started up the stairs.

"And we're running down some leads. Connecting one to this William Early guy is a real long shot. But ya never know. Gotta be in the ballpark to hit the home run." He barked a derisive laugh. "At least we're in the dugout."

CHAPTER 66

They closed and locked the bedroom door to prevent sale gawkers from entering while they pushed aside the bookcase to reveal the safe. Goodwin knelt to study it. "Uh-huh. Looks like a good one, although with enough determination any safe can be cracked one way or another."

"You're not very reassuring."

"In my business, you don't see secure safes; you see the one's broken into. But I'd like to think you're okay here."

"Really?" Jennifer asked, thinking of the staggering amount of Venuti's cash inside.

"Well, hey. I can't guarantee it, but this looks solid."

"Do you know much about safes?" Becca asked cautiously.

He brushed aside her concern. "Enough for government work. Now let's talk about something else. We got you at the hotel under your own name, right?"

"Because you said with Roderick in jail, we didn't need further protection."

"Right. But I didn't know about this William Early then. Of course, somebody could follow you there from here because they know you're here. This Early guy came to your front door right here?"

"Yes, but we haven't noticed anybody following us."

"Nah, you wouldn't see them. They're good. See, if he wants what you have and he's got plenty of cash, he's hired private eyes to shadow you."

"Are you trying to scare us?"

"No, no." He shook his head and started again. "Chelsea told you about her self-defense class. The idea is to make sensible decisions instead of risky ones about where you go and what you do. That way you're part of the solution, not part of the problem. So if you know you're shadowed you can make better choices than if you don't know. That's what I'm trying to tell you. During these last three days, play your cards close to your vest. Don't take chances. Even if this feels contrary to your real nature, these are special circumstances. You get my drift?"

"Thank you, Deputy Goodwin, for wanting to help. I understand. Do you, Becca?"

She grinned, "Well, youngsters like me still feel immortal and irrepressible. But I *will* try."

"Better than that, you must succeed, young lady." Jennifer wasn't smiling.

"Whoa," Becca scoffed. "That's my momster talking."

Before Jennifer could respond, Goodwin interjected. "Okay, let's push the bookcase back, unlock the door and head in our separate directions."

They did and when Becca went down the stairs first, Jennifer turned to Goodwin. "You started to tell me about Anthony Venuti earlier."

"Yeah, well, I was in a soft-hearted mood because of your mother's involvement. She's a gracious lady who's been through a lot, so I took a personal interest, which cops shouldn't do."

"I don't have to tell her what you know, but maybe I can better protect her if I know the truth."

He sighed, making a decision. "Okay. Now this is strictly confidential because I like the way your family works. You care about each other. Sure, it's out there, but the kind of work I do...I don't see it much.

"My FBI friend said Anthony Venuti came to them with information they needed to take down Mafia criminals. When things got hot for him and The Hand put out a hit on him, they moved him into a witness protection program. My friend said he went kicking and screaming because he wanted to take his ladylove with him, but they convinced him it wasn't fair to force her to abandon her family and friends for a life on the lam with him. Still, she might find comfort knowing he's alive. That's how you can feel for someone you love.

"Okay, I'm telling you all this because you introduced me to someone special and then you saved Chelsea from a vicious predator. I...I owe you something beyond solving your case, although..." he laughed, "I hope to do that, too."

She put a hand on his shoulder. "Thank you, Cliff, for telling me. I don't know how, but if the time comes, it might comfort my mother. You are kind to share this."

He turned to amble down the stairs just as her cellphone rang. "Hello," she said to the phone while waving goodbye to Goodwin.

"It's Mary Ann. Is this a good time to talk?"

That's an abrupt segue, Jennifer thought, but instead she said, "Sure, Mary Ann, how are you?"

"Oh, Jen, my life's evolving in such unexpected and exciting ways. What a total contrast from two years ago when Dan died and I wasn't sure I could go on. Life looked bleak. I didn't dream of the thrill of a man in my life again. But Charlie is my dream come true. How could I possibly be this lucky?"

"Wonderful to hear you happy, Mary Ann."

"Jen, I could only reveal this to you, but...well, we're intimate." Jennifer could almost feel the blush over the phone. "At first I felt scandalized. But then I thought 'I'm in the fourth quarter of my life. What am I waiting for? Why waste precious time?'"

"Wow!"

"Wow hardly covers it. Jen, I'm putting my whole self into this relationship to fan this miraculous flame. Just when I felt almost dead myself after Dan's death, suddenly I'm tingling with life. I feel like a teenager again. Oh wait, here he is. Would you like to say hello?"

"Well, I...sure."

"Hellew, Jennifah," said a baritone British-accented voice. "Mary Ahn tells me yoah huh best friend. Delighted to talk with you."

"Hello to you, Charlie. Are you two having fun together?"

"Quite so. Didn't think I'd evah meet someone like Mary Ahn. I heah we're going to get togethah with you and Jason when you return. When's that?"

"I drive north Monday, arriving Wednesday, if all goes as planned."

"Well, let's put something on the calendah soon aftah. Meantime, safe travel to you and yoahs."

"Thanks, Charlie. Nice to talk with you. Bye."

"Ta-ta, Jennifah. See you soon."

Mary Ann's voice came on. "Can't wait for you to meet him, Jen."

"Meantime, enjoy each other, you two."

Mary Ann giggled. "Don't need encouragement for that, dear friend."

Signing off, Jennifer marveled at her friend's transformation from quiet and uncertain after her husband's death, to this positive, enthusiastic person. Her friend's personality change in two years, from grief and despair to euphoria, seemed impossible. But, why not? Isn't happiness the thermometer for how well your life's going? Still, she worried that her friend's vulnerability made her susceptible to a predator's clutch. But, surely not in this case....

She thought of her own life, marveling at her good luck at most of life's intersections and especially in marrying Jason. In their forty-one years together, they'd shared the usual joys and sorrows, but grown together in new ways enriching them both.

Spontaneously she dialed his number. When he answered, she wasted no time. "Hi, Jay. Just feeling a wave of love for you and wanted to tell you so."

"Well, you caught me at a good time because I'm feeling a wave of love for you. How's it going in sunny Florida?"

She briefed him on major events and described the imminent trip home. She omitted the William Early part, which she knew would only worry him since he couldn't protect her from 1,100 miles away. She told him about Mary Ann and Charlie, preparing him for their proposed upcoming double date.

Jason added, "The movers expect to arrive Thursday with your mother's stuff."

"Perfect timing," she observed, "because we arrive the day before to direct them bringing in furniture at Donnegans' house."

"Miss you, Jay."

"Love you, Jen."

CHAPTER 67

Next morning while Becca recovered from another late night with her new friends, Jennifer and Grammy arrived to let Peggy's team into the house at 8:45. Several buyers' cars parked in front awaiting the sale opening in fifteen minutes.

"The sale did well yesterday," Peggy told her. "The weekend should be busy, too. Hello, Mrs. Ryerson. Going to stay awhile today?"

Grammy nodded and smiled, unsure how she'd react at watching her belongings sold.

Jen and Grammy had locked their purses in the car and settled onto kitchen chairs, sipping coffee they'd brought in paper cups.

When one customer carried a stack of books to the checkout table and another a box of china, Grammy said, "Nice to see others will enjoy books I won't read again and china I haven't had out of the cupboard for years. They'll be appreciated once more, whereas I stored them on shelves at this stage of my life. Most things I use daily are in the moving van going north."

This relieved Jennifer's initial doubts, but she didn't want Grammy to stay long enough to change her mind. When they left for lunch, Jennifer told Peggy they wouldn't be back until time to lock up when the sale ended at 4:00.

Becca joined them for lunch at Mira Mare, where they ogled the sunlight sparkling on the channel's ripples as power boats noodled along the waterway just beyond their terrace table.

Jennifer's cellphone rang. "Deputy Goodwin here. Got some news. Convenient to meet now?"

"Sure." She told him where they were. "If you haven't had lunch, please join us. Our treat."

Ten minutes later, he ambled in.

"What's up?" Becca asked.

"Remember I said tracing the snakes was a long shot? Well, sometimes you get lucky."

"What?" Grammy leaned forward with interest. Becca pulled back.

"We got a call from a guy who said he was the elderly caretaker at William Early's property here in Naples. His hobby is herpetology and he works with the Conservancy to rescue snakes, which he cages at his carriage house on the acreage. Eastern diamondbacks are his specialty. He said men who work for Early's private detectives forcibly stole three of his snakes, put each one in a canvas bag, and hauled them away. When he protested, they knocked him down and kicked him hard enough that he had to go to the ER."

Becca's eyes grew large as she listened, tucking her legs protectively beneath her on her chair. "Three snakes?" Her voice quavered. "But we only know about one with Birdsong." She thought of their garage. "Maybe two. That means there might still be..."

Jennifer speculated. "Was the one in the garage an unrelated accident or part of a larger pattern?"

Goodwin continued: "After the hospital patched him up, he called Early to describe what had happened. Early blew him off, said he'd release the snakes when he finished with them, which is what the Conservancy intended anyway. When the caretaker asked what they'd be used for, Early said it was none of his business. This made him mad enough to call the police, because he says he's lost all respect for Early."

"Why doesn't he just quit the caretaker job if he hates his employer?"

"I asked. He said it's more complicated than that."

"Why?" Grammy asked.

"Because he's William Early's father."

The three women gaped at Goodwin.

Jennifer's memory raced back to a previous hospital ER incident when she waited for her mother's diagnosis and saw an old man waiting for Early. She recalled the old man pushed away

Early's offer to help him. Father and son weren't on friendly terms even then.

"When I went out to interview this guy, he unloaded. Says his son's a business shark and Civil War nut who uses the same ruthless tactics in business and getting relics he wants." He turned to Jennifer. "Which leads him to you."

"Uh-oh." She grimaced.

"He told his father he's after a woman's documents, ones which could lead to the biggest find in recent Civil War history and he intends seeing them, one way or another. I wanted to bring him in for questioning, but his father says he left Naples on a private plane early this morning. And not his own plane, although he has one. No, he hitched a ride on a friend's plane to hide his trail. We know the plane's flight plan takes it to Culpeper, Virginia, but it already landed and their ground personnel say those arriving passengers left. So right now, we don't know where he is.

"Maybe he's gone but his 'associates,' as he calls the men he hires to carry out his orders, could turn up anywhere. Even if we find him, for certain he'll lawyer-up, so we'll have little chance to get the information we need."

"Where does this leave us?" Grammy asked, a hand protectively over her heart.

"With only circumstantial evidence, we can't declare Birdsong's death a homicide to throw all-out effort into finding Early. No, but we do have one advantage. We have bait."

"Bait?" Becca puzzled.

He looked straight at Jennifer. *"You."*

CHAPTER 68

"Who have you told about your travel plans to Virginia?" Goodwin asked the three of them.

They each considered his question.

"Peggy and her staff and the neighbor across the street," Grammy offered.

Becca nibbled a bite from her lunch plate. "The new friends I spend evenings with in Naples."

"The Realtor," Jennifer added, "and the hotel knows when we're leaving."

"Then change those plans and tell no one."

"But..."

Goodwin nodded. "I mean change your plans enough to confuse anyone wanting to follow you. You told me Early's associates questioned your neighbors in McLean to locate you in Florida, so he knows where you live in Virginia. We can't undo that. But if he doesn't know your travel schedule or exact arrival date, you gain a brief safety edge, at least for the trip. Virginia is another matter. Meantime, the smartest solution might be chartering a private plane to fly you there. I think the sheriff's department could facilitate arrangements to keep your names off the radar to casual hackers."

Grammy spoke up immediately. "Let's do it."

Jennifer glanced her way, wondering at the huge expense, until she remembered Anthony Venuti's gift to her mother made this decision financially viable. And this solution protected them much better than an easy-to-trail auto trip.

"When did you plan to leave?" Goodwin asked.

"Monday morning," Grammy said.

"Okay, how about Sunday evening instead?"

Jennifer nodded. "We could do that. The estate sale ends at four. We could finish up last-minute tasks at the house," her nod reminded Grammy and Becca about emptying the safe, "and fly out that evening."

"If you all agree, I'll make the arrangements. Another benefit is you can take on board those valuables in carry-on suitcases that you planned to guard on your road trip." Goodwin finished his meal. "I have to go. Besides your case, I have three others on at the moment. You'll hear from me soon about the flight arrangements. Tomorrow is Sunday. We don't have much time."

As he rose to go, Jennifer touched his arm. "Thank you, Detective, for the *many* ways you've guided us through this harrowing experience."

"I should be the one thanking you. Sometimes doing my job brings me a bonus. Knowing you—and Chelsea—rates as that bonus for me."

The three finished lunch, paid the bill and looked in on the estate sale before returning to the hotel. At the hotel desk, Jennifer said, "We're due to check out on Monday, but we may decide to stay an extra day or two. Is that a problem?"

"In high season here, it would be impossible, but now it's summer and no problem," the desk clerk confirmed. "We'll keep your reservation open-ended."

In fact, Jennifer knew they'd disappear Sunday night, but this tactic provided a different path for nosy pursuers to follow.

"Guess this is the last night with my Tony and other new friends," Becca noted. "I won't tell him, but I'll know it."

"Important that you say nothing," Jennifer reminded her. "Our safety rides on this new travel plan."

"I understand, Mom. The sooner the better because I have zero desire to face the third snake, if that's what they have in mind. You can count on me."

After Tony Venuti came for Becca, Jennifer and Grammy sipped a glass of wine on their balcony overlooking the Gulf of Mexico.

"This is my last night in Naples." Grammy's voice quavered. "Why don't we have a quiet evening together? Maybe order room service right here, just the two of us, and watch sunset afterward."

"Mom, what a perfect idea. Let's do it."

"And get to bed at a reasonable hour for a good sleep since tomorrow guarantees excitement."

That night Jennifer experienced not a vision but a dream, although this time it was a nightmare.

"I know why you're digging that hole." An ominous voice spoke from the surrounding nighttime darkness. She turned. The lantern light revealed an evil-faced man clad in a Union blue uniform standing menacingly close. She gasped. William Early! Not possible, yet here he stood. Glancing down in confusion, she looked in astonishment at her own 1860s clothes – long skirt and long-sleeved blouse. In her hands, she held an ancient shovel with which she dug at the ground.

Jennifer had been transported back 150 years to the time of the Civil War? But how? Why?

Her instincts underscored this dreaded man's sinister intention, but she had no weapon to protect herself. She couldn't outrun him or hide in the dark. And why was she digging out here alone at night with no weapon or companion to defend her?

"You stupid woman," he sneered. "You led me right to the treasure." He gave a derisive laugh. "I didn't need your map or riddle after all. I only needed dumb, gullible you. You can even do the work. Continue digging. I always want the most for the least. In this case, I'll own the reward but leave no witness to speak of what happens here tonight."

Jennifer quivered. He intended killing her and stealing the treasure. Desperate to figure a way out of this situation, her mind raced while she dug.

Suddenly the shovel blade pinged, striking something solid yet invisible. A stone? Metal? They both understood the sound's implications.

"I'll take it from here." Early elbowed her aside. Grabbing away her shovel, he plunged it into the ground, levering out a great clod of earth. Below it, metal glinted in the lantern light. He dropped the shovel, fell to his knees and clawed feverishly with his hands. With a grunt of satisfaction, he lifted out a glistening golden goblet. He lifted it high as he knelt on the ground. "Yes," he cried his elation into the night. "I found Mosby's treasure."

Surreptitiously, Jennifer had edged toward the shovel. Deftly retrieving it, she raised it to slam down on Early's head. But in an impossible undulating wave of movement, he morphed into the form of a huge eastern diamondback rattler, coiled around the goblet, beady eyes fastened on Jennifer. She knew the snake could strike faster than her downward bash of the shovel attempting to dispatch it. What to do?

Just then, the lantern illuminated a rodent, scampering across the clearing right toward the snake. The serpent shifted focus from immobile Jennifer to moving prey it savored. As it struck the rodent, she brought the shovel down sideways. When the snake, mouse in its fangs, hesitated, she plunged the sharp point of the shovel to sever the reptilian head from the body. Trapped in the snake's disembodied head, the rodent's legs trilled with the effort to escape.

Stepping back in horror, she screamed for help, but her screams echoed into the dark night with no one to hear them. She turned and ran full out through the dark forest, unable to see her way around trees, past rocks and over rises and swales, yet on she went, certain something crashed through brush close at her heels.

Suddenly she tripped, twisting onto her back as she fell in order to look up at her attacker. Early's blue-uniformed body stood menacingly over her, but from beneath the Union cap stared eyes in a serpent's head.

Jennifer lurched bolt-upright in bed, gasping. Her heart thudded and she felt drenched with sweat. Gradually displacing the Virginia woods with her hotel bedroom, she slowed her hysterical breathing to normal. Wide awake now, she got out of bed and wandered through the suite to the balcony, where slivers of moonlight danced on the Gulf's rhythmic waves.

In stark contrast to this timeless beauty, what did her terrifying fantasy mean?

CHAPTER 69

"Time to wake up, dear." Grammy touched Jennifer's shoulder next morning. "It's eight o'clock. We need to let Peggy into the house in forty-five minutes for the sale's last day. You're usually the first one awake. Are you okay?"

Jennifer jumped out of bed. "Sorry, Mom. A rough night," she yawned, "but I'll be ready fast."

Armed with coffee and donuts from a fast food drive-through, they arrived at the house to admit Peggy's group.

"Yesterday went very well." Peggy gestured toward the rooms. "We're down to less than a third of your belongings. Today we'll get bargain hunters because, as we discussed, we reduce most prices the last day. You're leaving tomorrow morning then?"

Jennifer and Grammy exchanged glances.

"Yes," Grammy confirmed this false information to cloak their true plans. "Remind me again when you send the check for my percentage of sales."

"The contract reads within ten days, but experience shows it's more like five. Your check comes with a full accounting of each sale, backed up by the individual receipts."

"Very thorough." Jennifer smiled.

"Do you want our company to dispose of whatever remains after the sale?"

Grammy considered. "I'll make that decision when we know what's left. But it's possible."

"Why don't we wander around the house, Mom, to see what's left?" They went upstairs.

"The movers took two bedrooms, but look, two more are empty," Grammy marveled. "And the linen closet."

"And the hall decorations and the plant on the landing." Jennifer added as they investigated the upstairs.

Back on the main floor, Grammy noted. "Oh my, your father's desk is gone and most of the other den furniture as well. Just a few books left in here."

They strolled through the other rooms, commenting on the estate sale's success.

"Do you think we should warn Peggy about a possible snake attack?" Grammy whispered. "I mean, Detective Goodwin told us three snakes were stolen but only two have surfaced. And remember, Early came to this very house before to scare us. If I were in Peggy's shoes, I'd want to know what could happen."

"I hear your caution, Mom, but wouldn't it scare them all unnecessarily? What if the last snake escaped from the men who stole it and is no longer an issue? Or what if they intended it for something else? The sale's going so well, and we have no real knowledge they plan another incident here. I understand your protective instinct, but I vote no. In fact, I'll surreptitiously collect the wasp spray containers and dispose of them later at the hotel."

"Hope you're right, dear. But speaking of the hotel, I think I'd be more comfortable there. Do you mind dropping me off? Then you might even sail off on some other estate sale shopping of your own in Naples. It is our last day here."

Back at the hotel, they found Becca's note: *Away for several hours with my friends. Back at 4pm for our 6pm appointment.* They all knew "appointment" meant departure for their seven o'clock airport charter tonight.

"Any last-minute errands I can do for you while I'm out, Mom?"

"Don't think so. This gives me relaxed time to pack and be ready to visit my home one last time to empty the safe into our carry-ons. And then on to the airport."

"Okay, I'm a cellphone call away if you need me. Like Becca, I'll be back by four o'clock. It'll take no time for me to pack. I'll just shove everything I brought into my bag."

"On your way, then."

When Jennifer left, Grammy puttered around, watched TV and studied the room-service menu for a lunch order. At a knock on the door, she approached and asked, "Who is it?"

"Housekeeping," said a female voice.

Grammy opened the door to a woman with a cleaning cart and a stack of clean towels in her arms.

As their eyes locked, they recognized each other. Both froze in a moment of shock and fear.

"YOU!" shouted the chambermaid.

"YOU!" cried Grammy. "You and Max left me to die in that closet, Jane. How could you do that? How did you get here?"

"I work at this hotel. I'm desperate for money while Max rots in jail because *you* had him arrested." She rammed her cart through the door, forcing Grammy inside as the cart pressed against her. "You destroyed my life when you destroyed my man." Jane kicked the door shut behind them. "I hate you, you horrible old woman."

"Jane, stop. Think. He *used* you. You're just another victim because he's conned seniors many times using this handyman-housekeeper scam. Police have a rap sheet on him for these very incidents. You helped him this time, but other women he abandoned helped him other times. Don't you realize I didn't destroy your relationship? He would have left you when you were no longer convenient for him."

"You lie. He loved me. The minute he escaped, he came directly to me."

"But why? Because you are the love of his life or because he needed your safe place to hide while he worked on his own revenge — revenge causing his second arrest?"

"He protected me when they interrogated him."

"Because he might need you again? To write him letters and pay for lawyers as the years of incarceration spread before him? To bring him cookies in prison?"

Jane screamed. "How dare you say this to me!"

"Jane, it's awful to admit a woman could love a cheating loser. It's hard to accept they'd sacrifice us to save themselves. It's insulting and humiliating to give a man our all and have him take it and walk away, leaving us with nothing. It's an ancient, heart-wrenching story for women. I'm an old woman who's seen this happen many times. I forgive you for what you did to me because I understand you did it for Max. But now you must realize he was the mistake. This requires strength, but you can do it."

"You're deranged. He loves me and only me." Tears glistened in her eyes.

"Jane, think. You have a choice. Stay on Max's bad road or turn onto a new road. You decide what happens next."

Enraged, Jane grabbed a broken tumbler from the trash sack on her cart. "I'll show you, you crazy old woman. My love for Max gives me the power to deal with you." She grasped the broken glass in her hand, intent upon inflicting a gory wound upon whatever part of Grammy she could strike.

Grammy's hand reached for one of the many aerosol cans sprinkled helter-skelter throughout the hotel suite.

"If you try to hurt me, I'll protect myself, Jane. Then police come and you'll end up in jail like Max. Is this really what you want? You can stop this nightmare right now."

Jane lifted the broken glass and rushed forward toward the old woman as Grammy pressed the wasp spray trigger.

CHAPTER 70

Jennifer's cell rang. "Goodwin here. Look, we have an incident at the hotel. Can you get over here?"

"What? Who?"

"Your mother. An intruder."

Jennifer's heart raced. "Is she okay?"

"Yes, but hurry if you can," Goodwin encouraged.

"An intruder?"

"Not William Early."

"But…"

"More when you arrive." Goodwin closed his phone.

Jennifer rushed to her car and careened toward the hotel. What could have happened? How much more trouble could any of them take before they left for Virginia?

Braced for chaos when she reached the hotel suite, Jennifer walked instead into a quiet, controlled scene. Her mother seemed calm and unhurt. The intruder had gone. "What?" she cried.

Goodwin explained the situation, summarizing, "So we arrested Jane for assault. One more road block out of your way and an important puzzle piece for us in the Roderick case."

As Jennifer sank into a chair, Goodwin ambled closer to talk privately with her. "At the Naples Airport tonight, if you leave the keys under the driver-side floor mat of your unlocked car, one of my men will deliver the vehicle to the rental company tomorrow morning. If anyone's nosy, this eliminates one clue to your departure. Tomorrow you call the hotel to describe your unexpected hasty check out and pay your bill over the phone."

Jennifer nodded. "Got it. I...I thank you *again*, Deputy, for rescuing Mom one more time."

Grammy added, "...and for advising us to charter a plane and quietly leave Naples without alerting that nasty Mr. Early. And bonus: it's even the safest way to take along our valuables."

Goodwin chuckled. "I'd say that daughter of yours is a problem-solver and now I'm keeping an eye on your beautician, who's pretty smart, too. Look, I like you folks. Glad I could help."

He shook their hands and moved briskly toward the door. "Try to stay out of trouble up in Virginia," he said over his shoulder.

After Goodwin and his team left, Jennifer sighed. "Let's order a room service lunch and finish packing. When Becca comes at four o'clock, we'll be ready to roll."

They were.

* * * * *

Jason met them at Dulles Airport, barely cramming all their suitcases and carry-ons into his vehicle.

The next morning the moving truck occupied most of their day as Grammy's familiar belongings filled the empty first floor of the Donnegans' house. While Jennifer helped her unpack suitcases, made her bed and put her towels in the bathroom, Becca bought groceries and arranged them in Grammy's refrigerator and pantry.

When everyone felt tired by dinnertime, Becca revealed, "I bought fixings for a large salad just in case we order pizza tonight."

Jason smiled. "Now there's a gal who thinks ahead."

After their pizza feast, Jennifer looked for the cloth originals of her map and riddle, hidden behind vases in the laundry room cabinet. Relieved, she found them undisturbed.

Later in the dark in their bedroom, Jennifer told Jason about William Early.

He sat up and turned on the bedside lamp. "The threats, the snakes. Why didn't you tell me about this before?"

"I knew you'd worry and you were a thousand miles away where you couldn't help."

"Jen, does this mean you...our family...we're all at risk again?"

"Honey, I didn't plan it this way. Maybe we'll never see Early again."

He gave a mirthless laugh. "Doesn't sound that way to me. Jen, Jen. I want to protect us all. Do you think what's written on pieces of cloth is worth endangering everything we hold dear? Why not give the cloths to Early? Better yet, to a museum where experts can decipher clues and have the proper authority to find and dig up X. Even if there's a treasure and you find it, it's either on public land or private property. You can't just dig wherever you like. And whoever owns that property also owns X."

"I hadn't thought of it that way."

"Well, you need to. Look, sweetheart, you've been gone a month and I'm so happy you're back, the last thing I want is an argument, but you have to agree this Early guy is determined, unpredictable and, if he murdered John Birdsong, he's a *killer*. The longer you keep the cloths, the greater our risk that he'll do something crazy to get them from us. What if he kidnaps one of the kids or grands for leverage? Wouldn't you give him the cloths to save the life of someone we love?"

She nodded sheepishly. "Of course, but…"

"Well, then let's get rid of them *before* we have a catastrophe instead of wishing we had when it's too late."

"It's just…just such a rare opportunity to open a window to the past."

"Yes, but the same holds true if a museum finds X. And remember, Jen, X may not be what we hope. This could be someone's buried laundry or garbage. This could be a hoax. If we agree Early shouldn't have the cloths and a museum should, then don't you see a reasonable plan for us to follow?"

"I admit the way you describe it makes sense."

"Look, how about this. We've spent a super busy day moving your mom and we're very tired now. Why not sleep on it tonight and tomorrow wake up with a solution?"

"I'll try, Jay, but I'm confused."

He chuckled. "More like stubborn."

They both laughed as she curled up against him, but she noticed he laughed louder and longer. "I love you, Jay."

"Love you, too, honey. Welcome home. I missed you big time."

CHAPTER 71

The next morning, Jennifer put the two cloths on the table beside her paper copies. "What do you make of these, Jay?"

While he studied them, Grammy arrived from across the street to share breakfast with them as planned. They'd barely finished when the phone rang.

"Who calls at eight o'clock?" Grammy clucked.

"Anybody who knows we're always up early." Jennifer spoke into the phone, punching the speaker button. "Hello."

Jennifer heard silence on the other end of the line, followed by a sob. "Hello? Hello! Who is this?"

"Mary Ann," mumbled a broken voice.

"Sweetie, you don't sound good. Are you...are you all right?"

"Jen, I'm wounded. I'm bleeding. He's gone...Charlie's gone. My life is over. He took my love, my life, my dreams and everything in my bank account. I want to die, Jen."

"Mary Ann. Don't move. Should I call an ambulance right now?"

"...No, it's...it's my broken heart that's bleeding."

"Stay put. I'll be right over."

Quickly explaining the situation to the others, she grabbed her cellphone and dashed out the door.

Worried at what she might find, she pounded on Mary Ann's door before a push showed it wasn't locked. She rushed inside. "Mary Ann?" she ran around the downstairs rooms. "Mary Ann?" she shouted.

"In here..." came the frail voice.

Jennifer followed it to the sun porch, where her friend lay on a rattan couch. She hurried over to see the situation for herself. Relieved at finding no blood, she hurried to kneel beside the couch. "Mary Ann, what happened?"

Mary Ann moaned. "My world is shattered. My life is over. He's gone. It isn't enough he destroyed my hopes and dreams, my future. He broke my heart. He *used* me, Jen. He used me *emotionally*, he used me *physically* and he used me *financially*." Her voice rose an octave. "*He stole all my money*. I'm ruined. I'm devastated. I can't go on."

Jennifer eyed the empty Crown Royal bottle and glass on the coffee table. "How long have you been drinking?"

"Since yesterday late afternoon, when my bank called to say I'm overdrawn. But there isn't enough alcohol in the world to make this pain go away."

"Let's call your daughter. Sibyle will want to be here with you."

"NO! It's too humiliating to reveal to anyone else. I told you only you because you're open-minded. After five children, nothing shocks you anymore. You're the only one I want to know about this."

"Mary Ann, unscrupulous men luring women with love and conning them with scams like this is as old as human history. You're just the latest one in the hands of this selfish criminal. It isn't your fault. You're the victim here, the trusting victim. You've done nothing wrong except being gullible, which we do when we love someone. *He's* the problem and we need to get the police involved quickly to follow your money and maybe get it back. You know my son-in-law is a Fairfax County police detective. He can put us in touch with the right law enforcement to help you. Instead of being the victim here, it's time to stand up and fight back."

For the first time Mary Ann looked up at Jennifer. "Fight back?"

"You bet. He's counting on you knuckling under rather than prosecuting him. But instead, go after him so he can't do this to anyone else. Do it for yourself. Do it for the others he's duped before and the ones he'll cheat next."

"I...I don't think..."

"Yes, you can. For your own peace of mind and to make society better. Here, let's call Sibyle right now. She can walk you through this fighting-back process."

"You think it's the right thing to do?"

"I know it's the right thing to do. And so do you. Here's my cellphone. Just dial her number."

Mary Ann studied the phone as if unsure what it was. Slowly, Jennifer's words penetrated her brain and she pressed buttons. But when Sibyle answered, Mary Ann handed the phone to Jennifer.

"Sibyle, it's Jennifer Shannon, your Mom's neighbor and friend. She needs you because she's had a devastating shock. Instead of the wonderful, loving man she thought him to be, Charlie has disappeared, breaking her heart and stealing her money. She's very upset. How fast can you get over here?"

"Geez, Jen, is she okay?"

"No. She needs you, your understanding, your love and your help involving police to find Charlie and charge him with the crime."

"I.... Okay, I...I'll be right over."

"...and bring your toothbrush."

"What?"

"Plan to stay as long as it takes to help her through this."

"Oh, my. Can you stay at least until I get there?"

"I just returned from a long trip and can't stay. You're close, in Vienna. You can be here in fifteen minutes. I'll wait that long. Hurry!"

When Sibyle arrived, Jennifer explained what she knew. "Your mother knows all the details. Call me if you need me. Here's Adam's number. He's the police detective. He'll tell you what department to call."

Back at home, she explained Mary Ann's plight. When her mother wiped away tears, Jennifer guessed she mourned for her own lost love, Anthony Venuti. But rather than steal her money, he made her a millionaire. When they were alone in the kitchen, she touched her mother's arm.

"What's bothering you this morning?"

"Tony. I agonize over what happened to him—what horrible end he suffered without me there to comfort him. At least Mary Ann's love is all right somewhere. She might wish he's dead, but my dear Tony really is. If only I knew what really happened I could put my mind at ease."

"Mom, I hope you forgive me, but I asked Deputy Goodwin to find out what he could about Tony." She explained what she'd learned, uncertain what reaction to expect.

First her mother's face registered shock, then disbelief as she absorbed the information. Then a smile lighted her expression.

"Oh, Jen, thank God he's alive and well. How much courage it must have taken for him not to ask me to go with him into witness protection. This was his final gift of love to me. This anguish about his final days has weighed me down for years. Now I can think of his sunny smile lighting up a room somewhere this very minute. He's alive." She beamed.

Jennifer comforted her mother, holding her hand. But her own mind raced. Would they ever know the real truth? Was Tony Venuti the selfless, brave hero, facing the future without the woman he truly loved rather than wrench her from her friends and family for a life on the run?

Or was his story a version of Charlie's? Did he choose a future without her, leaving his money with her only because the witness protection window swept him away too fast to retrieve the cash box in her keeping?

Her mother would never know which option was the truth, but she could forever cherish the version she chose.

CHAPTER 72

Jennifer left her mother's side to answer the phone, putting it on Speaker so the others could hear. "Hi, Mom. It's Hannah. We'd like to invite you, Dad, Grammy and Becca to visit our property this morning to see what we've accomplished. You were in Florida a month and you won't believe our progress. In two weeks, we start construction of our new house. "

"When do you want us?"

"The sooner the better. How about an hour, at ten o'clock? I've planned a picnic lunch for us."

Jennifer glanced out the window. "It's overcast today. Have you a rain plan?"

"The old house is gone, of course, but we could eat in the barn or the garage if we had to."

Jennifer looked at the others, eyebrows raised in inquiry. They nodded. "It's a yes, although I don't know whether Becca will come since she isn't awake yet. When we returned, Nathan was over here like a rocket. Almost seems like he lives here. But let's talk about you, honey. You sound like such a happy girl."

"Oh, Mom, this is an exciting time in our lives. We want to share our happiness with the people we love."

"Okay, see you soon. Love you."

She no sooner hung up than Becca shuffled in, eyes barely open but hand outstretched for a coffee cup, which Jennifer guided into it.

The doorbell rang. Jason answered, returning to the kitchen with Nathan. "Morning everyone...Becca. Good to see you all again."

Becca winced, "You're seeing me at my worst—in the morning BC."

"BC?" Nathan looked puzzled.

"Before coffee."

He laughed. "I'm from a big family. Hard to scare me."

"Coffee for you, Nathan?" Jennifer asked.

"Sure." He kissed Becca's cheek. "Hey, what's this you have spread across the table?"

Jennifer described the frame, the riddle and the map, surprised at his interest.

"My dad's a Civil War buff," Nathan said. "He has a whole collection of stuff he found in past years with his metal detector."

This caught Jennifer's attention. "He has one and knows how to use it?"

"You bet he does. Me, too. I guess it still works. He hasn't used it for years because he says getting permission from landowners is nearly impossible. And if you're caught using it on parkland I think the fine is $160,000. But he knows the ropes if you need advice."

"Hannah invited us all to see progress on their property this morning and…"

Nathan continued her thought. "…and that property hasn't been disturbed for many years. My Dad says all of northern Virginia was once Civil War territory. If I had the metal detector we might find something interesting."

Jason munched on a peach. "You'll have no trouble getting their permission. This could be fun."

"Then why don't I see if I can get the detector working and meet you at the Iversons' property? Did you say about an hour?"

"Good," Becca mumbled. "That gives me just enough time to get ready." She walked Nathan to the door. "See you there." From habit in Florida, she locked the door when he left.

* * * * *

An hour later, as their car turned up the long driveway into 3508 Winding Trail, Jennifer fought a tinge of unease. With this property Hannah and Adam's permanent home, she needed to shake for good the memory of her awful experience here with Ruger Yates. Once the mind connects a location with terror, the warning flag flies. She must put that episode behind her.

Jason nudged Jennifer back to the present. "Did you bring the things we're taking to the Smithsonian when we finish here?"

She nodded, tight-lipped. "It's all in the trunk...the frame, the riddle and map. I'll show them the framed picture, but I'm keeping it."

At the top of the driveway, Hannah and Adam greeted them. After hugs, Adam explained, "You can get an overview from up here, but the yard is the size of a football field, so the best look requires a walk."

Nathan drove up, removing the metal detector. "Not working perfectly, but we might find something with it. Do I have your permission to look for metal in your yard?"

"Sure," Adam agreed. "But if you find something exciting, let's share the loot."

"Suits me."

"I think I'll look from up here," Grammy decided. "See, I brought a portable chair." They settled her. "Did this house burn down?" She gestured toward the charred skeleton of irregular timbers and the blackened roof listing into the basement."

"Mom, I phoned you about it when it happened," Jennifer reminded her. "Remember, Hannah and Adam were inside?"

"I remember now. Somehow, I'd forgotten. What an awful scare." Grammy grimaced. "I'll hug them even tighter, realizing I almost lost them. I'll never forget it now that I've seen this gutted building."

Hannah led the way as they started down the sloping yard. "We had the bush-hogger leave all the big trees and most flowering bushes like these lilacs and rhododendrons, but he removed the brambles and thickets."

"And," Adam added, "we discovered a creek running down that side. We hadn't known about it before, but it's a nature spot where our children can find tadpoles someday. We have at least fifteen kinds of tall trees: maples, elms, three huge oaks, some locust, firs and hawthorns and wait until you see the pines. Really beautiful now that we can enjoy what's here. Do you think we should put in grass or leave the ground natural?"

"I vote for natural," Becca said.

"Eliminates mowing," Nathan observed.

Jason scooped up a stone. "Natural's 'in' now and practical, as Nathan says. How about this rock. Quartz?" Crystals beneath the stone's rough surface glinted as he rotated it in the sunlight. "Almost looks like it came from another planet."

Adam picked up on that. "If you want mystique, wait till you see what's up ahead."

As they came upon a clearing, Jennifer gasped.

"Mom, what's wrong?" Becca touched her mother's elbow with concern. Jennifer pointed and they all followed her stare to a circle of pine trees around a large boulder with a smaller one atop.

"This...this is the place."

"The place?" Jason asked. "What place?"

CHAPTER 73

// "This is the place in the painting."

"The place in *what* painting?" Adam asked.

Recovering from surprise, Jennifer managed, "I can't believe it. I must be mistaken. Jay, would you mind getting the painting from the car?"

"You're sure?"

"Well, I think so, but it can't be."

As he walked back up the hill, they heard Nathan's metal detector ping. They all watched as he narrowed the pinging to one spot, forced his weed digger into the spot and levered up a divot of soil. Crumbling the dirt away with his hand, he crowed, "Look, it's an old bullet." They crowded around him for a look.

Adam walked ahead. "Here's the place we want to show you. This opening in the trees. "The big rocks inside almost look like an altar. How do you think that smaller crescent-shaped rock fits in? Don't stumble against it. It's sharp."

Becca stepped into the circle and just as she climbed on to the boulder, rays of sunlight cut through the overcast, spilled through the trees and haloed her with its glow. "What is it?" she asked, seeing their amazed faces.

"There's...," Nathan searched for words, "...there's an other-worldly feel here."

To her surprise, Jennifer said, "Indians thought this a holy place. Now I see why."

Jason gave her a sharp look. "And how would you know that? Have you seen this place before?"

"Only in the painting and...my dreams."

Jason shook his head. "In her dreams? What next?" Switching to a subject he understood, he asked Adam. "What's your construction plan?"

As he answered, Adam led the way toward the stream. "First, excavators will remove the burn debris and dig up the old foundation. Hannah wants to save those original stones to use in the new fireplace and in our rock garden. Then the builder lays the new foundation. I'll show you our blueprints up in the barn, in case you have suggestions. We want a walk-out basement with big windows to bring in sunlight—no dank subterranean feel like...," he faltered as a twinge of boyhood memory flickered across his mind, "like the one in the original house."

"When do they begin?"

"Two weeks. Nice little creek, huh?" As they studied the gently running little stream, the metal detector pinged again. Nathan again focused on the exact spot and dug in with his tool.

This time, as the chunk of earth in his hand crumbled away, he held up a belt buckle."

Nathan touched Adam's arm. "If we're finding things randomly like this, you really should measure it off in quadrants and go at this scientifically. This may have been a Civil War camp site."

"Could you show me how?"

"My dad sure could, and I could help."

Becca arrived with the framed picture and Jennifer held it up for them to see. "I think she's right," Hannah agreed. "It's an amateur drawing but no question it's this scene. Where did you get this, Mom?"

"At an estate sale in Great Falls."

They snickered. "Well, of course. We should have guessed. That's our Mom, the garage sale diva."

Adam looked up the hill. "Okay, if you've seen enough here, we have a picnic waiting up by the barn." He led the way.

When they reached the upper driveway, Jason helped lift coolers out of the car. "Will you keep the barn?"

"Only during house construction... to store materials and provide shade on hot days before the roof goes on the house. Then it comes down."

Becca mused, "Instead of bulldozing it, why not salvage the barn wood to panel the basement walls? That shabby-chic look makes a unique statement, and the weathered grain would give a soft, gray textured background."

Hannah smiled broadly. "Oh, I like the idea. Unique *and* practical."

"Some people buy used bricks and wood from old building demolitions," Jennifer added, "to preserve the materials but keep them functional."

Hannah tucked the cooler into shade near the barn. "They call materials salvaged from old houses 'architectural artifacts'. All kinds of stuff like hardware, stained glass, doors, chandeliers, columns, statues and more."

Becca put the food baskets in the shade also. "So you've already looked into it?"

"When you're about to build a house, which you do maybe once in your lifetime, you research a lot. Architectural magazines are full of ideas for using these artifacts. Some owners find a round window or stained glass feature or other odd pieces they insist their builder or designer fit into construction. That's too fancy for what we have in mind, but I really like Becca's idea about the barn wood."

Jennifer couldn't resist. "And salvaged artifacts are another way to recycle things instead of junking them."

Becca turned to Nathan. "Uh-oh, Mom's on her soapbox again. Recycling is one of her excuses for haunting those garage and estate sales."

Nathan turned to Jennifer. "You know, my mother's a garage saler, too."

"Well then, she and I have more in common than thinking you're a nice guy."

"Why, thank ya, ma'am." Nathan gave a convincing John Wayne imitation, thumbs stuck into his waistband.

Grammy winked at John Wayne. "You know the famous Will Rogers quote?"

Nathan shook his head.

"'Never squat with your spurs on.'"

When the others within earshot stopped chuckling at the quote, Hannah asked Grammy, "How was the trip from Florida to Virginia?"

"After all the confusion surrounding the move, getting here was the easy part."

Jason asked Grammy, "Do you plan to buy a new car to replace your Mercedes?"

She considered this. "Jury's out, but probably not. I don't expect to drive much anymore. You and others offered to take me places while I live across the street, and the senior place where I move will offer transportation service. So I guess I'll just hang on to the insurance money when it comes."

Several murmured encouragement for that decision.

Adam turned to Nathan. "Want to take a closer look at the burned house?"

Activating his metal detector, Nathan cautioned, "The ground around the outside of the burn site is solid, but poking around in the ruins is risky and dirty — those black soot smudges are hard to wash off. Ask me how I know."

Becca swatted him playfully. "You little fireman, you."

"Shall I bring along the detector?"

"Absolutely," Adam said as all but Grammy walked to the site.

Jason tried chipping away at one of the foundation rocks. "This isn't a poured slab and cinderblock basement. These are stones and mortar and they're in solid. How old was the house?"

Adam scratched his chin. "Records don't go back about the original house because there was no building code then. People could slap together whatever they wanted on their land. The Yates family owned this farm property over a hundred years and two other farmers owned it in sequence before that. As for the house, looks like each owner added on instead of tearing down and starting over."

"So this original foundation could be a couple hundred years old?" Jason calculated.

Adam kicked the wall. "They built them to last back then. Not the kind of construction some contractors get away with now."

Jason admired the workmanship. "When you build it yourself, as this owner must have, only his best effort would do."

"Or what was at hand that he could afford. Although Hannah and I have grand ideas for our house, many special features are too expensive for us. But we do plan to take turns coming every day to watch our builder's progress, so we expect good results."

Jason looked at the stones. "Think of it: this structure survived a couple hundred years of thunderstorms without a lightning strike burning it down. But you two moved here, and it finally happened.

"Think of old cobblestone streets and dwellings in Europe dating back centuries, and eroding pyramids, intended to last forever. Each constructed one stone at a time by human hands — just like this old foundation."

He put an arm around his son-in-law's shoulder. "If home is where the heart is, yours will be a fine one indeed."

CHAPTER 74

Down in the yard, Jennifer looked pensive. "Adam, does your stream run all the way down the north side of your property?" When he nodded, she asked. "How far is the Potomac River?"

"Don't know exactly. Maybe twenty miles?"

"I want to show you something." She pulled out her paper copy of the map cloth slated for the museum.

He studied it a few minutes before shaking his head. "What am I looking for?"

"I don't know exactly. See this place on the map—the hut with the odd multi-layered flat roof and the circle of dots around it? It's crude, but instead of a hut, could that represent the boulders in your glen? Could the dots be those trees?"

"Well...if you look at it that way..." Recognition lighted his face as he pointed to the map. "The road here says 'winding path' and the name of my street is Winding Trail." Their eyes locked.

"Are you thinking what I'm thinking?"

"Quick, get the others. Let's get their take."

"Hey, everybody," Adam shouted. "Please come here for a quick conference."

Except for Grammy, the rest convened, studying landmarks shown on the paper and hustling around the property to discover what else might correspond.

"So with the stream over there, the Indian rocks down here and if this is the winding path…and that stone wall down from the creek," Adam puzzled, "where's X?"

Becca turned in a circle, holding the paper, and suddenly pointed. "Could the square shown here be the old Yates house basement?" She pointed toward the blackened planks and roofing, tumbled askew by the fire into and around the old stone foundation.

Hannah thought a minute. "Adam, don't we have shovels in the barn?" He nodded.

"I'll get them, if you tell me where they are," Jason offered.

"Inside the barn door on the left. All the tools are on that wall."

Jason took off up the hill, calling over his shoulder, "I'll check on Grammy while I'm up there."

"Nathan, would the metal detector work here?" Becca asked.

"Don't know. Let's see." He brought the detector to the place on the foundation that appeared to match the map. "Here goes."

When he activated the machine, they heard intermittent pinging, not concentrated pings identifying a hit. He hovered the machine over the parts of the foundation he could reach before apologizing. "This probably doesn't penetrate deep enough. I think it's only designed for up to fifteen inches. You get what you pay for, and Dad's only an amateur relic hunter, so I'm sure he didn't buy the most expensive detector."

"Then why don't we just dig?" Hannah suggested. "In two weeks, construction workers will remove this entire old house so nothing needs saving. Why not have some fun today?"

Becca took out her cellphone. "I wanted to take some family pictures today anyway, but shouldn't we do before-and-after shots of this dig site? I mean, if this turns into a history-making moment, shouldn't we record it?"

"Great idea," Adam agreed. "While Dad's getting shovels, let's snap that Indian altar and any other possible landmarks relating to the map. They hurried away on their task.

Five minutes later, Jason returned, carrying two shovels in one hand and helping Grammy with the other. She gripped a garden trowel and a plastic bucket.

"I don't want to miss out on this excitement," she explained.

Jennifer consulted the map. "This may be a dry run, but if we're guessing right, X might be here." She tapped the hill of dirt tamped against one wall of the foundation.

The two young men pulled away pieces of burned debris to clear access to that wall.

Jason's engineer's eyes studied the situation. "This foundation wall formed the basement, so it should be about six or seven feet high. We don't know how deep X is buried, so we probably should dig down from the top of the foundation until we find something." He chuckled. "Doing it without machinery will take a while. When you get tired, I'll take a turn with the shovel."

Becca added: "Me, too."

"Let's dump excavated dirt over here," Nathan grunted, carrying a shovelful to a spot fifteen feet away.

"I'll bring some bottled water for our laborers," Hannah offered, starting up the hill.

"And please bring my folding chair," Grammy said, leaning against a tree.

"Here, Hannah, let me help carry the water." Jennifer followed her daughter toward the car.

An hour later, Adam wiped his brow. "This stuff's like concrete."

Jason nodded. "If the house is as old as we think, Adam, the original builder tamped the soil down hard to begin with. Then rain and snow compacted it further for another couple centuries."

"Yeah," Nathan huffed. "I can vouch for that."

The others returned and Grammy adjusted herself in her chair. "But look, in an hour you've made a good dent. At that rate, will you reach bottom yet today?"

This thought discouraged the weary diggers but energized the willing bystanders.

"Here, Dad, your turn. I need a break." Adam handed his shovel to Jason and Becca took Nathan's while the two tired diggers sagged to the ground for a well-deserved rest.

Adam took a deep swig of water. "Won't we feel stupid after all this work if there is no X?"

"Or if this isn't the right place..." Nathan added wearily.

"Or it's someone's buried trash," Becca called over from the dig site.

"At least none of you will need to visit the gym for a while," Jennifer said, laughing.

An hour later, when they traded off again, Becca snapped more pictures of the digging operation. The resulting 4'x 4' hole in the ground meant they now hefted dirt out of the excavation with the bucket.

Hannah said, "I'm going to serve the picnic lunch here by the dig. Mom, would you give me a hand?"

"I'll help, too." Nathan followed the two of them up to the driveway.

As they returned with the food, they heard Jason shout, "Bingo!"

Everyone rushed to see. Becca raised her cellphone for the picture as her father lifted out a dirty fork. "Is this part of X or somebody's buried lunch?"

Adam handed the fork to Grammy to evaluate. "Here, Dad, you catch your breath while I take over." Adam climbed into the hole. "Pass me the trowel." Ten minutes later he held up a necklace and a candlestick."

A cheer rose from the group. Jennifer and Hannah danced in a circle and Grammy grinned ear-to-ear as Adam lifted out a small tarnished silver bowl and a brooch.

"I can't believe this," Jennifer marveled.

"Here's another old cloth in the crate, but it's in really bad shape. He put the damp tatters into Jennifer's outstretched hand. She thought she saw writing scratched on some of the threads, but the decomposition made it illegible.

Jennifer remembered the Dead Sea scrolls. "I can't read it, but let's save all the fragments in case an expert can."

Becca snapped a picture of the cloth shreds in her mother's hand while Hannah spread blankets on the ground and turned to the diggers.

"Why not rinse your hands in the creek and join us? Or I have sanitizer."

Nathan laughed. "For those of us with shovels, lunch is a saner way to 'dig in.'"

This brought groans from the group sitting cross-legged on the blankets, starting on the feast.

Becca waved a pickle. "Hannah, this is a fabulous picnic."

"Just wait, you chocaholic, until you see the dessert," Hannah tantalized her sister.

"You don't mean? Not your famous..."

"*Yes*, double fudge brownies!" Hannah confirmed.

"Heaven can wait."

CHAPTER 75

" A lpha Echo to Charlie Bravo," the camouflaged man hidden in the woods whispered into his phone. Hearing the correct response, he continued. "Seven individuals in sight, evidence of possible valuables from their dig visible on the blanket. When do reinforcements arrive…? Okay. Here are my coordinates and here are theirs." He read them off.

"Meet me in the woods but quiet. We want surprise. Did you report the situation to #1…? Roger. Will he join in the take…? Okay. When…? Ten minutes from the road where you conceal your vehicle to my position…. Thick undergrowth…. Okay, twenty minutes to conceal your vehicle, ten minutes to me. Then we go in together."

Ending the call, the camouflaged man again lifted binoculars to his eyes.

As minutes ticked, he watched the Shannon family visiting together at their picnic, including the old lady in the folding chair. If they continued digging out the treasure, his group need only scoop and bag it. But the longer they waited, the likelier the dynamics could change. On the plus side, some family members might depart, leaving fewer for his crew to confront. On the negative side, more might arrive. His crew needed a decision in—he glanced at his watch—seventeen minutes.

As he watched, the two younger men at the picnic rose. One, carrying a shovel and trowel, disappeared into the hole while the other emptied buckets of earth handed to him—along with occasional shiny objects. The women collected these on one end of a blanket.

When his watch showed seventeen minutes had passed, the camouflaged man's phone vibrated.

He listened and said, "Good. Now ten minutes to me. Situation unchanged."

* * * * *

Becca looked at the buckets of dirt and artifacts Adam and Nathan had removed from the hole. "Hannah, we could easily do that. No hard shoveling, just exposing the items and lifting them out. Let's give the boys a break."

When Adam and Nathan joined the others on the blanket, Adam said, "At first I saw only one crumbling crate, but I think I just uncovered the edge of another one. We don't know how many are buried. It's early afternoon and we'll be lucky to get all the stuff out by dark. How will you protect what we've found and what's still buried?"

Jennifer looked at the objects on the blanket. "We could put these in the safe in our house, except Grammy's almost filled it with her valuables from Florida. We could hide what we've found somewhere in the house where nobody would find it. But who could we get to stay out here in the woods all night to guard what's left?"

Adam raised a hand. "Look, I'm not a police detective for nothing. I can't stop thinking about this Early guy who had you followed. What if someone's still trailing you—maybe watching you right now? If he knows you've found what Early wants, he could carjack you on the way home or burglarize your house if you take the stuff there. He could send someone here tonight to dig up the rest."

Nervously, they glanced at the surrounding wood. Seeing nothing ominous, their attention returned to each other, but they felt uneasy.

Adam continued. "Most of my squad's at a firing range shoot today but off-duty when they finish. I could call them to come over here, maybe even help with the excavation. They could provide you armed escort home with the stuff you've found. Some of them moonlight with security jobs. One might stay here all night for a reasonable charge, or at least give you the name of a security guard to hire."

Jennifer hesitated. "Don't you think the fewer who know about this, the better?"

Jason shifted uncomfortably. "Jen, this whole treasure hunt invites danger, and we don't even know from what direction to protect ourselves. We're out here in the open, vulnerable, digging up something a known villain will kill to get. Yes, Adam, please call your police buddies to escort us home. I'll be happy to hire a couple of them to guard our house tonight and more to watch this site."

"All right, sir. I'll take care of it right now." Adam walked away, dialing his phone.

Jason turned to Jennifer. "If you went straight to the museum now with your painting, your riddle, your map and what you've found today in that hole, they'd be happy and we'd be safe. Otherwise, you endanger everyone you love, including me."

Grammy clucked, "Your husband just wheeled out the big cannons, Jen." In a softer voice, she asked, "What are you going to do, dear?"

Jennifer sighed. "Everything you say makes sense, Jay. I...I can't argue with logic, so I guess I agree."

"Geez, what a relief." Jason hugged his wife. "Thank you." He kissed her forehead and turned to his son-in-law. "Adam, how soon will your friends come?"

"They just finished so maybe twenty minutes or so?"

"Then let's get as much out of the hole as we can and photograph it before they get here. Please call the Smithsonian so we know exactly where to go. Adam, could your friends escort us there to be sure nothing happens en route?"

"We'll have to ask them, but I'm armed and you can count on me."

CHAPTER 76

The mercenary team approached so stealthily that the camouflaged man heard nothing and realized they'd arrived through the bushes only seconds before they materialized at his side.

As they knelt beside him, he reported, "Same seven targets."

They focused their own binoculars on Jennifer's group.

"They're still digging, but this scenario could change any minute — better if some leave, worse if more come."

"I'll make that decision," spoke a voice the camouflaged man didn't recognize. He looked up to see a new man also dressed in camos: William Early, whose face he knew from photographs. #1 had arrived.

"Yes, sir, Mr. 'E'."

"Chief," Early spoke to one of the men, "review your plan again."

"Sir, we go in armed when the seven are together in one spot, get all at once, no loose ends. We surprise the hell out of them. We disarm and immobilize them. We dig and collect your relics. We leave. You pay us the balance due."

Early's face creased into a feral grin. "*Yes.* At last." He turned to the soldier. "You brought the item?"

"Yes, sir."

"Give it to me." Chief handed him a large bag, which he clipped onto his belt. Early trained his binoculars on the Shannon family. "I see six."

"One's digging inside the hole."

"What do you recommend, Chief?"

"I doubt the situation can improve. We should roll."

"Do it."

Chief stood to give his men a hand signal. They moved forward, fanning out toward the family by the old house foundation. Guns in hand at the ready, they crept closer, tightening the arc until they encircled the Shannons.

Chief shouted, "Hands on your heads. Kneel down and no one gets hurt."

Stunned, the Shannon group froze.

Jason stood. "What the…" But even as he uttered the question, he realized the answer.

"I said *kneel*," the camouflaged man barked, knocking Jason to his knees.

Jennifer felt fear and a shudder of guilt. She had brought this danger to her loved ones.

Adam and Nathan had also jumped to their feet, ready to defend their turf, but were thrown to the ground by the mercenaries.

Hannah hurried to protect Grammy. Slowly they knelt on the blanket together.

"Get the other one out of the hole," Chief ordered.

Another mercenary did so, jerking Becca over to join the others, kneeling now on the blanket.

Before lifting his hands, Adam surreptitiously reached into his pocket to speed dial his cellphone with a code his fingers knew by heart.

One of the mercenaries kicked him. "I said hands on your *head*."

Early's men frisked them all for weapons, including Grammy.

"Here's one," a camo-suited man held Adam's pistol aloft before tucking it into this own belt.

"Get their cellphones," another ordered his team." They threw these into a pile.

"Hey, this phone's turned on."

"Then turn it off."

"Now on your knees. Keep those hands on your head. You, too, old lady."

Grammy struggled to comply.

William Early strode imperiously onto the scene. "Well, what have we here?" he sneered at Jennifer. "Let's see what you've found."

He knelt to examine the pile of excavated valuables. They heard his sharp intake of breath. "My God, this is it. I recognize the plantation mark on this bowl. Remarkable," he gloated. "And this knife — could it be...?" He feverishly scraped away the dirt and peered at it closely. "*Yes*, the JSM initials on the handle. *Mosby's treasure*, and now it's mine."

So she *had* truly found it. Early's authentication clinched that. Yet her shame at creating peril for her family and her fear of what might happen next overshadowed her sense of accomplishment.

"Now all of you, face down on the blankets."

They heard digging commence, accompanied by various orders. "Hand me the steel digging bar," and "Over here with our sharp shovel," and "Lift out this whole crate because a second one's buried next to it," and "Get it into the bags."

They knew Early's men intended taking the treasure with them.

Each family member lay on the blanket with his own thoughts: Grammy doubting why she came to Virginia; Jason awash in frustration at allowing his family to become endangered; Becca fearing her exciting, promising life about to end; Nathan realizing he never wanted to lose Becca; Hannah praying for survival for herself and her new secret; Jennifer torn with guilt over putting her family at risk; and Adam, hoping his last-ditch phone effort might have worked.

Adam lifted his head to glance sideways, noting weapons trained on them by Early and one of his men. The rest worked at the treasure site. However, Adam knew change was imminent when he heard a digger say, "Here's the second crate. Nothing more down..."

But his sentence stopped short at the sound of a single siren, followed by many more.

The mercenaries exchanged looks. They knew what to do. Their contract did not include capture and rotting in prison.

Early saw them prepare to leave. "Stop. I'll...I'll double your money if you salvage my treasure." As they continued toward the woods, he shouted, "Chief, I'll triple your money."

The sirens increased to an ear-splitting volume, closing in.

"Chief, I ORDER you to stop!" Early screamed.

But at Chief's hand signal, the men turned and disappeared into the woods as abruptly as they'd appeared. Adam jumped to his feet.

At this sudden movement, Early spun around, pointing his gun close range at the young man's heart. Adam halted in his tracks, holding open hands at his side in supplication as the other family members slowly rose to their feet.

"Don't move," Early shouted, his pointed gun wavering toward one and then another as they stood.

Suddenly, eight policemen materialized in the clearing. A voice boomed, "POLICE. DON'T MOVE. DROP YOUR WEAPON."

His world crumbling around him, Early reached to grab the nearest hostage. He jerked Jennifer in front of him, making her a human shield. Gripping her waist so tightly she could barely breathe, he backed them both toward the woods until they disappeared into the trees.

CHAPTER 77

Early jerked Jennifer along with him, then spun her around, jammed the gun in her back and growled, "Show me the way out of here."

Realizing buying time might give her a chance to escape, she said, "Follow the creek downhill."

"*Go.*" He prodded her before him. She moved along, desperate to invent a plan. Could she outrun him? Did his own need to get away mean if she bolted, he wouldn't follow her? Or would he shoot her dead and escape anyway?

Suddenly she saw the clearing ahead with the circle of trees and odd boulder configuration. On impulse, she turned that way and he followed. As they entered the circle of trees and approached the Indian altar, Early tripped and fell on the sharp rock they'd all carefully avoided. The bag clipped to his waist protected his leg from a deeper gash, but it ripped open in the process. As Early struggled to regain his footing, a large snake slithered out of the torn canvas. Jennifer immediately recognized the now-familiar markings of the eastern diamondback rattler. She scrambled quickly atop the boulder.

Early was unaware of his close proximity to the escaped snake. The diamondback coiled effortlessly into strike mode and froze in this position, awaiting the right moment. Early had dropped his weapon when he fell and, turning to find it, he came face-to-face with the snake. Seeing no other defense, he kicked at the serpent to frighten it into retreat. But the diamondback retaliated, rearing and striking Early. Its needle-sharp fangs drove into his ankle.

He yelled at the searing pain, gripping the reptile's body with one hand and clawing its head from his ankle with the other. During this desperate struggle, Early fell again. The powerful snake released the ankle. Its eyes focused intently on Early as its body coiled for another strike.

As Early twisted away on the ground, it lunged again, its fangs plunging deep into his neck. He writhed, scratching at the two pinpoints of blood near his throat as the rattler withdrew. The snake froze for a moment, as if surveying the situation. Then it slithered out of the clearing, melting invisibly into the bushes.

Atop the boulder, Jennifer frantically tried to think what to do. As her eyes darted around the clearing, she spied Early's gun where it landed when he tripped. She crept down from the big rock, skirting where he thrashed and moaned on the ground. His gun in her hand, she climbed back up on the boulder, safe from him and the snake. She snapped off the safety, trained the weapon on Early and shouted, "I'VE GOT HIM. COME HELP ME." She heard people rushing down the hill toward her.

Just as they reached her, the sun came out, flooding the clearing with the same eerie light they'd noticed before. For a freakish moment, her rescuers stood at the edge of the circle of trees, staring at her, open-mouthed.

Confused by their hesitation, she broke the silence. "A poisonous snake bit him twice." This seemed to break the spell.

An approaching policeman called, "Ma'am, did you see the snake to identify for the medics?"

"Eastern diamondback rattlesnake. They're not native here but the bite's very toxic. He'll need the antivenin quickly. He got a double dose.

Jason rushed to her and helped her down from the boulder. He wrapped his arms around her. "Oh Jen, my Jen. I thought I'd lost you."

"You okay, ma'am?" another policeman asked with concern.

"We're all okay now because you police came at the exact right moment. Thanks for your rescue. Any sign of Early's men who got away?"

"No, but we hope to learn more about them when we question him."

A stretcher arrived. The bearers lifted Early onto it and carried him up the hill. The rest followed back up toward the driveway.

When the ambulance left, Adam talked with his police friends as the others collected the picnic blankets and paraphernalia. He turned to the group. "The on-duty cops have to go back, but my buddies and I will give you an armed escort wherever you're going next."

Hannah turned to Jennifer. "Mom, what do we do with these bags of stuff from the dig?"

"Let's take it all back to our house to decide what to do next." She put an arm around Grammy. "How are you holding up, Mom?"

"When you're old you think you've seen it all, but I forgot what life's like being around you, honey. Despite all that happened to us in Florida, digging up buried treasure and attacked by armed camouflaged men is hard to match. I hope I can survive the next ten years here with you."

They laughed together, grateful this latest close call ended well.

Becca retrieved her cellphone from the pile on the blanket. "Before you move anything, let me get a picture of the ones still in the crate for the documentary."

"Documentary?" Nathan puzzled.

Becca grinned. "Yes, I just thought of this great idea."

Nathan winced and shook his head. "Are you going to be like your mother?"

Jennifer arched an eyebrow. "And what does that mean?"

"I…I …" he stammered.

But Jason clapped Nathan on the back, gave him a sympathetic nod and shrugged. "Not easy, lad, but seems like it's part of the deal. Mostly a great deal, but…well, not always."

Jennifer winked at Becca and whispered, "If life with us is a magic carpet ride, buckle up, boys."

CHAPTER 78

Returning to the Shannon home, they protected the dining room table with a blanket and spread the dirt-flecked treasure across it.

Then the phone rang. Jennifer recognized the voice of their aged family friend with psychic powers. "Veronika, I'm putting you on Speaker so we can all hear. How are you?"

"Worried, Jennifer. I had two visions about you this morning and I must warn you about the first one. This morning I saw you surrounded by terrible danger, but the next part makes no sense. In my vision, this danger comes from a snake-man. I know this sounds crazy, but it's what I saw: a man's body with a snake's head. Impossible as this is, the threat's power frightened me and I needed to let you know. Does this make any sense to you?"

Jennifer shivered. "I'm afraid it does." She told Veronika what happened.

"Ah, a happy ending then," Veronika said. "Well, the other reason I'm calling is my second vision—you're bringing me a gift."

Embarrassed, Jennifer could think of nothing she'd brought from Florida for Veronika. "What...what kind of gift?"

"That's the unusual part. The gift is a person, but who?"

Suddenly Jennifer knew the answer. "I brought you my eighty-seven-year old mother—to McLean from Naples."

"Italy?"

Jennifer laughed. "No, Florida."

"Well," Veronika continued undeterred, "I thought perhaps a handsome prince, because according to my vision, this person and I will become very close friends."

"Then let's get this friendship started. Would you like to come over now to meet my mother and continue with us this evening for dinner at Kazan Restaurant? Do you like Turkish food?"

"Why, Jennifer, thank you. My tastes are international, and I am happy to come. I'd suggest Serbian Crown, but they closed. Tragic since also gone are their fine Russian food and the slushy iced vodka I so adored. But Einstein reminds us, 'Life is like riding a bicycle. To keep your balance you must keep moving forward.' So now I am eager to try this Kazan instead."

"Good. How soon can you come to our house?"

"My driver knows your address. Maybe forty-five minutes?"

"Wonderful. See you then."

Ending the call, Jennifer turned to Grammy. "Mom, I wanted you to meet Veronika soon anyway. You're both seniors and about the same age. I think you'll enjoy each other."

Grammy smiled. "Apparently so, if we're destined to become close friends, as her vision suggests. What can you tell me about her?"

Becca grinned. "Other than she saved Mom's life during Milo's kidnapping, what else would you like to know about her?"

But before Grammy could answer, Hannah spoke up. "Veronika Verontsova's a magnificent lady who looks like Mother Earth. She wears long skirts and has thick gray hair she wears in a single braid. She moved here from Russia as a little girl and has lived on her father's horse estate in Great Falls since then. He's dead now, so she's there alone except for servants. Lilacs are her favorite flower. Want to know why?" Grammy nodded. "Because the scent of lilacs makes her aware a vision is coming. She can't gin one up at will; she has to wait until one comes to her."

Adam couldn't resist. "Actually, I met her first when she came to the police station to report a disturbing repeated vision about nearby terrorists. While she waited in the police lobby, she saw a picture in a local newspaper and told me, 'The woman in that picture is involved somehow with those terrorists.' Can you imagine how my jaw dropped when she pointed to a photo of Jennifer, my *mother-in-law*?"

They all laughed at this, even Jason. But then he whispered to Jennifer. "The truth is, having you in danger doesn't really amuse me."

She understood. Protecting the family was her job, too. But her personality infused her with curiosity about people and things. It also sparked her natural inclination to follow clues where they led. She never anticipated danger related to so simple a hobby as attending garage and estate sales. She thought the riddle and map might lead her on a harmless merry chase, unlike the scary paths some of her other garage-sale-adventures had taken. But not so, as it turned out...

"You're right, danger isn't funny. But I never look for trouble, Jay; things just seem to happen," she whispered.

Becca stood. "Why don't we all help rinse and dry these beautiful treasure pieces for Veronika to see and for whatever else is in their future?"

Jennifer jumped up. "I'll wash if the rest of you will dry. Becca, would you pass around dishtowels for anybody who wants to help? Jay, would you call to see if Zeynel Uzun has room at Kazan for a table of eight tonight at six?" She explained to Grammy. "He's the owner."

Treating each item carefully, they carried the valuables to the kitchen. Meantime, Hannah whisked away the dirt-flecked blanket, substituting a tablecloth for the soon-to-be-clean artifacts.

"Add a little silver polish and they'll shine as treasure should," Grammy said.

Jennifer crooked her finger at Adam. He came over. "Would you please bring down the dragon figurine on my bedroom night stand?"

"A dragon on your nightstand? As I keep telling the guys, I married into a strange family. Sure, where shall I put it when I bring it down?"

"How about on the dining room buffet, back by the mirror?"

"Will do."

Just then, the doorbell rang.

CHAPTER 79

Veronika Verontsova stood on the front porch. Jennifer greeted her warmly and guided her friend inside. She introduced Grammy. "I think you know everyone else," but repeated their names to be sure.

"Veronika, would you like to sit here next to my mother?"

"I would be proud to do so."

They engaged in lively conversation until Veronika pointed to the dining room table display. "Well, here is the elephant in the room. Please tell me about it."

They took turns around the table with show-and-tell about the garage sale purchase with hidden cloths, the efforts to decode them, William Early's involvement, the discovery at Iversons' property, the armed attack, the police rescue and security escort home.

"How exciting." Veronika examined a silver bowl near her with enthusiasm, turning it upside down to see the maker's mark. "Sterling silver. Look at this unusual filigreed workmanship around the edges. What happens to this treasure now?"

Becca said, "Good question. You solved the riddle, Mom, and found the treasure by yourself. Is it finders-keepers?"

Jennifer toyed with her necklace. "Actually we found it on Adam and Hannah's property, so technically, I think it belongs to them."

Hannah giggled. "How about fifty-fifty?"

Adam leaned toward Jennifer. "Without your map and riddle, we'd never have known it existed. Would excavators even notice it when they dug out the old foundation in two weeks? Or report it to us if they did? I think ownership is more like ninety-ten, with the large number on your side."

Grammy looked around the table. "So what happens next?"

Jennifer considered this. "When I first realized the cloths formed a two-part treasure map, it electrified the little child in me. I wanted to find buried treasure. After all, isn't part of each of us still a little kid?"

She heard a few chuckles. "But then I began reading about the Civil War, how seriously many take it and what this discovery would mean to historians. I thought if ever I *did* find it, I'd give the treasure to a museum because this piece of American history belongs to everyone. William Early's intention to keep it secret, hidden away in his private collection, reinforced my museum plan."

She nodded toward Jason. "Then your dad reminded me I couldn't dig just anywhere on private or public land, so even if I discovered the treasure's location, a museum had authority I didn't to excavate it. But when clues unexpectedly led to Hannah and Adam's property and we actually *found* it there, the digging restrictions disappeared. And now here it is."

Becca leaned forward. "So you could split the treasure with the Iversons and make the discovery public with pictures of the pieces. The country would own the knowledge, but you'd own the valuables."

"And if you keep what you divide," Nathan pointed out, relic hunters like my dad would vie to purchase every piece. It would be worth a fortune. That war and anything concerning it are almost sacred to many folks."

Jason spread his hands on the table. "Jennifer and I prefer to avoid publicity." He gave his family members around the table "the look," reminding them wordlessly of their on-going risk, without revealing it in front of guests. Family members knew of Homeland Security's warning to keep an invisible profile to avoid attracting the interest of Middle-Eastern terrorists. This terrorist vendetta still threatened the unknown person who took their diamonds, worth millions. The money from selling those diamonds was to fund their explosive plot against America. That unknown person was Jennifer. If they found her, they'd eliminate her. They'd warned: their memories were long.

"So," he continued, "if we donate this treasure to a museum it must be anonymous. Or perhaps it could be from you two." He nodded to Hannah and Adam.

Becca jumped to her feet. "But the pictures I've taken document this historic find. Think of a PBS Civil War film featuring this new information. The public deserves to see the excavation pictures, even if the voice-over doesn't describe where they were found."

As the rest talked about this, Hannah whispered to Adam. When she finished, he stared at her, a grin lighting his face.

Hannah addressed the group. "My parents choose to remain anonymous and although the treasure was buried on our land, we feel the same way. We don't want curiosity seekers or historians poking around our private property where we live and will raise our family. So if a museum donation happens, our role also remains anonymous."

"Anonymous but with photographic evidence?" Becca pleaded.

Jennifer explored middle ground. "As long as no one can trace the photos or their buried location, could we present a photo-and-treasure package to the museum as part of the anonymous donation?"

"*Yes!*" Becca pumped her fist in the air.

Those around the table nodded at this seemingly reasonable compromise.

"Once you put all this together for the museum, who anonymously takes it there?" Nathan asked.

All eyes turned toward him.

"How about *you*?" Jennifer suggested. "To insure there's no connection to any of us."

Adam leaned forward with a wry smile. "Good thing you have a police detective here. You're overlooking what detective work could uncover about your anonymous donation. A determined person, say a Civil War zealot, could tail Nathan to find out where he goes and who he sees and follow that trail.

"William Early knows the truth and he could broadcast it any time to implicate the Shannon family. As could the band of mercenaries he hired. So do the police who rescued you this afternoon. Plenty of witnesses out there. They may not know the story behind it yet, but they know what they saw this afternoon. Besides witnesses are forensics: Becca's photos, the paper they're printed on and so on. A dedicated detective could gather enough separate puzzle pieces to put the picture together. You wouldn't be anonymous for long."

Grammy frowned. "So is that an argument for keeping the treasure instead of donating it?"

Nobody offered an answer.

CHAPTER 80

V eronica turned her attention to the beautiful items on the table. "In Europe, we often trace historical evidence back ten centuries or more. Dating these beautiful pieces to the Civil War makes them at least 150 years old, but who knows when or where they originated? Maybe European settlers brought them on the Mayflower, or any foreign visitor or merchant since."

She held up a fancy serving fork. "Maybe some were family heirlooms, each with its own fascinating tale. Maybe some came from shops in large southern cities, which sold antiques from around the world. But besides their tangible worth and story behind every piece on this table is another important value: how this discovery amplifies American history."

Jennifer mused. "And trained museum researchers could probably trace each piece of treasure back to its origins — to the plantation owning it and even before."

Jason said, "Let's face it, we couldn't do that."

Becca shifted in her chair. "Besides the artifacts themselves, Mom's tantalizing map and riddle add big-time intrigue to capture public attention. If my photo documentary showed the painting inside the frame where you found the cloths, someone might recognize this location — the one Mom called the 'Indian holy place.' We know that location and the treasure are related, but whoever hid the cloths could have used any handy, unrelated frame. So even if a detective learned the pictured location exists on Iverson property, it wouldn't necessarily mean the treasure was buried nearby."

Veronika touched various items on the table before picking up a golden plate. "Now this attracts me. If you decide to donate, you might want to keep this one for the souvenir."

"The souvenir?" Jennifer asked with surprise.

"But, of course. My Old World understanding about such things is when a discoverer chooses to share his archaeological find with the world, he quietly keeps at least one item as a memento of his triumph. He's earned it for his mental and physical work, plus his time, and often his money. This is especially so if he gives the rest to a museum instead of keeping it all for himself. Of course, you do as you wish. This is only an idea."

Jennifer eyed the treasure in a new light. "What else interests you and why?"

"This sterling tea set surely graced many plantation gatherings–fancy breakfasts, lavish luncheons, tea at three, elegant dinners. And look at these beautiful serving utensils," she held up two large silver spoons with baroque handles. "And," she pointed, "those marvelous candlesticks."

Becca reached for a necklace. "Don't overlook the jewelry."

Hannah slipped a bracelet on her wrist. "Lovely to wear, historical artifacts and souvenirs of your adventure. These are three-fers."

Nathan pointed to an old pistol. "I bet this has a story. Do you think a museum could trace this weapon's history?"

Grammy picked up the gold plate. "Veronika, what drew you to this particular item?"

Veronika sighed. "I'm more American than European, but I've traveled a lot and have relatives abroad, so that colors what I say. Historically, gold's important in every human culture where it's available and discovered. Think about it: rare, malleable, lustrous, tarnish- and rust-proof; you can melt or fuse or cast it. No wonder it's called a precious metal. I've read about records valuing gold against silver dating back to 3310 BC."

Becca raised her hand. "In college I learned the Incas called their gold 'the tears of the sun.'"

Veronika smiled. "What an enchanting way to express it."

Jason examined the gold plate for the first time. "True, gold retains value through time and catastrophes. How about this recent fever to buy gold for cash? Those ads are everywhere. Sure, the price of gold fluctuates, but buyers know in the long run they stockpile a dependable commodity."

Veronika nodded. "Yes, it's the very reason war-ravaged countries like Europe and the Middle East coveted gold, and diamonds, for centuries. If you've seen the gold room at the Hermitage Museum in St. Petersburg, you're hooked. Every Russian longs to find the Romanov family's missing gold heirlooms or Napoleon's lost treasure."

Adam smiled at Veronika. "That gold plate is here on our table because a Union general knew what you know."

Grammy looked thoughtful. "Isn't seeing a real treasure here in front of us more exciting than Russian treasures in our imaginations."

Veronika gave a hearty laugh. "Wise you are, Frances. Are you sure you're not part Russian?"

CHAPTER 81

A dam's phone rang. "Iverson here…. When…? Cause…? Okay, thanks for letting me know." He turned to the others. "William Early died five minutes ago. They didn't get enough of the particular antivenin in time to save him."

Grammy looked pensive. "I guess we should even be glad for the difficult people in our lives—learning from them exactly who we don't want to be."

"Amen," Jennifer agreed.

Moving to a lighter topic, Jason glanced at his watch as he cleared his throat. "It's the cocktail hour. May I offer you all wine, beer or most other choices?"

Veronika raised a hand. "Have you vodka? The colder the better."

"I do indeed. Grey Goose?"

Veronika nodded and he took orders from the rest.

Nathan jumped to his feet. "Here, sir, let me help you." The two disappeared into the kitchen, took appropriate glasses from the cupboard and began pouring from different bottles. Out of earshot from the dining room, Nathan said. "Sir, besides giving you a hand with the drinks, I…I…."

Jason stopped mid-pour and looked up at the young firefighter medic who was six inches taller than he. "You…?" Jason encouraged.

He took a deep breath. "Sir, I…I'm in love with your daughter, Becca. I want to ask her to marry me but I…I talked to my dad and he suggested I speak with you about it first. I make a good salary and now that she's graduated, she'll have a job soon, too. So we're on solid financial ground. If you agree and if she says 'yes' — although I'm not sure she will — I'll be the happiest guy in Virginia."

Jason grinned. "Nathan, you're a fine young man and we'd be happy for you to join our family. But she's a live wire, so life won't always be easy. Speaking as a man married to one, I can attest that you'll rarely know dull moments. It takes courage to choose someone like Becca, but you are guaranteed a full and exciting life."

"I know, sir, and that's part of her irresistible charm."

Jason handed him a tray of drinks and picked up the second one himself. They started for the dining room but just before they left the kitchen, Jason whispered to Nathan, "Marriage is the most expensive way to get your laundry done for free."

"What are you two laughing about?" Becca inquired as they entered the dining room.

"Just a little joke," Jason said, passing out the beverages. When everyone had a glass, Jason held his high. "A toast to Grammy for bravely moving to McLean and to Veronika for sharing time with us tonight and to the treasure finder, my clever wife," he bowed to her, "and to Adam, who brought us police assistance when we needed it most. And to all of you who helped dig up Mosby's treasure and bring it here safely." They raised their glasses and sipped.

"Za zdorovye," Veronika offered the classic Russian toast. "To your health." They sipped a second time.

"So, Frances, how long is your visit to Virginia?" Veronika asked.

"Forever," she chuckled. "Jennifer will help me find a nice upscale senior apartment community for my new home. It's time for me to return to my family."

A shadow crossed Veronika's wrinkled old face. "Wise choice for you, but unfortunately for me, I have no family nearby."

"Why not join ours?" Grammy invited.

"Why not? What do you think?" Veronika asked the others jovially.

"Great idea," Jennifer said with enthusiasm. "The more the merrier."

"Then it's done." Grammy spoke with finality. She raised her glass. "To Veronika, the newest member of the Shannon family."

They all sipped again.

All except Hannah. Jennifer noticed she'd pushed away her still full wine glass. Hannah and Adam were wine enthusiasts, even considering growing grapes and making their own. "Honey, are you all right?"

Hannah smiled. "Yes, just giving up alcohol for a while."

At Jennifer's puzzled expression, Hannah added, "Adam and I want to share with everyone here that a little Iverson is on the way and should be our Christmas present for the family."

Everyone cheered and crowded around Hannah and Adam.

"Now you see," Veronika confided to the group, "that not all valuables are silver and gold. These two bring us a true treasure."

A few minutes later when the excitement about the baby quieted, Veronika turned to Grammy. "Frances, please tell me more about this upscale senior community you have in mind, because I like the idea. It's beautiful at my estate but also lonely and isolated. Why don't we search together? If we find just the right place, we could become neighbors there."

Jason whispered to Jennifer. "Those two have really hit it off."

She whispered back, "At their ages, aren't friends and fun pretty important?"

"Or at any age," he winked. "Just ask your HVADH."

"HVADH?"

"Handsome, virile and devoted husband."

She giggled, arching her eyebrows.

Veronika stood and spoke again. "My new family, here is a possible solution for you. If you decide to take some souvenirs and give the rest of the treasure to a museum..." she turned to Becca, "with whatever photo documentation our police detective concludes is safe to provide, then why don't I be your anonymous donor? I live on a large estate where people may imagine the treasure originated, but I will never reveal any details and no one can search my private property without my permission.

"Any museum will gratefully accept the donation and display the pieces to the public while their researchers explore each item's origins. This discovery will enrich American history and delight Civil War enthusiasts like Nathan's father. Jennifer and Jason can continue their low public profile while Hannah and Adam raise their new baby on their own property without nosy Rebel or Yankee enthusiasts bothering them. Mr. Early is gone now and so can make no more trouble for you. What do you think?"

Jennifer grinned and Jason nodded a smile of relief. Jennifer rose. "This is not only a solution, it's the perfect one. Thank you, dear Veronika, for making this wonderful offer."

Everyone cheered as they toasted the new plan. Jason and Nathan refilled glasses.

Veronika bowed good-naturedly, enjoying the lively social exchange so different from her quiet life on the estate. But suddenly she froze, then sniffed the air to the left and then to the right. "Do you smell lilacs?" she asked.

The rest exchanged anxious looks. Didn't this scent precede her visions? Veronika groped blindly for the chair behind her and sat down hard, her gaze fixed. As her trance-like stare continued, her head jerked several times as if an invisible hand had bumped her forehead.

The rest sat motionless in their seats, afraid any movement might adversely affect whatever gripped her.

Minutes passed. Then as suddenly as the spell began, she relaxed. Her shoulders drooped, her head nodded forward, her breathing deepened. Had she fallen asleep?

Just as Grammy reached out to touch her shoulder to ask if she was all right, her head rose and she looked around the room as if nothing had happened.

"Oh my," she mumbled to herself. "But what could it mean?" She seemed lost in thought.

"Are you okay?" Grammy asked, concern playing across her face.

"Yes, I...I had a vision, but it's very confusing."

"Would you tell us about it?"

"I...I found myself in ancient China in the time of the Yellow Emperor. A man named King Yu shrank back in fear as the Yellow River, named for the Emperor, flooded its banks with growing force. The rising water had already soaked the hem of his tunic. He knew his people and their crops would perish if he couldn't stop this flood, yet it grew worse every second.

"'Ying-long,' he cried out in desperation. 'Wherever you are, can you help me? Can you save us?' Suddenly a noise like a distant drumbeat filled the air and increased as a speck in the sky grew larger as it rocketed toward them.

"The sound wasn't a drumbeat, but the flapping of wings as something huge approached. Coming into view Yu saw the enormous dragon he had aided years ago when it was injured. Of all the Chinese dragons, this was the only kind with wings. His five toes proved him an Imperial Dragon, belonging only to the Emperor.

"'Ying-long,' he cried, 'Thank you, Great One, for coming so swiftly and to the Emperor for allowing it. Can you stop this murderous river from killing my people and ruining our land?' The dragon studied the situation and immediately began digging long channels with his gigantic tail. The flooding water spilled into these drainage canals and flowed harmlessly away. "Oh, thank you, Great Ying-long. You and the emperor you serve have saved us this day.

"But when the dragon coiled and roared as if to destroy him, Yu wasn't sure Ying-long remembered him from their early days. When he saw the dragon lift a mighty arm as if to smite him, King Yu said, 'I willingly sacrifice myself if that is your price for saving my people and their fields.'

"He closed his eyes, waiting for the terrible blow, but instead he felt a soft touch on his arm as one of the dragon's claws gently stroked him in memory of their earlier friendship. They looked together at the miracle Ying-long had accomplished and exchanged respectful bows. Then the dragon's powerful wings lifted him into the air and carried him quickly away."

Veronika shook her head in bewilderment. "My vision says it's the answer... but what is the question?"

Jennifer walked to the buffet where Nathan had tucked her dragon statue. "The question triggering your vision must be the one I've asked over and over: 'What kind of dragon is this favorite I found at a garage sale?' No one knew the answer until now. Thank you, dear Veronika."

All eyes turned to Jennifer's dragon. Clutching the pearl of wisdom in the talons of one claw, he appeared to look wisely upon his new family with his large, all-knowing eyes.

Jennifer cradled him in her arms.

Jason shook his head in disbelief. "What explains your uncanny connection to this odd creature?"

Jennifer wasn't sure they'd understand, but she smiled. "I think the answer is 'Here be dragons'..."

READING GROUP DISCUSSION QUESTIONS

1. Did this story expand your awareness of problems confronting senior citizens? If so, please give examples from the book.
2. Did the Civil War passages in this story trigger new interest for you into this time in our history?
3. Can you share examples from your family or others you know who have tried solving problems affecting their senior members?
4. Do coincidences in your life suggest such events are random or designed?
5. What would you do with a strange riddle and mysterious map you found hidden in a garage sale purchase?
6. Did you learn something new about dragons? If so, what interested you most?

ACKNOWLEDGMENTS

Sarah Altman, Orange County Sheriff's Office TRIAD Coordinator, and **Patrick Lawrence**, 3rd Degree Black Belt Tai Kwan Do in Orange, Virginia, conducted a self-defense class series that I attended. Some of their techniques are in my story.

Marc Birdsong, of Lake of the Woods, Virginia, shared with me his family's ancestral history in Virginia, dating to the 1700s, and encouraged me to use his family's name in my story.

Brian Bunce, a former antiques dealer in Michigan, now a resident of Naples, Florida, shared a Civil War letter he discovered in a shoebox purchased from a flea market. The letter, written in 1865 by a young woman to her soldier beau, offered useful insights into courting manners and speech of the time.

Rebecca "Becky" Celestial, hair stylist in San Diego, California, for forty-five years (during eighteen of which she owned her own salon), gave me valuable insights about beautician/client relationships and her experiences with aging customers at a senior center.

Colleen Eggie, Customer Service Representative for Able Moving & Storage in Manassas, Virginia, provided me with moving company information.

Dan Hartwick, a man who loves Civil War history, an avid Civil War relic hunter, a member of Rappahannock Civil War Round Table in Fredericksburg, Virginia, on Board of Directors of the Civil War Study Group at Lake of the Woods, Virginia. Dan lent me many books on this topic, demonstrated his metal detector and showed me metal buttons, bullets and other Civil War relics he found using it.

Angela Larson, Supervisor of the Naples, Florida, Sheriff Office Victim Advocate and Senior Advocacy Unit, gave me information, statistics and stories about senior abuse in Florida. She also offered helpful suggestions about sheriff deputy protocol and practice in various crime scene situations.

Tom and Marie O'Day. After one of my library talks, they chatted with me, revealing they collect books, art and dragon artifacts/literature. Immediately intrigued because of my dragon in this book, I visited their home, where they graciously shared their knowledge, collections and passion for dragons. They also lent me several dragon books for my research.

Dr. Pete Rainey, the author of two books about the Civil War, member of Orange County Historical Society, Culpeper Minute Men Chapter of the Virginia Society Sons of the American Revolution, charter member of Spotswood Family Descendants and Chairman of the Civil War Study Group at Lake of the Woods, Virginia, helped with accuracy in my Mosby chapters. His ancestors, farmers and merchants from Northern Ireland, came to Virginia in the 1700s.

Bruce B. Rosenblatt, with thirty years' experience with senior housing facilities and consulting, shared his knowledge with me. His company Senior Housing Solutions (www.seniorhousingsolutions. com) collects no referral fees or commissions from any senior facilities, thus remaining objective and unbiased in advising individual clients what best fits their unique needs.

Paulette Salmon (Doctor of Veterinary Medicine) and her husband, **Tom Rayhart, Jr.** (a wildlife biologist) introduced me to and educated me about Florida's venomous eastern diamondback rattlesnakes.

Jennifer Stuth, MD received her medical degree from the University of Missouri and completed her residency in Emergency Medicine at the University of Nebraska Medical Center, serving as chief resident. After residency, she moved to northern Virginia for a fellowship and master's degree in Disaster Medicine and Emergency Medical Services at George Washington University. She currently practices Emergency Medicine in Arlington, Virginia.

W. "Bill" Rosser Wilson, retired head & neck surgeon, pointed me in the Civil War direction. When he heard my idea for a garage sale purchase containing a map to a historical discovery, he suggested a Confederate trove, possibly a valuable large cache of weapons buried by Confederates just before the South's surrender. A fiction author himself (the C. D. Washington Mystery Series), his Civil War fascination springs from his great-grand-uncle (his grandmother's mother's brother), General Thomas Rosser, C.S.A.

Detective Ryan R. Young of the Criminal Investigations Section of Fairfax County Police Department specializes in uncovering criminal exploitation of seniors in the county, but also on prevention programs. He worked on home improvement scams, gathering evidence to prosecute these criminals. He also emphasized social or cultural vulnerability of seniors (especially if isolated or with disabilities). He described the county's efforts to protect seniors from abuse, neglect or exploitation before they're preyed upon, although police often learn about these situations only after a crime has occurred.

Lisanne Zabka, a United Airlines Flight Attendant, showed me her extensive collection of Far Eastern memorabilia, including dragon china sets, platters and wall art. Her regular flights to China offer exciting opportunities to browse their markets and shops for unique treasures and additions to her dragon collection. She gifted me with a cherished dragon necklace.

BIBLIOGRAPHY

Ranger Mosby, by Virgil Carrington Jones, EPM Publications, Inc., McLean, Virginia,1906, University of North Carolina Press, Chapel Hill, NC 1944

Mosby's Rangers, by Jeffry D. Wert, A Touchstone Book, Division of Simon & Schuster, New York, 1990

Mosby's Rangers, by James J. Williamson, Ralph G. Kenyon, Publisher, New York, 1896

Gray Ghost: The Life of Col. John Singleton Mosby by James A. Ramage, The University Press of Kentucky, 1999

The Memoirs of Colonel John S. Mosby, edited by Charles Wells Russell, Indiana University Press, Bloomington, 1959

Ready...Aim...Fire! Small Army Ammunition in the Battle of Gettysburg, by Dean S. Thomas, Thomas Publications, Gettysburg, PA, 1993

The Civil War Collector's Price Guide, Millennium Edition, North South Traders Civil War, a Division of Publishers Press, Orange, VA, 2000

The Complete Guide to Caring for Aging Loved Ones, The Official Book of Focus on The Family Physicians Resource Council, Tyndale House Publishers, Inc., Wheaton, Illinois, 2002

Stonewall's Gold: A Novel of the Civil War, Robert J. Mrazek, Thomas Dunne Books, St. Martin's Griffin, New York, 1999

Armchair Reader: Civil War, Untold Tales of the Blue and Gray, West Side Publishing, a Division of Publications International, Ltd., 2008

Civil War Handbook, by William H. Price, L.B. Prince Co., Inc., 8900 Lee Highway, Fairfax, VA, 1961

Book of Dragons, by H. Gustavo Ciruelo Cabral, Sterling: Reprint Edition, 20112

A Practical Guide to Dragons, by Lisa Trumbauer, Mirrorstone, 2006

The Complete Book of Dragons: A Guide to Dragon Species, by Cressida Cowel, Little, Brown Books for Young readers, 2014

Dragonology, The Complete Book of Dragons, by Dr. Ernest Drake and Dugold A. Steer, Candlewick, 2013

If you have not had the chance to read Suzi Weinert's other books from *The Garage Sale Mystery Series,* here is your opportunity to read more stories about Jennifer Shannon's thrilling adventures springing from garage sale shopping. The first title is *Garage Sale Stalker,* available from www.bluewaterpress.com/GSS and her second title is *Garage Sale Diamonds,* found at www.bluewaterpress.com/GSD. Both of these tales will keep you on the edge throughout your reading.